Galactic Dreamers

RANDOM HOUSE NEW YORK

Galactic Dreamers

Science Fiction as Visionary Literature

EDITED AND INTRODUCED BY

Robert Silverberg

Y. A.

Acknowledgments

"Common Time," by James Blish, Copyright 1953 by Columbia Publications, Inc. Reprinted by permission of the author and his agent, Robert P. Mills, Ltd.

"The New Prime," by Jack Vance, Copyright 1951 by Jack Vance. Reprinted by permission of the author and his agents, Scott Meredith Literary Agency, Inc.

"Incentive," by Brian W. Aldiss, Copyright © 1958 by Nova Publications, Ltd. Reprinted by permission of the author and Faber & Faber Ltd. First published in *New Worlds,* 1958.

"The Waiting Grounds," by J. G. Ballard, Copyright © 1959 by Nova Publications, Ltd. Reprinted by permission of the author and his agent Scott Meredith Literary Agency, Inc.

"Sky," by R. A. Lafferty, Copyright © 1971 by Robert Silverberg. Reprinted by permission of the author and his agent, Virginia Kidd.

"Night," by John W. Campbell, Jr. Copyright 1935 by Street & Smith Publications, Inc. Reprinted by permission of the author's Estate and its agents, Scott Meredith Literary Agency, Inc.

"The Dead Lady of Clown Town," by Cordwainer Smith, Copyright © 1964 by Galaxy Publishing Corporation. Reprinted by permission of the author's Estate and its agents, Scott Meredith Literary Agency, Inc.

"Breckenridge and the Continuum," by Robert Silverberg, Copyright © 1973 by Robert Silverberg. Reprinted by permission of the author and his agents, Scott Meredith Literary Agency, Inc.

CONTENTS

INTRODUCTION

Science fiction is many things to many people—political satire to some, ingenious gadget-filled technological speculation to others, fast-paced and violent adventure stories to still others. I admire such worthy examples of each type as Pohl and Kornbluth's *The Space Merchants,* Asimov's *The Caves of Steel,* and van Vogt's *The World of Null-A* as much as anyone, but my keenest interest, as a science-fiction reader, goes not to the satirical nor to the cerebral nor to the adventurous, but rather to the visionary, to the mystical, to the psychedelic—to the stories that show me the cosmos in all its dazzling splendor.

The first two science-fiction books I read, before I was ten years old, imprinted me with that love of the consciousness-expanding qualities of the genre. When I was seven or eight

I came upon Verne's *Twenty Thousand Leagues Under the Sea,* and some trip it was for me, as with Captain Nemo as my guide I glided through polar seas, spied on monsters of the deep, even visited the ruins of sunken Atlantis: Verne gave me, for the first time, that tingle of the spine that tells of infinite possibilities, of access to all the wonders of this wondrous planet. Not much later I discovered Wells' *The Time Machine,* which repeated the Verne impact but even more intensely, for now not merely the depths of the sea but all of time lay open to me. The doings of the Eloi and the Morlocks were of fair interest to me, but the really over-whelming moment came later, in the closing pages of the book, when Wells' time traveler journeys to the far reaches of the future, to a time when "the sun, red and very large, halted motionless upon the horizon, a vast dome glowing with a dull heat," and the sky is almost black, and on a deso-late beach crawls "a monstrous crablike creature . . . as large as yonder table, with its many legs moving slowly and uncer-tainly, its big claws swaying, its long antennae, like carters' whips, waving and feeling. . . ." Wells' stony beach, his dead sky, his thin painful air, his slow scuttling crabs at the end of time, moved and transformed me. I have never forgotten those images of darkness and decline, that vision of millennia to come, and much of my later reading has been a quest to experience once again that chilly sense of widening percep-tions, of looking beyond the barriers of space and time, that Wells gave me.

I have found that sense often since then, though I can never have the intensity of it that the first time brought. The novels of Olaf Stapledon gave it to me, notably *Last and First Men* and *The Starmaker;* I found it in S. Fowler Wright's *The World Below,* William Hope Hodgson's enormous *The Night Land,* Walter de la Mare's *The Three Mulla-Mulgars,* John Taine's *Before the Dawn,* and a few other books that I hunted down in the public libraries just after World War II. Then I discovered science-fiction magazines, and the whole specialist genre of science-fiction books that emerged from them late in the 1940's; and while the mind-expanding element was too often diluted here by pages and pages of mere plot-spinning or pulp-magazine action-formulas, there were moments, there were keen moments, when I tasted the real thing. I found it in Arthur C. Clarke's *Against the Fall of Night* and *Childhood's End*, in Theodore Sturgeon's *More than Human*, in Hal Clement's *Mission of Gravity*, in the stories John W. Campbell wrote as "Don A. Stuart." Long before I had ever heard the word "transcendental," I was seeking and finding an analogue of transcendental experience in the pages of magazines with awful names like *Thrilling Wonder Stories* and *Astounding Science Fiction.*

As I left adolescence and began my own career as a writer, some of the joy of reading inevitably went from me; learning my craft, I became so concerned with examining the way established writers achieved their plot crises and resolutions and interplay of characters and all the rest that I nearly forgot about the search for the tingles of the spine that had begun the whole thing. Still, preoccupied as I was with the mechanics of writing, I still could respond—accidentally, as it were—when I came upon the story that aroused in me that fundamental science-fictional ecstasy. So it was when I read Cordwainer Smith, when Brian Aldiss' *The Long Afternoon of Earth* appeared, when Jack Vance sent me into the remote future with *The Dying Earth*. And, when I dared, I tried to write stories that would bring to others that essential science-fiction thing that so turned me on, such stories as "Sundance" and "Nightwings" and "Hawksbill Station" and above all the novel *Son of Man.*

And what was that essential science-fiction thing? Why, no more than to show the reader something he has never been able to see with his own eyes, something strange and unique, beautiful and troubling, which draws him for the moment out of himself, places him in contact with the vastness of the universe, gives him for a sizzling moment a communion with the fabric of space and time, and leaves him forever transformed, forever enlarged. It is, if you will, a psychedelic experience; at its most profound it can be a spiritual experience as well. Though I value the achievements of science-fiction's gadget-makers and trend-identifiers and yarn-spinners, they are for me lesser achievements than those which open the walls of the universe.

In this anthology I have assembled eight stories which have succeeded in sparking that visionary flash in me. Some manage it only for a few sentences, but it is enough; some attain an eerie power for nearly their entire length. I doubt that any reader will respond to all of them as affirmatively as I did, but I doubt, also, that there will be many who, reading through the entire group, fail to come away having known moments of wonder, terror, awe, and transformation. I read science fiction in the hope of encountering more such experiences; I write it in an attempt to codify and share my own encounters with the infinite; I have compiled this collection by way of expressing, by example, what it is about science fiction that holds so many of us in so rapt a spell.

Robert Silverberg

Galactic Dreamers

COMMON TIME

James Blish

This story first appeared more than twenty years ago in an obscure, long-forgotten magazine called Science Fiction Quarterly. *The magazine is known today only by collectors of science-fiction esoterica; the Blish story itself lives on, a classic of its genre, for rarely has a work conveyed so intensely a sense of the* strangeness *that mankind will encounter when explorers finally venture into the darker reaches of space. "Common Time" has the icy clarity of an exceptionally vivid dream—not an unpleasant dream, but one that is passing strange.*

James Blish was a significant figure in modern science fiction for nearly thirty years. His best-known works include the Hugo-winning novel A Case of Conscience, *the vast epic published under the collective title of* Cities in Flight, *and the historical novel,* Doctor Mirabilis. *American-born and educated, he lived for some years in Great Britain with his wife, the artist and writer Judith A. Lawrence. He died in 1975.*

I.

DON'T MOVE.

It was the first thought that came into Garrard's mind when he awoke, and perhaps it saved his life. He lay where he was, strapped against the padding, listening to the round hum of the engines. That in itself was wrong; he should be unable to hear the overdrive at all.

He thought to himself: Has it begun already?·

Otherwise everything seemed normal. The DFC-3 had crossed over into interstellar velocity, and he was still alive, and the ship was still functioning. The ship should at this moment be travelling at 22.4 times the speed of light—a neat 4,157,000 miles per second.

Somehow Garrard did not doubt that it was. On both previous tries, the ships had whiffed away toward Alpha Centauri at the proper moment when the overdrive should have cut in, and the split-second of residual image after they had vanished, subjected to spectroscopy, showed a Doppler shift which tallied with the acceleration predicted for that moment by Haertel.

The trouble was not that Brown and Cellini hadn't gotten away in good order. It was simply that neither of them had ever been heard from again.

Very slowly, he opened his eyes. His eyelids felt terrifically heavy. As far as he could judge from the pressure of the couch against his skin, the gravity was normal; nevertheless, moving his eyelids seemed almost an impossible job.

After long concentration he got them fully open. The instrument chassis was directly before him, extended over his diaphragm on its elbow-joint. Still without moving anything but his eyes, and those only with the utmost patience, he checked each of the meters. Velocity: 22.4 c. Operating temperature: normal. Ship temperature: 37° C. Air pressure: 778 mm. Fuel: No. 1 tank full, No. 2 tank full, No. 3 tank full, No. 4 tank nine-tenths full. Gravity: 1 g. Calendar: stopped.

He looked at it closely, though his eyes seemed to focus very slowly, too. It was, of course, something more than a calendar—it was an all-purpose clock, designed to show him the passage of seconds, as well as of the ten months his trip was supposed to take to the double star. But there was no doubt about it: the second-hand was motionless.

That was the second abnormality. Garrard felt an impulse to get up and see if he could start the clock again. Perhaps the trouble had been temporary and safely in the past. Immediately there sounded in his head the injunction he had drilled into himself for a full month before the trip had begun—

Don't move!

Don't move until you know the situation as far as it can be known without moving. Whatever it was that had snatched Brown and Cellini irretrievably beyond human ken was potent and totally beyond anticipation. They had both been excellent men, intelligent, resourceful, trained to the point of diminishing returns and not a micron beyond that point, the best men in the Project; and preparations for every knowable kind of trouble had been built into their ships, as they had been built into the DFC-3. Therefore, if there was nevertheless something wrong, it would be something that might strike from some commonplace quarter—and strike only once.

He listened to the humming. It was even and placid, and not very loud, but it disturbed him deeply. The overdrive was supposed to be inaudible, and the tapes from the first unmanned test vehicles had recorded no such hum. The noise did not appear to interfere with the overdrive's operation, or to indicate any failure in it. It was just an irrelevancy for which he could find no reason.

But the reason existed. Garrard did not intend to move until he found out what it was.

While he lay thinking about it, he noticed for the first time that he was not breathing. Though he felt not the slightest discomfort, the discovery called up so overwhelming a flash of panic that he very nearly sat bolt upright on the couch. Luckily—or so it seemed after the panic had begun to ebb— the curious lethargy which had affected his eyelids seemed to involve his whole body, for the impulse was gone before he could summon the energy to answer it. And the panic, poignant though it had been for an instant, turned out to be wholly intellectual. In a moment he was observing that his failure to breathe in no way discommoded him as far as he could tell—it was just there, waiting to be explained—

Or to kill him. But it hadn't, yet.

Engines hum; eyelids heavy; breathing absent; calendar stopped. The four facts added up to nothing. The temptation to move something, even if it were only a big toe, was strong, but he fought it back. He had been awake only a short while, half an hour at most, and already had noticed four abnormalities. There were bound to be more, anomalies more subtle than these four, but available to close examination before he had to move. Nor was there anything in particular that he had to do, aside from caring for his own wants: the Project, on the chance that Brown's and Cellini's failures to return had resulted from some tampering with the overdrive, had made everything in the DFC-3 subject only to the computer, so that Garrard was in a very real sense just along for the ride. Only when the overdrive was off could he—

Pock.

It was a soft, low-pitched noise, rather like a cork coming out of a wine bottle. It seemed to have come just from the right of the control chassis. He halted a sudden jerk of his head on the cushions toward it with a flat fiat of will. Slowly, he moved his eyes in that direction.

He could see nothing that might have caused the sound. The ship's temperature dial showed no change, which ruled out a heat-noise from differential contraction or expansion, the only possible explanation he could bring to mind.

He closed his eyes—a process which turned out to be just as difficult as opening them had been—and tried to visualize what the calendar had looked like when he had first come out of anesthesia. After he got a clear and, he was almost sure, accurate picture, he opened his eyes again.

The sound had been the calendar, advancing one second. It was now motionless again, apparently stopped.

He did not know how long it normally took the second-hand to make that jump. The question had never come up. Certainly the jump, when it came at the end of each second, had been too fast for the eye to follow.

Belatedly, he realized what all this cogitation was costing him in terms of essential information. The calendar had moved. Above all and before anything else, he *must* know exactly how long it took it to move again—

He began to count, allowing an arbitrary five seconds lost. One-and-a-six, one-and-a-seven, one-and-a-eight—

Garrard had gotten only that far when he found himself plunged into Hell.

First, and utterly without reason, a sickening fear flooded swiftly through his veins, becoming more and more intense. His bowels began to knot, with infinite slowness. His whole body became a field of small, slow pulses, not so much shaking him as putting his limbs into contrary joggling motions and making his skin ripple gently under his clothing. Against the hum another sound became audible, a nearly subsonic thunder which seemed to be inside his head. Still the fear mounted, and with it came the pain, and the tenesmus—a board-like stiffening of his muscles, particularly across his abdomen and his shoulders, but affecting his forearms almost as grievously. He felt himself beginning, very gradually, to double at the middle, a motion about which he could do precisely nothing, a terrifying kind of dynamic paralysis . . .

It lasted for hours. At the height of it, his mind, even his very personality, was washed out utterly; he was only a vessel of horror. When some few trickles of reason began to return over that burning desert of reasonless emotion, he found that he was sitting up on the cushions, and that with one arm he had thrust the control chassis back on its elbow so that it no longer jutted over his body. His clothing was wet with perspiration which stubbornly refused to evaporate or to cool him. And his lungs ached a little, although he could still detect no breathing.

What under God had happened? Was it this that had killed Brown and Cellini? For it would kill him too, of that he was sure, if it happened often—or even if it happened only twice more, if the next two such things followed the first one closely. At the very best it would make a slobbering idiot of him, and though the computer might bring him and the ship back to Earth, it would not be able to tell the Project about this tornado of senseless fear.

The calendar said that the eternity in hell had taken three seconds. As he looked at it in academic indignation, it said *Pock* and condescended to make the total seizure four seconds long. With grim determination, Garrard began again to count.

He took care to establish the counting as an absolutely even, automatic process which would not stop at the back of his mind no matter what other problem he tackled along with it, or what emotional typhoons should interrupt him. Really compulsive counting cannot be stopped by anything, not the transports of love nor the agonies of empires. Garrard knew the dangers in deliberately setting up such a mechanism in his mind, but he also knew how desperately he needed to time that clock-tick. He was beginning to understand what had happened to him—but he needed exact measurement before he could put that understanding to use.

Of course there had been plenty of speculation on the possible effect of the overdrive on the subjective time of the pilot, but none of it had come to much. At any speed below the velocity of light, subjective and objective time were exactly the same as far as the pilot was concerned. For an observer on Earth, time aboard the ship would appear to be vastly slowed at near-light speeds, but for the pilot himself there would be no apparent change.

Since flight beyond the speed of light was impossible, although for slightly differing reasons, by both the current theories of relativity, neither theory had offered any clue as to what would happen on board a trans-light ship. They would not allow that any such ship could even exist. The Haertel transformation, on which, in effect, the DFC-3 flew, was nonrelativistic: it showed that the apparent elapsed time of a trans-light journey should be identical in ship time and in the time of observers at both ends of the trip.

But since ship and pilot were part of the same system, both covered by the same expression in Haertel's equation, it had never occurred to anyone that the pilot and the ship might keep different times. The notion was ridiculous.

One-and-a-sevenhundredone, one-and-a-sevenhundred-two, one-and-a-sevenhundredthree, one-and-a-sevenhun-dredfour . . .

The ship was keeping ship time, which was identical with observer time. It would arrive at the Alpha Centauri system in ten months. But the pilot was keeping Garrard time, and it was beginning to look as though he wasn't going to arrive at all.

It was impossible, but there it was. Something—almost certainly an unsuspected physiological side-effect of the overdrive field on human metabolism, an effect which naturally could not have been detected in the preliminary, robot-piloted tests of the overdrive—had speeded up Garrard's subjective apprehension of time, and had done a thorough job of it.

The second-hand began a slow, preliminary quivering as the calendar's innards began to apply power to it. Seventy-hundred-forty-one, seventy-hundred-forty-two, seventy-hundred-forty-three . . .

At the count of 7,058 the second-hand began the jump to the next graduation. It took it several apparent minutes to get across the tiny distance, and several more to come completely to rest. Later still, the sound came to him:

Pock.

In a fever of thought, but without any real physical agitation, his mind began to manipulate the figures. Since it took him longer to count an individual number the larger the number became, despite the dropping of the compensating "one-and-a" as soon as the numbers passed one thousand, the interval between the two calendar-ticks probably was closer to 7,200 seconds than to 7,058. Figuring backward brought him quickly to the equivalence he wanted:

One second in ship time was two hours in Garrard time.

Had he really been counting for what was, for him, two whole hours? There seemed to be no doubt about it. It looked like a long trip ahead.

Just how long it was going to be struck him with stunning force. Time had been slowed for him by a factor of 7200. He would get to Alpha Centauri in just 720,000 months.

Which was—

Six thousand years!

II.

Garrard sat motionless for a long time after that, the Nessus-shirt of warm sweat swathing him persistently, refusing even to cool. There was, after all, no hurry.

Six thousand years. There would be food and water and air for all that time, or for sixty or six hundred thousand years; the ship would synthesize his needs as a matter of course for as long as the fuel lasted, and the fuel bred itself. Even if Garrard ate a meal every three seconds of objective or ship time (which, he realized suddenly, he wouldn't be able to do, for it took the ship several seconds of objective time to prepare and serve up a meal once it was ordered; he'd be lucky if he ate once a day, Garrard time), there would be no reason to fear any shortage of supplies. That had been one of the earliest of the possibilities for disaster that the Project engineers had ruled out in the design of the DFC-3.

But nobody had thought to provide a mechanism which would indefinitely refurbish Garrard. After six thousand years, there would be nothing left of him but a faint film of dust on the DFC-3's dully-gleaming horizontal surfaces. His corpse might outlast him a while, since the ship itself was sterile—but eventually he would be consumed by the bacteria which he carried in his own digestive tract, the bacteria which he needed to synthesize part of his B-vitamin needs while he lived, but which would consume him without compunction once he had ceased to be as complicated and delicately balanced a thing as a pilot—or as any other kind of life.

He was, in short, to die before the DFC-3 had gotten fairly away from Sol; and when, after 12,000 apparent years, the DFC-3 returned to Earth, not even his mummy would be still aboard.

The chill that went through him at that seemed almost unrelated to the way he thought he felt about the discovery: it lasted an enormously long time, and insofar as he could characterize it at all, it seemed to be a chill of urgency and excitement, not at all the kind of chill he should be feeling at a virtual death sentence. Luckily it was not as intolerably violent as the last such emotional convulsion, and when it was over, two clock-ticks later, it left behind a residuum of doubt.

Suppose that this effect of time-stretching was only mental? The rest of his bodily processes might still be keeping ship time; he had no immediate reason to believe otherwise. If so, he would be able to move about only on ship time, too; it would take many apparent months to complete the simplest task.

But he would live, if that were the case. His mind would arrive at Alpha Centauri six thousand years older, and perhaps madder, than his body, but he would live.

If, on the other hand, his bodily movements were going to be as fast as his mental processes, he would have to be enormously careful. He would have to move slowly and exert as little force as possible. The normal human hand movement, in such a task as lifting a pencil, took the pencil from a state of rest to another state of rest by imparting to it an acceleration of about two feet per second per second—and, of course, decelerated it by the same amount. If Garrard were to attempt to impart to a two-pound weight which was keeping ship time an acceleration of 14,400 ft/sec² in his time, he'd have to exert a force of 900 pounds on it.

The point was not that it couldn't be done—but that it would take as much effort as pushing a stalled jeep. He'd never be able to lift that pencil with his forearm muscles alone; he'd have to put his back into the task.

And the human body wasn't engineered to maintain stresses of that magnitude indefinitely. Not even the most powerful professional weight-lifter is forced to show his prowess throughout every minute of every day.

Pock.

That was the calendar again; another second had gone by. Or another two hours. It had certainly seemed longer than a second, but less than two hours, too. Evidently subjective time was an intensively recomplicated measure—even in this world of micro-time in which his mind, at least, seemed to be operating, he could make the lapses between calendar-ticks seem a little shorter by becoming actively interested in some problem or other. That would help, during the waking hours, but it would help only if the rest of his body were *not* keeping the same time as his mind. If it were not, then he would lead an incredibly active, but perhaps not intolerable mental life during the many centuries of his awake-time, and would be mercifully asleep for nearly as long.

Both problems—that of how much force he could exert with his body, and how long he could hope to be asleep in his mind—emerged simultaneously into the forefront of his consciousness while he still sat inertly on the hammock, their terms still much muddled together. After the single tick of the calendar, the ship—or the part of it that Garrard could see from here—settled back into complete rigidity. The sound of the engines, too, did not seem to vary in frequency or amplitude, at least as far as his ears could tell. He was still not breathing. Nothing moved, nothing changed.

It was the fact that he could still detect no motion of his diaphragm or his rib cage that decided him at last. His body had to be keeping ship time, otherwise he would have blacked out from anoxia long before now. That assumption explained, too, those two incredibly prolonged, seemingly sourceless saturnalias of emotion through which he had suffered: they had been nothing more nor less than the response of his endocrine glands to the purely intellectual reactions he had experienced earlier. He had discovered that he was not breathing, had felt a flash of panic and had tried to sit up; long after his mind had forgotten those two impulses, they had inched their way from his brain down his nerves to the glands and muscles involved, and actual, *physical* panic had supervened; when that was over, he actually *was* sitting up, though the flood of adrenalin had prevented his noticing the motion as he had made it. The later chill, less violent and only apparently associated with the discovery that he might die long before the trip was completed, actually had been his body's response to a much earlier mental command—the abstract fever of interest he had felt while computing the time-differential had been responsible for it.

Obviously, he was going to have to be very careful with apparently cold and intellectual impulses of any kind—or he would pay for them later with a prolonged and agonizing glandular reaction. Nevertheless, the discovery gave him considerable satisfaction, and he allowed it free play; it certainly could not hurt him to feel pleased for a few hours, and the glandular pleasure might even prove helpful if it caught him at a moment of mental depression. Six thousand years, after all, provided a considerable number of opportunities for feeling down in the mouth, so it would be best to encourage all pleasure-moments and let the after-reaction last as long as it might. It would be the instants of panic, of fear, of gloom which he would have to regulate sternly the moment they came into his mind; it would be those which would otherwise plunge him into four, five, six, perhaps even ten Garrard-hours of emotional inferno.

Pock.

There now, that was very good: there had been two Garrard-hours which he had passed with virtually no difficulty of any kind, and without being especially conscious of their passage. If he could really settle down and become used to this kind of scheduling, the trip might not be as bad as he had at first feared. Sleep would take immense bites out of it, and during the waking periods he could put in one hell of a lot of creative thinking.

During a single day of ship time, Garrard could get in more thinking than any philosopher of Earth could have managed during an entire lifetime. Garrard could, if he disciplined himself sufficiently, devote his mind for a century to running down the consequences of a single thought, down to the last detail, and still have millennia left to go on to the next thought. What panoplies of pure reason could he not have assembled by the time 6,000 years had gone by? With sufficient concentration, he might come up with the solution to the Problem of Evil between breakfast and dinner of a single ship's day, and in a ship's month might put his finger on the First Cause!

Pock.

Not that Garrard was sanguine enough to expect that he would remain logical or even sane throughout the trip. The vista was still grim in much of its detail. But the opportunities, too, were there. He felt a momentary regret that it hadn't been Haertel, rather than himself, who had been given such an opportunity—

Pock.

—for the old man could certainly have made better use of it than Garrard could; the situation demanded someone trained in the highest rigors of mathematics to be put to the best conceivable use. Still and all Garrard began to feel—

Pock.

—that he would give a good account of himself, and it tickled him to realize that (as long as he held onto his essential sanity) he would return—

Pock.

—to Earth after ten Earth months with knowledge centuries advanced beyond anything—

Pock.

—that Haertel knew, or that anyone could know—

Pock.

—who had to work within a normal lifetime. *Pock.* The whole prospect tickled him. *Pock.* Even the clock-tick seemed more cheerful. *Pock.* He felt fairly safe now *Pock* in disregarding his drilled-in command *Pock* against moving *Pock,* since in any *Pock* event he *Pock* had already *Pock* moved *Pock* without *Pock* being *Pock* harmed *Pock Pock Pock Pock Pockpockpockpockpockpockpockpock* . . .

He yawned, stretched, and got up. It wouldn't do to be too pleased, after all. There were certainly many problems that still needed coping with, such as how to keep the impulse toward getting a ship-time task performed going while his higher centers were following the ramifications of some purely philosophical point. And besides . . .

And besides, he had just moved.

More than that: he had just performed a complicated maneuver with his body *in normal time!*

Before he looked at the calendar itself, the message it had been ticking away at him had penetrated. While he had been enjoying the protracted, glandular backwash of his earlier feeling of satisfaction, he had failed to notice, at least consciously, that the calendar was accelerating.

Goodbye, vast ethical systems which would dwarf the Greeks. Goodbye, calculi aeons advanced beyond the spinor-calculus of Dirac. Goodbye, cosmologies by Garrard which would allot God a job as third-assistant-waterboy in an n-dimensional backfield. Goodbye, also, to a project he had once tried to undertake in college—to describe and count the positions of love, of which, according to under-the-counter myth, there were supposed to be at least 48. Garrard had never been able to carry his tally beyond 20, and he had just lost what was probably his last opportunity to try again.

The micro-time in which he had been living had worn off, only a few objective minutes after the ship had gone into overdrive and he had come out of the anesthetic. The long intellectual agony, with its glandular counterpoint, had come to nothing. Garrard was now keeping ship time.

Garrard sat back down on the hammock, uncertain whether to be bitter or relieved. Neither emotion satisfied him in the end; he simply felt unsatisfied. Micro-time had been bad enough while it lasted, but now it was gone, and everything seemed normal. How could so transient a thing have killed Brown and Cellini? They were stable men, more stable, by his own private estimation, than Garrard himself. Yet he had come through it. Was there more to it than this?

And if there was—what, conceivably, could it be?

There was no answer. At his elbow, on the control chassis which he had thrust aside during that first moment of infinitely protracted panic, the calendar continued to tick. The engine noise was gone. His breath came and went in natural rhythm. He felt light and strong. The ship was quiet, calm, unchanging.

The calendar ticked, faster and faster. It reached and passed the first hour, ship time, of flight in overdrive.

Pock.

Garrard looked up in surprise. The familiar noise, this time, had been the hour-hand jumping one unit. *The minute-hand was already sweeping past the half-hour.*

The second-hand was whirling like a propeller—and while he watched it, it speeded up to complete invisibility—

Pock.

Another hour. The half-hour already passed. *Pock.* Another hour. *Pock.* Another. *Pock. Pock. Pock, Pock, Pock, Pock, Pock-pock-pock-pock-pockpockpockpock . . .*

The hands of the calendar swirled toward invisibility as

time ran away with Garrard. Yet the ship did not change. It stayed there, rigid, inviolate, invulnerable. When the date-tumblers reached a speed at which Garrard could no longer read them, he discovered that once more he could not move —and that, although his whole body seemed to be aflutter like that of a humming bird, nothing coherent was coming to him through his senses. The room was dimming, becoming redder; or no, it was . . .

But he never saw the end of the process, never was allowed to look from the pinnacle of macro-time toward which the Haertel overdrive was taking him.

The pseudo-death took him first.

III.

That Garrard did not die completely and within a comparatively short time after the DFC-3 had gone into overdrive was due to the purest of accidents, but Garrard did not know that. In fact, he knew nothing at all for an indefinite period, sitting rigid and staring, his metabolism slowed down to next to nothing, his mind almost utterly inactive. From time to time a single wave of low-level metabolic activity passed through him—what an electrician might have termed a "maintenance turnover"—in response to the urgings of some occult survival urge, but these were of so basic a nature as to reach his consciousness not at all.

This was the pseudo-death.

Then, it was as if a single dim light had been turned on in the midst of an enormous cavern. He was—no, not conscious again, but at least he was once more alive, and in the deep levels of his mind that fact registered. He began to breathe normally. An observer might have judged him to be asleep, as in fact he was. The sleep was very deep, but at least it was no longer the pseudo-death.

When the observer actually arrived, however, Garrard woke. He could make very little sense out of what he saw or felt even now, but one fact was clear: the overdrive was off —and with it the crazy alterations in time-rates—and there was strong light coming through one of the ports. The first leg of the trip was over. It had been these two changes in his environment which had restored him to life.

The thing or things which had restored him to consciousness, however, was—it was what? It made no sense. It was a construction, a rather fragile one, which completely surrounded his hammock. No, it wasn't a construction, but evidently something alive, a living being, organized horizontally, that had arranged itself in a circle about him. No, it was a number of beings. Or a combination of all of these things.

How it had gotten into the ship was a mystery, but there it was. Or there they were.

"How do you hear?" the creature said abruptly. Its voice, or their voices, came at equal volume from every point in the circle, but not from any particular point in it. Garrard could think of no reason why that should be unusual.

"I—" he said. "Or we—we hear with our ears. Here."

His answer, with its unintentionally long chain of open vowel-sounds, rang ridiculously. He wondered why he was speaking such an odd language.

"We-they wooed to pitch you-yours thiswise," the creature said. With a thump, a book from the DFC-3's ample library fell to the deck beside the hammock. "We wooed there and there and there for a many. You are the being-Garrard. We-they are the clinesterton beademung, with all of love."

"With all of love," Garrard echoed. The beademung's use of the language they both were speaking was odd, but again Garrard could find no logical reason why the beademung's usage should be considered wrong.

"Are—are you-they from Alpha Centauri?" he said hesitantly.

"Yes, we hear the twin radioceles, that show there beyond the gift-orifices. We-they pitched that the being-Garrard wooed with most adoration these twins and had mind to them, soft and loud alike. How do you hear?"

This time the being-Garrard understood the question. "I hear Earth," he said. "But that is very. soft, and does not show."

"Yes," said the beademung. "It is a harmony, not a first, as ours. The All-Devouring listens to lovers there, not on the radioceles. Let me-mine pitch you-yours so to have mind of the rodalent beademung and other brothers and lovers, along the channel which is fragrant to the being-Garrard."

Garrard found that he understood the speech without difficulty. The thought occurred to him that to understand a language on its own terms, without having to put it back into English in one's own mind, is an ability that is won only with difficulty and long practice; but instantly his mind said, But it *is* English; which of course it was. The offer the clinesterton beademung had just made was enormously hearted, and he in turn was much minded and of love, to his own delighting as well as to the beademungen; that almost went without saying.

There were many matings of ships after that, and the being-Garrard pitched the harmonies of the beademungen, leaving his ship with the many gift orifices in harmonic for the All-Devouring to love, while the beademungen made show of they-theirs.

He tried, also, to tell how he was out of love with the overdrive, which wooed only spaces and times, and made featurelings. The rodalent beademung wooed the overdrive, but it did not pitch he-them.

Then the being-Garrard knew that all the time was devoured, and he must hear Earth again.

"I pitch you-them to fullest love," he told the beademungen. "I shall adore the radioceles of Alpha and Proxima Centauri, 'on Earth as it is in Heaven.' Now the overdrive my-other must woo and win me, and make me adore a featureling much like silence."

"But you will be pitched again," the clinesterton beademung said. "After you have adored Earth. You are much loved by Time, the All-Devouring. We-they shall wait for this othering."

Privately Garrard did not faith as much, but he said, "Yes, we-they will make a new wooing of the beademungen at some other radiant. With all of love."

On this the beademungen made and pitched adorations, and in the midst the overdrive cut in. The ship with the many gift orifices and the being-Garrard him-other saw the twin radioceles sundered away.

Then, once more, came the pseudo-death.

IV.

When the small candle lit in the endless cavern of Garrard's pseudo-dead mind, the DFC-3 was well inside the orbit of Uranus. Since the sun was still very small and distant, it made no spectacular display through the nearby port, and nothing called him from the post-death sleep for nearly two days.

The computers waited patiently for him. They were no longer immune to his control; he could now tool the ship back to Earth himself if he so desired. But the computers were also designed to take into account the fact that he might be truly dead by the time the DFC-3 got back. After giving him a solid week, during which time he did nothing but sleep, they took over again. Radio signals began to go out, tuned to a special channel.

An hour later, a very weak signal came back. It was only a directional signal, and it made no sound inside the DFC-3 —but it was sufficient to put the big ship in motion again.

It was that which woke Garrard. His conscious mind was still glazed over with the icy spume of the pseudo-death, and as far as he could see the interior of the cabin had not changed one whit, except for the book on the deck—

The book. The clinesterton beademung had dropped it

there. But what under God was a clinesterton beademung? And what was he, Garrard, crying about? He did not understand. He remembered dimly some kind of experience out there by the Centauri twins—

—the twin radioceles—

There was another one of those words. It seemed to have Greek roots, but he knew no Greek—and besides, why would Centaurians speak Greek?

He leaned forward and actuated the switch which would roll the shutter off the front port, actually a telescope with a translucent viewing screen. It showed a few stars and a faint nimbus off on one edge which might be the Sun. At about one o'clock on the screen was a planet about the size of a pea which had tiny projections, like tea-cup handles, on each side. The DFC-3 hadn't passed Saturn on its way out; at that time the planet had been on the other side of the sun from the route the starship had had to follow. But Saturn was certainly difficult to mistake.

He was on his way home—and he was still alive and sane. Or was he still sane? These fantasies about Centaurians, which still seemed to have such a profound emotional effect upon him, did not argue very well for the stability of his mind.

But they were fading rapidly. When he discovered, clutching at the handiest fragments of the "memories," that the plural of *beademung* was *beademungen,* he stopped taking the problem seriously. Obviously a race of Centaurians who spoke Greek wouldn't also be forming weak German plurals. The whole garbled business had obviously been thrown up by his unconscious.

But what *had* he found by the Centaurus stars?

There was no answer to that question but that incomprehensible mumbo-jumbo about love, the All-Devouring, and beademungen. Possibly he had never seen the Centaurus stars at all, but had been lying here cold as a mackerel for the entire twenty months.

Or had it been 12,000 years? After the tricks the overdrive had played with time, there was no way to tell what the objective date actually was. Frantically Garrard put the telescope into action. Where was the Earth? After 12,000 years—

The Earth was there. Which, he realized swiftly, proved nothing. The Earth had lasted for many millions of years; 12,000 years was nothing to a planet. The Moon was there, too; both were plainly visible, on the far side of the Sun, but not too far to pick them out clearly with the telescope at highest power. Garrard could even see a clear sun-highlight on the Atlantic Ocean, not far east of Greenland; evidently the computers were bringing the DFC-3 in on the Earth from about 23° north of the plane of the ecliptic.

The Moon, too, had not changed. He could even see on its face the huge splash of white, mimicking the sun-highlight on Earth's ocean, which was the magnesium hydroxide landing beacon which had been dusted over the Mare Vaporum in the earliest days of spaceflight, with a dark spot on its southern edge which could only be the crater Monilius.

But that again proved nothing. The Moon never changed. A film of dust laid down by modern man on its face would last for millennia—what, after all, existed on the Moon to blow it away? The Mare Vaporum beacon covered more than 4000 square miles; age would not dim it, nor could man himself undo it either accidentally or on purpose in anything under a century. When you dust an area that large on a world without atmosphere, it stays dusted.

He checked the stars against his charts. They hadn't moved; why should they have, in only 12,000 years? The pointer-stars in the Dipper still pointed to Polaris. Draco, like a fantastic bit of tape, wound between the two Bears and Cepheus and Cassiopeia as it always had done. These constellations told him only that it was spring in the northern hemisphere of Earth.

But spring of what year?

Then, suddenly, it occurred to him that he had a method of finding the answer. The Moon causes tides in the Earth, and action and reaction are always equal and opposite. The Moon cannot move things on Earth without itself being affected—and that effect shows up in the Moon's angular momentum. The Moon's distance from the Earth increases steadily by 0.6 inches every year. At the end of 12,000 years, it should be 600 feet farther away from the Earth than it had been when Garrard left it.

Was it possible to measure? Garrard doubted it, but he got out his ephemeris and his dividers anyhow, and took pictures. While he worked, the Earth grew nearer. By the time he had finished his first calculation, which was indecisive because it allowed a margin for error greater than the distances he was trying to check, Earth and Moon were close enough in the telescope to permit much more accurate measurements.

Which were, he realized wryly, quite unnecessary. The computer had brought the DFC-3 back, not to an observed sun or planet, but simply to a calculated point. That Earth and Moon would not be near that point when the DFC-3 returned was not an assumption that the computer could make. That the Earth was visible from here was already good and sufficient proof that no more time had elapsed than had been calculated for from the beginning.

This was hardly new to him; it had simply been retired to the back of his mind. Actually he had been doing all this figuring for one reason, and one reason only: because deep in his brain, set to work by himself, there was a mechanism that demanded counting. Long ago, while he was still trying to time the ship's calendar, he had initiated compulsive counting—and it appeared that he had been counting ever since. That had been one of the known dangers of deliberately starting such a mental mechanism, and now it was bearing fruit in these perfectly useless astronomical exercises.

The insight was healing. He finished the figures roughly, and that unheard moron deep inside his brain stopped counting at last. It had been pawing its abacus for twenty months now, and he imagined that it was as glad to be retired as he was to feel it go.

His radio squawked and said anxiously, "DFC-3, DFC-3. Garrard, do you hear me? Are you still alive? Everybody's going wild down here. Garrard, if you hear me, call us!"

It was Haertel's voice. Garrard closed the dividers so convulsively that one of the points nipped into the heel of his hand.

"Haertel, I'm here. DFC-3 to the Project. This is Garrard." And then, without knowing quite why, he added: "With all of love."

Haertel, after all the hoopla was over, was more than interested in the time-effects. "It certainly enlarges the manifold in which I was working," he said. "But I think we can account for it in the transformation. Perhaps even factor it out, which would eliminate it as far as the pilot is concerned. We'll see, anyhow."

Garrard swirled his highball reflectively. In Haertel's cramped old office in the Project's administration shack, he felt both strange and as old and compressed, constricted. He said, "I don't think I'd do that, Adolph. I think it saved my life."

"How?"

"I told you that I seemed to die after a while. Since I got home I've been reading, and I've discovered that the psychologists take far less stock in the individuality of the human psyche than you and I do. You and I are physical scientists, so we think about the world as being all outside our skins, something which is to be observed, but which doesn't alter the essential *I*. But evidently that old solipsistic position isn't quite true. Our very personalities, really, depend in large part upon all the things in our environment, large and small, that exist outside our skins. If by some means you could cut a human being off from every sense impression that comes to him from outside, he would cease to exist as a personality within two or three minutes. Probably he would die."

"Unquote: Harry Stack Sullivan," Haertel said, drily. "So?"

"So," Garrard said, "think of what a monotonous environment the inside of a spaceship is. It's perfectly rigid, sterile, unchanging, lifeless. In ordinary interplanetary flight in such an environment, even the most hardened spaceman may go off his rocker now and then. You know the typical spaceman's psychosis as well as I do, I suppose. The man's personality goes rigid, just like his surroundings. It used to happen to submariners, too. Usually he recovers as soon as he makes port and makes contact with a more or less normal world again.

"But in the DFC-3, I was cut off from the world around me much more severely. I couldn't look outside the ports—I was in overdrive and there was nothing to see. I couldn't communicate with home, because I was going faster than light. And then I found I couldn't move, too, for an enormous long while, and that even the instruments that are in constant change for the usual spaceman wouldn't be in motion for me. Even those were fixed.

"After the time rate began to pick up, I found myself in an even more impossible box. The instruments moved, all right, but they moved too *fast* for me to read them. The whole situation was now utterly rigid—and, in effect, *I died.* I froze as solid as the ship around me, and stayed that way as long as the overdrive was on."

"By that showing," Haertel said drily, "the time effects were hardly your friends."

"But they were, Adolph. Look. Your engines act on subjective time; they keep it varying along continuous curves, from far-too-slow to far-too-fast, and, I suppose, back down again. Now, this is a *situation of continuous change.* It wasn't marked enough, in the long run, to keep me out of pseudo-death; but it was sufficient to protect me from being obliterated altogether, which I think is what happened to

Brown and Cellini. Those men knew that they could shut down the overdrive if they could just get to it, and they killed themselves trying. But I knew that I just had to sit and take it—and, by my great good luck, your sine-curve time-variation made it possible for me to survive."

"Ah, ah," Haertel said. "A point worth considering—though I doubt that it will make interstellar travel very popular!"

He dropped back into silence, his thin mouth pursed. Garrard took a grateful pull at his drink. At last Haertel said: "Why are you in trouble with the authorities over these Centaurians? It seems to me that you have done a good job. It was nothing that you were a hero, any fool can be brave, but I see also that you thought, where Brown and Cellini evidently only reacted. Is there some secret about what you found when you reached those two stars?"

"Yes, there is," Garrard said. "But I've already told you what it is. When I came out of the pseudo-death, I was just a sort of plastic palimpsest upon which anybody could have made a mark. My own environment, my ordinary Earth environment, was a hell of a long way away. My present surroundings were nearly as rigid as they had ever been. When I met the Centaurians—if I did, and I'm not at all sure of that —*they* became the most important thing in my world, and my personality changed to accommodate and understand them. That was a change about which I couldn't do a thing.

"Possibly I did understand them. But the man who understood them wasn't the same man you're talking to now, Adolph. Now that I'm back on Earth, I don't understand that man. He even spoke English in a way that's gibberish to me. If I can't understand myself during that period—and I can't, I don't even believe that that man was the Garrard I know —what hope have I of telling you or the Project about the Centaurians? They found me in a controlled environment, and they altered me by entering it. Now that they're gone, nothing comes through; I don't even understand why I think they spoke English!"

"Did they have a name for themselves?"

"Sure," Garrard said. "They were the beademungen."

"What did they look like?"

"I never saw them."

Haertel leaned forward. "Then how—"

"I heard them. I think." Garrard shrugged, and tasted his Scotch again. He was home, and on the whole he was pleased.

But in his malleable mind he heard someone say, *On Earth, as it is in Heaven:* and then, in another voice, which might also have been his own (why had he thought "him-other"?), *It is later than you think.*

"Adolph," he said, "is this all there is to it? Or are we going to go on with it from here? How long will it take to make a better starship, a DFC-4?"

"Many years," Haertel said, smiling kindly. "Don't be anxious, Garrard. You've come back, which is more than the others managed to do, and nobody will ask you to go out again. I really think that it's hardly likely that we'll get another ship built during your lifetime, and even if we do, we'll be slow to launch it. We really have very little information about what kind of a playground you found out there."

"I'll go," Garrard said. "I'm not afraid to go back—I'd like to go. Now that I know how the DFC 3 behaves, I could take that again, bring you back proper maps, tapes, photos."

"Do you really think," Haertel said, his face suddenly serious, "that we could let the DFC-3 go out again? Garrard, we're going to take that ship apart practically molecule by molecule; that's preliminary to the building of any DFC-4. And no more can we let you go. I don't mean to be cruel, but has it occurred to you that this desire to go back may be the result of some kind of post-hypnotic suggestion? If so, the more badly you want to go back, the more dangerous to us all you may be. We are going to have to examine you just as thoroughly as we do the ship. If these beademungen wanted you to come back, they must have had a reason—and we have to know that reason."

Garrard nodded, but he knew that Haertel could see the

slight movement of his eyebrows and the wrinkles forming in his forehead, the contractions of the small muscles which stop the flow of tears only to make grief patent on the rest of the face.

"In short," he said, *"don't move."*

Haertel looked politely puzzled. Garrard, however, could say nothing more. He had returned to humanity's common time, and would never leave it again.

Not even, for all his dimly remembered promise, with all there was left in him of love.

THE NEW PRIME

Jack Vance

Jack Vance is a native Californian, sturdy and stolid, who delights in felling timber, building boats, and cruising the Pacific for months at a time. These may seem curiously rugged pursuits for a writer whose prose is marked by astonishing delicacy of effect and richness of poetic detail, but Vance himself sees no contradiction between Vance the outdoorsman and Vance the stylist, and neither should we: let us rejoice, rather, that we have among us someone equally at home at the tiller and in the ivory tower. He has been a professional writer since 1945, and much of his work has been science fiction, and much of that is soaring, visionary fantasy, set in remote places and times. Would that we could include here such long Vance works as To Live Forever, The Dying Earth, *or the award-winning novellas, "The Dragon*

Masters" and "The Last Castle." But the story that follows displays, in a smaller compass, Vance's ingenuity, his breadth of vision, and his elegance of style.

MUSIC, carnival lights, the slide of feet on waxed oak, perfume, muffled talk and laughter.

Arthur Caversham of twentieth-century Boston felt air along his skin, and discovered himself to be stark naked.

It was at Janice Paget's coming-out party: three hundred guests in formal evening-wear surrounded him.

For a moment he felt no emotion beyond vague bewilderment. His presence seemed the outcome of logical events, but his memory was fogged and he could find no definite anchor of certainty.

He stood a little apart from the rest of the stag line, facing the red and gold calliope where the orchestra sat. The buffet, the punch bowl, the champagne wagons, tended by clowns, were to his right; to the left, through the open flap of the circus tent, lay the garden, now lit by strings of colored lights, red, green, yellow, blue, and he caught a glimpse of a merry-go-round across the lawn.

Why was he here? He had no recollection, no sense of purpose. . . . The night was warm; the other young men in the full-dress suits must feel rather sticky, he thought. . . . An idea tugged at a corner of his mind. There was a significant aspect of the affair that he was overlooking.

He noticed that the young men nearby had moved away from him. He heard chortles of amusement, astonished exclamations. A girl dancing past saw him over the arm of her escort; she gave a startled squeak, jerked her eyes away, giggling and blushing.

Something was wrong. These young men and women were startled and amazed by his naked skin to the point of embarrassment. The gnaw of urgency came closer to the surface. He must do something. Taboos felt with such intensity might not be violated without unpleasant consequences; such was his understanding. He was lacking garments; these he must obtain.

He looked about him, inspecting the young men who watched him with ribald delight, disgust, or curiosity. To one of these latter he addressed himself.

"Where can I get some clothing?"

The young man shrugged. "Where did you leave yours?"

Two heavyset men in dark blue uniforms entered the tent; Arthur Caversham saw them from the corner of his eye, and his mind worked with desperate intensity.

This young man seemed typical of those around him. What sort of appeal would have meaning for him? Like any other human being, he could be moved to action if the right chord were struck. By what method could he be moved?

Sympathy?

Threats?

The prospect of advantage or profit?

Caversham rejected all of these. By violating the taboo he had forfeited his claim to sympathy. A threat would excite derision, and he had no profit or advantage to offer. The stimulus must be more devious. . . . He reflected that young men customarily banded together in secret societies. In the thousand cultures he had studied this was almost infallibly true. Long-houses, drug-cults, tongs, instruments of sexual initiation—whatever the name, the external aspects were near-identical: painful initation, secret signs and passwords, uniformity of group conduct, obligation to service. If this young man were a member of such an association, he might react to an appeal to this group-spirit.

Arthur Caversham said, "I've been put in this taboo situation by the brotherhood; in the name of the brotherhood, find me some suitable garments."

The young man stared, taken aback. "Brotherhood? . . . You mean fraternity?" Enlightenment spread over his face. "Is this some kind of hell-week stunt?" He laughed. "If it is, they sure go all the way."

"Yes," said Arthur Caversham. "My fraternity."

The young man said, "This way, then—and hurry, here comes the law. We'll take off under the tent. I'll lend you my topcoat till you make it back to your house."

The two uniformed men, pushing quietly through the dancers, were almost upon them. The young man lifted the flap of the tent, Arthur Caversham ducked under, his friend followed. Together they ran through the many-colored shadows to a little booth painted with gay red and white stripes that was near the entrance to the tent.

"You stay back, out of sight," said the young man. "I'll check out my coat."

"Fine," said Arthur Caversham.

The young man hesitated. "What's your house? Where do you go to school?"

Arthur Caversham desperately searched his mind for an answer. A single fact reached the surface.

"I'm from Boston."

"Boston U? or MIT? Or Harvard?"

"Harvard."

"Ah." The young man nodded. "I'm Washington and Lee myself. What's your house?"

"I'm not supposed to say."

"Oh," said the young man, puzzled but satisfied. "Well— just a minute. . . ."

Bearwald the Halforn halted, numb with despair and exhaustion. The remnants of his platoon sank to the ground around him, and they stared back to where the rim of the night flickered and glowed with fire. Many villages, many wood-gabled farmhouses had been given the torch, and the Brands from Mount Medallion reveled in human blood.

The pulse of a distant drum touched Bearwald's skin, a deep *thrumm-thrumm-thrumm*, almost inaudible. Much closer he heard a hoarse human cry of fright, then exultant killing-calls, not human. The Brands were tall, black, man-shaped but not men. They had eyes like lamps of red glass, bright white teeth, and tonight they seemed bent on slaughtering all the men of the world.

"Down," hissed Kanaw, his right arm-guard, and Bearwald crouched. Across the flaring sky marched a column of tall Brand warriors, rocking jauntily, without fear.

Bearwald said suddenly, "Men—we are thirteen. Fighting arm to arm with these monsters we are helpless. Tonight their total force is down from the mountain; the hive must be near deserted. What can we lose if we undertake to burn the home-hive of the Brands? Only our lives, and what are these now?"

Kanaw said, "Our lives are nothing; let us be off at once."

"May our vengeance be great," said Broctan the left arm-guard. "May the home-hive of the Brands be white ashes this coming morn . . ."

Mount Medallion loomed overhead; the oval hive lay in Pangborn Valley. At the mouth of the valley, Bearwald divided the platoon into two halves, and placed Kanaw in the van of the second. "We move silently twenty yards apart; thus if either party rouses a Brand, the other may attack from the rear and so kill the monster before the vale is roused. Do all understand?"

"We understand."

"Forward then, to the hive."

The valley reeked with an odor like sour leather. From the direction of the hive came a muffled clanging. The ground was soft, covered with runner moss; careful feet made no sound. Crouching low, Bearwald could see the shapes of his men against the sky—here indigo with a violet rim. The angry glare of burning Echevasa lay down the slope to the south.

A sound. Bearwald hissed, and the columns froze. They waited. *Thud-thud-thud-thud* came the steps—then a hoarse cry of rage and alarm.

"Kill, kill the beast!" yelled Bearwald.

The Brand swung his club like a scythe, lifting one man,

carrying the body around with the after-swing. Bearwald leapt close, struck with his blade, slicing as he hewed; he felt the tendons part, smelled the hot gush of Brand blood.

The clanging had stopped now, and Brand cries carried across the night.

"Forward," panted Bearwald. "Out with your tinder, strike fire to the hive. Burn, burn, burn . . ."

Abandoning stealth he ran forward; ahead loomed the dark dome. Immature Brands came surging forth, squeaking and squalling, and with them came the genetrices—twenty-foot monsters crawling on hands and feet, grunting and snapping as they moved.

"Kill!" yelled Bearwald the Halforn. "Kill! Fire, fire, fire!"

He dashed to the hive, crouched, struck spark to tinder, puffed. The rag, soaked with saltpeter, flared; Bearwald fed it straw, thrust it against the hive. The reed-pulp and withe crackled.

He leapt up as a horde of young Brands darted at him. His blade rose and fell; they were cleft, no match for his frenzy. Creeping close came the great Brand genetrices, three of them, swollen of abdomen, exuding an odor vile to his nostrils.

"Out with the fire!" yelled the first. "Fire, out. The Great Mother is tombed within; she lies too fecund to move. . . . Fire, woe, destruction!" And they wailed, "Where are the mighty? Where are our warriors?"

Thrumm-thrumm-thrumm came the sound of skindrums. Up the valley rolled the echo of hoarse Brand voices.

Bearwald stood with his back to the blaze. He darted forward, severed the head of a creeping genetrix, jumped back. . . . Where were his men? "Kanaw!" he called. "Laida! Theyat! Gyorg! Broctan!"

He craned his neck, saw the flicker of fires. "Men! Kill the creeping mothers!" And leaping forward once more, he hacked and hewed, and another genetrix sighed and groaned and rolled flat.

The Brand voices changed to alarm; the triumphant drumming halted; the thud of footsteps came loud.

At Bearwald's back the hive burnt with a pleasant heat. Within came a shrill keening, a cry of vast pain.

In the leaping blaze he saw the charging Brand warriors. Their eyes glared like embers, their teeth shone like white sparks. They came forward, swinging their clubs, and Bearwald gripped his sword, too proud to flee.

After grounding his air sled Ceistan sat a few minutes inspecting the dead city Therlatch: a wall of earthen brick a hundred feet high, a dusty portal, and a few crumbled roofs lifting above the battlements. Behind the city the desert spread across the near, middle, and far distance to the hazy shapes of the Allune Mountains at the horizon, pink in the light of the twin suns Mig and Pag.

Scouting from above he had seen no sign of life, nor had he expected any, after a thousand years of abandonment. Perhaps a few sand-crawlers wallowed in the heat of the ancient bazaar. Otherwise the streets would feel his presence with great surprise.

Jumping from the air sled, Ceistan advanced toward the portal. He passed under, stood looking right and left with interest. In the parched air the brick buildings stood almost eternal. The wind smoothed and rounded all harsh angles; the glass had been cracked by the heat of day and chill of night; heaps of sand clogged the passageways.

Three streets led away from the portal and Ceistan could find nothing to choose between them. Each was dusty, narrow, and each twisted out of his line of vision after a hundred yards.

Ceistan rubbed his chin thoughtfully. Somewhere in the city lay a brassbound coffer, containing the Crown and Shield Parchment. This, according to tradition, set a precedent for the fiefholder's immunity from energy-tax. Glay, who was

Ceistan's liege-lord, having cited the parchment as justification for his delinquency, had been challenged to show validity. Now he lay in prison on charge of rebellion, and in the morning he would be nailed to the bottom of an air sled and sent drifting into the west, unless Ceistan returned with the parchment.

After a thousand years, there was small cause for optimism, thought Ceistan. However, the lord Glay was a fair man and he would leave no stone unturned. . . . If it existed, the chest presumably would lie in state, in the town's Legalic, or the Mosque, or in the Hall of Relics, or possibly in the Sumptuar. He would search all of these, allowing two hours per building; the eight hours so used would see the end to the pink daylight.

At random he entered the street in the center and shortly came to a plaza at whose far end rose the Legalic, the Hall of Records and Decisions. At the façade Ceistan paused, for the interior was dim and gloomy. No sound came from the dusty void save the sigh and whisper of the dry wind. He entered.

The great hall was empty. The walls were illuminated with frescoes of red and blue, as bright as if painted yesterday. There were six to each wall, the top half displaying a criminal act and the bottom half the penalty.

Ceistan passed through the hall, into the chambers behind. He found but dust and the smell of dust. Into the crypts he ventured, and these were lit by embrasures. There was much litter and rubble, but no brass coffer.

Up and out into the clean air he went, and strode across the plaza to the Mosque, where he entered under the massive architrave.

The Nunciator's Confirmatory lay wide and bare and clean, for the tesselated floor was swept by a powerful draft. A thousand apertures opened from the low ceiling, each communicating with a cell overhead; thus arranged so that the devout might seek counsel with the Nunciator as he passed below without disturbing their attitudes of supplication. In the center of the pavilion a disk of glass roofed a recess. Below was a coffer and in the coffer rested a brass-bound chest. Ceistan sprang down the steps in high hopes.

But the chest contained jewels—the tiara of the Old Queen, the chest vellopes of the Gonwand Corps, the great ball, half emerald, half ruby, which in the ancient ages was rolled across the plaza to signify the passage of the old year.

Ceistan tumbled them all back in the coffer. Relics on this planet of dead cities had no value, and synthetic gems were infinitely superior in luminosity and water.

Leaving the Mosque, he studied the height of the suns. The zenith was past, the moving balls of pink fire leaned to the west. He hesitated, frowning and blinking at the hot earthen walls, considering that not impossibly both coffer and parchment were fable, like so many others regarding dead Ther-latch.

A gust of wind swirled across the plaza and Ceistan choked on a dry throat. He spat, and an acrid taste bit his tongue. An old fountain opened in the wall nearby; he examined it wistfully, but water was not even a memory along these dead streets.

Once again he cleared his throat, spat, turned across the city toward the Hall of Relics.

He entered the great nave, past square pillars built of earthen brick. Pink shafts of light struck down from the cracks and gaps in the roof, and he was like a midge in the vast space. To all sides were niches cased in glass, and each held an object of ancient reverence: the armor in which Plange the Forewarned led the Blue Flags; the coronet of the First Serpent; an array of antique Padang skulls; Princess Thormosterallam's bridal gown on woven cobweb palladium, as fresh as the day she wore it; the original Tablets of Legality; the great conch throne of an early dynasty; a dozen other objects. But the coffer was not among them.

Ceistan sought for entrance to a possible crypt, but except where the currents of dusty air had channeled grooves in the porphyry, the floor was smooth.

Out once more into the dead streets, and now the suns had passed behind the crumbled roofs, leaving the streets in magenta shadow.

With leaden feet, burning throat, and a sense of defeat, Ceistan turned to the Sumptuar, on the citadel. Up the wide steps, under the verdigris-fronted portico into a lobby painted with vivid frescoes. These depicted the maidens of ancient Therlatch at work, at play, amid sorrow and joy: slim creatures with short, black hair and glowing ivory skin, as graceful as water vanes, as round and delectable as chermoyan plums. Ceistan passed through the lobby with many side-glances, reflecting that these ancient creatures of delight were now the dust he trod under his feet.

He walked down a corridor which made a circuit of the building, and from which the chambers and apartments of the Sumptuar might be entered. The wisps of a wonderful rug crunched under his feet, and the walls displayed moldy tatters, once tapestries of the finest weave. At the entrance to each chamber a fresco pictured the Sumptuar maiden and the sign she served; at each of these chambers Ceistan paused, make a quick investigation, and so passed on to the next. The beams slanting in through the cracks served him as a gauge of time, and they flattened ever more toward the horizontal.

Chamber after chamber after chamber. There were chests in some, altars in others, cases of manifestos, triptychs, and fonts in others. But never the chest he sought.

And ahead was the lobby where he had entered the building. Three more chambers were to be searched, then the light would be gone.

He came to the first of these, and this was hung with a new curtain. Pushing it aside, he found himself looking into an outside court, full in the long light of the twin suns. A fountain of water trickled down across steps of apple-green jade into a garden as soft and fresh and green as any in the north. And rising in alarm from a couch was a maiden, as vivid and delightful as any in the frescoes. She had short, dark hair, a face as pure and delicate as the great white frangipani she wore over her ear.

For an instant Ceistan and the maiden stared eye to eye; then her alarm faded and she smiled shyly.

"Who are you?" Ceistan asked in wonder. "Are you a ghost or do you live here in the dust?"

"I am real," she said. "My home is to the south, at the Palram Oasis, and this is the period of solitude to which all maidens of the race submit when aspiring for Upper Instruction. . . . So without fear may you come beside me, and rest, and drink of fruit wine and be my companion through the lonely night, for this is my last week of solitude and I am weary of my aloneness."

Ceistan took a step forward, then hesitated. "I must fulfill my mission. I seek the brass coffer containing the Crown and Shield Parchment. Do you know of this?"

She shook her head. "It is nowhere in the Sumptuar." She rose to her feet, stretching her ivory arms as a kitten stretches. "Abandon your search, and come let me refresh you."

Ceistan looked at her, looked up at the fading light, looked down the corridor to the two doors yet remaining. "First I must complete my search; I owe duty to my lord Glay, who will be nailed under an air sled and sped west unless I bring him aid."

The maiden said with a pout, "Go then to your dusty chamber; and go with a dry throat. You will find nothing, and if you persist so stubbornly, I will be gone when you return."

"So let it be," said Ceistan.

He turned away, marched down the corridor. The first chamber was bare and dry as a bone. In the second and last, a man's skeleton lay tumbled in a corner; this Ceistan saw in the last rosy light of the twin suns.

There was no brass coffer, no parchment. So Glay must die, and Ceistan's heart hung heavy.

He returned to the chamber where he had found the

maiden, but she had departed. The fountain had been stopped, and moisture only filmed the stones.

Ceistan called, "Maiden, where are you? Return; my obligation is at an end. . . ."

There was no response.

Ceistan shrugged, turned to the lobby and so outdoors, to grope his way through the deserted twilight street to the portal and his air sled.

Dobnor Daksat became aware that the big man in the embroidered black coat was speaking to him.

Orienting himself to his surroundings, which were at once familiar and strange, he also became aware that the man's voice was condescending, supercilious.

"You are competing in a highly advanced classification," he said. "I marvel at your . . . ah, confidence." And he eyed Daksat with a gleaming and speculative eye.

Daksat looked down at the floor, frowned at the sight of his clothes. He wore a long cloak of black-purple velvet, swinging like a bell around his ankles. His trousers were of scarlet corduroy, tight at the waist, thigh, and calf, with a loose puff of green cloth between calf and ankle. The clothes were his own, obviously: they looked wrong and right at once, as did the carved gold knuckle-guards he wore on his hands.

The big man in the dark cloak continued speaking, looking at a point over Daksat's head, as if Daksat were nonexistent.

"Clauktaba has won Imagist honors over the years. Bel-Washab was the Korsi Victor last month; Tol Morabait is an acknowledged master of the technique. And then there is Ghisel Ghang of West Ind, who knows no peer in the creation of fire-stars, and Pulakt Havjorska, the Champion of the Island Realm. So it becomes a matter of skepticism whether you, new, inexperienced, without a fund of images, can do more than embarrass us all with your mental poverty."

Daksat's brain was yet wrestling with his bewilderment, and he could feel no strong resentment at the big man's evident contempt. He said, "Just what is all this? I'm not sure that I understand my position."

The man in the black cloak inspected him quizzically. "So, now you commence to experience trepidation? Justly, I assure you." He sighed, waved his hands. "Well, well—young men will be impetuous, and perhaps you have formed images you considered not discreditable. In any event, the public eye will ignore you for the glories of Clauktaba's geometrics and Ghisel Ghang's star-bursts. Indeed, I counsel you, keep your images small, drab, and confined; you will so avoid the faults of bombast and discord. . . . Now, it is time to go to your Imagicon. This way, then. Remember, grays, browns, lavenders, perhaps a few tones of ocher and rust; then the spectators will understand that you compete for the schooling alone, and do not actively challenge the masters. This way then. . . ."

He opened a door and led Dobnor Daksat up a stair and so out into the night.

They stood in a great stadium, facing six great screens forty feet high. Behind them in the dark sat tier upon tier of spectators—thousands and thousands, and their sounds came as a soft crush. Daksat turned to see them, but all their faces and their individualities had melted into the entity as a whole.

"Here," said the big man, "this is your apparatus. Seat yourself and I will adjust the ceretemps."

Daksat suffered himself to be placed in a heavy chair, so soft and deep that he felt himself to be floating. Adjustments were made at his head and neck and the bridge of his nose. He felt a sharp prick, a pressure, a throb, and then a soothing warmth. From the distance, a voice called out over the crowd:

"Two minutes to gray mist! Two minutes to gray mist! Attend, Imagists, two minutes to gray mist!"

The big man stooped over him. "Can you see well?"

Daksat raised himself a trifle. "Yes . . . all is clear."

"Very well. At 'gray mist,' this little filament will glow.

When it dies, then it is your screen, and you must imagine your best."

The far voice said, "One minute to gray mist! The order is Pulakt Havjorska, Tol Morabait, Ghisel Ghang, Dobnor Daksat, Clauktaba, and Bel-Washab. There are no handicaps; all colors and shapes are permitted. Relax then, ready your lobes, and now—gray mist!"

The light glowed on the panel of Daksat's chair, and he saw five of the six screens light to a pleasant pearl-gray, swirling a trifle as if agitated, excited. Only the screen before him remained dull. The big man, who stood behind him, reached down, prodded. "Gray mist, Daksat; are you deaf and blind?"

Daksat thought gray mist, and instantly his screen sprang to life, displaying a cloud of silver-gray, clean and clear.

"Humph," he heard the big man snort. "Somewhat dull and without interest—but I suppose good enough.... See how Clauktaba's rings with hints of passion already, quivers with emotion."

And Daksat, noting the screen to his right, saw this to be true. The gray, without actually displaying color, flowed and filmed as if suppressing a vast flood of light.

Now, to the far left, on Pulakt Havjorska's screen, color glowed. It was a gambit image, modest and restrained—a green jewel dripping a rain of blue and silver drops which struck a black ground and disappeared in little orange explosions.

Then Tol Morabait's screen glowed: a black and white checkerboard with certain of the squares flashing suddenly green, red, blue, and yellow—warm, searching colors, pure as shafts from a rainbow. The image disappeared in a flush mingled of rose and blue.

Ghisel Ghang wrought a circle of yellow which quivered, brought forth a green halo, which in turn bulged giving rise to a larger band of brilliant black and white. In the center formed a complex kaleidoscopic pattern. The pattern suddenly vanished in a brilliant flash of light; on the screen for an instant or two appeared the identical pattern in a complete new suit of colors. A ripple of sound from the spectators greeted this *tour de force.*

The light on Daksat's panel died. Behind him he felt a prod. "Now."

Daksat eyed the screen and his mind was blank of ideas. He ground his teeth. Anything. Anything. A picture . . . he imagined a view across the meadowlands beside the River Melramy.

"Hm," said the big man behind him. "Pleasant. A pleasant fantasy, and rather original."

Puzzled, Daksat examined the picture on the screen. So far as he could distinguish, it was an uninspired reproduction of a scene he knew well. Fantasy? Was that what was expected? Very well, he'd produce fantasy. He imagined the meadows glowing, molten, white-hot. The vegetation, the old cairns slumped into a viscous seethe. The surface smoothed, became a mirror which reflected the Copper Crags.

Behind him the big man grunted. "A little heavy-handed, that last, and thereby you destroyed the charming effect of those unearthly colors and shapes. . . ."

Daksat slumped back in his chair, frowning, eager for his turn to come again.

Meanwhile Clauktaba created a dainty white blossom with purple stamens on a green stalk. The petals wilted, the stamens discharged a cloud of swirling yellow pollen.

Then Bel-Washab, at the end of the line, painted his screen a luminous underwater green. It rippled, bulged, and a black irregular blot marred the surface. From the center of the blot seeped a trickle of hot gold that quickly meshed and veined the black blot.

Such was the first passage.

There was a pause of several seconds. "Now," breathed the voice behind Daksat, "now the competition begins."

On Pulakt Havjorska's screen appeared an angry sea of color: waves of red, green, blue, an ugly mottling. Dramatically, a yellow shape appeared at the lower right, vanquished the chaos. It spread over the screen, the center went lime-green. A black shape appeared split, bowed softly and easily to both sides. Then turning, the two shapes wandered into the background, twisting, bending with supple grace. Far down a perspective they merged, darted forward like a lance, spread out into a series of lances, formed a slanting pattern of slim black bars.

"Superb!" hissed the big man. "The timing, so just, so exact!"

Tol Morabait replied with a fuscous brown field threaded with crimson lines and blots. Vertical green hatching formed at the left, strode across the screen to the right. The brown field pressed forward, bulged through the green bars, pressed hard, broke, and segments flitted forward to leave the screen. On the black background behind the green hatching, which now faded, lay a human brain, pink, pulsing. The brain sprouted six insectlike legs, scuttled crabwise back into the distance.

Ghisel Ghang brought forth one of his fire-bursts—a small pellet of bright blue exploding in all directions, the tips working and writhing through wonderful patterns in the five colors, blue, violet, white, purple, and light green.

Dobnor Daksat, rigid as a bar, sat with hands clenched and teeth grinding into teeth. Now! Was not his brain as excellent as those of the far lands? Now!

On the screen appeared a tree, conventionalized in greens and blues, and each leaf was a tongue of fire. From these fires wisps of smoke arose on high to form a cloud which worked and swirled, then emptied a cone of rain about the tree. The flames vanished and in their places appeared star-shaped white flowers. From the cloud came a bolt of lightning, shattering the tree to agonized fragments of glass. Another bolt into the brittle heap and the screen exploded in a great gout of white, orange, and black.

The voice of the big man said doubtfully, "On the whole, well done, but mind my warning, and create more modest images, since—"

"Silence!" said Dognor Daksat in a harsh voice.

So the competition went, round after round of spectacles, some sweet as canmel honey, others as violent as the storms that circle the poles. Color strove with color, patterns evolved and changed, sometimes in glorious cadence, sometimes in the bitter discord necessary to the strength of the image.

And Daksat built dream after dream, while his tension vanished, and he forgot all save the racing pictures in his mind and on the screen, and his images became as complex and subtle as those of the masters.

"One more passage," said the big man behind Daksat, and now the imagists brought forth the master-dreams: Pulakt Havjorska, the growth and decay of a beautiful city; Tol Morabait, a quiet composition of green and white interrupted by a marching army of insects who left a dirty wake, and who were joined in battle by men in painted leather armor and tall hats, armed with short swords and flails. The insects were destroyed and chased off the screen; the dead warriors became bones and faded to twinkling blue dust. Ghisel Ghang created three fire-bursts simultaneously, each different, a gorgeous display.

Daksat imagined a smooth pebble, magnified it to a block of marble, chipped it away to create the head of a beautiful maiden. For a moment she stared forth and varying emotions crossed her face—joy at her sudden existence, pensive thought, and at last fright. Her eyes turned milky opaque blue, the face changed to a laughing sardonic mask, black-cheeked with a fleering mouth. The head tilted, the mouth spat into the air. The head flattened into a black background, the drops of spittle shone like fire, became stars, constellations, and one of these expanded, became a planet with configurations dear to Daksat's heart. The planet hurtled off into darkness, the constellations faded. Dobnor Daksat relaxed. His last image. He sighed, exhausted.

The big man in the black cloak removed the harness in brittle silence. At last he asked, "The planet you imagined in the last screening, was that a creation or a remembrance of actuality? It was none of our system here, and it rang with the clarity of truth."

Dobnor Daksat stared at him, puzzled, and the words faltered in his throat. "But it is—home! This world! Was it not this world?"

The big man looked at him strangely, shrugged, turned away. "In a moment now the winner of the contest will be made known and the jeweled brevet awarded."

The day was gusty and overcast, the galley was low and black, manned by the oarsmen of Beleclaw. Ergan stood on the poop, staring across the two miles of bitter sea to the coast of Racland, where he knew the sharp-faced Racs stood watching from the headlands.

A gout of water erupted a few hundred yards astern.

Ergan spoke to the helmsman. "Their guns have better range than we bargained for. Better stand offshore another mile and we'll take our chances with the current."

Even as he spoke, there came a great whistle and he glimpsed a black pointed projectile slanting down at him. It struck the waist of the galley, exploded. Timber, bodies, metal flew everywhere, and the galley laid its broken back into the water, doubled up and sank.

Ergan, jumping clear, discarded his sword, casque, and greaves almost as he hit the chill gray water. Gasping from the shock, he swam in circles, bobbing up and down in the chop; then, finding a length of timber, he clung to it for support.

From the shores of Racland a longboat put forth and approached, bow churning white foam as it rose and fell across the waves. Ergan turned loose the timber and swam as rapidly as possible from the wreck. Better drowning than capture; there would be more mercy from the famine-fish that swarmed the waters than from the pitiless Racs.

So he swam, but the current took him to the shore, and at last, struggling feebly, he was cast upon a pebbly beach.

Here he was discovered by a gang of Rac youths and marched to a nearby command post. He was tied and flung into a cart and so conveyed to the city Korsapan.

In a gray room he was seated facing an intelligence officer of the Rac secret police, a man with the gray skin of a toad, a moist gray mouth, eager, searching eyes.

"You are Ergan," said the officer. "Emissary to the Bargee of Salomdek. What was your mission?"

Ergan stared back eye to eye, hoping that a happy and convincing response would find his lips. None came, and the truth would incite an immediate invasion of both Belaclaw and Salomdek by the tall, thin-headed Rac soldiers, who wore black uniforms and black boots.

Ergan said nothing. The officer leaned forward. "I ask you once more; then you will be taken to the room below." He said "Room Below" as if the words were capitalized, and he said it with soft relish.

Ergan, in a cold sweat, for he knew of the Rac torturers, said, "I am not Ergan; my name is Ervard; I am an honest trader in pearls."

"This is untrue," said the Rac. "Your aide was captured, and under the compression pump he blurted up your name with his lungs."

"I am Ervard," said Ergan, his bowels quaking.

The Rac signaled. "Take him to the Room Below."

A man's body, which has developed nerves as outposts against danger, seems especially intended for pain, and cooperates wonderfully with the craft of the torturer. These characteristics of the body had been studied by the Rac specialists, and other capabilities of the human nervous system had been blundered upon by accident. It had been found that certain programs of pressure, heat, strain, friction, torque, surge, jerk, sonic and visual shock, vermin, stench, and vileness created cumulative effects, whereas a single method, used to excess, lost its stimulation thereby.

All this lore and cleverness was lavished upon Ergan's citadel of nerves, and they inflicted upon him the entire gamut of pain: the sharp twinges, the dull, lasting joint-aches which groaned by night, the fiery flashes, the assaults of filth and lechery, together with shocks of occasional tenderness when he would be allowed to glimpse the world he had left.

Then back to the Room Below.

But always: "I am Ervard the trader." And always he tried to goad his mind over the tissue barrier to death, but always the mind hesitated at the last toppling step, and Ergan lived.

The Racs tortured by routine, so that the expectation, the approach of the hour, brought as much torment as the act itself. And then the heavy, unhurried steps outside the cell, the feeble thrashing around to evade, the harsh laughs when they cornered him and carried him forth, and the harsh laughs when three hours later they threw him sobbing and whimpering back to the pile of straw that was his bed.

"I am Ervard," he said, and trained his mind to believe that this was the truth, so that never would they catch him unaware. "I am Ervard! I am Ervard, I trade in pearls!"

He tried to strangle himself on straw, but a slave watched always, and this was not permitted.

He attempted to die by self-suffocation, and would have been glad to succeed, but always as he sank into blessed numbness, so did his mind relax and his motor nerves take up the mindless business of breathing once more.

He ate nothing, but this meant little to the Racs, as they injected him full of tonics, sustaining drugs, and stimulants, so that he might always be keyed to the height of his awareness.

"I am Ervard," said Ergan, and the Racs gritted their teeth angrily. The case was now a challenge; he defied their ingenuity, and they puzzled long and carefully upon refinements and delicacies, new shapes to the iron tools, new types of jerk ropes, new directions for the strains and pressures. Even when it was no longer important whether he was Ergan or Ervard, since war now raged, he was kept and maintained as a problem, an ideal case; so he was guarded and cosseted with even more than usual care, and the Rac torturers mulled over their techniques, making changes here, improvements there.

Then one day the Belaclaw galleys landed and the feather-crested soldiers fought past the walls of Korsapan.

The Racs surveyed Ergan with regret. "Now we must go, and still you will not submit to us."

"I am Ervard," croaked that which lay on the table. "Ervard the trader."

A splintering crash sounded overhead.

"We must go," said the Racs. "Your people have stormed the city. If you tell the truth, you may live. If you lie, we kill you. So there is your choice. Your life for the truth."

"The truth?" muttered Ergan. "It is a trick—" And then he caught the victory chant of the Belaclaw soldiery. "The truth? Why not? . . . Very well." And he said, "I am Ervard," for now he believed this to be the truth.

Galactic Prime was a lean man with reddish-brown hair, sparse across a fine arch of skull. His face, undistinguished otherwise, was given power by great dark eyes flickering with a light like fire behind smoke. Physically, he had passed the peak of his youth; his arms and legs were thin and loose-jointed; his head inclined forward as if weighted by the intricate machinery of his brain.

Arising from the couch, smiling faintly, he looked across the arcade to the eleven Elders. They sat at a table of polished wood, backs to a wall festooned with vines. They were grave men, slow in their motions, and their faces were lined with wisdom and insight. By the ordained system, Prime was the executive of the universe, the Elders the deliberative body, invested with certain restrictive powers.

"Well?"

The Chief Elder without haste raised his eyes from the computer. "You are the first to arise from the couch."

Prime turned a glance up the arcade, still smiling faintly. The others lay variously: some with arms clenched, rigid as bars; others huddled in fetal postures. One had slumped from the couch half to the floor; his eyes were open, staring at remoteness.

Prime returned his gaze to the Chief Elder, who watched him with detached curiosity. "Has the optimum been established?"

The Chief Elder consulted the computer. "Twenty-six thirty-seven is the optimum score."

Prime waited, but the Chief Elder said no more. Prime stepped to the alabaster balustrade beyond the couches. He leaned forward, looked out across the vista—miles and miles of sunny haze, with a twinkling sea in the distance. A breeze blew past his face, ruffling the scant russet strands of his hair. He took a deep breath, flexed his fingers and hands, for the memory of the Rac torturers was still heavy on his mind. After a moment he swung around, leaned back, resting his elbows upon the balustrade. He glanced once more down the line of couches; there were still no signs of vitality from the candidates.

"Twenty-five seventy-four," said the Chief Elder. "The computer judged Bearwald the Halforn's final defiance of the Brand warriors unprofitable."

Prime considered. "The point is well made. Obstinacy serves no purpose unless it advances a predetermined end. It is a flaw I must seek to temper." He looked along the line of Elders, from face to face. "You make no enunciations, you are curiously mute."

He waited; the Chief Elder made no response.

"May I inquire the high score?"

"Twenty-five seventy-four."

Prime nodded. "Mine."

"Yours is the high score," said the Chief Elder.

Prime's smile disappeared: a puzzled line appeared across his brow. "In spite of this, you are still reluctant to confirm my second span of authority; there are still doubts among you."

"Doubts and misgivings," replied the Chief Elder.

Prime's mouth pulled in at the corners, although his brows were still raised in polite inquiry. "Your attitude puzzles me. My record is one of selfless service. My intelligence is phenomenal, and in this final test, which I designed to dispel your last doubts, I attained the highest score. I have proved my social intuition and flexibility, my leadership, devotion to duty, imagination, and resolution. In every commensurable aspect, I fulfill best the qualifications for the office I hold."

The Chief Elder looked up and down the line of his fellows. There were none who wished to speak. The Chief Elder squared himself in his chair, sat back.

"Our attitude is difficult to represent. Everything is as you say. Your intelligence is beyond dispute, your character is exemplary, you have served your term with honor and devotion. You have earned our respect, admiration, and gratitude. We realize also that you seek this second term from praiseworthy motives: you regard yourself as the man best able to coordinate the complex business of the galaxy."

Prime nodded grimly. "But you think otherwise."

"Our position is perhaps not quite so blunt."

"Precisely what is your position?" Prime gestured along the couches. "Look at these men. They are the finest of the galaxy. One man is dead. That one stirring on the third couch has lost his mind; he is a lunatic. The others are sorely shaken. And never forget that this test has been expressly designed to measure the qualities essential to the Galactic Prime."

"This test has been of great interest to us," said the Chief Elder mildly. "It has considerably affected our thinking."

Prime hesitated, plumbing the unspoken overtones of the words. He came forward, seated himself across from the line of Elders. With a narrow glance he searched the faces of the eleven men, tapped once, twice, three times with his fingertips on the polished wood, leaned back in the chair.

"As I have pointed out, the test has gauged each candidate for the exact qualities essential to the optimum conduct of office, in this fashion: Earth of the twentieth century is a planet of intricate conventions; on Earth the candidate, as

Arthur Caversham, is required to use his social intuition—a quality highly important in this galaxy of two billion suns. On Belotsi, Bearwald the Halforn is tested for courage and the ability to conduct positive action. At the dead city Therlatch on Praesepe Three, the candidate, as Ceistan, is rated for devotion to duty, and as Dobnor Daksat at the Imagicon on Staff, his creative conceptions are rated against the most fertile imaginations alive. Finally as Ergan, on Chankozar, his will, persistence, and ultimate fiber are explored to their extreme limits.

"Each candidate is placed on the identical set of circumstances by a trick of temporal, dimensional, and cerebroneural meshing, which is rather complicated for the present discussion. Sufficient that each candidate is objectively rated by his achievements, and that the results are commensurable."

He paused, looked shrewdly along the line of grave faces. "I must emphasize that although I myself designed and arranged the test, I thereby gained no advantage. The mnemonic synapses are entirely disengaged from incident to incident, and only the candidate's basic personality acts. All were tested under precisely the same conditions. In my opinion the scores registered by the computer indicate an objective and reliable index of the candidate's ability for the highly responsible office of Galactic Executive."

The Chief Elder said, "The scores are indeed significant."

"Then—you approve my candidacy?"

The Chief Elder smiled. "Not so fast. Admittedly you are intelligent, admittedly you have accomplished much during your term as Prime. But much remains to be done."

"Do you suggest that another man would have achieved more?"

The Chief Elder shrugged. "I have no conceivable way of knowing. I point out your achievements, such as the Glenart civilization, the Dawn Time on Masilis, the reign of King Karal on Aevir, the suppression of the Arkid Revolt. There are many such examples. But there are also shortcomings:

the totalitarian governments on Earth, the savagery on Belotsi and Chankozar, so pointedly emphasized in your test. Then there is the decadence of the planets in the Eleven Hundred Ninth Cluster, the rise of the priest-kings on Fiir, and much else."

Prime clenched his mouth and the fires behind his eyes burnt more brightly.

The Chief Elder continued. "One of the most remarkable phenomena of the galaxy is the tendency of humanity to absorb and manifest the personality of the Prime. There seems to be a tremendous resonance which vibrates from the brain of the Prime through the minds of man from Center to the outer fringes. It is a matter which should be studied, analyzed, and subjected to control. The effect is as if every thought of the Prime is magnified a billion-fold, as if every mood sets the tone for a thousand civilizations, every facet of his personality reflects in the ethics of a thousand cultures."

Prime said tonelessly, "I have remarked this phenomenon and have thought much on it. Prime's commands are promulgated in such a way as to exert subtle rather than overt influence; perhaps here is the background of the matter. In any event, the fact of this influence is even more reason to select for the office a man of demonstrated virtue."

"Well put," said the Chief Elder. "Your character is indeed beyond reproach. However, we of the Elders are concerned by the rising tide of authoritarianism among the planets of the galaxy. We suspect that this principle of resonance is at work. You are a man of intense and indomitable will, and we feel that your influence has unwittingly prompted an irruption of autarchies."

Prime was silent a moment. He looked down the line of couches where the other candidates were recovering awareness. They were men of various races: a pale Northkin of Palast, a stocky red Hawolo, a gray-haired gray-eyed Islander from the Sea Planet—each the outstanding man of the planet of his birth. Those who had returned to consciousness sat quietly, collecting their wits, or lay back on the couch, trying to expunge the test from their minds. There had been a toll taken: one lay dead, another bereft of his wits crouched whimpering beside his couch.

The Chief Elder said, "The objectionable aspects of your character are perhaps best exemplified by the test itself."

Prime opened his mouth; the Chief Elder held up his hand. "Let me speak; I will try to deal fairly with you. When I am done, you may say your say.

"I repeat that your basic direction is displayed by the details of the test that you devised. The qualities you measured were those which you considered the most important: that is, those ideals by which you guide your own life. This arrangement I am sure was completely unconscious, and hence completely revealing. You conceive the essential characteristics of the Prime to be social intuition, aggressiveness, loyalty, imagination, and dogged persistence. As a man of strong character you seek to exemplify these ideals in your own conduct; therefore it is not at all surprising that in this test, designed by you, with a scoring system calibrated by you, your score should be highest.

"Let me clarify the idea by an analogy. If the Eagle were conducting a test to determine the King of Beasts, he would rate all the candidates on their ability to fly; necessarily he would win. In this fashion the Mole would consider ability to dig important; by his system of testing *he* would inevitably emerge King of Beasts."

Prime laughed sharply, ran a hand through his sparse red-brown locks. "I am neither Eagle nor Mole."

The Chief Elder shook his head. "No. You are zealous, dutiful, imaginative, indefatigable—so you have demonstrated, as much by specifying tests for these characteristics as by scoring high in these same tests. But conversely, by the very absence of other tests you demonstrate deficiencies in your character."

"And these are?"

"Sympathy. Compassion. Kindness." The Chief Elder settled back in his chair. "Strange. Your predecessor two times removed was rich in these qualities. During his term, the great humanitarian systems based on the idea of human brotherhood sprang up across the universe. Another example of resonance—but I digress."

Prime said with a sardonic twitch of his mouth, "May I ask this: have you selected the next Galactic Prime?"

The Chief Elder nodded. "A definite choice has been made."

"What was his score in the test?"

"By your scoring system—seventeen eighty. He did poorly as Arthur Caversham; he tried to explain the advantages of nudity to the policeman. He lacked the ability to concoct an instant subterfuge; he has little of your quick craft. As Arthur Caversham he found himself naked. He is sincere and straightforward, hence tried to expound the positive motivations for his state, rather than discover the means to evade the penalties."

"Tell me more about this man," said Prime shortly.

"As Bearwald the Halforn, he led his band to the hive of the Brands on Mount Medallion, but instead of burning the hive, he called forth to the queen, begging her to end the useless slaughter. She reached out from the doorway, drew him within and killed him. He failed—but the computer still rated him highly on his forthright approach.

"At Therlatch, his conduct was as irreproachable as yours, and at the Imagicon his performance was adequate. Yours approached the brilliance of the Master Imagists, which is high achievement indeed.

"The Rac tortures are the most trying element of the test. You knew well you could resist limitless pain; therefore you ordained that all other candidates must likewise possess this attribute. The new Prime is sadly deficient here. He is sensitive, and the idea of one man intentionally inflicting pain upon another sickens him. I may add that none of the candidates achieved a perfect count in the last episode. Two others equaled your score—"

Prime evinced interest. "Which are they?"

The Chief Elder pointed them out—a tall hard-muscled man with rock-hewn face standing by the alabaster balustrade gazing moodily out across the sunny distance, and a man of middle age who sat with his legs folded under him, watching a point three feet before him with an expression of imperturbable placidity.

"One is utterly obstinate and hard," said the Chief Elder. "He refused to say a single word. The other assumes an outer objectivity when unpleasantness overtakes him. Others among the candidates fared not so well; therapy will be necessary in almost all cases."

Their eyes went to the witless creature with vacant eyes who padded up and down the aisle, humming and muttering quietly to himself.

"The tests were by no means valueless," said the Chief Elder. "We learned a great deal. By your system of scoring, the competition rated you most high. By other standards which we Elders postulated, your place was lower."

With a tight mouth, Prime inquired, "Who is this paragon of altruism, kindliness, sympathy, and generosity?"

The lunatic wandered close, fell on his hands and knees, crawled whimpering to the wall. He pressed his face to the cool stone, stared blankly up at Prime. His mouth hung loose, his chin was wet, his eyes rolled apparently free of each other.

The Chief Elder smiled in great compassion; he stroked the mad creature's head. "This is he. Here is the man we select."

The old Galactic Prime sat silent, mouth compressed, eyes burning like far volcanoes.

At his feet the new Prime, Lord of Two Billion Suns, found a dead leaf, put it into his mouth and began to chew.

INCENTIVE

Brian W. Aldiss

The encounter between humanity and intelligent alien beings is one of science fiction's earliest and most persistent themes, but the site of the encounter keeps moving outward. In the time of H. G. Wells, it was sufficient to place it on the moon; succeeding generations of writers exploited the possibilities of alien life on the other planets of our solar system; when Martians and Jovians began to look scientifically implausible, writers turned to the stars, which are infinite and infinitely suitable to any sort of imaginative thrust, infinities being nicely designed to include all conceivable possibilities. The theme of galactic empire is a vast and mind-expanding one, which writers have approached from many sides. This brief and relatively early story by Oxford's Brian Aldiss, author of such splendid visionary works as The

Long Afternoon of Earth, Non-Stop, *and* Barefoot in the Head, *offers an incisive look at what it may mean to become a citizen of the galaxy.*

THE OCEAN seemed to be breathing shallowly, like a child asleep, when the first lemmings reached it. In all the wide sea, no hint of menace existed. Yet the first lemmings paused daintily on the very verge of the water, peering out to sea and looking about as though in indecision. Unavoidably, the pressure of the marching column behind pushed them into the tiny wavelets. When their paws became wet, it was as if they resigned themselves to what was to come. Swimming strongly, the leaders of the column set off from the shore. All the other lemmings followed, only their heads showing above water. A human observer would have said they swam bravely; and unavoidably he would have asked himself: to what goal did the lemmings imagine they were headed? For what grand illusion were they prepared to throw away their lives?

All down the waterway, craft moved. Farrow Westerby stood at the forward port of his aquataxi, staring ahead and ignoring the water traffic moving by him. His two fellow Isolationists stood slightly apart, not speaking. Farrow's eye was on the rising structure on the left bank ahead. When the aquataxi moored as near to this structure as possible Farrow stepped ashore; glancing back rather impatiently, he waited for one of his companions to pay the fare.

"Wonderful, isn't it?" the taxi man said, nodding towards the strange building as he cast off. "I can't ever see us putting up anything like it."

"No," Farrow said flatly, walking away ahead of his friends.

They had disembarked in that sector of the capital called Horby Clive Island. Located in the governmental center of

New Union, most of it had been ceded to the Galactics a year ago. In that brief time, using Earth labor for the rough work, they had transformed the place. Six of their large, irregular buildings were already completed. The seventh was now going up, creating a new wonder for the world.

"We will wait here for you, Farrow," one of the two men said, extending his hand formally. "Good luck with the Galactic Minister. As the only Isolationist with an extensive knowledge of the Galactic tongue, Galingua, you represent, as you know, our best chance of putting our case for Earth's remaining outside the Multi-Planet Federation."

As Farrow thanked him and accepted the proffered hand, the other man, a stooping septuagenarian with a pale voice, gripped Farrow's arm. "And the case is clear enough," he said. "These aliens pretend they offer us Federation out of altruism. Most people swallow that, because they believe Earth ingenuity must be a valuable asset anywhere in the galaxy. So it may be, but we Isolationists claim there must be some ulterior motive for a superior race's wanting to welcome in a junior one as they appear to welcome us. If you can get a hint from this Minister Jandanagger as to what that motive is, you'll have done more than well."

"Thank you; I think I have the situation pretty clear," Farrow said sharply, regretting his tone of voice at once. But the other two were wise enough to make allowance for nervousness in times of stress. When he left them to make his way towards the Galactic buildings, their faces held only sincere smiles of farewell.

As Farrow pushed through the crowds of sightseers who stood here all day watching the new building develop, he listened with interest and some contempt to their comments. Many of them were discussing the current announcement on Federation.

"I think their goodness of heart is proved by the way they've let us join. It's nothing but a friendly gesture."

"It shows what respect they must have for Earth."

"You can't help seeing the future's going to be wonderful,

now we can export goods all over the galaxy. I tell you, we're in for a boom all round."

"Which goes to prove that however advanced the race, they can't do without the good old Earth know-how. Give the Galactics the credit for spotting that!"

The seventh building round which so many idle spectators clustered was nearing completion. It grew organically, like some vast succulent plant, springing from a flat metal matrix, thrusting along curved girders, encompassing them. Its color was a natural russet which seemed to take its tones from the tones of the sky overhead.

Grouped round the base of this extraordinary structure were distilleries, sprays, excavators, and other machines, the function of which was unknown to Farrow. They provided the raw material from which the building drew its bulk.

To one side of these seven well-designed eccentricities lay the space field. There, too, was another minor mystery. Earth governments had ceded—willingly when they sniffed the prizes to be won from Federation!—five such centers as the Horby Clive center in various parts of the globe. Each center was being equipped as a space port and educational unit, in which terrestrials would learn to understand the antiphonal complexities of Galingua and to behave as citizens of a well-populated galaxy.

Even granting vast alien resources, it was a formidable project. According to latest estimates, at least eight thousand Galactics were at present working on Earth. Yet on the space field sat only one craft, an unlikely-looking polyhedron with Arcturan symbols on its hull. The Galactics, in short, seemed to have remarkably few spaceships.

That was a point he would like to investigate, Farrow thought, speculatively eyeing the inert beacons round the perimeter of the field.

He skirted them, avoiding the crowds as far as possible, and arrived at the entrance of one of the other six Galactic buildings quite as eccentric in shape as its unfinished brother. As he walked in, an Earthman in a dark grey livery came deferentially forward.

"I have an appointment with Galactic Minister Jandanagger Laterobinson," Farrow announced, pronouncing the strange name awkwardly. "I am Farrow Westerby, Special Deputy of the Isolationist League."

Directly he heard the phrase "Isolationist League," the receptionist's manner chilled. Setting his lips, he beckoned Farrow over to a small side apartment, the doors of which closed as Farrow entered. The apartment, the Galactic equivalent of a lift, began to move through the building, traveling upwards on what Farrow judged to be an elliptical path. It delivered him into Jandanagger Laterobinson's room.

Standing up, the Galactic Minister greeted Farrow with amiable reserve, giving the latter an opportunity to sum up his opponent. Laterobinson was unmistakeably humanoid; he might, indeed, have passed for an Earthman, were it not for the strangeness of his eyes, set widely apart in his face and half-hidden by the peculiar configuration of an epicanthic fold of skin. This minor variation of feature nevertheless gave Jandanagger what all his race seemed to possess: a watchful, tensely withdrawn air.

"You know the reason for my visit, Minister," Farrow said, when he had introduced himself. He spoke carefully in Galingua, the language he had spent so many months so painfully learning; initially, its wide variation in form from any terrestial tongue had all but baffled him.

"Putting it briefly, you represent a body of people who fear contact with the other races in the Galaxy unlike must of your fellows on Earth," Jandanagger said easily. Expressed like that, the idea sounded absurd.

"I would rather claim to represent a body of people who have thought more deeply about the present situation than perhaps their fellows have done."

"Since your views are already known to me through the

newly established Terrestial-Galactic Council, I take it you wish us to discuss this matter personally?"

"That is so."

Jandanagger returned to his chair, gesturing Farrow into another.

"My role on Earth is simply to talk and to listen," he said, not without irony. "So do please feel free to talk."

"Minister, I represent ten percent of the people of Earth. If this sounds a small number, I would point out that that percentage contains some of the most eminent men in the world. Our position is relatively simple. You first visited Earth over a year ago; after investigation, you decided we were sufficiently advanced to become probationary members of the Galactic Federation. As a result, certain advantages and disadvantages will naturally accrue; although both sides will reap advantages, we shall suffer all the disadvantages—and they may well prove fatal to us."

Pausing, he scrutinized Jandanagger, but nothing was to be learned from the Minister's continued look of friendly watchfulness. He continued speaking.

"Let me briefly outline these advantages and disadvantages. To begin with, the advantages to you. You will have here a convenient base, dock and administrative seat in a region of space you say you have yet to explore and develop. Also, it is possible that when arrangements are worked out between us, terrestrials may be engaged to help colonize the new worlds you expect to find in this region. We shall be a cheap manufacturing area for you. We shall produce such items as plastics, clothes, foodstuffs, and simple tools which it will be easier for you to buy from us than transport from your distant home planets. Is this correct?"

"As you point out, Mr. Westerby, Earth occupies a key position in the Federation's present thousand-year plan for expansion. Although at present you can only regard yourselves as a frontier world, at the end of that period you may well be a key world. At the end of ten thousand years—well, your peoples are full of confidence; the omens are good."

"In short, there is promotion ahead if we behave ourselves?"

The acid note in Farrow's voice merely brought a slight smile to Jandanagger's lips.

"One is not made head prefect in one's first few days at school."

"Let me then enumerate the advantages, as opposed to the promises, which Earth will enjoy from entering the Federation. In the first place, we shall enjoy material benefits: new machines, new toys, new gadgets and some new techniques, like your vibro-molecular system of building—which produces, if I may say so, some excruciatingly ugly structures."

"One's tastes, Mr. Westerby, have to be trained to appreciate anything of aesthetic worth."

"Quite. Or to regard the hideous as normal. However, that brings us to the nonmaterial assets inherent in belonging to your Federation. You plan to revolutionize our educational systems. From nursery school to university, you will inculcate mores, matters and methods foreign to us; Earth will be invaded not by soldiers but by teachers—which is the surest way of gaining a bloodless victory."

The wide eyes regarded him calmly, but still as if from behind a barricade.

"How else are we to help you to become citizens of a complex civilization? For a start, it is essential your peoples learn Galingua. Education is a science and an art towards which you have not yet begun to formulate the rules. The whole question is enormously complicated, and quite beyond brief explanation—not that I could explain it, for I am not an educational specialist; those specialists will arrive here when my work is done, and the formal membership charters signed. But to take just one simple point. Your children first go to school at, say, five years old. They go into a class with other children and are quite separate from their homes; learning becomes at once an isolated part of life, something done in certain hours. And their first lesson is to obey the teacher. Thus, if their education is rated a success, it is because, to whatever extent, they have learned obedience and forfeited independence of mind; and they are probably set at permanent odds with their home environment.

"Our methods differ radically. We allow no children to enter our schools before the age of ten—but by that time, thanks to certain instructive toys and devices they have been familiar with for years, they will come knowing at least as much as your child of school-leaving age. And not only knowing. Behaving, Feeling, Understanding."

Farrow was at a disadvantage. "I feel like a heathen being told by a missionary that I should be wearing clothes."

The other man smiled, got up, and came over to him. "Be consoled that that's a false analogy," he said. "You are *demanding* the clothes. And when you wear them, you are certain to admire the cut."

All of which, Farrow reflected, made the two of them no less heathen and missionary.

"Don't look so disconcerted, Mr. Westerby. You have a perfect right to be distressed at the thought of your planet being depersonalized. But that is something we would not dream of doing. Depersonalized, you are nothing to yourselves or us. We need worlds capable of making their best personal contribution. If you would care to come with me, I should like to give you perhaps a better idea of how the civilized galaxy functions."

Farrow rose to his feet. It consoled him that he was slightly taller than the Minister. Jandanagger stood courteously aside, ushered his guest through a door. As they walked down a silent corridor, Farrow found his tongue again. "I haven't fully explained why I think that Federation would be such a bad thing for Earth. We are progressing on our own. Eventually, we should develop our own method of space travel, and come to join you on a more equal footing."

"Space travel—travel between different star systems—is not just a matter of being able to build starships. Any postnuclear culture can stumble on that trick. Space travel is a state of mind. The journey's always hell, and you never find a planet, however lovely, that suits you as well as the one you were born on. You need an incentive."

"What sort of an incentive?"

"Have you any idea?"

"I take it you are not referring to interstellar trading or conquest?"

"Correct."

"I'm afraid I don't know what sort of an incentive you mean."

The Minister gave something like a chuckle and said, "I'll try and show you presently. You were going to tell me why Federation would be a bad thing for Earth."

"No doubt it has been to your purpose to learn something of our history. It is full of dark things. Blood; war; lost causes, forgotten hopes; ages in chaos and days when even desperation died. It is no history to be proud of. Though many men individually seek good, collectively they lose it as soon as it is found. Yet we have one quality which always gives cause for hope that tomorrow may be better: initiative. Initiative has never faded, even when we crawled from what seemed the last ditch.

"But if we know that there exists a collective culture of several hundred worlds which we can never hope to emulate, what is to prevent us sinking back into despair forever?"

"An incentive, of course."

As he spoke, Jandanagger led the way into a small, boomerang-shaped room with wide windows. They sank onto a low couch, and at once the room moved. The dizzy view from the window shifted and rolled beneath them. The room was airborn.

"This is our nearest equivalent to your trains. It runs on a nucleonically bonded track. We are only going as far as the next building; there is some equipment there I would like you to inspect."

No reply seemed to be required; Farrow sat silent. He had known an electric moment of fear when the room first moved. In no more than ten seconds they swooped to the branch of another Galactic building, becoming part of it.

Once more leading the way, Jandanagger escorted him to a lift, which took them down into a basement room. They had arrived. The equipment of which Jandanagger had spoken was not particularly impressive to look at. Before a row of padded seats ran a counter, above which a line of respirator-like masks hung, with several cables trailing from them into the wall.

The Galactic Minister seated himself, motioning Farrow into the adjoining seat.

"What is this?" Farrow asked, unable to keep a slight tinge of anxiety from his tone.

"It is a type of wave-synthesizer. In effect, it renders down many of the wavelengths which man cannot detect by himself, translating them into paraphrased terms which he can. At the same time it feeds in objective and subjective impressions of the universe. That is to say, you will experience—when you fit the mask and I switch on—instrumental recordings of the universe (visual and aural and so on) as well as human impressions of it.

"I should warn you that owing to your lack of training, you may unfortunately gather a rather confused impression from the synthesizer. All the same, I fancy that it will give you a better rough idea of what the galaxy is like than you would get from a long star journey."

"Let's go," Farrow said.

Now the entire column of lemmings had embarked into the still water. They swam smoothly and silently, their communal wake soon dissolving into the grandly gentle motion of the sea. Gradually the column attenuated, as the stronger animals drew further ahead and the weaker ones dropped behind. One by one, inevitably, these weaker animals drowned; yet until their sleek heads finally disappeared below the surface, they still pressed forward with bulging eyes fixed upon the far and empty horizon.

No human spectator, however devoid of anthropomorphic feeling, could have failed to ask himself: what might be the nature of that goal that prompted such a sacrifice?

The inside of the mask was cold. It fitted loosely over his face, covering his ears and leaving only the back of his head free. Again a touch of unreasoning fear shot through him.

"The switch is by your hand," the Minister said. "Press it."

Farrow pressed the switch. Darkness submerged him.

"I am with you," the Minister said. "I have a mask on too, and can see and feel what you do."

A spiral was curling out into the darkness, boring its way through nothing: an opaque, smothering nothing as warm as flesh. Materializing from the spiral issued a growing cluster of bubbles, dark as polyhedric grapes, multiplying and multiplying as if breathed from an inexhaustible bubble pipe. The lights on their surfaces, glittering, changing, spun a misty web which gradually veiled the operation.

"Cells are being formed, beaten out in endless duplication on the microscopic anvils of creation. You witness the beginning of a new life," Jandanagger said, his voice sounding distant.

Like a curtain by an open window, the cells trembled behind their veil, awaiting life. And the moment of its coming was not perceptible. Only now the veil had something to conceal within itself; its translucence dimmed, its surface patterned, a kind of blind purpose shaped it into more definite outline. No longer was it beautiful.

Consciousness simmered inside it, a pinpoint of instinct-plus without love or knowledge, an eye trying to see through a lid of skin. It was not inert; instead, it struggled on the verge of terror, undergoing the trauma of coming-into-being, fighting, scrabbling, lest it fell back again into the gulf of not-being.

"Here is the Afterlife your religions tell of," Jandanagger's voice said. "This is the purgatory everyone of us must undergo. Only it comes not after but before life. The spirit that will become us has to tread the billion years of the past before it reaches the present it can be born into. One might almost say there was something it had to expiate."

The fetus was all Farrow's universe; it filled the mask, filled him. He suffered with it, for it obviously suffered. Pressures wracked it, the irremediable pressures of time and biochemistry, the pain of which it strove to lessen by changing shape. It writhed from worm- to slug-hood, it grew gills and a tail. Fishlike, and then no longer fishlike, it toiled up the steep slope of evolution, mouselike, piglike, apelike, babylike.

"This is the truth the wisest man forgets: that he has done all this."

Now the environment changed. The fetus, exerting itself, had become a baby, and the baby could only become a man by the proddings of a thousand new stimuli. And all these stimuli, animal, vegetable, or mineral, lived too, in their different way. They competed. They inflicted constant challenges on the man creature; some of them, semi-sentient, invaded his flesh and bred there, creating their own life cycles; others, nonsentient, were like waves that passed unceasingly through his mind and his body. He seemed hardly an entity, merely a focal point of forces, constantly threatened with dissolution.

So complete was the identification between the image and the receiver, that Farrow felt he was the man. He recognized that everything happening to the man happened to him; he sweated and writhed like the fetus, conscious of the salt water in his blood, the unstoppable rays in the marrow of his bones. Yet the mind was freer than it had been in the fetus stage; during the wrenching moment of fear when environments had changed the eye of consciousness had opened its lids.

"And now the man changes environments again, to venture away from his own planet," the Galactic Minister said.

But space was not space as Farrow had reckoned it. It struck his eyes like slate: not a simple nothingness, but an unfathomable web of forces, a creeping blend of stresses and fields in which stars and planets hung like dew amid spiders' webs. No life was here, only the same interaction of planes and pressures that had attended the man all along. Nonetheless, his perceptions reached a new stage, the light of consciousness burnt more steadily.

Again he was reaching out, swimming towards the confines of his galaxy. About him, proportions changed, slid, dwindled. In the beginning, the womb had been everywhere, equipped with all the menace and coercion of a full-scale universe; now the galaxy was revealed as smaller than the womb—a pintsized goldfish bowl in which a tiddler swam, unaware of the difference between air and water. For there was no spanning the gulfs between galaxies: there was nothing And the man had never met nothing before. Freedom was not a condition he knew.

As he swam up to the surface, something stirred beyond the yellow rim of the galaxy. The something could hardly be seen; but it was there, wakeful and clawed, a creature with senses though insensate. It registered half as sight, half as noise: a smouldering and delayed series of pops, like the sound of bursting arteries. It was big. Farrow screamed into the blackness of his mask.

The creature was waiting for the man. Stretching, it stretched right round the galaxy, round the goldfish bowl, its supernatent bat's wings groping for purchase.

Farrow screamed again.

"I'm sorry," he said weakly, as he felt the Minister removing his mask for him. "I'm sorry."

The Minister patted his shoulder. Shuddering, Farrow buried his face in his hands, trying to erase the now loathsome contact of the mask. That thing beyond the galaxy—it seemed to have entered and found a permanent place in his mind.

At last, gathering himself together, he stood up. Weakness floated in every layer of him. Moistening his lips, he spoke. "So you inveigle us into the Federation to face that!"

Jandanagger took his arm.

"Come back to my room. There is a point I can now make clear to you which I could not before: Earth has not been inveigled into the Federation. With your Earth-bound eyes, I know how you see the situation. You fancy that despite the evidence before your eyes of Galactic superiority, there must be some vital point on which Earth can offer something unbeatable. You fancy there must be some factor for which we need terrestrial help—a factor it does not yet suit us to reveal; isn't that so?"

Farrow avoided the other's wide eyes as they ascended in the lift to the top of the building. "There are other things beside the material ones," he said evasively. "Think for instance of the great heritage of literature in the world; to a truly civilized race, that might appear invaluable."

"That depends upon what you mean by civilized. The senior races of the Galaxy, having lost the taste for the spectacle of mental suffering, would be unlikely to find much attraction in your literatures."

This gently administered rebuke silenced Farrow. After a pause, the Galactic Minister continued, "No, you have no secret virtues, alas, for which we are gulling you into the Federation. The boot is on the other foot. We are taking you in as a duty, because you need looking after. I apologize for putting the matter so bluntly; but such may be the best way."

Stopping gently, the lift released them into the boomerang-shaped room. In a minute, they were speeding back to the building Farrow had first entered, with the crowded Horby Clive sector below them. Farrow closed his eyes, still feeling sick and shattered. The implications of what Jandanagger had said were momentarily beyond his comprehension. "I understand nothing," he said. "I don't understand why it should be your duty to look after Earth."

"Then already you do begin to understand," Jandanagger said, and for the first time personal warmth tempered his voice. "For not only are our sciences beyond yours, so are our philosophies and thought disciplines. All our mental abilities have been keyed semantically into the language in which you have learnt to converse with me, Galingua."

The flying room was reabsorbed; they became again merely one leaf tip of the giant building growing towards the grey clouds.

"Your language is certainly comprehensive and complex," Farrow said. "but perhaps my knowledge of it is too elementary for me to recognize the extra significances of which you speak."

"That is only because you have still to be shown how Galingua is more than a language: it is a way of life, our means of space travel itself! Concentrate on what I am telling you, Mr. Westerby."

Confusedly, Farrow shook his head as the other spoke; blood seemed to be congesting at the base of his skull. The odd idea came to him that he was losing his character, his identity. Wisps of meaning, hints of a greater comprehension, blew through his brain like streamers in the draught of a fan. As he tried to settle them, keep them steady, his own language became less like the bedrock of his being; his knowledge of Galingua, coupled with the experiences of the last hour, gradually assumed a dominant tone. With Jandanagger's grave eyes upon him, he began to think in the tongue of the galaxy.

For Jandanagger was talking, and with increasing rapidity. Although his meanings seemed clear, it felt to Farrow as if they were being comprehended only by a level below his conscious one. It was like partial drunkeness, when the grand simplicities of the world are revealed in wine and the mind skates over the thin ice of experience.

For Jandanagger was talking of many things at once, shifting things that could not be spoken of in terrestrial tongues, dissolving mental disciplines never formulated through terrestrial voices. Yet all these things balanced together in one sentence like jugglers' balls, enhancing each other.

For Jandanagger was talking of only one thing: the thrust of creation. He spoke of what the synthesizer had demonstrated: that man was never a separate entity, merely a solid within a solid—or better still, a flux within a flux. That he had only a subjective identity. That the wheeling matter of the galaxy was one with him.

And he spoke in the same breath of Galingua, which was merely a vocal representation of that flux, of whose cadences followed the great spiral of life within the flux. As he spoke it, he unlocked the inner secret of it to Farrow, so that what before had been a formal study became an orchestration, with every cell another note.

With a wild exultation, Farrow was answering now, merging with the spiral of talk. The new language was like a great immaterial *stupa,* its base broad, rooted in the ground of the ego, its spire high, whirling up into the sky. And by it, Farrow gradually ascended with Jandanagger: or rather, the proportions and perspectives about him changed, slid, dwindled, as they had done in the synthesizer. With no sense of alarm, he found himself high above the gaping crowds, shooting upwards on an etheric spiral.

Within him was a new understanding of the stresses permeating all space. He rode upwards through the planes of the universe, Jandanagger close by, sharing the revelation.

Now it was clear why the Galactics needed few spaceships: their big polygonal vessels carried only material; man himself had found a safer way of traveling in the goldfish bowl of the galaxy.

Looking outwards, Farrow saw where the stars thinned. Out there was the thing with claws, popping silently like bursting blood vessels. Fear came to him again.

"The thing in the synthesizer . . ." he said to Jandanagger, "the thing that surrounds the galaxy—if man can ever get out, cannot it get in at us?"

For a long minute Jandanagger was silent, searching for the key phrases of explanation.

"You have learned as much as you have very rapidly," he said. "By not-understanding and then by well-understanding, you have made yourself one of the true citizens of the galaxy. But you have only taken leap X; now you must take leap X^{10}. Prepare yourself."

"I am prepared."

"All that you have learned is true. Yet there is a far greater truth, a truer truth. Nothing exists in the ultimate sense: all is illusion, a two-dimensional shadow play on the mist of space-time."

"But the thing . . ."

"The thing is why we fare ever further forward into the illusion of space. It is real. Only the galaxy as you previously misinterpreted it is unreal, being but a configuration of mental forces. That monster, that thing you sensed is the residue of the slime of the evolutionary past still lingering—not outside you!—but in your own mind. It is from that we must escape. We must grow from it."

More explanation followed, but it was beyond Farrow. In a flash, he saw that Jandanagger, with an eagerness to experiment, had driven him too far and too fast. He could not make the last leap; he was falling back, toppling into a not-being. Somewhere within him, the pop-thud-pop sound of bursting arteries began. Others would succeed where he had failed—

but meanwhile, the angry claws were reaching from the heavens for him.

And now the lemmings were scattered over a considerable area of sea. Few of the original column were left; the remaining swimmers, isolated from each other, were growing tired. Yet they pressed forward as doggedly as ever towards the unseen goal.

Nothing was ahead of them. They had launched themselves into a vast—but not infinite—world without landmarks. The cruel incentive urged them always on. And if an invisible spectator had asked himself the agonized 'why?' to it all, an answer might have occurred to him: that these creatures were not heading for some especial promise in their future, merely fleeing from some terrible fear in their past.

THE WAITING GROUNDS

J. G. Ballard

J. G. Ballard's passage through the universe of science fiction encompassed about a decade, from 1956 to 1966: he went by like some hyperbolic comet, filling the heavens with a strange and baleful light such as never had been seen before, and moved on to other realms. Born in Shanghai in 1930, interned in a Japanese prisoner-of-war camp during World War II, repatriated to England in 1946, Ballard studied medicine at Cambridge, turned to writing soon afterward, and by the late 1950's was dazzling and perplexing science-fiction readers with his dark and hypnotic stories and novels, typified by intelligent though passive characters in the grip of inexplicable cosmic catastrophes. The present story is a good example of Ballard's purely science-fictional writing, his preoccupation with immensities and cosmo-

graphic mysteries. During the 1960's, overtones of William Burroughs, Beckett, and other avant-garde writers began emerging in his work, and eventually he ceased to use the materials of science fiction altogether as his fiction, now often cryptic and hermetic, turned to such obsessive themes as political assassinations and automobile accidents. It seems doubtful that he will return to science fiction, but he has left in his wake a corpus of memorable and highly individual stories—"The Terminal Beach," "The Cage of Sand," "The Voices of Time," and dozens more—which open vistas beyond vistas of disturbing marvels.

WHETHER Henry Tallis, my predecessor at Murak Radio Observatory, knew about the Waiting Grounds I can't say. On the whole it seems obvious he must have done, and that the three weeks he spent handing the station over to me —a job which could easily have been done in three days— were merely to give him sufficient time to decide whether or not to tell me about them. Certainly he never did, and the implied judgment against me is one I haven't yet faced up to.

I remember that on the first evening after my arrival at Murak he asked me a question I've been puzzling over ever since. We were up on the lounge deck of the observatory, looking out at the sand reefs and fossil cones of the volcano jungle glowing in the false dusk, the great 250-foot steel bowl of the telescope humming faintly in the air above us. "Tell me, Quaine," Tallis suddenly asked, "where would you like to be when the world ends?"

"I haven't really thought about it," I admitted. "Is there any urgency?"

"Urgency?" Tallis smiled at me thinly, his eyes amiable but assessing me shrewdly. "Wait until you've been here a little longer."

He had almost finished his last tour at the observatory and I assumed he was referring to the desolation around us which he, after fifteen years, was leaving thanklessly to my entire care. Later, of course, I realized how wrong I was, just as I misjudged the whole of Tallis's closed, complex personality.

He was a lean, ascetic-looking man of about fifty, withheld and moody, as I discovered the moment I debarked from the freighter flying me in to Murak—instead of greeting me at the ramp he sat in the half-track a hundred yards away at the edge of the port, watching silently through dark glasses as I heaved my suitcases across the burning, lava-thick sunlight, legs weary after the massive deceleration, stumbling in the unfamiliar gravity.

The gesture seemed characteristic. Tallis's manner was aloof and sardonic; everything he said had the same deliberately ambiguous overtones, that air of private mystery recluses and extreme introverts assume as a defense. Not that Tallis was in any way pathological—no one could spend fifteen years, even with six-monthly leaves, virtually alone on a remote planetary clinker like Murak without developing a few curious mannerisms. In fact, as I all too soon realized, what was really remarkable about Tallis was the degree to which he had preserved his sanity, not surrendered it.

He listened keenly to the latest news from Earth.

"The first pilotless launchings to Proxima Centauri are scheduled for 2250 . . . The U.N. Assembly at Lake Success have just declared themselves a sovereign state . . . V-R Day celebrations are to be discontinued—you must have heard it all on the radiocasts."

"I haven't got a radio here," Tallis said. "Apart from the one up there, and that's tuned to the big spiral networks in Andromeda. On Murak we listen only to the important news."

I nearly retorted that by the time it reached Murak the news, however important, would be a million years old, but on that first evening I was preoccupied with adjusting myself to an unfamiliar planetary environment—notably a denser atmosphere, slightly higher (1.2 E) gravity, vicious temperature swings from –30° to +160°—and programming new routines to fit myself into Murak's 18-hour day.

Above all, there was the prospect of two years of near-absolute isolation.

Ten miles from Murak Reef, the planet's only settlement, the observatory was sited among the first hills marking the northern edge of the inert volcano jungle which spread southwards to Murak's equator. It consisted of the giant telescope and a straggling nexus of twenty or thirty asbestos domes which housed the automatic data processing and tracking units, generator and refrigerating plant, and a miscellany of replacement and vehicle stores, workshops and ancillary equipment.

The observatory was self-sufficient as regards electric power and water. On the nearby slopes farms of solar batteries had been planted out in quarter-mile strips, the thousands of cells winking in the sunlight like a field of diamonds, sucking power from the sun to drive the generator dynamos. On another slope, its huge mouth permanently locked into the rock face, a mobile water synthesizer slowly bored its way through the desert crust, mining out oxygen and hydrogen combined into the surface minerals.

"You'll have plenty of spare time on your hands," the Deputy Director of the Astrographic Institute on Ceres had warned me when I initialed the contract. "There's a certain amount of routine maintenance, checking the power feeds to the reflector traverses and the processing units, but otherwise you won't need to touch the telescope. A big digital does the heavy thinking, tapes all the data down in 2000-hour schedules. You fly the cans out with you when you go on leave."

"So apart from shovelling the sand off the doorstep there's virtually nothing for me to do?" I'd commented.

"That's what you're being paid for. Probably not as much as you deserve. Two years will seem a long time, even with three leave intervals. But don't worry about going crazy. You aren't alone on Murak. You'll just be bored. £2000 worth, to be exact. However, you say you have a thesis to write. And you never know, you may like it there. Tallis, the observer you're taking over from, went out in '03 for two years like yourself, and stayed fifteen. He'll show you the ropes. Pleasant fellow, by all accounts, a little whimsical, probably try to pull your leg."

Tallis drove me down to the settlement the first morning to collect my heavy vacuum baggage that had traveled spacehold.

"Murak Reef," he pointed out as the old '95 Chrysler half-track churned through the thick luminous ash silted over the metal road. We crossed a system of ancient lava lakes, flat grey discs half a mile wide, their hard crusts blistered and pocked by the countless meteor showers that had driven into Murak during the past million years. In the distance a group of long flat-roofed sheds and three high ore elevators separated themselves from the landscape.

"I suppose they warned you. One supplies depot, a radio terminal and the minerals concession. Latest reliable estimates put the total population at seven."

I stared out at the surrounding desert floor, cracked and tiered by the heat swings into what looked like huge plates of rusted iron, and at the massed cones of the volcano jungle yellowing in the sand haze. It was 4 o'clock local time—early morning—but the temperature was already over 80°. We drove with windows shuttered, sun curtain down, refrigerating unit pumping noisily.

"Must be fun on Saturday night," I commented. "Isn't there anything else?"

"Just the thermal storms, and a mean noon temperature of one hundred and sixty degrees."

"In the shade?"

Tallis laughed. "Shade? You must have a sense of humor. There isn't any shade on Murak. Don't ever forget it. Half an hour before noon the temperature starts to go up two degrees a minute. If you're caught out in it you'll be putting a match to your own pyre."

Murak reef was a dust hole. In the sheds backing onto the depot the huge ore crushers and conveyors of the extraction plants clanked and slammed. Tallis introduced me to the agent, a morose old man called Pickford, and to two young engineers taking the wraps off a new grader. No one made any attempt at small talk. We nodded briefly, loaded my luggage onto the half-track and left.

"A taciturn bunch," I said. "What are they mining?"

"Tantalum, columbium, the rare earths. A heart-breaking job, the concentrations are barely workable. They're tempted to Murak by fabulous commission rates, but they're lucky if they can even fill their norms."

"You can't be sorry you're leaving. What made you stay here fifteen years?"

"It would take me fifteen years to tell you," Tallis rejoined. "I like the empty hills and the dead lakes."

I murmured some comment, and aware that I wasn't satisfied he suddenly scooped a handful of grey sand off the seat, held it up and let it sift away through his fingers. "Prime archezoic loam. Pure bedrock. Spit on it and anything might happen. Perhaps you'll understand me if I say I've been waiting for it to rain."

"Will it?"

Tallis nodded. "In about two million years, so someone who came here told me."

He said it with complete seriousness.

During the next few days, as we checked the stores and equipment inventories and ran over the installation together, I began to wonder if Tallis had lost his sense of time. Most men left to themselves for an indefinite period develop some occupational interest: chess or an insoluble dream-game or merely a compulsive wood-whittling. But Tallis, as far as I could see, did nothing. The cabin, a three-story drum built round a central refrigerating column, was spartan and comfortless. Tallis's only recreation seemed to be staring out at the volcano jungle. This was an almost obsessive activity —all evening and most of the afternoon he would sit up on the lounge deck, gazing out at the hundreds of extinct cones visible from the observatory, their colors running the spectrum from red to violet as the day swung round into night.

The first indication of what Tallis was watching for came about a week before he was due to leave. He had crated up his few possessions and we were clearing out one of the small storage domes near the telescope. In the darkness at the back, draped across a pile of old fans, track links and beer coolers, were two pedal-powered refrigerator suits, enormous unwieldy sacks equipped with chest pylons and hand-operated cycle gears.

"Do you ever have to use these?" I asked Tallis, glumly visualizing what a generator failure could mean.

He shook his head. "They were left behind by a survey team which did some work out in the volcanos. There's an entire camp lying around in these sheds, in case you ever feel like a weekend on safari."

Tallis was by the door. I moved my flashlight away and was about to switch it off when something flickered up at me from the floor. I stepped over the debris, searched about and found a small circular aluminum chest, about two feet across by a foot deep. Mounted on the back was a battery pack, thermostat and temperature selector. It was a typical relic of an expensively mounted expedition, probably a cocktail cabinet or hat box. Embossed in heavy gold lettering on the lid were the initials "C.F.N."

Tallis came over from the door. "What's this?" he asked sharply, adding his flash to mine.

I would have left the case where it lay, but there was something in Tallis's voice, a distinct inflection of annoyance, that made me pick it up and shoulder past into the sunlight.

I cleaned off the dust, Tallis at my shoulder. Keying open the vacuum seals I sprung back the lid. Inside was a small tape recorder, spool racks and a telescopic boom mike that cantilevered three feet up into the air, hovering a few inches from my mouth. It was a magnificent piece of equipment, a single-order job hand-made by a specialist, worth at least £500 apart from the case.

"Beautifully tooled," I remarked to Tallis. I tipped the platform and watched it spring gently. "The air bath is still intact."

I ran my fingers over the range indicator and the selective six-channel reading head. It was even fitted with a sonic trip, a useful device which could be set to trigger at anything from a fly's foot-fall to a walking crane's.

The trip had been set; I wondered what might have strayed across it when I saw that someone had anticipated me. The tape between the spools had been ripped out, so roughly that one spool had been torn off its bearings. The rack was empty, and the two frayed tabs hooked to the spool axles were the only pieces of tape left.

"Somebody was in a hurry," I said aloud. I depressed the lid and polished the initials with my finger tips. "This must have belonged to one of the members of the survey. C.F.N. Do you want to send it on to him?"

Tallis watched me pensively. "No. I'm afraid the two members of the team died here. Just over a year ago."

He told me about the incident. Two Cambridge geologists had negotiated through the Institute for Tallis's help in establishing a camp ten miles out in the volcano jungle, where they intended to work for a year, analyzing the planet's core materials. The cost of bringing a vehicle to Murak was prohibitive, so Tallis had transported all the equipment to the camp site and set it up for them.

"I arranged to visit them once a month with power packs, water and supplies. The first time everything seemed all right. They were both over sixty, but standing up well to the heat. The camp and laboratory were running smoothly, and they had a small transmitter they could have used in an emergency.

"I saw them three times altogether. On my fourth visit they had vanished. I estimated that they'd been missing for about a week. Nothing was wrong. The transmitter was working, and there was plenty of water and power. I assumed they'd gone out collecting samples, lost themselves and died quickly in the first noon high."

"You never found the bodies?"

"No. I searched for them, but in the volcano jungle the contours of the valley floors shift from hour to hour. I notified the Institute and two months later an inspector flew in from Ceres and drove out to the site with me. He certified the deaths, told me to dismantle the camp and store it here. There were a few personal things, but I've heard nothing from any friends or relatives."

"Tragic," I commented. I closed the tape recorder and carried it into the shed. We walked back to the cabin. It was an hour to noon, and the parabolic sun bumper over the roof was a bowl of liquid fire.

I said to Tallis: "What on earth were they hoping to catch in the volcano jungle? The sonic trip was set."

"Was it?" Tallis shrugged. "What are you suggesting?"

"Nothing. It's just curious. I'm surprised there wasn't more of an investigation."

"Why? To start with, the fare from Ceres is £800, over £3000 from Earth. They were working privately. Why should anyone waste time and money doubting the obvious?"

I wanted to press Tallis for detail, but his last remark seemed to close the episode. We ate a silent lunch, then went out on a tour of the solar farms, replacing burnt-out thermocouples. I was left with a vanished tape, two deaths, and a silent teasing suspicion that linked them neatly together.

Over the next days I began to watch Tallis more closely, waiting for another clue to the enigma growing around him.

I did learn one thing that astonished me. I had asked him about his plans for the future; these were indefinite—he said something vague about a holiday, nothing he anticipated with any eagerness, and sounded as if he had given no thought whatever to his retirement. Over the last few days, as his departure time drew closer, the entire focus of his mind became fixed upon the volcano jungle; from dawn until late into the night he sat quietly in his chair, staring out at the ghostless panorama of disintegrating cones, adrift in some private time sea.

"When are you coming back?" I asked with an attempt at playfulness, curious why he was leaving Murak at all.

He took the question seriously. "I'm afraid I won't be. Fifteen years is long enough, just about the limit of time one can spend continuously in a single place. After that one gets institutionalized—"

"Continuously?" I broke in. "You've had your leaves?"

"No, I didn't bother. I was busy here."

"Fifteen years!" I shouted. "Good God, why? In this of all places! And what do you mean, 'busy'? You're just sitting here, waiting for nothing. What are you supposed to be watching for, anyway?"

Tallis smiled evasively, started to say something and then thought better of it.

The questions pressed round him. What *was* he waiting for? Were the geologists still alive? Was he expecting them to return or make some signal? As I watched him pace about the cabin on his last morning I was convinced there was something he couldn't quite bring himself to tell me. Almost melodramatically he watched out over the desert, delaying his departure until the thirty-minute take-off siren hooted from the port. As we climbed into the half-track I fully expected the glowing specters of the two geologists to come looming out of the volcano jungle, uttering cries of murder and revenge.

He shook my hand carefully before he went aboard. "You've got my address all right? You're quite sure?" For some reason, which confused my cruder suspicions, he had made a special point of ensuring that both I and the Institute would be able to contact him.

"Don't worry," I said. "I'll let you know if it rains."

He looked at me somberly. "Don't wait too long." His eyes strayed past my head towards the southern horizon, through the sand-haze to the endless sea of cones. He added: "Two million years is a long time."

I took his arm as we walked to the ramp. "Tallis," I asked quietly, "what are you watching for? There's something, isn't there?"

He pulled away from me, collected himself. "What?" he said shortly, looking at his wrist watch.

"You've been trying to tell me all week," I insisted. "Come on, man."

He shook his head abruptly, muttered something about the heat and stepped quickly through the lock.

I started to shout after him: "Those two geologists are out there...!" but the five-minute siren shattered the air and by the time it stopped Tallis had disappeared down the companionway and crewmen were shackling on the launching gantry and sealing the cargo and passenger locks.

I stood at the edge of the port as the ship cleared its take-off check, annoyed with myself for waiting until the last impossible moment to press Tallis for an explanation. Half an hour later he was gone.

Over the next few days Tallis began to slide slowly into the back of my mind. I gradually settled into the observatory, picked out new routines to keep time continuously on the move. Mayer, the metallurgist down at the mine, came over to the cabin most evenings to play chess and forget his pitifully low extraction rates. He was a big, muscular fellow of thirty-five who loathed Murak's climate, geology and bad company, a little crude but the sort of tonic I needed after an overdose of Tallis.

Mayer had met Tallis only once, and had never heard about the deaths of the two geologists. "Damned fools, what were they looking for? Nothing to do with geology, Murak hasn't got one."

Pickford, the old agent down at the depot, was the only person on Murak who remembered the two men, but time had garbled his memories.

"Salesmen, they were," he told me, blowing into his pipe. "Tallis did the heavy work for them. Should never have come here, trying to sell all those books."

"Books?"

"Cases full. Bibles, if I recall."

"Textbooks," I suggested. "Did you see them?"

"Sure I did," he said, puttering to himself. "Guinea moroccos." He jerked his head sharply. "You won't sell them here, I told them."

It sounded exactly like a dry piece of academic humor. I could see Tallis and the two scientists pulling Pickford's leg, passing off their reference library as a set of commercial samples.

I suppose the whole episode would eventually have faded, but Tallis's charts kept my interest going. There were about twenty of them, half million aerials of the volcano jungle within a fifteen-mile radius of the observatory. One of them was marked with what I assumed to be the camp site of the geologists and alternative routes to and from the observatory. The camp was just over ten miles away, across terrain that was rough but not over-difficult for a tracked car.

I still suspected I was getting myself wound up over nothing. A meaningless approach arrow on the charts, the faintest suggestion of a cryptic X, and I should have been off like a rocket after a geldspar mine or two mysterious graves. I was almost sure that Tallis had not been responsible, either by negligence or design, for the deaths of the two men, but that still left a number of unanswered questions.

The next clear day I checked over the half-track, strapped a flare pistol into my knee holster and set off, warning Pickford to listen out for a May Day call on the Chrysler's transmitter.

It was just after dawn when I gunned the half-track out of the observatory compound and headed up the slope between two battery farms, following the route mapped out on the charts. Behind me the telescope swung slowly on its bogies, tirelessly sweeping its great steel ear through the Cepheid talk. The temperature was in the low seventies, comfortably cool for Murak, the sky a fresh cerise, broken by lanes of indigo that threw vivid violet lights on the drifts of grey ash on the higher slopes of the volcano jungle.

The observatory soon fell behind, obscured by the exhaust dust. I passed the water synthesizer, safely pointed at ten thousand tons of silicon hydrate, and within twenty minutes reached the nearest cone, a white broad-backed giant two-hundred feet high, and drove round it into the first valley. Fifty feet across at their summits, the volcanos jostled together like a herd of enormous elephants, separated by narrow dust-filled valleys, sometimes no more than a hundred yards apart, here and there giving way to the flat mile-long deck of a fossil lava lake. Wherever possible the route took advantage of these, and I soon picked up the tracks left by the Chrysler on its trips a year earlier.

I reached the site in three hours. What was left of the camp stood on a beach overlooking one of the lakes, a dismal collection of fuel cylinders, empty cold stores and water tanks sinking under the tides of dust washed up by the low thermal winds. On the far side of the lake the violet-capped cones of the volcanos ranged southwards. Behind, a crescent of sharp cliffs cut off half the sky.

I walked round the site, looking for some trace of the two geologists. A battered tin field desk lay on its side, green paint blistered and scratched. I turned it over and pulled out its drawers, finding nothing except a charred notebook and a telephone, the receiver melted solidly into its cradle.

Tallis had done his job too well.

The temperature was over 100° by the time I climbed back into the half-track and a couple of miles ahead I had to stop as the cooling unit was draining power from the spark plugs and stalling the engine. The outside temperature was 130°, the sky a roaring shield reflected in the slopes around me so that they seemed to stream with molten wax. I sealed all the shutters and changed into neutral, even then having to race the ancient engine to provide enough current for the cooler. I sat there for over an hour in the dim gloom of the dashboard, ears deadened by the engine roar, right foot cramping, cursing Tallis and the two geologists.

That evening I unfurled some crisp new vellum, flexed my slide rule and determined to start work on my thesis.

One afternoon two or three months later, as we turned the board between chess games, Mayer remarked: "I saw Pickford this morning. He told me he had some samples to show you."

"TV tapes?"

"Bibles, I thought he said."

I looked in on Pickford the next time I was down at the settlement. He was hovering about in the shadows behind the counter, white suit dirty and unpressed.

He puffed smoke at me. "Those salesmen," he explained. "You were inquiring about. I told you they were selling Bibles."

I nodded. "Well?"

"I kept some."

I put out my cigarette. "Can I see them?"

He gestured me round the counter with his pipe. "In the back."

I followed him between the shelves, loaded with fans, radios and TV-scopes, all outdated models imported years earlier to satisfy the boom planet Murak had never become.

"There it is," Pickford said. Standing against the back wall of the depot was a three-by-three wooden crate, taped with metal bands. Pickford ferretted about for a wrench. "Thought you might like to buy some."

"How long has it been here?"

"About a year. Tallis forgot to collect it. Only found it last week."

Doubtful, I thought: more likely he was simply waiting for Tallis to be safely out of the way. I watched while he pried off the lid. Inside was a tough brown wrapping paper. Pickford broke the seals and folded the sides back carefully, revealing a layer of black morocco-bound volumes.

I pulled out one of them and held the heavily ribbed spine up to the light.

It was a Bible, as Pickford had promised. Below it were a dozen others.

"You're right," I said. Pickford pulled up a radiogram and sat down, watching me.

I looked at the Bible again. It was in mint condition, the King James Authorized Version. The marbling inside the end-boards was unmarked. A publisher's ticket slipped out onto the floor, and I realized that the copy had hardly come from a private library.

The bindings varied slightly. The next volume I pulled out was a copy of the Vulgate.

"How many crates did they have altogether?" I asked Pickford.

"Bibles? Fourteen, fifteen with this one. They ordered them all after they got here. This was the last one." He pulled out another volume and handed it to me. "Good condition, eh?"

It was a Koran.

I started lifting the volumes out and got Pickford to help me sort them on the shelves. When we counted them up there were ninety in all: thirty-five Holy Bibles (twenty-four Authorized Versions and eleven Vulgates), fifteen copies of the Koran, five of the Talmud, ten of the Bhagavat Gita and twenty-five of the Upanishads.

I took one of each and gave Pickford a £10 note.

"Any time you want some more," he called after me. "Maybe I can arrange a discount." He was chuckling to himself, highly pleased with the deal, one up on the salesmen.

When Meyer called round that evening he noticed the six volumes on my desk.

"Pickford's samples," I explained. I told him how I had found the crate at the depot and that it had been ordered by the geologists after their arrival. "According to Pickford they ordered a total of fifteen crates. All Bibles."

"He's senile."

"No. His memory is good. There were certainly other crates because this one was sealed and he knew it contained Bibles."

"Damned funny. Maybe they were salesmen."

"Whatever they were they certainly weren't geologists. Why did Tallis say they were? Anyway, why didn't he ever mention that they had ordered all these Bibles?"

"Perhaps he'd forgotten?"

"Fifteen crates? Fifteen crates of Bibles? Heavens above, what did they do with them?"

Mayer shrugged. He went over to the window. "Do you want me to radio Ceres?"

"Not yet. It still doesn't add up to anything."

"There might be a reward. Probably a big one. God, I could go home!"

"Relax. First we've got to find out what these so-called geologists were doing here, why they ordered this fantastic supply of Bibles. One thing: whatever it was, I swear Tallis knew about it. Originally I thought they might have discovered a geldspar mine and been double-crossed by Tallis— that sonic trip was suspicious. Or else that they'd deliberately faked their own deaths so that they could spend a couple of years working the mine, using Tallis as their supply source. But all these Bibles mean we must start thinking in completely different categories."

Round the clock for three days, with only short breaks for sleep hunched in the Chrysler's driving seat, I systematically swept the volcano jungle, winding slowly through the labyrinth of valleys, climbing to the crest of every cone, carefully checking every exposed quartz vein, every rift or gulley that might hide what I was convinced was waiting for me.

Mayer deputized at the observatory, driving over every afternoon. He helped me recondition an old diesel generator in one of the storage domes and we lashed it on to the back of the half-track to power the cabin heater needed for the $-30°$ nights and the three big spot lights fixed on the roof, providing a $360°$ traverse. I made two trips with a full cargo of fuel out to the camp site, dumped them there and made it my base.

Across the thick glue-like sand of the volcano jungle, we calculated, a man of sixty could walk at a maximum of one mile an hour, and spend at most two hours in $70°$ or above sunlight. That meant that whatever there was to find would be within twelve square miles of the camp site, three square miles if we included a return journey.

I searched the volcanos as exactingly as I could, marking each cone and the adjacent valleys on the charts as I covered them, at a steady five miles an hour, the great engine of the Chrysler roaring ceaselessly, from noon, when the valleys filled with fire and seemed to run with lava again, round to midnight, when the huge cones became enormous mountains of bone, somber graveyards presided over by the fantastic colonnades and hanging galleries of the sand reefs, suspended from the lake rims like inverted cathedrals.

I forced the Chrysler on, swinging the bumpers to uproot any suspicious crag or boulder that might hide a mine shaft, ramming through huge drifts of fine white sand that rose in soft clouds around the half-track like the dust of powdered silk.

I found nothing. The reefs and valleys were deserted, the volcano slopes untracked, craters empty, their shallow floors littered with meteor debris, rock sulphur and cosmic dust.

I decided to give up just before dawn on the fourth morning, after waking from a couple of hours of cramped and restless sleep.

"I'm coming in now," I reported to Mayer over the transmitter. "There's nothing out here. I'll collect what fuel there is left from the site and see you for breakfast."

Dawn had just come up as I reached the site. I loaded the fuel cans back onto the half-track, switched off the spotlights and took what I knew would be my last look round. I sat down at the field desk and watched the sun arcing upwards through the cones across the lake. Scooping a handful of ash off the desk, I scrutinized it sadly for geldspar.

"Prime archezoic loam," I said, repeating Tallis's words aloud to the dead lake. I was about to spit on it, more in anger than in hope, when some of the tumblers in my mind started to click.

About five miles from the far edge of the lake, silhouetted against the sunrise over the volcanos, was a long 100-foot high escarpment of hard slate-blue rock that lifted out of the desert bed and ran for about two miles in a low clean sweep across the horizon, disappearing among the cones in the southwest. Its outlines were sharp and well-defined, suggesting that its materials predated the planet's volcanic period. The escarpment sat squarely across the desert, gaunt and rigid, and looked as if it had been there since Murak's beginning, while the soft ashy cones and grey hillocks around it had known only the planet's end.

It was no more than an uninformed guess, but suddenly I would have bet my entire two years' salary that the rocks of the escarpment were archezoic. It was about three miles outside the area I had been combing, just visible from the observatory.

The vision of a geldspar mine returned sharply!

The lake took me nearly halfway there. I raced the Chrysler across it at forty, wasted thirty minutes picking a route through an elaborate sand reef, and then entered a long steeply walled valley which led directly towards the escarpment.

A mile away I saw that the escarpment was not, as it first seemed, a narrow continuous ridge, but a circular horizontal table. A curious feature was the almost perfect flatness of the table top, as if it had been deliberately levelled by a giant sword. Its slides were unusually symmetrical; they sloped at exactly the same angle, about 35°, and formed a single cliff unbroken by fissures or crevices.

I reached the table in an hour, parked the half-track at its foot and looked up at the great rounded flank of dull blue rock sloping away from me, rising like an island out of the grey sea of the desert floor.

I changed down into bottom gear and floored the accelerator. Steering the Chrysler obliquely across the slope to minimize the angle of ascent, I roared slowly up the side, tracks skating and racing, swinging the half-track around like a frantic pendulum.

Scaling the crest, I leveled off and looked out over a plateau about two miles in diameter, bare except for a light blue carpet of cosmic dust.

In the center of the plateau, at least a mile across, was an enormous metallic lake, heat ripples spiralling upwards from its dark smooth surface.

I edged the half-track forward, held out of the side window, watching carefully, holding down the speed that picked up too easily. There were no meteorites or rock fragments lying about; presumably the lake surface cooled and set at night, to melt and extend itself as the temperature rose the next day.

Although the roof seemed hard as steel I stopped about 300 yards from the edge, cut the engine and climbed up onto the cabin.

The shift of perspective was slight but sufficient. The lake vanished, and I realized I was looking down at a shallow basin, about half a mile wide, scooped out of the roof.

I swung back into the cab and slammed in the accelerator. The basin, like the table top, was a perfect circle, sloping smoothly to the floor about one hundred feet below its rim, in imitation of a volcanic crater.

I braked the half-track at the edge and jumped out.

Four hundred yards away, in the basin's center, five gigantic rectangular slabs of stone reared up from a vast pentagonal base.

This, then, was the secret Tallis had kept from me.

The basin was empty, the air warmer, strangely silent after three days of the Chrysler's engine roaring inside my head.

I lowered myself over the edge and began to walk down the slope towards the great monument in the center of the basin. For the first time since my arrival on Murak I was unable to see the desert and the brilliant colors of the volcano jungle. I had strayed into a pale blue world, as pure and exact as a geometric equation, composed of the curving floor, the pentagonal base and the five stone rectangles towering up into the sky like the temple of some abstract religion.

It took me nearly three minutes to reach the monument. Behind me, on the skyline, the half-track's engine steamed faintly. I went up to the base stone, which was a yard thick and must have weighed over a thousand tons, and placed my palms on its surface. It was still cool, the thin blue grain closely packed. Like the megaliths standing on it, the pentagon was unornamented and geometrically perfect.

I heaved myself up and approached the nearest megalith. The shadows around me were enormous parallelograms, their angles shrinking as the sun blazed up into the sky. I walked slowly round into the center of the group, dimly aware that neither Tallis nor the two geologists could have carved the megaliths and raised them onto the pentagon, when I saw that the entire inner surface of the nearest megalith was covered by row upon row of finely chiseled hieroglyphs.

Swinging round, I ran my hands across its surface. Large patches had crumbled away, leaving a faint indecipherable tracery, but most of the surface was intact, packed solidly with pictographic symbols and intricate cuneiform glyphics that ran down it in narrow columns.

I stepped over to the next megalith. Here again, the inner face was covered with tens of thousands of minute carved symbols, the rows separated by finely cut dividing rules that fell the full fifty-foot height of the megalith.

There were at least a dozen languages, all in alphabets I had never seen before, strings of meaningless ciphers among which I could pick out odd cross-hatched symbols that seemed to be numerals, and peculiar serpentine forms that might have represented human figures in stylized poses.

Suddenly my eye caught:

CYR*RK VII   A*PHA LEP**IS   *D 1317

Below was another, damaged but legible.

AMEN*TEK LC*V   *LPHA LE*ORIS   AD 13**

There were blanks among the letters, where time had flaked away minute grains of the stone.

My eyes raced down the column. There were a score more entries:

PONT*AR*H *CV   ALPH* L*PORIS   A* *318
MYR*K LV*   A**HA LEPORI*   AD 13*9
KYR** XII   ALPH* LEP*RIS   AD 1*19

. . . .
. . . .

The list of names, all from Alpha Leporis, continued down the column. I followed it to the base, where the names ended three inches from the bottom, then moved along the surface, across rows of hieroglyphs, and picked up the list three or four columns later.

M*MARYK XX*V	A*PHA LEPORI*	AD 1389
CYRARK IX	ALPHA *EPORIS	AD 1390
. . . . .	. . . . .	. . . .

I went over to the megalith on my left and began to examine the inscriptions carefully.

Here the entries read:

MINYS-259	DELT* ARGUS	AD 1874
TYLNYS-413	DELTA ARGUS	*D 1874
. . . . .	. . . . .	. . . .

There were fewer blanks; to the right of the face the entries were more recent, the lettering sharper. In all there were five distinct languages, four of them, including Earth's, translations of the first entry running down the left-hand margin of each column.

The third and fourth megaliths recorded entries from Gamma Grus and Beta Trianguli. They followed the same pattern, their surfaces divided into eighteen-inch-wide columns, each of which contained five rows of entries, the four hieroglyphic languages followed by Earth's, recording the same minimal data in the same terse formula: Name—Place —Date.

I had looked at four of the megaliths. The fifth stood with its back to the sun, its inner face hidden.

I walked over to it, crossing the oblique panels of shadow withdrawing to their sources, curious as to what fabulous catalogue of names I should find.

The fifth megalith was blank.

My eyes raced across its huge unbroken surface, marked only by the quarter-inch-deep grooves of the dividing rules some thoughtful master mason from the stars had chiseled to tabulate the entries from Earth that had never come.

I returned to the other megaliths and for half an hour read at random, arms outstretched involuntarily across the great inscription panels, finger tips tracing the convolutions of the hieroglyphs, seeking among the thousands of signatures some clue to the identity and purpose of the four stellar races.

COPT*C LEAGUE MLV	BETA TRIANGULI	*D 1723
ISARI* LEAGUE* VII	BETA *RIANGULI	AD 1724
MAR-5-GO	GAMMA GRUS	AD 1959
VEN-7-GO	GAMMA GRUS	AD 1960
TETRARK XII	ALPHA LEPORIS	AD 2095

Dynasties recurred again and again, Cyrark's, Minys-'s, -Go's, separated by twenty- or thirty-year intervals that appeared to be generations. Before AD 1200 all entries were illegible. This represented something over half the total. The surfaces of the megaliths were almost completely covered, and initially I assumed that the first entries had been made roughly 2200 years earlier, shortly after the birth of Christ. However the frequency of the entries increased algebraically: in the fifteenth century there were one or two a year, by the twentieth century there were five or six, and by the present year the number varied from twenty entries from Delta Argus to over thirty-five from Alpha Leporis.

The last of these, at the extreme bottom right corner of the megalith, was

CYRARK CCCXXIV   ALPHA LEPORIS   AD 2218

The letters were freshly incised, perhaps no more than a day old, even a few hours. Below, a free space of two feet reached to the floor.

Breaking off my scrutiny, I jumped down from the base stone and carefully searched the surrounding basin, sweeping the light dust carpet for vehicle or foot marks, the remains of implements or scaffolding.

But the basin was empty, the dust untouched except for the single file of prints leading down from the half-track.

I was sweating uncomfortably, and the thermo-alarm strapped to my wrist rang, warning me that the air temperature was 85°, ninety minutes to noon. I reset it to 100°, took a last look round the five megaliths, and then made my way back to the half-track.

Heat waves raced and glimmered round the rim of the basin, and the sky was a dark inflamed red, mottled by the thermal pressure fields massing overhead like storm clouds. I jogged along at a half run, in a hurry to contact Mayer. Without his confirmation the authorities on Ceres would treat my report as the fantasy of a sand-happy lunatic. In addition, I wanted him to bring his camera; we could develop the reels within half an hour and radio a dozen stills as indisputable proof.

More important, I wanted someone to share the discovery, provide me with at least some cover in numbers. The frequency of entries on the megaliths, and the virtual absence of any further space—unless the reverse sides were used, which seemed unlikely—suggested a climax was soon to be reached, probably the climax for which Tallis had been waiting. Hundreds of entries had been made during his fifteen years on Murak; watching all day from the observatory he must have seen every landing.

As I swung into the half-track the emergency light on the transceiver above the windscreen was pulsing insistently. I switched to audio and Mayer's voice snapped into my ear. "Quaine? Is that you? Where the hell are you, man? I nearly put out a May Day for you!"

He was at the camp site. Calling in from the observatory when I failed to arrive, he assumed I had broken down and abandoned the half-track, and had come out searching for me.

I picked him up at the camp site half an hour later, retroversed the tracks in a squealing circle of dust and kicked off again at full throttle. Mayer pressed me all the way back but I told him nothing, driving the Chrysler hard across the lake, paralleling the two previous sets of tracks and throwing up a huge cloud of dust 150 feet into the air. It was now over

95°, and the ash hills in the valley at the end of the lake were beginning to look angry and boiled.

Eager to get Mayer down into the basin, and with my mind spinning like a disintegrating flywheel, it was only as the half-track roared up the table slope that I felt a first chilling pang of fear. Through the windscreen I hesitantly scanned the tilting sky. Soon after reaching the basin we would have to shut down for an hour, two of us crammed together in the fume-filled cabin, deafened by the engine, sitting targets with the periscope blinded by the glare.

The center of the plateau was a pulsing blur as the air trapped in the basin throbbed upwards into the sun. I drove straight towards it, Mayer stiffening in his seat. A hundred yards from the basin's edge the air suddenly cleared and we could see the tops of the megaliths. Mayer leaped up and swung out of the door onto the running board as I cut the engine and slammed the half-track to a halt by the rim. We jumped down, grabbing flare pistols and shouting to each other, slid into the basin and sprinted through the boiling air to the megaliths looming up in the center.

I half-expected to find a reception party waiting for us, but the megaliths were deserted. I reached the pentagon fifty yards ahead of Mayer, climbed up and waited for him, gulping in the molten sunlight.

I helped him up and led him over to one of the megaliths, picked a column and began to read out the entries. Then I took him round the others, recapitulating everything I had discovered, pointing out the blank tablet reserved for Earth.

Mayer listened, broke away and wandered off, staring up dully at the megaliths. "Quaine, you've really found something," he muttered softly. "Crazy, must be some sort of temple."

I followed him round, wiping the sweat off my face and shielding my eyes from the glare reflected off the great slabs. "Look at them, Mayer! They've been coming here for ten thousand years! Do you know what this means?"

Mayer tentatively reached out and touched one of the

megaliths. " 'Argive League xxv . . . Beta Tri-' " he read out. "There are others then. God Almighty. What do you think they look like?"

"What does it matter? Listen. They must have leveled this plateau themselves, scooped out the basin and cut these tablets from the living rock. Can you even imagine the tools they used?"

We crouched in the narrow rectangle of shadow in the lee of the sunward megalith. The temperature climbed, forty-five minutes to noon, 105°.

"What is all this, though?" Mayer asked. "Their burial ground?"

"Unlikely. Why leave a tablet for Earth? If they've been able to learn our language they'd know the gesture was pointless. Anyway, elaborate burial customs are a sure sign of decadence, and there's something here that suggests the exact opposite. I'm convinced they expect that some time in the future we'll take an active part in whatever is celebrated here."

"Maybe, but what? Think in new categories, remember?" Mayer squinted up at the megaliths. "This could be anything from an ethnological bill of lading to the guest list at an all-time cosmic house party."

He noticed something, frowned, then suddenly wrenched away from me. He leapt to his feet, pressed his hands against the surface of the slab behind us and ran his eyes carefully over the grain.

"What's worrying you?" I asked.

"Shut up!" he snapped. He scratched his thumbnail at the surface, trying to dislodge a few grains. "What are you talking about, Quaine, these slabs aren't made of stone!"

He slipped out his jack knife, sprung the blade and stabbed viciously at the megalith, slashing a two-foot long groove across the inscriptions.

I stood up and tried to restrain him but he shouldered me

away and ran his finger down the groove, collecting a few fragments. He turned on me angrily. "Do you know what this is? *Tantalum oxide!* Pure ninety-nine percent paygold. No wonder our extraction rates are fantastically small. I couldn't understand it, but these people"— he jerked his thumb furiously at the megalith —"have damn well milked the planet dry to build these crazy things!"

It was 115°. The air was beginning to turn yellow and we were breathing in short exhausted pants.

"Let's get back to the truck," I temporized. Mayer was losing control, carried away by his rage. With his big burly shoulders hunched in anger, staring up blindly at the five great megaliths, face contorted by the heat, he looked like an insane subman pinned in the time trophy of a galactic superhunter.

He was ranting away as we stumbled through the dust towards the half-track.

"What do you want to do?" I shouted. "Cut them down and put them through your ore crushers?"

Mayer stopped, the blue dust swirling about his legs. The air was humming as the basin floor expanded in the heat. The half-track was only fifty yards away, its refrigerated cabin a cool haven.

Mayer was watching me, nodding slowly. "It could be done. Ten tons of Hy-Dyne planted round those slabs would crack them into small enough pieces for a tractor to handle. We could store them out at the observatory, then sneak them later into my refining tanks."

I walked on, shaking my head with a thin grin. The heat was hitting Mayer, welling up all the irrational bitterness of a year's frustration. "It's an idea. Why don't you get in touch with Gamma Grus? Maybe they'll give you the lease."

"I'm serious, Quaine," Mayer called after me. "In a couple of years we'd be rich men."

"You're crazy!" I shouted back at him. "The sun's boiling your brains."

I began to scale the slope up to the rim. The next hour in the cabin was going to be difficult, cooped up with a maniac eager to tear the stars apart. The butt of the flare pistol swinging on my knee caught my eye; a poor weapon, though, against Mayer's physique.

I had climbed almost up to the rim when I heard his feet thudding through the dust. I started to turn round just as he was on me, swinging a tremendous blow that struck me on the back of the head. I fell, watched him close in and then stood up, my skull exploding, and grappled with him. We stumbled over each other for a moment, the walls of the basin diving around us like a switchback, and then he knocked my hands away and smashed a heavy right cross into my face.

I fell on my back, stunned by the pain; the blow seemed to have loosened my jaw and damaged all the bones on the left side of my face. I managed to sit up and saw Mayer running past. He reached one hand to the rim, pulled himself up and lurched over to the half-track.

I dragged the flare pistol out of its holster, snapped back the bolt and trained it at Mayer. He was thirty yards away, turning the near-side door handle. I held the butt with both hands and fired as he opened the door. He looked round at the sharp detonation and watched the silver shell soar swiftly through the air towards him, ready to duck.

The shell missed him by three feet and exploded against the cabin roof. There was a brilliant flash of light that resolved itself a fraction of a second later into a fireball of incandescent magnesium vapor ten feet in diameter. This slowly faded to reveal the entire driving cabin, bonnet and forward side-panels of the half-track burning strongly with a loud, heavy crackling. Out of this maelstrom suddenly plunged the figure of Mayer, moving with violent speed, blackened arms across his face. He tripped over the rim, catapulted down into the dust and rolled for about twenty yards before he finally lay still, a shapeless bundle of smoking rags.

I looked numbly at my wrist watch. It was ten minutes to noon. The temperature was 130°. I pulled myself to my feet and trudged slowly up the slope towards the half-track, head thudding like a volcano, uncertain whether I would be strong enough to lift myself out of the basin.

When I was ten feet from the rim I could see that the windscreen of the half-track had melted and was dripping like treacle onto the dashboard.

I dropped the flare pistol and turned round.

It was five minutes to noon. Around me, on all sides, enormous sheets of fire were cascading slowly from the sky, passing straight through the floor of the basin, and then rising again in an inverted torrent. The megaliths were no longer visible, screened by curtains of brilliant light, but I groped forward, following the slope, searching for what shade would still be among them.

Twenty yards further on I saw that the sun was directly overhead. It expanded until the disc was as wide as the basin, and then lowered itself to about ten feet above my head, a thousand rivers of fire streaming across its surface in all directions. There was a terrifying roaring and barking noise, overlaid by a dull, massive pounding as all the volcanos in the volcano jungle began to erupt again. I walked on, in a dream, shuffling slowly, eyes closed to shut out the furnace around me. Then I discovered that I was sitting on the floor of the basin, which started to spin, setting up a high-pitched screaming.

A strange vision swept like a flame through my mind.

For eons I plunged, spiraling weightlessly through a thousand whirling vortexes, swirled and buffeted down chasmic eddies, splayed out across the disintegrating matrix of the continuum, a dreamless ghost in flight from the cosmic Now. *Then a million motes of light prickled the darkness above me, illuminating enormous curving causeways of time and space veering out past the stars to the rim of the galaxy.*

My dimensions shrank to a metaphysical extension of astral zero, I was propelled upwards to the stars. Aisles of light broke and splintered around me, I passed Aldebaran, soared over Betelgeuse and Vega, zoomed past Antares, finally halted a hundred light years above the crown of Canopus.

Epochs drifted. Time massed on gigantic fronts, colliding like crippled universes. Abruptly, the infinite worlds of tomorrow unfolded before me—ten thousand years, a hundred thousand, unnumbered millennia raced past me in a blur of light, an iridescent cataract of stars and nebulae, interlaced by flashing trajectories of flight and exploration, I entered deep time.

Deep Time: 1,000,000 mega-years. I saw the Milky Way, a wheeling carousel of fire, and Earth's remote descendants, countless races inhabiting every stellar system in the galaxy. The dark intervals between the stars were a continuously flickering field of light, a gigantic phosphorescent ocean, filled with the vibrating pulses of electromagnetic communication pathways.

To cross the enormous voids between the stars they have progressively slowed their physiological time, first ten, then a hundred-fold, so accelerating stellar and galactic time. Space has become alive with transient swarms of comets and meteors, the constellations have begun to dislocate and shift, the slow majestic rotation of the universe itself is at last visible.

Deep Time: 10,000,000 mega-years. Now they have left the Milky Way, which has started to fragment and dissolve. To reach the island galaxies they have further slowed their time schemes by a factor of 10,000, and can thus communicate with each other across vast intergalactic distances in a subjective period of only a few years. Continuously expanding into deep space, they have extended their physiological dependence upon electronic memory banks which store the atomic and molecular patterns within their bodies, transmit them outwards at the speed of light, and later reassemble them.

Deep Time: 100,000,000 mega-years. They have spread now to all the neighboring galaxies, swallowing thousands of nebulae. Their time schemes have decelerated a million-fold, they have become the only permanent forms in an ever-changing world. In a single instant of their lives a star emerges and dies, a subuniverse is born, a score of planetary life systems evolve and vanish. Around them the universe sparkles and flickers with myriad points of light, as untold numbers of constellations appear and fade.

Now, too, they have finally shed their organic forms and are composed of radiating electromagnetic fields, the primary energy substratum of the universe, complex networks of multiple dimensions, alive with the constant tremor of the sentient messages they carry, bearing the lifeways of the race.

To power these fields, they have harnessed entire galaxies riding the wave-fronts of the stellar explosions out towards the terminal helixes of the universe.

Deep Time: 1,000,000,000, mega-years. They are beginning to dictate the form and dimensions of the universe. To girdle the distances which circumscribe the cosmos they have reduced their time period to 0.00000001 of its previous phase. The great galaxies and spiral nebulae which once seemed to live for eternity are now of such brief duration that they are no longer visible. The universe is now almost filled by the great vibrating mantle of ideation, a vast shimmering harp which has completely translated itself into pure wave form, independent of any generating source.

As the universe pulses slowly, its own energy vortices flexing and dilating, so the force-fields of the ideation mantle flex and dilate in sympathy, growing like an embryo within the womb of the cosmos, a child which will soon fill and consume its parent.

Deep Time: 10,000,000,000 mega-years. The ideation-field has now swallowed the cosmos, substituted its own dynamic, its own spatial and temporal dimensions. All primary time and energy fields have been engulfed. Seeking the final extension of itself within its own bounds the mantle has reduced its time period to an almost infinitesimal 0.00000000 ... n of its previous interval. Time has virtually ceased to exist, the ideation-field is nearly stationary, infinitely slow eddies of sentience undulating outward across its mantles.

Ultimately it achieves the final predicates of time and space, eternity and infinity, and slows to absolute zero. Then with a cataclysmic eruption it disintegrates, no longer able to contain itself. Its vast energy patterns begin to collapse, the whole system twists and thrashes in its mortal agony, thrusting outwards huge cataracts of fragmenting energy. In parallel, time emerges.

Out of this debris the first proto-galactic fields are formed, coalescing to give the galaxies and nebulae, the stars encircled by their planetary bodies. Among these, from the elemental seas, based on the carbon atom, emerge the first living forms.

So the cycle renews itself ...

The stars swam, their patterns shifting through a dozen constellations, novas flooded the darkness like blind-

ing arcs, revealing the familiar profiles of the Milky Way, the constellations Orion, Coma Berenices, Cygnus.

Lowering my eyes from the storm-tossed sky I saw the five megaliths. I was back on Murak. Around me the basin was filled with a great concourse of silent figures, ranged upwards along the darkened slopes, shoulder to shoulder in endless ranks, like spectators in a spectral arena.

Beside me a voice spoke, and it seemed to have told me everything I had witnessed of the great cosmic round.

Just before I sank into consciousness for the last time I tried to ask the question ever-present in my drifting mind, but it answered before I spoke, the star-littered sky, the five megaliths and the watching multitude spinning and swirling away into a dream as it said:

"Meanwhile we wait here, at the threshold of time and space, celebrating the identity and kinship of the particles within our bodies with those of the sun and the stars, of our brief private times with the vast periods of the galaxies, with the total unifying time of the cosmos . . ."

I woke lying face downwards in the cool evening sand, shadows beginning to fill the basin, the thermal winds blowing a crisp refreshing breeze across my head and back. Below, the megaliths rose up into the thin blue air, their lower halves cut by the shadow-line of the sinking sun. I lay quietly, stirring my legs and arms tentatively, conscious of the gigantic rifts that had been driven through my mind. After a few minutes I pulled myself to my feet and gazed round at the slopes curving away from me, the memory of the insane vision vivid in my mind.

The vast concourse that had filled the basin, the dream of the cosmic cycle, the voice of my interlocutor—were still real to me, a world in parallel I had just stepped from, and the door to which hung somewhere in the air around me.

Had I dreamed everything, assembling the entire fantasy

in my mind as I lay raving in the noon heat, saved by some thermodynamic freak of the basin's architecture?

I held my thermo-alarm up to the fading light, checking the maximum and minimum levels. The maximum read: 162°. Yet I had survived! I felt relaxed, restored, almost rejuvenated. My hands and face were unburnt—a temperature of over 160° would have boiled the flesh off my bones, left my skin a blackened crisp.

Over my shoulder I noticed the half-track standing on the rim. I ran towards it, for the first time remembering Mayer's death. I felt my cheekbones, testing my jaw muscles. Surprisingly Mayer's heavy punches had left no bruise.

Mayer's body had gone! A single line of footsteps led down from the half-track to the megaliths, but otherwise the carpet of light blue dust was untouched. Mayer's prints, all marks of our scuffle, had vanished.

I quickly scaled the rim and reached the half-track, peering under the chassis and between the tracks. I flung open the cabin door, found the compartment empty.

The windscreen was intact. The paintwork on the door and bonnet was unmarked, the metal trim around the windows unscratched. I dropped to my knees, vainly searched for any flakes of magnesium ash. On my knee the flare pistol lodged securely in its holster, a primed star shell in the breach.

I left the Chrysler, jumped down into the basin and ran over to the megaliths. For an hour I paced round them, trying to resolve the countless questions that jammed my mind.

Just before I left I went over to the fifth tablet. I looked up at the top left corner, wondering whether I should have qualified for its first entry had I died that afternoon.

A single row of letters, filled with shadow by the falling light, stood out clearly.

I stepped back and craned up at them. There were the symbols of the four alien languages, and then, proudly against the stars:

CHARLES FOSTER NELSON   EARTH   AD 2217

"Tell me, Quaine, where would you like to be when the world ends?"

In the seven years since Tallis first asked me this question I must have reexamined it a thousand times. Somehow it seems the key to all the extraordinary events that have happened on Murak, with their limitless implications for the people of Earth (to me a satisfactory answer contains an acceptable statement of one's philosophy and beliefs, an adequate discharge of the one moral debt we owe ourselves and the universe).

Not that the world is about to "end." The implication is rather that it has already ended and regenerated itself an infinite number of times, and that the only remaining question is what to do with ourselves in the meantime. The four stellar races who built the megaliths chose to come to Murak. What exactly they are waiting for here I can't be certain. A cosmic redeemer, perhaps, the first sight of the vast mantle of ideation I glimpsed in my vision. Recalling the period of two million years Tallis cited for life to appear on Murak it may be that the next cosmic cycle will receive its impetus here, and that we are advance spectators, five kings come to attend the genesis of a super-species which will soon outstrip us.

That there are others here, invisible and sustained by preternatural forces, is without doubt. Apart from the impossibility of surviving a Murak noon, I certainly didn't remove Mayer's body from the basin and arrange to have him electrocuted by one of the data-processing units at the observatory. Nor did I conceive the vision of the cosmic cycle myself.

It looks as if the two geologists stumbled upon the Waiting Grounds, somehow divined their significance, and then let Tallis in on their discovery. Perhaps they disagreed, as Mayer and I did, and Nelson may have been forced to kill his companion, to die himself a year later in the course of his vigil.

Like Tallis I shall wait here if necessary for fifteen years. I go out to the Grounds once a week and watch them from the observatory the rest of the time. So far I have seen nothing, although two or three hundred more names have been added to the tablets. However, I am certain that whatever we are waiting for will soon arrive. When I get tired or impatient, as I sometimes do, I remind myself that they have been coming to Murak and waiting here, generation upon generation, for 10,000 years.

Whatever it is, it must be worth waiting for.

SKY

R. A. Lafferty

Raphael Aloysius Lafferty lives in Oklahoma, used to be an electrical engineer, and these days writes stories so idiosyncratic that one need read only two or three sentences to identify an unlabeled piece as his work. His style is playful, his erudition is formidable, his vision is fey, and—for all his gaudy craziness—his world view is firmly anchored to a surprisingly strong and consistent moral-philosophical base: though Lafferty is all lightness, he is "heavy" in the current colloquial meaning of the word. Which has won a passionate following for such novels as Past Master and Fourth Mansions, for his scores of short stories (collected in Nine Hundred Grandmothers and Strange Doings), and for his major excursion to date outside the field of fantasy, the historical novel Okla Hannali. His short story "Eurema's Dam" won a

Hugo in 1973; the story reprinted here was a runner-up for the award the year before.

THE SKY-SELLER was Mr. Furtive himself, fox-muzzled, ferret-eyed, slithering along like a snake, and living under the Rocks. The Rocks had not been a grand place for a long time. It had been built in the grand style on a mephitic plot of earth (to transform it), but the mephitic earth had won out. The apartments of the Rocks had lost their sparkle as they had been divided again and again, and now they were shoddy. The Rocks had weathered. Its once pastel hues were now dull grays and browns.

The five underground levels had been parking places for motor vehicles when those were still common, but now these depths were turned into warrens and hovels. The Sky-Seller lurked and lived in the lowest and smallest and meanest of them all.

He came out only at night. Daylight would have killed him: he knew that. He sold out of the darkest shadows of the night. He had only a few (though oddly select) clients, and nobody knew who his supplier was. He said that he had no supplier, that he gathered and made the stuff himself.

Welkin Alauda, a full-bodied but light-moving girl (it was said that her bones were hollow and filled with air), came to the Sky-Seller just before first light, just when he had become highly nervous but had not yet bolted to his underground.

"A sack of Sky from the nervous mouse. Jump, or the sun will gobble your house!" Welkin sang-song, and she was already higher than most skies.

"Hurry, hurry!" the Sky-Seller begged, thrusting the sack to her while his black eyes trembled and glittered (if real light should ever reflect into them he'd go blind).

Welkin took the sack of Sky, and scrambled money notes into his hands which had furred palms. (Really? Yes, really.)

"World be flat and the Air be round, wherever the Sky

grows underground," Welkin intoned, taking the sack of Sky and soaring along with a light scamper of feet (she hadn't much weight, her bones were hollow). And the Sky-Seller darted head-first down a black well-shaft thing to his depths.

Four of them went Sky-Diving that morning, Welkin herself, Karl Vlieger, Icarus Riley, Joseph Alzarsi; and the pilot was—(no, not who you think, he had already threatened to turn them all in; they'd use that pilot no more)—the pilot was Ronald Kolibri in his little crop-dusting plane.

But a crop-duster will not go up to the frosty heights they liked to take off from. Yes it will—if everybody is on Sky. But it isn't pressurized, and it doesn't carry oxygen. That doesn't matter, not if everybody is on Sky, not if the plane is on Sky too.

Welkin took Sky with Mountain Whizz, a carbonated drink. Karl stuffed it into his lip like snuff. Icarus Riley rolled it and smoked it. Joseph Alzarsi needled it, mixed with drinking alcohol, into his main vein. The pilot Ronny tongued and chewed it like sugar dust. The plane named Shrike took it through the manifold.

Fifty thousand feet— You can't go that high in a crop-duster. Thirty below zero— Ah, that isn't cold! Air too thin to breathe at all—with Sky, who needs such included things as air?

Welkin stepped out, and went up, not down. It was a trick she often pulled. She hadn't much weight; she could always get higher than the rest of them. She went up and up until she disappeared. Then she drifted down again, completely enclosed in a sphere of ice crystal, sparkling inside it and making monkey-faces at them.

The wind yelled and barked, and the divers took off. They all went down, soaring and gliding and tumbling; standing still sometimes, it seemed; even rising again a little. They went down to clouds and spread out on them: black-white clouds with the sun inside them and suffusing them both from above and below. They cracked Welkin's ice-crystal sphere and she stepped out of it. They ate the thin pieces of it, very cold and brittle and with a tang of ozone. Alzarsi took off his shirt and sunned himself on a cloud.

"You will burn," Welkin told him. "Nobody burns so as when sunning himself on a cloud." That was true.

They sank through the black-whiteness of these clouds and came into the limitless blue concourse with clouds above and below them. It was in this same concourse that Hippodameia used to race her horses, there not being room for such coursers to run on earth. The clouds below folded up and the clouds above folded down, forming a discrete space.

"We have our own rotundity and sphere here," said Icarus Riley (these are their Sky-Diver names, not their legal names), "and it is apart from all worlds and bodies. The worlds and the bodies do not exist for as long a time as we say that they do not exist. The axis of our present space is its own concord. Therefore, it being in perfect concord, Time stops."

All their watches had stopped, at least.

"But there *is* a world below," said Karl. "It is an abject world, and we can keep it abject forever if we wish. But it has at least a shadowy existence, and later we will let it fill out again in our compassion for lowly things. It is flat, though, and we must insist that it remain flat."

"This is important," Joseph said with the deep importance of one on Sky. "So long as our own space is bowed and globed, the world must remain flat or depressed. But the world must not be allowed to bow its back again. We are in danger if it ever does. So long as it is truly flat and abject it cannot crash ourselves to it."

"How long could we fall," Welkin asked, "—if we had not stopped time, if we let it flow at its own pace, or at ours? How long could we fall?"

"Hephaestus once tumbled through space all day long," Icarus Riley said, "and the days were longer then."

Karl Vlieger had gone wall-eyed from an interior-turned

sexual passion that he often experienced in diving. Icarus Riley seemed to be on laughing gas suddenly; this is a sign that Sky is not having perfect effect. Joseph Alzarsi felt a cold wind down his spine and a series of jerky little premonitions.

"We are not perfect," Joseph said. "Tomorrow or the next day we may be, for we *do* approach perfection. We win a round. And we win another. Let us not throw away our victory today through carelessness. The earth has bowed his old back a little bit, and we make ready for him! Now, guys, now!"

Four of them (or maybe only three of them) pulled the rings. The chutes unpeeled, flowered, and jerked. They had been together like a sheaf in close conversation. But suddenly, on coming to earth, they were spread out over five hundred yards.

They assembled. They packed their chutes. That would be all the diving for that day.

"Welkin, how did you pack your chute so quickly?" Icarus asked her suspiciously.

"I don't know."

"You are always the slowest one of us, and the sloppiest. Someone always has to re-roll your chute for you before it is used again. And you were the last one to land just now. How were you the first one to be packed? How did you roll it so well? It has the earmarks of my own rolling, just as I rolled it for you before we took off this morning."

"I don't know, Icarus. Oh, I think I'll go up again, straight up."

"No, you've sailed and dived enough for one morning. Welkin, did you even open your chute?"

"I don't know."

High on Sky, they went up again the next morning. The little plane named Shrike flew up as no plane had ever flown before, up through Storm. The storm-shrouded earth shrank to the size of a pea-doogie.

"We will play a trick on it," said Welkin. "When you're on Sky you can play a trick on anything and make it abide by it. I will say that the pea-doogie that was the world is nothing. See, it is gone. Then I will select another pea-doogie, that one there, and I will call it the world. And that *is* the world that we will come down to in a little while. I've switched worlds on the world, and it doesn't know what happened to it."

"It's uneasy, though." Joseph Alzarsi spoke through flared nostrils. "You shook it. No wonder the world has its moments of self-doubt."

They were one million feet high. The altimeter didn't go that high, but Ronald Kolibri the pilot wrote out the extended figure in chalk to make it correct. Welkin stepped out. Karl and Icarus and Joseph stepped out. Ronald Kolibri stepped out, but only for a while. Then he remembered that he was the pilot and got back in the plane. They were so high that the air was black and star-filled instead of blue. It was so cold that the empty space was full of cracks and potholes. They dived half a million feet in no time at all. They pulled up laughing.

It was invigorating, it was vivifying. They stamped on the clouds, and the clouds rang like frosty ground. This was the ancestral country of all hoarfrost, of all grained-snow and glare-ice. Here was weather-maker, here was wind-son. They came into caves of ice mixed with moraine; they found antler hatchets and Hemicyon bones; they found coals still glowing. The winds bayed and hunted in packs through the chasms. These were the cold Fortean clouds, and their location is commonly quite high.

They came down below Storm, finding new sun and new air. It was pumpkin-summer, it was deep autumn in the sky.

They dropped again, miles and millennia, to full Sky-summer: the air so blue that it grew a violet patina on it to save the surface. Their own space formed about them again, as it did every day, and time stopped.

But not motion! Motion never stopped with them. Do you not realize that nothingness in a void can still be in motion?

And how much more they of the great centrality! There was Dynamic; there was sustaining vortex; there was the high serenity of fevered motion.

But is not motion merely a relationship of space to time? No. That is an idea that is common to people who live on worlds, but it is a subjective idea. Here, beyond the possible influence of any worlds, there was living motion without reference.

"Welkin, you look quite different today," Joseph Alzarsi spoke in wonder. "What is it?"

"I don't know. It's wonderful to be different and I'm wonderful."

"It is something missing from you," said Icarus. "I believe it is a defect missing."

"But I hadn't any, Icarus."

They were in central and eternal moment, and it did not end, it could not end, it goes on yet. Whatever else seems to happen, it is merely in parentheses to that moment.

"It is time to consider again," Icarus mused after a while. There is no time or while in the Moment, but there is in the parentheses. "I hope it is the last time we will ever have to consider. We, of course, are in our own space and beyond time or tangent. But the earth, such as it is, is approaching with great presumption and speed."

"But it's *nothing* to us!" Karl Vlieger suddenly raged out in a chthonic and phallic passion. "We can shatter it! We can shoot it to pieces like a clay pigeon! It cannot rush onto us like a slashing dog. Get down, world! Heel, you cur! Heel, I say!"

"We say to one world 'rise' and it rises, and to another one 'heel' and it heels," Icarus sky-spoke in his dynamic serenity.

"Not yet," Joseph Alzarsi warned. "Tomorrow we will be total. Today we are not yet. Possibly we *could* shatter the world like a clay pigeon if we wished, but we would not be lords of it if we had to shatter it."

"We could always make another world," said Welkin reasonably.

"Certainly, but this one is our testing. We will go to it when

it is crouched down. We cannot allow it to come ravening to
us. Hold! Hold there, we order you!"
    And the uprushing world halted, cowed.
    "We go down," said Joseph.
    "We will let it come up only when it is properly broken."
("And they inclined the heavens and came down.")

    Once more, three of them pulled the rings. And the
chutes unpeeled, flowered, and jerked. They had been like
a sheaf together in their moment; but now, coming to earth,
they were suddenly scattered out over five hundred yards.

    "Welkin, you didn't have your chute at all today!"
Icarus gaped with some awe when they had assembled again.
"That is what was different about you."
    "No, I guess I didn't have it. There was no reason to have
it if I didn't need it. Really, there was never any reason for
me to have used one at all ever."
    "Ah, we *were* total today and didn't know it," Joseph ven-
tured. "Tomorrow none of us will wear chutes. This is easier
than I had believed."

    Welkin went to the Sky-Seller to buy new Sky that
night. Not finding him in the nearer shadows of the Rocks,
she went down and down, drawn by the fungoid odor and the
echoing dampness of the underground. She went through
passages that were man-made, through passages that were
natural, through passages that were unnatural. Some of these
corridors, it is true, had once been built by men, but now
they had reverted and become most unnatural deep-earth
caverns. Welkin went down into the total blackness where
there were certain small things that still mumbled out a faint
white color; but it was the wrong color white, and the things
were all of a wrong shape.

There was the dead white shape of Mycelium masses, the grotesqueness of Agaricus, the deformity of Deadly Amanita and of Morel. The gray-milky Lactarius glowed like lightless lanterns in the dark; there was the blue-white of the Deceiving Clitocybe and the yellow-white of the Caesar Agaric. There was the insane ghost-white of the deadliest and queerest of them all, the Fly Amanita, and a mole was gathering this.

"Mole, bring Sky for the Thing Serene, for the Minions tall and the Airy Queen," Welkin jangled. She was still high on Sky, but it had begun to leave her a little and she had the veriest touch of the desolate sickness.

"Sky for the Queen of the buzzing drones, with her hollow heart and her hollow bones," the Sky-Seller intoned hollowly.

"And fresh, Oh I want it fresh, fresh Sky!" Welkin cried.

"With these creatures there is no such thing as fresh," the Sky-Seller told her. "You want it stale, Oh so stale! Ingrown and aged and with its own mold grown moldy."

"Which is it?" Welkin demanded. "What is the name of the one you gather it from?"

"The Fly Amanita."

"But isn't that simply a poisonous mushroom?"

"It has passed beyond that. It has sublimated. Its simple poison has had its second fermenting into narcotic."

"But it sounds so cheap that it be merely narcotic."

"Not merely narcotic. It is something very special in narcotic."

"No, no, not narcotic at all!" Welkin protested. "It is liberating, it is world-shattering. It is Height Absoluto. It is motion and detachment itself. It is the ultimate. It is mastery."

"Why, then it is mastery, lady. It is the highest and lowest of all created things."

"Take it, take it," the Sky-Seller growled, "and be gone. Something begins to curl up inside me."

"I go!" Welkin said, "and I will be back many times for more."

"No, you will not be. Nobody ever comes back many times for Sky. You will be back never. Or one time. I think that you will be back one time."

They went up again the next morning, the last morning. But why should we say that it was the last morning? Because there would no longer be divisions or days for them. It would be one last eternal day for them now, and nothing could break it.

They went up in the plane that had once been named Shrike and was now named Eternal Eagle. The plane had repainted itself during the night with new name and new symbols, some of them not immediately understandable. The plane snuffled Sky into its manifolds, and grinned and roared. And the plane went up.

Oh! Jerusalem in the Sky! How it went up!

They were all certainly perfect now and would never need Sky again. *They were Sky.*

"How little the world is!" Welkin rang out. "The towns are like fly-specks and the cities are like flies."

"It is wrong that so ignoble a creature as the Fly should have the exalted name," Icarus complained.

"I'll fix that," Welkin sang. "I give edict: That all the flies on earth be dead!" And all the flies on earth died in that instant.

"I wasn't sure you could do that," said Joseph Alzarsi. "The wrong is righted. Now we ourselves assume the noble name of Flies. There are no Flies but us!"

The five of them, including the pilot Ronald Kolibri, stepped chuteless out of the Eternal Eagle.

"Will you be all right?" Ronald asked the rollicking plane.

"Certainly," the plane said. "I believe I know where there are other Eternal Eagles. I will mate."

It was cloudless, or else they had developed the facility of seeing through clouds. Or perhaps it was that, the earth having become as small as a marble, the clouds around it were insignificant.

Pure light that had an everywhere source! (The sun also had become insignificant and didn't contribute much to the light.) Pure and intense motion that had no location reference. They weren't going anywhere with their intense motion (they already *were* everywhere, or at the super-charged center of everything).

Pure cold fever. Pure serenity. Impure hyper-space passion of Karl Vlieger, and then of all of them; but it was purely rampant at least. Stunning beauty in all things along with a towering cragginess that was just ugly enough to create an ecstasy.

Welkin Alauda was mythic with nenuphars in her hair. And it shall not be told what Joseph Alzarsi wore in his own hair. An always-instant, a million or a billion years!

Not monotony, no! Presentation! Living sets! Scenery! The scenes were formed for the splinter of a moment; or they were formed forever. Whole worlds formed in a pregnant void: not spherical worlds merely, but dodeka-spherical, and those much more intricate than that. Not merely seven colors to play with, but seven to the seventh and to the seventh again.

Stars vivid in the bright light. You who have seen stars only in darkness be silent! Asteroids that they ate like peanuts, for now they were all metamorphic giants. Galaxies like herds of rampaging elephants. Bridges so long that both ends of them receded over the light-speed edges. Waterfalls, of a finer water, that bounced off galaxy clusters as if they were boulders.

Through a certain ineptitude of handling, Welkin extinguished the old sun with one such leaping torrent.

"It does not matter," Icarus told her. "Either a million or a billion years had passed according to the time-scale of the bodies, and surely the sun had already come onto dim days. You can always make other suns."

Karl Vlieger was casting lightning bolts millions of parsecs long and making looping contact with clustered galaxies with them.

"Are you sure that we are not using up any time?" Welkin asked them with some apprehension.

"Oh, time still uses itself up, but we are safely out of the reach of it all," Joseph explained. "Time is only one very inefficient method of counting numbers. It is inefficient because it is limited in its numbers, and because the counter by such a system must die when he has come to the end of his series. That alone should weigh against it as a mathematical system; it really shouldn't be taught."

"Then nothing can hurt us ever?" Welkin wanted to be reassured.

"No, nothing can come at us except inside time and we are outside it. Nothing can collide with us except in space and we disdain space. Stop it, Karl! As you do it, that's buggery."

"I have a worm in my own tract and it gnaws at me a little," the pilot Ronald Kolibri said. "It's in my internal space and it's crunching along at a pretty good rate."

"No, no, that's impossible. Nothing can reach or hurt us," Joseph insisted.

"I have a worm of my own in a still more interior tract," said Icarus, "the tract that they never quite located in the head or the heart or the bowels. Maybe this tract always was outside space. Oh, my worm doesn't gnaw, but it stirs. Maybe I'm tired of being out of reach of everything."

"Where do these doubts rise from?" Joseph sounded querulous. "You hadn't them an instant ago, you hadn't them as recently as ten million years ago. How can you have them now when there isn't any now?"

"Well, as to that—" Icarus began—(and a million years went by)—"as to that I have a sort of cosmic curiosity about an object in my own past—"—(another million years went by)—"an object called world."

"Well, satisfy your curiosity then," Karl Vlieger snapped. "Don't you even know how to make a world?"

"Certainly I know how, but will it be the same?"

"Yes, if you're good enough. It will be the same if you make it the same."

Icarus Riley made a world. He wasn't very good at it and it wasn't quite the same, but it did resemble the old world a little.

"I want to see if some things are still there," Welkin clamored. "Bring it closer."

"It's unlikely your things are still there," Joseph said. "Remember that billions of years may have passed."

"The things will be there if I put them there," Icarus insisted.

"And you cannot bring it closer since all distance is now infinite," Karl maintained.

"At least I can focus it better," Icarus insisted, and he did. The world appeared quite near.

"It remembers us like a puppy would," Welkin said. "See, it jumps up at us."

"It's more like a lion leaping for a treed hunter just out of reach," Icarus grudged. "But we are *not* treed."

"It can't ever reach us, and it wants to," Welkin piqued. "Let's reach down to it."

("And they inclined the heavens and went down.")

A most peculiar thing happened to Ronald Kolibri as he touched earth. He seemed to have a seizure. He went slack-faced, almost horror-faced, and he would not answer the others.

"What is it, Ronald?" Welkin begged in kindred anguish. "Oh, what is it? Somebody help him!"

Then Ronald Kolibri did an even more peculiar thing. He began to fold up and break up from the bottom. Bones slowly splintered and pierced out of him and his entrails gushed out. He compressed. He shattered. He splashed. Can a man splash?

The same sort of seizure overtook Karl Vlieger: the identical slack-face horror-face, the same folding up and breaking up from the bottom, the same hideous sequence.

And Joseph Alzarsi went into the same sundering state, baffled and breaking up.

"Icarus, what's happened to them?" Welkin screamed. "What is that slow loud booming?"

"They're dead. How could that be?" Icarus puzzled trembling. "Death is in time, and we are not."

Icarus himself passed through time as he crashed earth, breaking up, spilling out more odiously than any of them.

And Welkin touched earth, crashed, then what? She heard her own slow loud booming as she hit.

(Another million years went by, or some weeks.)

A shaky old woman on crutches was going down the middle-of-the-night passages that are under the Rocks. She was too old a woman to be Welkin Alauda, but not too old for a Welkin who had lived millions of years outside of time.

She had not died. She was lighter than the others, and besides she had done it twice before unscathed. But that was before she had known fear.

Naturally they had told her that she would never walk again; and now most unnaturally she was walking with crutches. Drawn by the fungoid odor and the echoing dampness she went down in the total dark to where small things were glowing with the wrong color white and were all of the wrong shape. She wanted one thing only, and she would die without it.

"Sky for salving the broken Crone! Sky for the weal of my hollow bone!" she crackled in an old-woman voice. But it was only her own voice that echoed back to her.

Should a Sky-Seller live forever?

NIGHT

John W. Campbell

Beyond any doubt the dominant figure in the development of modern American science fiction was John W. Campbell, who edited Astounding Science Fiction *(now called* Analog*) from 1937 until his death thirty-four years later. A tall, massive man whose active, crackling mind never seemed to rest, Campbell in his long reign as editor discovered most of the major writers of his time—such people as Robert A. Heinlein, Isaac Asimov, Theodore Sturgeon, A. E. van Vogt, and L. Sprague de Camp—and cunningly goaded them to exceed their own considerable capabilities by constantly setting stimulating literary challenges for them. Though best known as a brilliant, cantankerous, often eccentric editor, Campbell had earlier been the outstanding science fiction writer of the 1930's, or, rather, the* two *outstanding science*

*fiction writers of the 1930's. Under his own name he pub-
lished a long series of straightforward space-adventure stories, dense with technological speculation, starting at the age
of twenty in 1930; though these "heavy-science" works were
immensely popular, he began later in the decade to write
very different stories, moody and haunting, under the
pseudonym of "Don A. Stuart," and it is the Stuart stories
that continue to hold readers after more than forty years—
"Twilight," "Blindness," "Dead Knowledge," and the story
offered here. The powerful novella "Who Goes There?" was
the last important Stuart story, in 1938; after that Campbell
virtually abandoned his own writing to concentrate on his
editorial tasks, freely passing the ideas he conceived to his
most gifted contributors. Our loss, but also our great gain.*

CONDON was staring through the glasses with a face
tense and drawn, all his attention utterly concentrated on
that one almost invisible speck infinitely far up in the blue
sky, and saying over and over again in the most horribly
absent-minded way, "My Lord—my Lord—"

Suddenly he shivered and looked down at me, sheer agony
in his face. "He's never coming down. Don, he's never coming down—"

I knew it, too—knew it as solidly as I knew the knowledge
was impossible. But I smiled and said: "Oh, I wouldn't say
that. If anything, I'd fear his coming down. What goes up
comes down."

Major Condon trembled all over. His mouth worked horribly for a moment before he could speak. "Talbot—I'm scared
—I'm horribly scared. You know—you're his assistant—you
know he's trying to defeat gravity. Men aren't meant to—it's
wrong—wrong—"

His eyes were glued on those binoculars again, with the
same terrible tensity, and now he was saying over and over
in that absent-minded way, "Wrong—wrong—wrong—"

Simultaneously he stiffened and stopped. The dozen or so other men standing on that lonely little emergency field stiffened; then the major crumpled to the ground. I've never before seen a man faint, let alone an army officer with a D. S. medal. I didn't stop to help him, because I knew something had happened. I grabbed the glasses.

Far, far up in the sky was that little orange speck—far, where there is almost no air, and he had been forced to wear a stratosphere suit with a little alcohol heater. The broad, orange wings were overlaid now with a faint-glowing, pearl-gray light. And it was falling. Slowly, at first, circling aimlessly downward. Then it dipped, rose, and somehow went into a tail spin.

It was horrible. I know I must have breathed, but it didn't seem so. It took minutes for it to fall those miles, despite the speed. Eventually it whipped out of that tail spin—through sheer speed, whipped out and into a power dive. It was a ghastly, flying coffin, hurtling at more than half a thousand miles an hour when it reached the Earth, some fifteen miles away.

The ground trembled, and the air shook with the crash of it. We were in the cars and roaring across the ground long before it hit. I was in Bob's car, with Jeff, his laboratory technician— Bob's little roadster he'd never need again. The engine picked up quickly, and we were going seventy before we left the field, jumped a shallow ditch and hit the road— the deserted, concrete road that led off toward where he must be. The engine roared as Jeff clamped down on the accelerator. Dimly, I heard the major's big car coming along behind us.

Jeff drove like a maniac, but I didn't notice. I knew the thing had done ninety-five but I think we must have done more. The wind whipped tears in my eyes so I couldn't be sure whether I saw mounting smoke and flame or not. With diesel fuel there shouldn't be—but that plane had been doing things it shouldn't. It had been trying out Carter's antigravity coil.

We shot up the flat, straight road across wide, level country, the wind moaning a requiem about the car. Far ahead I saw the side road that must lead off toward where Bob should be, and lurched to the braking of the car, the whine and sing of violently shrieking tires, then to the skidding corner. It was a sand road; we slithered down it and for all the lightness and power, we slowed to sixty-five, clinging to the seat as the soft sand gripped and clung.

Violently Jeff twisted into a branching cow path, and somehow the springs took it. We braked to a stop a quarter of a mile from the plane.

It was in a fenced field of pasture and wood lot. We leaped the fence and raced toward it: Jeff got there first, just as the major's car shrieked to a stop behind ours.

The major was cold and pale when he reached us. "Dead," he stated.

And I was very much colder and probably several times as pale. "I don't know!" I moaned. "He isn't there!"

"Not there!" The major almost screamed it. "He must be —he has to be. He has no parachute—wouldn't take one. They say he didn't jump—"

I pointed to the plane and wiped a little cold sweat from my forehead. I felt clammy all over, and my spine prickled. The solid steel of the huge diesel engine was driven through the stump of a tree, down into the ground perhaps eight or nine feet, and the dirt and rock had splashed under that blow like wet mud.

The wings were on the other side of the field, flattened, twisted straws of dural alloy. The fuselage of the ship was a perfect silhouette—a longitudinal projection that had flattened in on itself, each separate action stopping only as it hit the ground.

The great torus coil with its strangely twined wrappings of hair-fine bismuth wire was intact! And bent over it, twisted, utterly wrecked by the impact, was the main-wing stringer

—the great dural-alloy beam that supported most of the ship's weight in the air. It was battered, crushed on those hair-fine, fragile bismuth wires—and not one of them was twisted or displaced or so much as skinned. The back frame of the ponderous diesel engine—the heavy supercharger was the anvil of that combination—was cracked and splintered. And not one wire of the hellish bismuth coil was strained or skinned or displaced.

And the red pulp that should have been there—the red pulp that had been a man—wasn't. It simply wasn't there at all. He hadn't left the plane. In the clear, cloudless air, we could see that. He was gone.

We examined it, of course. A farmer came, and another, and looked, and talked. Then several farmers came in old, dilapidated cars with their wives and families, and watched.

We set the owner of the property on watch and went away —went back to the city for workmen and a truck with a derrick. Dusk was falling. It would be morning before we could do anything, so we went away.

Five of us—the major of the army air force, Jeff Rodney, the two Douglas Company men whose names I never remembered and I—sat in my—our—room. Bob's and Jeff's and mine. We'd been sitting there for hours trying to talk, trying to think, trying to remember every little detail, and trying to forget every ghastly detail. We couldn't remember the detail that explained it, nor forget the details that rode and harried us.

And the telephone rang. I started, then slowly got up and answered. A strange voice, flat and rather unpleasant, said, "Mr. Talbot?"

"Yoo."

It was Sam Gantry, the farmer we'd left on watch. "There's a man here."

"Yes? What does he want?"

"I dunno. I dunno where he came from. He's either dead or out cold. Gotta funny kind of an aviator suit on, with a glass face on it. He looks all blue, so I guess he's dead."

"Lord! Bob! Did you take that helmet off?" I roared.

"No, sir, no—no, sir. We just left him the way he was."

"His tanks have run out. Listen. Take a hammer, a wrench, anything, and break that glass faceplate! Quick! We'll be there."

Jeff was moving. The major was, too, and the others. I made a grab for the half-empty bottle of Scotch, started out, and ducked back into the closet. With the oxygen bottle under my arm I jumped into the crowded little roadster just as Jeff started it moving. He turned on the horn, and left it that way.

We dodged, twisted, jumped and stopped with jerks in traffic, then leaped into smooth, roaring speed out toward the farmer's field. The turns were familiar now; we scarcely slowed for them, sluing around them. This time Jeff charged through the wire fence. A headlight popped; there was a shrill scream of wire, the wicked *zing* of wire scratching across the hood and mud guards, and we were bouncing across the field.

There were two lanterns on the ground; three men carried others; more men squatted down beside a still figure garbed in a fantastic, bulging, airproof stratosphere suit. They looked at us, open-mouthed as we skidded to a halt, moving aside as the major leaped out and dashed over with the Scotch. I followed close behind with the oxygen bottle.

Bob's faceplate was shattered, his face blue, his lips blue and flecked with froth. A long gash across his cheek from the shattered glass bled slowly. The major lifted his head without a word, and glass tinkled inside the helmet as he tried to force a little whisky down his throat.

"Wait!" I called. "Major, give him artificial respiration, and this will bring him around quicker—better." The major nodded, and rose, rubbing his arm with a peculiar expression.

"That's cold!" he said, as he flipped Bob over, and straddled his back. I held the oxygen bottle under Bob's nose as the major swung back in his arc, and let the raw, cold oxygen gas flow into his nostrils.

In ten seconds Bob coughed, gurgled, coughed violently, and took a deep shuddering breath. His face turned pink almost instantly under that lungful of oxygen, and I noticed with some surprise that he seemed to exhale almost nothing, his body absorbing the oxygen rapidly.

He coughed again; then "I could breathe a heck of a sight better if you'd get off my back," he said. The major jumped up, and Bob turned over and sat up. He waved me aside, and spat. "I'm—all right," he said softly.

"Lord, man, what happened?" demanded the major.

Bob sat silent for a minute. His eyes had the strangest look —a hungry look—as he gazed about him. He looked at the trees beyond and at the silent, watching men in the light of the lanterns; then up, up to where a myriad stars gleamed and danced and flickered in the clear night sky.

"I'm back," he said softly. Then suddenly he shivered, and looked horribly afraid. "But—I'll have to be—then—too."

He looked at the major for a minute, and smiled faintly. And at the two Douglas Company men. "Your plane was all right. I started up on the wings, as arranged, went way up, till I thought surely I was at a safe height, where the air wasn't too dense and the field surely wouldn't reach to Earth —Lord!—reach to Earth! I didn't guess how far that field extended. It touched Earth—twice.

"I was at forty-five thousand when I decided it was safe, and cut the engine. It died, and the stillness shocked me. It was so quiet. So quiet.

"I turned on the coil circuit, and the dynamotor began to hum as the tubes warmed up. And then—the field hit me. It paralyzed me in an instant. I never had a chance to break the circuit, though I knew instantly something was wrong—terribly wrong. But the very first thing it did was to paralyze me, and I had to sit there and watch the instruments climb to positions and meanings they were never meant for.

"I realized I alone was being affected by that coil—I alone, sitting directly over it. I stared at the meters and they began to fade, began to seem transparent, unreal. And as they faded into blankness I saw clear sky beyond them; then for a hundredth of a second, like some effect of persistence of vision, I thought I saw the plane falling, twisting down at incredible speed, and the light faded as the Sun seemed to rocket suddenly across the sky and vanish.

"I don't know how long I was in that paralyzed condition, where there was only blankness—neither dark nor light, nor time nor any form—but I breathed many times. Finally, form crawled and writhed into the blankness, and seemed to solidify beneath me as, abruptly, the blankness gave way to a dull red light. I was falling.

"I thought instantly of the forty-five thousand feet that lay between me and the solid Earth, and stiffened automatically in terror. And at the same instant I landed in a deep blanket of white snow, stained by the red light that lighted the world.

"Cold. Cold—it tore into me like the fang of a savage animal. What cold! The cold of ultimate death. It ripped through that thick, insulated suit and slashed at me viciously, as though there were no insulation there. I shivered so violently I could scarcely turn up the alcohol valves. You know I carried alcohol tanks and catalyst grids for heating, because the only electric fields I wanted were those of the apparatus. Even used a diesel instead of gas engine.

"I thanked the Lord for that then. I realized that whatever had happened I was in a spot indescribably cold and desolate. And in the same instant, realized that the sky was black. Blacker than the blackest night, and yet before me the snow field stretched to infinity, tainted by the blood-red light, and my shadow crawled in darker red at my feet.

"I turned around. As far as the eye could see in three directions the land swept off in very low, very slightly rolling hills, almost plains—red plains of snow dyed with the dripping light of sunset, I thought.

"In the fourth direction, a wall—a wall that put the Great Wall of China to shame—loomed up half a mile—a blood-red wall that had the luster of metal. It stretched across the horizon and looked a scant hundred yards away, for the air was utterly clear. I turned up my alcohol burners a bit more and felt a little better.

"Something jerked my head around like a giant hand—a sudden thought. I stared at the sun and gulped. It was four times—six times—the size of the sun I knew. And it wasn't setting. It was forty-five degrees from the horizon. It was red. Blood-red. And there wasn't the slightest bit of radiant heat reaching my face from it. That sun was cold.

"I'd just automatically assumed I was still on Earth, whatever else might have happened, but now I knew I couldn't be. It must be another planet of another sun—a frozen planet —for that snow was frozen air. I knew it absolutely. A frozen planet of a dead sun.

"And then I changed even that. I looked up at the black sky above me, and in all the vast black bowl of the heavens, not three-score stars were visible. Dim, red stars, with one single sun that stood out for its brilliance—a yellowish-red sun perhaps a tenth as bright as our Sun, but a monster here. It was another—a dead—space. For if that snow was frozen air, the only atmosphere must have been neon and helium. There wasn't any hazy air to stop the light of the stars, and that dim, red sun didn't obscure them with its light. The stars were gone.

"In that glimpse, my mind began working by itself; I was scared.

"Scared? I was so scared I was afraid I was going to be sick. Because right then I knew I was never coming back. When I felt that cold, I'd wondered when my oxygen bottles would give out, if I'd get back before they did. Now it was not a worry. It was simply the limiting factor on an already-determined thing, the setting on the time bomb. I had just so much more time before I died right there.

"My mind was working out things, working them out all by itself, and giving answers I didn't want, didn't want to know about. For some reason it persisted in considering this was Earth and the conviction became more and more fixed. It was right. That was Earth. And it was old Sol. Old—old Sol. It was the time axis that coil distorted—not gravity at all. My mind worked that out with a logic as cold as that planet.

"If it was time it had distorted, and this was Earth, then it had distorted time beyond imagining to an extent as meaningless to our minds as the distance a hundred million light years is. It was simply vast—incalculable. The sun was dead. The Earth was dead. And Earth was already, in our time, two billion of years old, and in all that geological time, the sun had not changed measurably. Then how long was it since my time? The sun was dead. The very stars were dead. It must have been, I thought even then, billions on billions of years. And I grossly underestimated it.

"The world was old—old—old. The very rocks and ground radiated a crushing aura of incredible age. It was old, older than—but what is there? Older than the hills? Hills? Gosh, they'd been born and died and been born and worn away again, a million, a score of million times! Old as the stars? No, that wouldn't do. The stars were dead—then.

"I looked again at the metal wall and set out for it, and the aura of age washed up at me and dragged at me and tried to stop this motion when all motion should have ceased. And the thin, unutterably cold wind whined in dead protest at me, and pulled at me with the ghost hands of the million million million that had been born and lived and died in the countless ages before I was born.

"I wondered as I went. I didn't think clearly, for the dead aura of the dead planet pulled at me. Age. The stars were dying, dead. They were huddled there in space, like decrepit old men, huddling for warmth. The galaxy was shrunk. So tiny, it wasn't a thousand light years across, the stars were separated by miles where there had been light years. The magnificent, proudly sprawling universe I had known, that flung itself across a million million light years, that flung radiant energy through space by the millions of millions of tons was—gone.

"It was dying—a dying miser that hoarded its last broken dregs of energy in a tiny cramped space. It was broken and shattered. A thousand billion years before the cosmical constant had been dropped from that broken universe. The cosmical constant that flung giant galaxies whirling apart with ever greater speed had no place here. It had hurled the universe in broken fragments, till each spattered bit felt the chill of loneliness, and wrapped space about itself, to become a universe in itself while the flaming galaxies vanished.

"That had happened so long ago that the writing it had left in the fabric of space itself had worn away. Only the gravity constant remained, the hoarding constant, that drew things together, and slowly the galaxy collapsed, shrunken and old, a withered mummy.

"The very atoms were dead. The light was cold; even the red light made things look older, colder. There was no youth in the universe. I didn't belong, and the faint protesting rustle of the infinitely cold wind about me moved the snow in muted, futile protest, resenting my intrusion from a time when things were young. It whinnied at me feebly and chilled the youth of me.

"I plodded on and on, and always the metal wall retreated, like one of those desert mirages. I was too stupefied by the age of the thing to wonder; I just walked on.

"I was getting nearer, though. The wall was real; it was fixed. As I drew slowly nearer, the polished sheen of the wall died and the last dregs of hope died. I'd thought there might be some one still living behind that wall. Beings who could build such a thing might be able to live even here. But I couldn't stop then; I just went on. The wall was broken and cracked. It wasn't a wall I'd seen; it was a series of broken walls, knitted by distance to a smooth front.

"There was no weather to age them, only the faintest stirring of faint, dead winds—winds of neon and helium, inert and uncorroding—as dead and inert as the universe. The city had been dead a score of billions of years. That city was dead for a time ten times longer than the age of our planet today. But nothing destroyed it. Earth was dead—too dead to suffer the racking pains of life. The air was dead, too dead to scrape away metal.

"But the universe itself was dead. There was no cosmic radiation then to finally level the walls by atomic disintegration. There had been a wall—a single metal wall. Something —perhaps a last wandering meteor—had chanced on it in a time incalculably remote, and broken it. I entered through the great gap. Snow covered the city—soft, white snow. The great red sun stood still just where it was. Earth's restless rotation had long since been stilled—long, long since.

"There were dead gardens above, and I wandered up to them. That was really what convinced me it was a human city, on Earth. There were frozen, huddled heaps that might once have been men. Little fellows with fear forever frozen on their faces huddled helplessly over something that must once have been a heating device. Dead perhaps, since the last storm old Earth had known, tens of billions of years before.

"I went down. There were vastnesses in that city. It was huge. It stretched forever, it seemed, on and on, in its deadness. Machines, machines everywhere. And the machines were dead, too. I went down, down where I thought a bit of light and heat might linger. I didn't know then how long death had been there; those corpses looked so fresh, preserved by the eternal cold.

"It grew dark down below, and only through rents and breaks did that bloody light seep in. Down and down, till I was below the level of the dead surface. The white snow persisted, and then I came to the cause of that final, sudden death. I could understand then. More and more I had puzzled, for those machines I'd seen I knew were far and beyond anything we ever conceived—machines of perfection, self-repairing, and self-energizing, self-perpetuating. They could make duplicates of themselves, and duplicate other, needed machines; they were intended to be eternal, ever-lasting.

"But the designers couldn't cope with some things that were beyond even their majestic imaginations—the imaginations that conceived these cities that had lived beyond—a million times beyond—what they had dreamed. They must have conceived some vague future. But not a future when the Earth died, and the sun died, and even the universe itself died.

"Cold had killed them. They had heating arrangements, devices intended to maintain forever the normal temperature despite the wildest variations of the weather. But in every electrical machine, resistances, balance resistances, and induction coils, balance condensers, and other inductances. And cold, stark, spatial cold, through ages, threw them off. Despite the heaters, cold crept in colder—cold that made their resistance balances and their induction coils superconductors! That destroyed the city, Superconduction—like the elimination of friction, on which all things must rest. It is a drag and a thing engineers fight forever. Resistance and friction must finally be the rest and the base of all things, the force that holds the great bed bolts firm and the brakes that stop the machines when needed.

"Electrical resistance died in the cold and the wonderful machines stopped for the replacement of defective parts. And when they were replaced, they, too, were defective. For what months must that constant stop—replacement—start—stop—replacement have gone on before, at last defeated forever, those vast machines must bow in surrender to the inevitable? Cold had defeated them by defeating and removing the greatest obstacle of the engineers that built them—resistance.

"They must have struggled forever—as we would say—

through a hundred billion years against encroaching harshness of nature, forever replacing worn, defective parts. At last, defeated forever, the great power plants, fed by dying atoms, had been forced into eternal idleness and cold. Cold conquered them at last.

"They didn't blow up. Nowhere did I see a wrecked machine; always they had stopped automatically when the defective resistances made it impossible to continue. The stored energy that was meant to restart those machines after repairs had been made had long since leaked out. Never again could they move, I knew.

"I wondered how long they had been, how long they had gone on and on, long after the human need of them had vanished. For that vast city contained only a very few humans at the end. What untold ages of lonely functioning perfection had stretched behind those at-last-defeated mechanisms?

"I wandered out, to see perhaps more, before the necessary end came to me, too. Through the city of death. Everywhere little self-contained machines, cleaning machines that had kept that perfect city orderly and neat, stood helpless and crushed by eternity and cold. They must have continued functioning for years after the great central power stations failed, for each contained its own store of energy, needing only occasional recharge from the central stations.

"I could see where breaks had occurred in the city, and clustered about those breaks were motionless repair machines, their mechanisms in positions of work, the debris cleared away and carefully stacked on motionless trucks. The new beams and plates were partly attached, partly fixed and left, as the last dregs of their energy was fruitlessly expended in the last, dying attempts of that great body to repair itself. The death wounds lay unmended.

"I started back up. Up to the top of the city. It was a long climb, an infinite, weary climb, up half a mile of winding ramps, past deserted, dead homes; past, here and there, shops and restaurants; past motionless little automotive passenger cars.

"Up and up, to the crowning gardens that lay stiff and brittle and frozen. The breaking of the roof must have caused a sudden chill, for their leaves lay green in sheaths of white, frozen air. Brittle glass, green and perfect to the touch. Flowers, blooming in wonderful perfection showed still; they didn't seem dead, but it didn't seem they could be otherwise under the blanket of cold.

"Did you ever sit up with a corpse?" Bob looked up at us —through us. "I had to once, in my little home town where they always did that. I sat with a few neighbors while the man died before my eyes. I knew he must die when I came there. He died—and I sat there all night while the neighbors filed out, one by one, and the quiet settled. The quiet of the dead.

"I had to again. I was sitting with a corpse then. The corpse of a dead world in a dead universe, and the quiet didn't have to settle there; it had settled a billion years ago, and only my coming had stirred those feeble, protesting ghosts of eon-dead hopes of that planet to softly whining protest—protest the wind tried to sob to me, the dead wind of the dead gases. I'll never be able to call them inert gases again. I know. I know they are dead gases, the dead gases of dead worlds.

"And above, through the cracked crystal of the roof, the dying suns looked down on the dead city. I couldn't stay there. I went down. Down under layer after layer of buildings, buildings of gleaming metal that reflected the dim, blood light of the Sun outside in carmine stains. I went down and down, down to the machines again. But even there hopelessness seemed more intense. Again I saw that agonizing struggle of the eternally faithful machines trying to repair themselves once more to serve the masters who were dead a million million years. I could see it again in the frozen, exhausted postures of the repair machines, stilled forever in their hopeless endeavors, the last poor dregs of energy spilled in fruitless conflict with time.

"It mattered little. Time himself was dying now, dying with the city and the planet and the universe he had killed.

"But those machines had tried so hard to serve again—and failed. Now they could never try again. Even they—the deathless machines—were dead.

"I went out again, away from those machines, out into the illimitable corridors, on the edge of the city. I could not penetrate far before the darkness became as absolute as the cold. I passed the shops where goods, untouched by time in this cold, still beckoned those strange humans, but humans for all that; beckoned the masters of the machines that were no more. I vaguely entered one to see what manner of things they used in that time.

"I nearly screamed at the motion of the thing in there, heard dimly through my suit the strangely softened sounds it made in the thin air. I watched it stagger twice—and topple. I cannot guess what manner of storage cells they had— save that they were marvelous beyond imagination. That stored energy that somehow I had released by entering was some last dreg that had remained through a time as old as our planet now. Its voice was stilled forever. But it drove me out —on.

"It had died while I watched. But somehow it made me more curious. I wondered again, less oppressed by utter death. Still, some untapped energy remained in this place, stored unimaginably. I looked more keenly, watched more closely. And when I saw a screen in one office, I wondered. It was a screen. I could see readily it was television of some type. Exploratively, I touched a stud. Sound! A humming, soft sound!

"To my mind leaped a picture of a system of these. There must be—interconnected—a vast central office somewhere with vaster accumulator cells, so huge, so tremendous in their power once, that even the little microfraction that remained was great. A storage system untouchable to the repair machines—the helpless, hopeless power machines.

"In an instant I was alive again with hope. There was a strange series of studs and dials, unknown devices. I pulled back on the stud I had pressed, and stood trembling, wondering. Was there hope?

"Then the thought died. What hope? The city was dead. Not merely that. It had been dead, dead for untold time. Then the whole planet was dead. With whom might I connect? There were none on the whole planet, so what mattered it that there was a communication system.

"I looked at the thing more blankly. Had there been—how could I interpret its multitudinous devices? There was a thing on one side that made me think of a telephone dial for some reason. A pointer over a metal sheet engraved with nine symbols in a circle under the arrow of the pointer. Now the pointer was over what was either the first or the last of these.

"Clumsily, in these gloves, I fingered one of the little symbol buttons inlaid in the metal. There was an unexpected click, a light glowed on the screen, a lighted image! It was a simple projection—but what a projection! A three-dimensional sphere floated, turning slowly before my eyes, turning majestically. And I nearly fell as understanding flooded me abruptly. The pointer was a selector! The studs beneath the pointer I understood! Nine of them. One after the other I pressed, and nine spheres—each different—swam before me.

"And right there I stopped and did some hard thinking. Nine spheres. Nine planets. Earth was shown first—a strange planet to me, but one I knew from the relative size and the position of the pointer must be Earth—then, in order, the other eight.

"Now—might there be life? Yes. In those nine worlds there might be, somewhere.

"Where? Mercury—nearest the Sun? No, the Sun was too dead, too cold, even for warmth there. And Mercury was too small. I knew, even as I thought, that I'd have one good chance because whatever means they had for communication wouldn't work without tremendous power. If those incredible storage cells had the power for even one shot, they had no more. Somehow I guessed that this apparatus might incorporate no resistance whatever. Here would be only very high frequency alternating current, and only condensers and inductances would be used in it. Supercooling didn't bother them any. It improved them. Not like the immense direct-current power machinery.

"But where to try? Jupiter? That was big. And then I saw what the solution must be. Cold had ruined these machines, thrown them off by making them too-perfect conductors. Because they weren't designed to defend themselves against spatial cold. But the machines—if there were any—on Pluto for instance, must originally have been designed for just such conditions! There it had always been cold. There it always would be cold.

"I looked at that thing with an intensity that should have driven my bare eyesight to Pluto. It was a hope. My only hope. But—how to signal Pluto? They could not understand! If there were any 'they.'

"So I had to guess—and hope. Somehow, I knew, there must be some means of calling the intelligent attendant, that the user might get aid. There was a bank of little studs— twelve of them—with twelve symbols, each different, in the center of the panel, grouped in four rows of three. I guessed. Duodecimal system.

"Talk of the problems of interplanetary communication! Was there ever such a one? The problem of an anachronism in the city of the dead on a dead planet, seeking life somewhere, somehow.

"There were two studs, off by themselves, separate from the twelve—one green, one red. Again I guessed. Each of these had a complex series of symbols on it, so I turned the pointer on the right to Pluto, wavered, and turned it to Neptune. Pluto was farther. Neptune had been cold enough; the machines would still be working there, and it would be, perhaps, less of a strain on the dregs of energy that might remain.

"I depressed the green symbol hoping I had guessed truly, that red still meant danger, trouble and wrongness to men when that was built—that it meant release and cancellation for a wrongly pressed key. That left green to be an operative call signal.

"Nothing happened. The green key alone was not enough. I looked again, pressed the green key and that stud I had first pressed.

"The thing hummed again. But it was a deeper note now, an entirely different sound, and there was a frenzied clicking inside. Then the green stud kicked back at me. The Neptune key under the pointer glowed softly; the screen began to shimmer with a grayish light. And, abruptly, the humming groaned as though at a terrific overload; the screen turned dull; the little signal light under Neptune's key grew dim. The signal was being sent—hurled out.

"Minute after minute I stood there, staring. The screen grew very slowly, very gently duller, duller. The energy was fading. The last stored driblet was being hurled away—away into space. 'Oh,' I groaned, 'it's hopeless—hopeless to—'

"I'd realized the thing would take hours to get to that distant planet, traveling at the speed of light, even if it had been correctly aligned. But the machinery that should have done that through the years probably had long since failed for lack of power.

"But I stood there till the groaning motors ceased altogether, and the screen was as dark as I'd found it, the signal light black. I released the stud then, and backed away, dazed by the utter collapse of an insane hope. Experimentally I pressed the Neptune symbol again. So little power was left now, that only the faintest wash of murky light projected the Neptune image, little energy as that would have consumed.

"I went out. Bitter. Hopeless. Earth's last picture was long, long since painted—and mine had been the hand that spent Earth's last poor resource. To its utter exhaustion, the eternal city had strived to serve the race that created it, and I, from the dawn of time had, at the end of time, drained its last poor atom of life. The thing was a thing done.

"Slowly I went back to the roof and the dying suns. Up the miles of winding ramp that climbed a half mile straight up. I went slowly—only life knows haste—and I was of the dead.

"I found a bench up there—a carved bench of metal in the midst of a riot of colorful, frozen towers. I sat down, and looked out across the frozen city to the frozen world beyond, and the freezing red Sun.

"I do not know how long I sat there. And then something whispered in my mind. 'We sought you at the television machine.'

"I leaped from the bench and stared wildly about me.

"It was floating in the air—a shining dirigible of metal, ruby-red in that light, twenty feet long, perhaps ten in diameter, bright, warm orange light gleaming from its ports. I stared at it in amazement.

" 'It—it worked!' I gasped.

" 'The beam carried barely enough energy to energize the amplifiers when it reached Neptune, however,' replied the creature in the machine.

"I couldn't see him—I knew I wasn't hearing him, but somehow that didn't surprise me.

" 'Your oxygen has almost entirely given out, and I believe your mind is suffering from lack of oxygen. I would suggest you enter the lock; there is air in here.'

"I don't know how he knew, but the gauges confirmed his statement. The oxygen was pretty nearly gone. I had perhaps another hour's supply if I opened the valves wide—but it was a most uncomfortably near thing, even so.

"I got in. I was beaming, joyous. There was life. This universe was not so dead as I had supposed. Not on Earth, perhaps, but only because they did not choose! They had spaceships! Eagerly I climbed in, a strange thrill running through my body as I crossed the threshold of the lock. The door closed behind me with a soft *shush* on its soft gaskets, locked, and a pump whined somewhere for a moment; then the inner door opened. I stepped in—and instantly turned off my alcohol burners. There was heat—heat and light and air!

"In a moment I had the outer lacings loose, and the inner zipper down. Thirty seconds later I stepped out of the suit and took a deep breath. The air was clean and sweet and warm, invigorating, fresh-smelling, as though it had blown over miles of green, sun-warmed fields. It smelled alive, and young.

"Then I looked for the man who had come for me. There was none. In the nose of the ship, by the controls, floated a four-foot globe of metal, softly glowing with a warm, golden light. The light pulsed slowly or swiftly with the rhythm of his thoughts, and I knew that this was the one who had spoken to me.

" 'You had expected a human?' he thought to me. 'There are no more. There have been none for a time I cannot express in your mind. Ah, yes, you have a mathematical means of expression, but no understanding of that time, so it is useless. But the last of humanity was allowed to end before the sun changed from the original G-O stage—a very, very long time ago.'

"I looked at him and wondered. Where was he from? Who —what—what manner of thing? Was it an armor-encased living creature or another of the perfect machines?

"I felt him watching my mind operate, pulsing softly in his golden light. And suddenly I thought to look out of the ports. The dim red suns were wheeling across those ports at an unbelievable rate. Earth was long since gone. As I looked, a dim, incredibly dim, red disk suddenly appeared, expanded —and I looked in awe at Neptune.

"The planet was scarcely visible when we were already within a dozen millions of miles. It was a jeweled world. Cities—the great, perfect cities—still glowed. They glowed in soft, golden light above, and below, the harsher, brighter blue of mercury vapor lighted them.

"He was speaking again. 'We are machines—the ultimate development of man's machines. Man was almost gone when we came.

" 'With what we have learned in the uncounted dusty megayears since, we might have been able to save him. We could not then. It was better, wiser, that man end than that he sink down so low as he must, eventually. Evolution is the rise under pressure. Devolution is the gradual sinking that comes when there is no pressure—and there is no end to it. Life vanished from this system—a dusty infinity I cannot sort in my memory—my type memory, truly, for I have complete all the memories of those that went before me that I replace. But my memory cannot stretch back to that time you think of—a time when the constellations—

" 'It is useless to try. Those memories are buried under others, and those still buried under the weight of a billion centuries.

" 'We enter'—he named a city; I cannot reproduce that name—'now. You must return to Earth, though, in some seven and a quarter of your days, for the magnetic axis stretches back in collapsing field strains. I will be able to inject you into it, I believe.'

"So I entered that city, the living city of machines, that had been when time and the universe were young.

"I did not know then that, when all this universe had dissolved away, when the last sun was black and cold, scattered dust in a fragment of a scattered universe, this planet with its machine cities would go on—a last speck of warm light in a long-dead universe. I did not know then.

" 'You still wonder that we let man die out?' asked the

machine. 'It was best. In another brief million years he would have lost his high estate. It was best.'

" 'Now we go on. We cannot end, as he did. It is automatic with us.'

"I felt it then, somehow. The blind, purposeless continuance of the machine cities I could understand. They had no intelligence, only functions. These machines—these living, thinking, reasoning investigators—had only one function, too. Their function was slightly different—they were designed to be eternally curious, eternally investigating. And their striving was the more purposeless of the two, for theirs could reach no end. The cities fought eternally only the blind destructiveness of nature; wear, decay, erosion.

"But their struggle had an opponent forever, so long as they existed. The intelligent—no, not quite intelligent, but something else—curious machines were without opponents. They had to be curious. They had to go on investigating. And they had been going on in just this way for such incomprehensible ages that there was no longer anything to be curious about. Whoever, whatever designed them gave them function and forgot purpose. Their only curiosity was the wonder if there might, somewhere, be one more thing to learn.

"That—and the problem they did not want to solve, but must try to solve, because of the blind functioning of their very structure.

"Those eternal cities were limited. The machines saw now that limit, and saw the hope of final surcease in it. They worked on the energy of the atom. But the masses of the suns were yet tremendous. They were dead for want of energy. The masses of the planets were still enormous. But they, too, were dead for want of energy.

"The machines there on Neptune gave me food and drink—strange, synthetic foods and drinks. There had been none on all the planet. They, perforce, started a machine, unused in a billion years and more, that I might eat. Perhaps they were glad to do so. It brought the end appreciably nearer, that vast consumption of mine.

"They used so very, very little, for they were so perfectly efficient. The only possible fuel in all the universe is one—hydrogen. From hydrogen, the lightest of elements, the heaviest can be built up, and energy released. They knew how to destroy matter utterly to energy, and could do it.

"But while the energy release of hydrogen compounding to the heavy elements is controllable, the destruction of matter to energy is a self-regenerative process. Started once, it spreads while matter lies within its direct, contiguous reach. It is wild, uncontrollable. It is impossible to utilize the full energy of matter.

"The suns had found that. They had burned their hydrogen until it was a remnant so small the action could not go on.

"On all Earth there was not an atom of hydrogen—nor was there on any planet, save Neptune. And there the store was not great. I used an appreciable fraction while I was there. That is their last hope. They can see the end, now.

"I stayed those few days, and the machines came and went. Always investigating, always curious. But there is in all that universe nothing to investigate save the one problem they are sure they cannot solve.

"The machine took me back to Earth, set up something near me that glowed with a peculiar, steady, gray light. It would fix the magnetic axis on me, on my location, within a few hours. He could not stay near when the axis touched again. He went back to Neptune, but a few millions of miles distant, in this shrunken mummy of the solar system.

"I stood alone on the roof of the city, in the frozen garden with its deceptive look of life.

"And I thought of that night I had spent, sitting up with the dead man. I had come and watched him die. And I sat up with him in the quiet. I had wanted someone, any one to talk to.

"I did then. Overpoweringly it came to me I was sitting up in the night of the universe, in the night and quiet of the universe, with a dead planet's body, with the dead, ashen hopes of countless, nameless generations of men and women. The universe was dead, and I sat up alone—alone in the dead hush.

"Out beyond, a last flicker of life was dying on the planet Neptune—a last, false flicker of aimless life, but not life. Life was dead. The world was dead.

"I knew there would never be another sound here. For all the little remainder of time. For this was the dark and the night of time and the universe. It was inevitable, the inevitable end that had been simply more distant in my day—in the long, long-gone time when the stars were mighty lighthouses of a mighty space, not the dying, flickering candles at the head of a dead planet.

"It had been inevitable then; the candles must burn out for all their brave show. But now I could see them guttering low, the last, fruitless dregs of energy expiring as the machines below had spent their last dregs of energy in that hopeless, utterly faithful gesture—to attempt the repair of the city already dead.

"The universe had been dead a billion years. It had been. This, I saw, was the last radiation of the heat of life from an already-dead body—the feel of life and warmth imitation of life by a corpse. Those suns had long and long since ceased to generate energy. They were dead, and their corpses were giving off the last, lingering life heat before they cooled.

"I ran. I think I ran—down away from the flickering, red suns in the sky. Down to the shrouding blackness of the dead city below, where neither light, nor heat, nor life, nor imitation of life bothered me.

"The utter blackness quieted me somewhat. So I turned off my oxygen valves, because I wanted to die sane, even here, and I knew I'd never come back.

"The impossible happened! I came to with that raw oxygen

in my face. I don't know how I came—only that here is warmth and life.

"Somewhere, on the far side of that bismuth coil, inevitable still, is the dead planet and the flickering, guttering candles that light the death watch I must keep at the end of time."

THE DEAD LADY OF CLOWN TOWN

Cordwainer Smith

"Cordwainer Smith" is the pseudonym that was used by Dr. Paul Linebarger, professor of political science at Johns Hopkins University, for the science fiction that he published between 1950 and his death in 1966. Because he kept his academic and literary lives so rigidly separate, there were few who knew the identity of the author of the Cordwainer Smith stories in his lifetime—and great was the speculation as such extraordinary works as "Scanners Live in Vain," "Alpha Ralpha Boulevard," "Under Old Earth," and "Think Blue, Count Two," appeared in the magazines. Most of Smith's stories were segments of an enormous portrait of the universe of thousands of years hence, a universe ruled by the mysterious and omnipotent Lords of the Instrumentality and populated by a variety of human and almost-human

creatures. He moved through his panorama of the imagina-
tion in an amazingly assured way, as though he were not
inventing it but merely writing down familiar myths and
historical fragments, which led some of us to speculate, only
half jokingly, that the author of the Smith works was actu-
ally a time traveler from the far future, earning his living
among us by pretending to write science fiction. "The Dead
Lady of Clown Town" is one of his last and longest stories;
though complete in itself, it is linked to other tales in his saga
of the future at half a dozen points, and affords an excellent
glimpse into that strange and baffling universe to come.

I

YOU already know the end—the immense drama of
the Lord Jestocost, seventh of his line, and how the cat-girl
C'mell initiated the vast conspiracy. But you do not know the
beginning, how the first Lord Jestocost got his name, because
of the terror and inspiration which his mother, the Lady
Goroke, obtained from the famous real-life drama of the
dog-girl D'joan. It is even less likely that you know the other
story—the one behind D'joan. This story is sometimes men-
tioned as the matter of the "nameless witch," which is absurd, because she really had a name. The name was "Elaine,"
an ancient and forbidden one.

Elaine was a mistake. Her birth, her life, her career were
all mistakes. The ruby was wrong. How could that have happened?

Go back to An-fang, the Peace Square at An-fang, the
Beginning Place at An-fang, where all things start. Bright it
was. Red square, dead square, clear square, under a yellow
sun.

This was Earth Original, Man-home itself, where Earth-port thrusts its way up through hurricane clouds that are higher than the mountains.

An-fang was near a city, the only living city with a preatomic name. The lovely meaningless name was Meeya Meefla, where the lines of ancient roadways, untouched by a wheel for thousands of years, forever paralleled the warm, bright, clear beaches of the Old South East.

The headquarters of the People Programmer was at An-fang, and there the mistake happened:

A ruby trembled. Two tourmaline nets failed to rectify the laser beam. A diamond noted the error. Both the error and the correction went into the general computer.

The error assigned, on the general account of births for Fomalhaut III, the profession of "lay therapist, female, intuitive capacity for correction of human physiology with local resources." On some of the early ships they used to call these people *witchwomen,* because they worked unaccountable cures. For pioneer parties, these lay therapists were invaluable; in settled post-Riesmannian societies, they became an awful nuisance. Sickness disappeared with good conditions, accidents dwindled down to nothing, medical work became institutional.

Who wants a witch, even a good witch, when a thousand-bed hospital is waiting with its staff eager for clinical experience . . . and only seven out of its thousand beds filled with real people? (The remaining beds were filled with lifelike robots on which the staff could practice, lest they lose their morale. They could, of course, have worked on underpeople —animals in the shape of human beings, who did the heavy and the weary work which remained as the *caput mortuum* of a really perfected economy—but it was against the law for animals, even when they were underpeople, to go to a human hospital. When underpeople got sick, the Instrumentality took care of them—in slaughterhouses. It was easier to breed new underpeople for the job than it was to repair sick ones. Furthermore, the tender, loving care of a hospital might give them ideas. Such as the idea that they were people. This would have been bad, from the prevailing point of view. Therefore the human hospitals remained almost empty while an underperson who sneezed four times or who vomited once was taken away, never to be ill again. The empty beds kept on with the robot patients, who went through endless repetitions of the human patterns of injury or disease.) This left no work for witches, bred and trained.

Yet the ruby had trembled; the program had indeed made a mistake; the birth-number for a "lay therapist, general, female, immediate use" had been ordered for Fomalhaut III.

Much later, when the story was all done down to its last historic detail, there was an investigation into the origins of Elaine. When the laser had trembled, both the original order and the correction were fed simultaneously into the machine. The machine recognized the contradiction and promptly referred both papers to the human supervisor, an actual man who had been working on the job for seven years.

He was studying music, and he was bored. He was so close to the end of his term that he was already counting the days to his own release. Meanwhile he was rearranging two popular songs. One was "The Big Bamboo," a primitive piece which tried to evoke the original magic of man. The other was about a girl, "Elaine, Elaine" whom the song asked to refrain from giving pain to her loving swain. Neither of the songs was important; but between them they influenced history, first a little bit and then very much.

The musician had plenty of time to practice. He had not had to meet a real emergency in all his seven years. From time to time the machine made reports to him, but the musician just told the machine to correct its own errors, and it infallibly did so.

On the day that the accident of Elaine happened, he was trying to perfect his finger work on the guitar, a very old instrument believed to date from the prespace period. He was playing "The Big Bamboo" for the hundredth time.

The machine announced its mistake with an initial musical chime. The supervisor had long since forgotten all the instructions which he had so worrisomely memorized seven long years ago. The alert did not really and truly matter, because the machine invariably corrected its own mistakes whether the supervisor was on duty or not.

The machine, not having its chime answered, moved into a second-stage alarm. From a loudspeaker set in the wall of the room, it shrieked in a high, clear human voice, the voice of some employee who had died thousands of years earlier: "Alert, alert! Emergency. Correction needed. Correction needed!"

The answer was one which the machine had never heard before, old though it was. The musician's fingers ran madly, gladly over the guitar strings and he sang clearly, wildly back to the machine a message strange beyond any machine's belief:

> Beat, beat the Big Bamboo!
> Beat, beat, beat the Big Bamboo for me...!

Hastily the machine set its memory banks and computers to work, looking for the code reference to "bamboo," trying to make that word fit the present context. There was no reference at all. The machine pestered the man some more.

"Instructions unclear. Instructions unclear. Please correct."

"Shut up," said the man.

"Cannot comply," stated the machine. "Please state and repeat, please state and repeat, please state and repeat."

"Do shut up," said the man, but he knew the machine would not obey this. Without thinking, he turned to his other tune and sang the first two lines twice over:

> Elaine, Elaine,
>   go cure the pain!
> Elaine, Elaine,
>   go cure the pain!

Repetition had been inserted as a safeguard into the machine, on the assumption that no real man would repeat an error. The name "Elaine" was not correct number code, but the fourfold emphasis seemed to confirm the need for a "lay therapist, female." The machine itself noted that a genuine man had corrected the situation card presented as a matter of emergency.

"Accepted," said the machine.

This word, too late, jolted the supervisor away from his music.

"Accepted what?" he asked.

There was no answering voice. There was no sound at all except for the whisper of slightly-moistened warm air through the ventilators.

The supervisor looked out the window. He could see a little of the blood-black red color of the Peace Square of An-fang; beyond lay the ocean, endlessly beautiful and endlessly tedious.

The supervisor sighed hopefully. He was young. "Guess it doesn't matter," he thought, picking up his guitar.

(Thirty-seven years later, he found out that it did matter. The Lady Goroke herself, one of the chiefs of the Instrumentality, sent a subchief of the Instrumentality to find out who had caused D'joan. When the man found that the witch Elaine was the source of the trouble, she sent him on to find out how Elaine had gotten into a well-ordered universe. The supervisor was found. He was still a musician. He remembered nothing of the story. He was hypnotized. He still remembered nothing. The subchief invoked an emergency and Police Drug Four ("clear memory") was administered to the musician. He immediately remembered the whole silly scene, but insisted that it did not matter. The case was referred to Lady Goroke, who instructed the authorities that the musician be told the whole horrible, beautiful story of D'joan at Fomalhaut—the very story which you are now being told—and he wept. He was not punished otherwise, but the Lady Goroke commanded that those memories be left in his mind for so long as he might live.)

The man picked up his guitar, but the machine went on about its work.

It selected a fertilized human embryo, tagged it with the freakish name "Elaine," irradiated the genetic code with strong aptitudes for witchcraft and then marked the person's card for training in medicine, transportation by sailship to Fomalhaut III and release for service on the planet.

Elaine was born without being needed, without being wanted, without having a skill which could help or hurt any existing human being. She went into life doomed and useless.

It is not remarkable that she was misbegotten. Errors do happen. Remarkable was the fact that she managed to survive without being altered, corrected or killed by the safety devices which mankind has installed in society for its own protection.

Unwanted, unused, she wandered through the tedious months and useless years of her own existence. She was well fed, richly clothed, variously housed. She had machines and robots to serve her, underpeople to obey her, people to protect her against one another or against herself, should the need arise. But she could never find work; without work, she had no time for love; without work or love, she had no hope at all.

If she had only stumbled into the right experts or the right authorities, they would have altered or retrained her. This would have made her into an acceptable woman; but she did not find the police, nor did they find her. She was helpless to correct her own programming, utterly helpless. It had been imposed on her at An-fang, way back at An-fang, where all things begin.

The ruby had trembled, the tourmaline failed, the diamond passed unsupported. Thus a woman was born doomed.

II

Much later, when people made songs about the strange case of the dog-girl D'joan, the minstrels and singers had tried to imagine what Elaine felt like, and they had made up "The Song of Elaine" for her. It is not authentic, but it shows how Elaine looked at her own life before the strange case of D'joan began to flow from Elaine's own actions:

> Other women hate me.
> Men never touch me.
> I am too much me.
>   I'll be a witch!
>
> Mama never towelled me.
> Daddy never growled me
> Little kiddies grate me
>   I'll be a bitch!
>
> People never named me
> Dogs never shamed me
> Oh, I am such me!
>   I'll be a witch.
>
> I'll make them shun me.
> They'll never run me.
> Could they even stun me?
>   I'll be a witch.
>
> Let them all attack me.
> They can only rack me.
> Me—I can hack me.
>   I'll be a witch.
>
> Other women hate me.
> Men never touch me.
> I am too much me.
>   I'll be a witch.

The song overstates the case. Women did not hate Elaine; they did not look at her. Men did not shun Elaine; they did not notice her either. There were no places on Fomalhaut III

where she could have met human children, for the nurseries
were far underground because of chancy radiation and fierce
weather. The song pretends that Elaine began with the
thought that she was not human, but underpeople, and had
herself been born a dog. This did not happen at the beginning of the case, but only at the very end, when the story of
D'joan was already being carried between the stars and developing with all the new twists of folklore and legend. She
never went mad.

("Madness" is a rare condition, consisting of a human mind
which does not engage its environment correctly. Elaine
approached it before she met D'joan. Elaine was not the only
case, but she was a rare and genuine one. Her life, thrust back
from all attempts at growth, had turned back on itself and
her mind had spiraled inward to the only safety she could
really know, psychosis. Madness is always better than X, and
X to each patient is individual, personal, secret and over-
whelmingly important. Elaine had gone normally mad; her
imprinted and destined career was the wrong one. "Lay
therapists, female" were coded to work decisively, autono-
mously, on their own authority and with great rapidity.
These working conditions were needed on new planets.
They were not coded to consult other people; most places,
there would be no one to consult. Elaine did what was set for
her at An-fang, all the way down to the individual chemical
conditions of her spinal fluid. She was herself the wrong and
she never knew it. Madness was much kinder than the real-
ization that she was not herself, should not have lived, and
amounted at the most to a mistake committed between a
trembling ruby and a young, careless man with a guitar.)

She found D'joan and the worlds reeled.

Their meeting occurred at a place nicknamed "the edge of
the world," where the undercity met daylight. This was itself
unusual; but Fomalhaut III was an unusual and uncomfortable planet, where wild weather and men's caprice drove
architects to furious design and grotesque execution.

Elaine walked through the city, secretly mad, looking for sick people whom she could help. She had been stamped, imprinted, designed, born, bred and trained for this task. There was no task.

She was an intelligent woman. Bright brains serve madness as well as they serve sanity—namely, very well indeed. It never occurred to her to give up her mission.

The people of Fomalhaut III, like the people of Manhome Earth itself, are almost uniformly handsome; it is only in the far-out, half-unreachable worlds that the human stock, strained by the sheer effort to survive, becomes ugly, weary or varied. She did not look much different from the other intelligent, handsome people who flocked the streets. Her hair was black, and she was tall. Her arms and legs were long, the trunk of her body short. She wore her hair brushed straight back from a high, narrow, square forehead. Her eyes were an odd deep blue. Her mouth might have been pretty, but it never smiled, so that no one could really tell whether it was beautiful or not. She stood erect and proud, but so did everyone else. Her mouth was strange in its very lack of communicativeness and her eyes swept back and forth, back and forth like ancient radar, looking for the sick, the needy, and stricken, whom she had a passion to serve.

How could she be unhappy? She had never had time to be happy. It was easy for her to think that happiness was something which disappeared at the end of childhood. Now and then, here and there, perhaps when a fountain murmured in sunlight or when leaves exploded in the startling Fomalhautian spring, she wondered that other people—people as responsible as herself by the doom of age, grade, sex, training and career number—should be happy when she alone seemed to have no time for happiness. But she always dismissed the thought and walked the ramps and streets until her arches ached, looking for work which did not yet exist.

Human flesh, older than history, more dogged than culture, has its own wisdom. The bodies of people are marked with the archaic ruses of survival, so that on Fomalhaut III,

Elaine herself preserved the skills of ancestors she never even thought about—those ancestors, who in the incredible and remote past, had mastered terrible Earth itself. Elaine was mad. But there was a part of her which suspected that she was mad.

Perhaps this wisdom seized her as she walked from Waterrocky Road toward the bright esplanades of the Shopping Bar. She saw a forgotten door. The robots could clean near it but, because of the old, odd, architectural shape, they could not sweep and polish right at the bottom line of the door. A thin hard line of old dust and caked polish lay like a sealant at the base of the doorline. It was obvious that no one had gone through for a long, long time.

The civilized rule was that prohibited areas were marked both telepathically and with symbols. The most dangerous of all had robot or underpeople guards. But everything which was not prohibited, was permitted. Thus Elaine had no right to open the door, but she had no obligation not to do so. She opened it—

By sheer caprice.

Or so she thought.

This was a far cry from the "I'll be a witch" motif attributed to her in the later ballad. She was not yet frantic, not yet desperate, she was not yet even noble.

That opening of a door changed her own world and changed life on thousands of planets for generations to come, but the opening was not itself strange. It was the tired caprice of a thoroughly frustrated and mildly unhappy woman. Nothing more. All the other descriptions of it have been improvements, embellishments, falsifications.

She did get a shock when she opened the door, but not for the reasons attributed backwards to her by balladists and historians.

She was shocked because the door opened on steps and the steps led down to landscape and sunlight—truly an unexpected sight on any world. She was looking from the New City to the Old City. The New City rose on its shell out over the old city, and when she looked "indoors" she saw the sunset in the city below. She gasped at the beauty and the unexpectedness of it.

There, the open door—*with another world beyond it.* Here, the old familiar street, clean, handsome, quiet, useless, where her own useless self had walked a thousand times.

There—something. Here, the world she knew. She did not know the words "fairyland" or "magic place," but if she had known them, she would have used them.

She glanced to the right, to the left.

The passerby noticed neither her nor the door. The sunset was just beginning to show in the upper city. In the lower city it was already blood-red with streamers of gold like enormous frozen flame. Elaine did not know that she sniffed the air; she did not know that she trembled on the edge of tears; she did not know that a tender smile, the first smile in years, relaxed her mouth and turned her tired tense face into a passing loveliness. She was too intent on looking around.

People walked about their business. Down the road, an underpeople type—female, possibly cat—detoured far around a true human who was walking at a slower pace. Far away, a police ornithopter flapped slowly around one of the towers; unless the robots used a telescope on her or unless they had one of the rare hawk-undermen who were sometimes used as police, they could not see her.

She stepped through the doorway and pulled the door itself back into the closed position.

She did not know it, but therewith unborn futures reeled out of existence, rebellion flamed into coming centuries, people and underpeople died in strange causes, mothers changed the names of unborn Lords and starships whispered back from places which men had not even imagined before. Space which had always been there, waiting for men's notice, would come the sooner—because of her, because of the door, because of her next few steps, what she would say and the child she would meet. (The ballad-writers told the whole story later on, but they told it backwards, from their own knowledge of D'joan and what Elaine had done to set the worlds afire. The simple truth is the fact that a lonely woman went through a mysterious door. That is all. Everything else happened later.)

At the top of the steps she stood, door closed behind her, the sunset gold of the unknown city streaming out in front of her. She could see where the great shell of the New City of Kalma arched out toward the sky; she could see that the buildings here were older, less harmonious than the ones she had left. She did not know the concept "picturesque," or she would have called it that. She knew no concept to describe the scene which lay peacefully at her feet.

There was not a person in sight.

Far in the distance, a fire-detector throbbed back and forth on top of an old tower. Outside of that there was nothing but the yellow-gold city beneath her, and a bird—was it a bird, or a large storm-swept leaf?—in the middle distance.

Filled with fear, hope, expectation and the surmisal of strange appetites, she walked downward. With quiet, unknown purpose.

III

At the foot of the stairs, nine flights of them there had been, a child waited—a girl, about five. The child had a bright blue smock, wavy red-brown hair, and the daintiest hands which Elaine had ever seen.

Elaine's heart went out to her. The child looked up at her and shrank away. Elaine knew the meaning of those handsome brown eyes, of that muscular supplication of trust, that recoil from people. It was not a child at all—just some animal in the shape of a person, a dog perhaps, which would later be taught to speak, to work to perform useful services.

The little girl rose, standing as though she were about to run. Elaine had the feeling that the little dog-girl had not decided whether to run toward her or from her. She did not wish to get involved with an underperson—what woman would?—but neither did she wish to frighten the little thing. After all, it was small, very young.

The two confronted each other for a moment, the little thing uncertain, Elaine relaxed. Then the little animal-girl spoke.

"Ask her," she said, and it was a command.

Elaine was surprised. Since when did animals command?

"Ask her!" repeated the little thing. She pointed at a window which had the words TRAVELERS' AID above it. Then the girl ran. A flash of blue from her dress, a twinkle of white from her running sandals, and she was gone.

Elaine stood quiet and puzzled in the forlorn and empty city.

The window spoke to her, "You might as well come on over. You will, you know."

It was the wise mature voice of an experienced woman—a voice with a bubble of laughter underneath its phonic edge, with a hint of sympathy and enthusiasm in its tone. The command was not merely a command. It was, even at its beginning, a happy private joke between two wise women.

Elaine was not surprised when a machine spoke to her. Recordings had been telling her things all her life. She was not sure of this situation, however.

"Is there somebody there?" she said.

"Yes and no," said the voice. "I'm 'Travelers' Aid' and I help everybody who comes through this way. You're lost or you wouldn't be here. Put your hand in my window."

"What I mean is," said Elaine, "are you a person or are you a machine?"

"Depends," said the voice. "I'm a machine, but I used to be a person, long, long ago. A Lady, in fact, and one of the Instrumentality. But my time came and they said to me, 'Would you mind if we made a machine print of your whole personality? It would be very helpful for the information booths.' So of course I said yes, and they made this copy, and I died, and they shot my body into space with all the usual honors, but here I was. It felt pretty odd inside this contraption, me looking at things and talking to people and giving good advice and staying busy until they built the new city. So what do you say? Am I me or aren't I?"

"I don't know, ma'am." Elaine stood back.

The warm voice lost its humor and became commanding. "Give me your hand, then, so I can identify you and tell you what to do."

"I think," said Elaine, "that I'll just go back upstairs and go through the door into the upper city."

"And cheat me," said the voice in the window, "out of my first conversation with a real person in four years?" There was demand in the voice, but there was still the warmth and the humor; there was loneliness too. The loneliness decided Elaine. She stepped up to the window and put her hand flat on the ledge.

"You're Elaine," cried the window. "You're *Elaine!* The worlds wait for you. You're from An-fang, where all things begin, the Peace Square at An-fang, on old Earth itself!"

"Yes," said Elaine.

The voice bubbled over with enthusiasm. "He is waiting for you. Oh, he has waited for you a long, long time. And the little girl you met. *That was D'joan herself.* The story has begun. 'The world's great age begins anew.' And I can die when it is over. So sorry, my dear. I don't mean to confuse you. I am the Lady Panc Ashash. You're Elaine. Your number originally ended 783 and you shouldn't even be on this planet. All the important people here end with the numbers 5 and 6. You're a lay therapist and you're in the wrong place, but your lover is already on his way, and you've never been in love yet, and it's all too exciting."

Elaine looked quickly around her. The old lower town was turning more red and less gold as the sunset progressed. The steps behind her seemed terribly high as she looked back, the door at the top very small. Perhaps it had locked on her when she closed it. Maybe she wouldn't ever be able to leave the old lower city.

The window must have been watching her in some way, because the voice of the Lady Panc Ashash became tender.

"Sit down, my dear," said the voice from the window. "When I was me, I used to be much more polite. I haven't been me for a long, long time. I'm a machine, and still I feel like myself. Do sit down, and do forgive me."

Elaine looked around. There was the roadside marble bench behind her. She sat on it obediently. The happiness which had been in her at the top of the steps bubbled forth anew. If this wise old machine knew so much about her, perhaps it could tell her what to do. What did the voice mean by "wrong planet"? By "lover"? By "he is coming for you now," or was that what the voice had actually said?

"Take a breath, my dear," said the voice of the Lady Panc Ashash. She might have been dead for hundreds or thousands of years, but she still spoke with the authority and kindness of a great lady.

Elaine breathed deep. She saw a huge red cloud, like a pregnant whale, getting ready to butt the rim of the upper city, far above her and far out over the sea. She wondered if clouds could possibly have feelings.

The voice was speaking again. What had it said?

Apparently the question was repeated. "Did you know you were coming?" said the voice from the window.

"Of course not." Elaine shrugged. "There was just this door, and I didn't have anything special to do, so I opened it. And here was a whole new world inside a house. It looked strange and rather pretty, so I came down. Wouldn't you have done the same thing?"

"I don't know," said the voice candidly. "I'm really a machine. I haven't been me for a long, long time. Perhaps I would have, when I was alive. I don't know that, but I know about things. Maybe I can see the future, or perhaps the machine part of me computes such good probabilities that it just seems like it. I know who you are and what is going to happen to you. You had better brush your hair."

"Whatever for?" said Elaine.

"He is coming," said the happy old voice of the Lady Panc Ashash.

"*Who* is coming?" said Elaine, almost irritably.

"Do you have a mirror? I wish you would look at your hair. It could be prettier, not that it isn't pretty right now. You want to look your best. Your lover; that's who is coming, of course."

"I haven't got a lover," said Elaine. "I haven't been authorized one, not till I've done some of my lifework, and I haven't even found my lifework yet. I'm not the kind of girl who would go ask a Subchief for the dreamies, not when I'm not entitled to the real thing. I may not be much of a person, but I have some self-respect." Elaine got so mad that she shifted her position on the bench and sat with her face turned away from the all-watching window.

The next words gave her gooseflesh down her arms, they were uttered with such real earnestness, such driving sincerity. *"Elaine, Elaine, do you really have no idea of who you are?"*

Elaine pivoted back on the bench so that she looked toward the window. Her face was caught redly by the rays of the setting sun. She could only gasp.

"I don't know what you mean . . ."

The inexorable voice went on. "Think, Elaine, think. Does the name 'D'joan' mean nothing to you?"

"I suppose it's an underperson, a dog. That's what the D is for, isn't it?"

"That was the little girl you met," said the Lady Panc Ashash, as though the statement were something tremendous.

"Yes," said Elaine dutifully. She was a courteous woman, and never quarreled with strangers.

"Wait a minute," said the Lady Panc Ashash, "I'm going to get my body out. God knows when I wore it last, but it'll make you feel more at easy terms with me. Forgive the clothes. They're old stuff, but I think the body will work all right. This is the beginning of the story of D'joan, and I want that hair of yours brushed even if I have to brush it myself. Just wait right there, girl, wait right there. I'll just take a minute."

The clouds were turning from dark red to liver-black. What could Elaine do? She stayed on the bench. She kicked her shoe against the walk. She jumped a little when the old-fashioned street lights of the lower city went on with sharp geometrical suddenness; they did not have the subtle shading of the newer lights in the other city upstairs, where day phased into the bright clear night with no sudden shift in color.

The door beside the little window creaked open. Ancient plastic crumbled to the walk.

Elaine was astonished.

Elaine knew she must have been unconsciously expecting a monster, but this was a charming woman of about her own height, wearing weird, old-fashioned clothes. The strange woman had glossy black hair, no evidence of recent or current illness, no signs of severe lesions in the past, no impairment evident of sight, gait, reach or eyesight. (There was no way she could check on smell or taste right off, but this was the medical check-up she had had built into her from birth on—the checklist which she had run through with every adult person she had ever met. She had been designed as a "lay therapist, female" and she was a good one, even when there was no one at all to treat.)

Truly, the body was a rich one. It must have cost the landing charges of forty or fifty planet-falls. The human shape was perfectly rendered. The mouth moved over genuine teeth; the words were formed by throat, palate, tongue, teeth and lips, and not just by a microphone mounted in the head. The body was really a museum piece. It was probably a copy of the Lady Panc Ashash herself in time of life. When the face smiled, the effect was indescribably winning. The lady wore the costume of a bygone age—a stately frontal dress of heavy blue material, embroidered with a square pattern of gold at hem, waist and bodice. She had a matching cloak of dark, faded gold, embroidered in blue with the same pattern of squares. Her hair was upswept and set with jeweled combs. It seemed perfectly natural, but there was dust on one side of it.

The robot smiled. "I'm out of date. It's been a long time since I was me. But I thought, my dear, that you would find this old body easier to talk to than the window over there . . ."

Elaine nodded mutely.

"You know this is not me?" said the body sharply.

Elaine shook her head. She didn't know; she felt that she didn't know anything at all.

The Lady Panc Ashash looked at her earnestly. "This is not me. It's a robot body. You looked at it as though it were a real person. And I'm not me, either. It hurts sometimes. Did you know a machine could hurt? I can. But—I'm not *me.*"

"Who are you?" said Elaine to the pretty old woman.

"Before I died, I was the Lady Panc Ashash. Just as I told you. Now I am a machine, and a part of your destiny. We will help each other to change the destiny of worlds, perhaps even to bring mankind back to humanity."

Elaine stared at her in bewilderment. This was no common robot. It seemed like a real person and spoke with such warm authority. And this thing, whatever it was, this thing seemed to know so much about her. Nobody else had ever cared. The nurse-mothers at the Childhouse on earth had said, "Another witch-child, and pretty too, they're not much trouble," and had let her life go by.

At last Elaine could face the face which was not really a face. The charm, the humor, the expressiveness were still there.

"What—what," stammered Elaine, "do I do now?"

"Nothing," said the long-dead Lady Panc Ashash, "except to meet your destiny."

"You mean my lover?"

"So impatient!" laughed the dead woman's record in a very human way. "Such a hurry. Lover first and destiny later. I was like that myself when I was a girl."

"But what do I do?" persisted Elaine.

The night was now complete above them. The street lights glared on the empty and unswept streets. A few doorways, not one of them less than a full street-crossing away, were illuminated with rectangles of light or shadow—light if they were far from the street lights, so that their own interior lights shone brightly, shadow if they were so close under the big lights that they cut off the glare from overhead.

"Go through this door," said the old nice woman.

But she pointed at the undistinguished white of an uninter-rupted wall. There was no door at all in that place.

"But there's no door there," said Elaine.

"If there were a door," said the Lady Panc Ashash, "you wouldn't need me to tell you to go through it. And you do need me."

"Why?" said Elaine.

"Because I've waited for you hundreds of years, that's why."

"That's no answer!" snapped Elaine.

"It is so an answer," smiled the woman, and her lack of hostility was not robot-like at all. It was the kindliness and composure of a mature human being. She looked up into Elaine's eyes and spoke emphatically and softly. "I know because I do know. Not because I'm a dead person—that doesn't matter any more—but because I am now a very old machine. You will go into the Brown and Yellow Corridor and you will think of your lover, and you will do your work, and men will hunt you. But you will come out happily in the end. Do you understand this?"

"No," said Elaine, "no, I don't." But she reached out her hand to the sweet old woman. The lady took her hand. The touch was warm and very human.

"You don't have to understand it. Just do it. And I know you will. So since you are going, go."

Elaine tried to smile at her, but she was troubled, more consciously worried than ever before in her life. Something real was happening to her, to her own individual self, at a very long last. "How will I get through the door?"

"I'll open it," smiled the Lady, releasing Elaine's hand, "and you'll know your lover when he sings you the poem."

"Which poem?" said Elaine, stalling for time and frightened by a door which did not even exist.

"It starts, 'I knew you and loved you, and won you, in Kalma . . .' You'll know it. Go on in. It'll be bothersome at first, but when you meet the Hunter, it will all seem different."

"Have you ever been in there, yourself?"

"Of course not," said the dear old Lady. "I'm a machine. That whole place is thoughtproof. Nobody can see, hear, think or talk in or out of it. It's a shelter left over from the ancient wars, when the slightest sign of a thought would have brought destruction on the whole place. That's why the Lord Englok built it, long before my time. But you can go in. And you will. Here's the door."

The old robot Lady waited no longer. She gave Elaine a strange friendly crooked smile, half proud and half apologetic. She took Elaine with firm fingertips holding Elaine's left elbow. They walked a few steps down toward the wall.

"Here, now," said the Lady Panc Ashash, and pushed.

Elaine flinched as she was thrust toward the wall. Before she knew it, she was through. Smells hit her like a roar of battle. The air was hot. The light was dim. It looked like a picture of the Pain Planet, hidden somewhere in space. Poets later tried to describe Elaine at the door with a verse which began,

> There were brown ones and blue ones
> And white ones and whiter,
>   In the hidden and forbidden
>   Downtown of Clown Town.
> There were horrid ones and horrider
> In the brown and yellow corridor.

The truth was much simpler.

Trained witch, born witch that she was, she perceived the truth immediately. All these people, all she could see, at least, were sick. They needed help. They needed herself.

But the joke was on her, for she could not help a single one of them. Not one of them was a real person. They were just animals, things in the shape of man. Underpeople. Dirt.

And she was conditioned to the bone never to help *them*.

She did not know why the muscles of her legs made her walk forward, but they did.

There are many pictures of that scene.

The Lady Panc Ashash, only a few moments in her past, seemed very remote. And the city of Kalma itself, the new city, ten stories above her, almost seemed as though it had never existed at all. This, this was real.

She stared at the underpeople.

And this time, for the first time in her life, they stared right back at her. She had never seen anything like this before.

They did not frighten her; they surprised her. The fright, Elaine felt, was to come later. Soon, perhaps, but not here, not now.

IV

Something which looked like a middle-aged woman walked right up to her and snapped at her.

"Are you death?"

Elaine stared. "Death? What do you mean? I'm Elaine."

"Be damned to that!" said the woman-thing. "Are you death?"

Elaine did not know the word "damned" but she was pretty sure that "death," even to these things, meant simply "termination of life."

"Of course not," said Elaine. "I'm just a person. A witch woman, ordinary people would call me. We don't have anything to do with you underpeople. Nothing at all." Elaine could see that the woman-thing had an enormous coiffure of soft brown sloppy hair, a sweat-reddened face and crooked teeth which showed when she grinned.

"They all say that. They never know that they're death. How do you think we die, if you people don't send contaminated robots in with diseases? We all die off when you do that, and then some more underpeople find this place again later on and make a shelter of it and live in it for a few generations until the death machines, things like you, come sweeping through the city and kill us off again. This is Clown Town, the underpeople place. Haven't you heard of it?"

Elaine tried to walk past the woman-thing, but she found her arm grabbed. This couldn't have happened before, not in the history of the world—an underperson seizing a real person!

"Let go!" she yelled.

The woman-thing let her arm go and faced toward the others. Her voice had changed. It was no longer shrill and excited, but low and puzzled instead. "I can't tell. Maybe it is a real person. Isn't that a joke? Lost, in here with us. Or maybe she *is* death. I can't tell. What do you think, Charley-is-my-darling?"

The man she spoke to stepped forward. Elaine thought, in another time, in some other place, that underperson might pass for an attractive human being. His face was illuminated by intelligence and alertness. He looked directly at Elaine as though he had never seen her before, which indeed he had not, but he continued looking with so sharp, so strange a stare that she became uneasy. His voice, when he spoke, was brisk, high, clear, friendly; set in this tragic place, it was the caricature of a voice, as though the animal had been programmed for speech from the habits of a human, persuader by profession, whom one saw in the storyboxes telling people messages which were neither good nor important, but merely clever. The handsomeness was itself deformity. Elaine wondered if he had come from goat stock.

"Welcome, young lady," said Charley-is-my-darling. "Now that you are here, how are you going to get out? If we turned her head around, Mabel," said he to the underwoman who had first greeted Elaine, "turned it around eight or ten times, it would come off. Then we could live a few weeks or months longer before our lords and creators found us and put us all to death. What do you say, young lady? Should we kill you?"

"Kill? You mean, terminate life? You cannot. It is against the law. Even the Instrumentality does not have the right to do that without trial. You can't. You're just underpeople."

"But we will die," said Charley-is-my-darling, flashing his quick intelligent smile, "if you go back out of that door. The police will read about the Brown and Yellow Corridor in your mind and they will flush us out with poison or they will spray disease in here so that we and our children will die."

Elaine stared at him.

The passionate anger did not disturb his smile or his persuasive tones, but the muscles of his eye-sockets and forehead showed the terrible strain. The result was an expression which Elaine had never seen before, a sort of self-control reaching out beyond the limits of insanity.

He stared back at her.

She was not really afraid of him. Underpeople could not twist the heads of real persons; it was contrary to all regulations.

A thought struck her. Perhaps regulations did not apply in a place like this, where illegal animals waited perpetually for sudden death. The being which faced her was strong enough to turn her head around ten times clockwise or counterclockwise. From her anatomy lessons, she was pretty sure that the head would come off somewhere during that process. She looked at him with interest. Animal-type fear had been conditioned out of her, but she had, she found, an extreme distaste for the termination of life under random circumstances. Perhaps her "witch" training would help. She tried to pretend that he was in fact a man. The diagnosis "hypertension: chronic aggression, now frustrated, leading to overstimulation and neurosis: poor nutritional record: hormone disorder probable" leapt into her mind.

She tried to speak in a new voice.

"I am smaller than you," she said, "and you can 'kill' me just as well later as now. We might as well get acquainted. I'm Elaine, assigned here from Manhome Earth."

The effect was spectacular.

Charley-is-my-darling stepped back. Mabel's mouth dropped open. The others gaped at her. One or two, more quickwitted than the rest, began whispering to their neighbors.

At last Charley-is-my-darling spoke to her. "Welcome, my lady. Can I call you my lady? I guess not. Welcome, Elaine. We are your people. We will do whatever you say. Of course you got in. The Lady Panc Ashash sent you. She has been telling us for a hundred years that somebody would come from Earth, a real person with an animal name, not a number, and that we should have a child named D'joan ready to take up the threads of destiny. Please, please sit down. Will you have a drink of water? We have no clean vessel here. We are all underpeople here and we have used everything in the place, so that it is contaminated for a real person." A thought struck him. "Baby-baby, do you have a new cup in the kiln?" Apparently he saw someone nod, because he went right on talking. "Get it out then, for our guest, with tongs. New tongs. Do not touch it. Fill it with water from the top of the little waterfall. That way our guest can have an uncontaminated drink. A clean drink." He beamed with a hospitality which was as ridiculous as it was genuine.

Elaine did not have the heart to say she did not want a drink of water.

She waited. They waited.

By now, her eyes had become accustomed to the darkness. She could see that the main corridor was painted a yellow, faded and stained, and a contrasting light brown. She wondered what possible human mind could have selected so ugly a combination. Cross-corridors seemed to open into it; at any rate, she saw illuminated archways further down and people walking out of them briskly. No one can walk briskly and naturally out of a shallow alcove, so she was pretty sure that the archways led to something.

The underpeople, too, she could see. They looked very much like people. Here and there, individuals reverted to the animal type—a horse-man whose muzzle had regrown to its ancestral size, a rat-woman with normal human features except for nylon-like white whiskers, twelve or fourteen on each side of her face, reaching twenty centimeters to either side. One looked very much like a person indeed—a beautiful young woman seated on a bench some eight or ten meters down the corridor, and paying no attention to the crowd, to Mabel, to Charley-is-my-darling or to herself.

"Who is that?" said Elaine, pointing with a nod at the beautiful young woman.

Mabel, relieved from the tension which had seized her when she had asked if Elaine were "death," babbled with a sociability which was outre in this environment. "That's Crawlie."

"What does she do?" asked Elaine.

"She has her pride," said Mabel, her grotesque red face now jolly and eager, her slack mouth spraying spittle as she spoke.

"But doesn't she *do* anything?" said Elaine.

Charley-is-my-darling intervened. "Nobody has to do anything here, Lady Elaine—"

"It's illegal to call me 'lady,' " said Elaine.

"I'm sorry, human being Elaine. Nobody *has* to do anything at all here. The whole bunch of us are completely illegal. This corridor is a thought-shelter, so that no thoughts can escape or enter it. Wait a bit! Watch the ceiling . . . Now!"

A red glow moved across the ceiling and was gone.

"The ceiling glows," said Charley-is-my-darling, "whenever anything *thinks* against it. The whole tunnel registers 'sewage tank: organic waste' to the outside, so that dim perceptions of life which may escape here are not considered too unaccountable. People built it for their own use, a million years ago."

"They weren't here on Fomalhaut III a million years ago," snapped Elaine. Why, she wondered, did she snap at him? He wasn't a person, just a talking animal who had missed being dropped down the nearest incinerator.

"I'm sorry, Elaine," said Charley-is-my-darling. "I should have said, a long time ago. We underpeople don't get much chance to study real history. But we use this corridor. Somebody with a morbid sense of humor named this place Clown Town. We live along for ten or twenty or a hundred years, and then people or robots find us and kill us all. That's why Mabel was upset. She thought you were death for this time. But you're not. You're *Elaine*. That's wonderful, wonderful." His sly, too-clever face beamed with transparent sincerity. It must have been quite a shock to him to be honest.

"You were going to tell me what the undergirl is for," said Elaine.

"That's Crawlie," said he. "She doesn't do anything. None of us really have to. We're all doomed anyhow. She's a little more honest than the rest of us. She has her pride. She scorns the rest of us. She puts us in our place. She makes everybody feel inferior. We think she is a valuable member of the group. We all have our pride, which is hopeless anyway, but Crawlie has her pride all by herself, without doing anything whatever about it. She sort of reminds us. If we leave her alone, she leaves us alone."

Elaine thought, You're funny things, so much like people, but so inexpert about it, as though you all had to "die" before you really learned what it is to be alive. Aloud, she could only say, "I never met anybody like that."

Crawlie must have sensed that they were talking about her, because she looked at Elaine with a short quick stare of blazing hatred. Crawlie's pretty face locked itself into a glare of concentrated hostility and scorn; then her eyes wandered and Elaine felt that she, Elaine, no longer existed in the thing's mind, except as a rebuke which had been administered and forgotten. She had never seen privacy as impenetrable as Crawlie's. And yet the being, whatever she might have been made from, was very lovely in human terms.

A fierce old hag, covered with mouse-gray fur, rushed up to Elaine. The mouse-woman was the Baby-baby who had been sent on the errand. She held a ceramic cup in a pair of long tongs. Water was in it.

Elaine took the cup.

Sixty to seventy underpeople, including the little girl in the blue dress whom she had seen outside, watched her as she sipped. The water was good. She drank it all. There was a universal exhalation, as though everyone in the corridor had waited for this moment. Elaine started to put the cup down but the old mouse-woman was too quick for her. She took the cup from Elaine, stopping her in midgesture and using the tongs, so that the cup would not be contaminated by the touch of an underperson.

"That's right, Baby-baby," said Charley-is-my-darling, "we can talk. It is our custom not to talk with a newcomer until we have offered our hospitality. Let me be frank. We may have to kill you, if this whole business turns out to be a mistake, but let me assure you that if I do kill you, I will do it nicely and without the least bit of malice. Right?"

Elaine did not know what was so right about it, and said so. She visualized her head being twisted off. Apart from the pain and the degradation, it seemed so terribly messy—to terminate life in a sewer with things which did not even have a right to exist.

He gave her no chance to argue, but went on explaining, "Suppose things turn out just right. Suppose that you are the Esther-Elaine-or-Eleanor that we have all been waiting for— the person who will do something to D'joan and bring us all help and deliverance—give us life, in short, *real life*—then what do we do?"

"I don't know where you get all these ideas about me. Why am I Esther-Elaine-or-Eleanor? What do I do to D'joan? Why me?"

Charley-is-my-darling stared at her as though he could not believe her question. Mabel frowned as though she could not think of the right words to put forth her opinions. Baby-baby, who had glided back to the group with swift mouselike suddenness, looked around as though she expected someone from the rear to speak. She was right. Crawlie turned her face toward Elaine and said, with infinite condescension:

"I did not know that real people were ill-informed or stupid. You seem to be both. We have all our information from the Lady Panc Ashash. Since she is dead, she has no prejudices against us underpeople. Since she has not had much of anything to do, she has run through billions and billions of probabilities for us. All of us know what most probabilities come to—sudden death by disease or gas, or maybe being hauled off to the slaughterhouses in big police ornithopters. But the Lady Panc Ashash found that perhaps a person with a name like yours would come, a human being with an old-name and not a number name, that that person would meet the Hunter, that she and the Hunter would teach the underchild D'joan a message and that the message would change the worlds. We have kept one child after another named D'joan, waiting for a hundred years. Now you show up. Maybe you are the one. You don't look very competent to me. What are you good for?"

"I'm a witch," said Elaine.

Crawlie could not keep the surprise from showing on her face. "A witch? Really?"

"Yes," said Elaine, rather humbly.

"I wouldn't be one," said Crawlie. "I have my pride." She turned her face away and locked her features in their expression of perennial hurt and disdain.

Charley-is-my-darling whispered to the group nearby, not caring whether Elaine heard his words or not, "That's wonderful, wonderful. She is a witch. A human witch. Perhaps the great day is here! Elaine," said he humbly, "will you please look at us."

Elaine looked. When she stopped to think about where she

was, it was incredible that the empty old lower city of Kalma should be just outside, just beyond the wall, and the busy new city a mere thirty-five meters higher. This corridor was a world to itself. It felt like a world, with the ugly yellows and browns, the dim old lights, the stenches of man and animal mixed under intolerably bad ventilation. Baby-baby, Crawlie, Mabel and Charley-is-my-darling were part of this world. They were real; but they were outside, outside, so far as Elaine herself was concerned.

"Let me go," she said. "I'll come back some day."

Charley-is-my-darling, who was so plainly the leader, spoke as if in a trance: "You don't understand, Elaine. The only 'going' you are going to go is death. There is no other direction. We can't let the old you go out of this door, not when the Lady Panc Ashash has thrust you in to us. Either you go forward to your destiny, to our destiny too, either you do that, and all works out all right, so that you love us, and we love you," he added dreamily, "or else I kill you with my own hands. Right here. Right now. I could give you another clean drink of water first. But that is all. There isn't much choice for you, human being Elaine. What do you think would happen if you went outside?"

"Nothing, I hope," said Elaine.

"Nothing!" snorted Mabel, her face regaining its original indignation. "The police would come flapping by in their ornithopter—"

"And they'd pick your brains," said Baby-baby.

"And they'd know about us," said a tall pale man who had not spoken before.

"And we," said Crawlie from her chair, "would all of us die within an hour or two at the longest. Would that matter to you, ma'am and Elaine?"

"And," added Charley-is-my-darling, "they would disconnect the Lady Panc Ashash, so that even the recording of that dear dead lady would be gone at last, and there would be no mercy at all left upon this world."

"What is 'mercy'?" asked Elaine.

"It's obvious you never heard of it," said Crawlie.

The old mouse-hag Baby-baby came close to Elaine. She looked up at her and whispered through yellow teeth. "Don't let them frighten you, girl. Death doesn't matter all that much, not even to you true humans with your four hundred years or to us animals with the slaughterhouse around the corner. Death is a *when*, not a *what*. It's the same for all of us. Don't be scared. Go straight ahead and you may find mercy and love. They're much richer than death, if you can only find them. Once you do find them, death won't be very important."

"I still don't know *mercy*," said Elaine, "but I thought I knew what *love* was, and I don't expect to find my lover in a dirty old corridor full of underpeople."

"I don't mean that kind of love," laughed Baby-baby, brushing aside Mabel's attempted interruption with a wave of her hand-paw. The old mouse face was on fire with sheer expressiveness. Elaine could suddenly imagine what Baby-baby had looked like to a mouse-underman when she was young and sleek and gray. Enthusiasm flushed the old features with youth as Baby-baby went on, "I don't mean love for a lover, girl. I mean love for yourself. Love for life. Love for all things living. Love even for me. Your love for me. Can you imagine that?"

Elaine swam through fatigue but she tried to answer the question. She looked in the dim light at the wrinkled old mouse-hag with her filthy clothes and her little red eyes. The fleeting image of the beautiful young mouse-woman had faded away; there was only this cheap, useless old thing, with her inhuman demands and her senseless pleading. People never loved underpeople. They used them, like chairs or doorhandles. Since when did a doorhandle demand the Charter of Ancient Rights?

"No," said Elaine calmly and evenly, "I can't imagine ever loving you."

"I knew it," said Crawlie from her chair. There was triumph in the voice.

Charley-is-my-darling shook his head as if to clear his sight. "Don't you even know who controls Fomalhaut III?"

"The Instrumentality," said Elaine. "But do we have to go on talking? Let me go or kill me or something. This doesn't make sense. I was tired when I got here, and I'm a million years tireder now."

Mabel said, "Take her along."

"All right," said Charley-is-my-darling. "Is the Hunter there?"

The child D'joan spoke. She had stood at the back of the group. "He came in the other way when she came in the front."

Elaine said to Charley-is-my-darling, "You lied to me. You said there was only one way."

"I did not lie," said he. "There is only one way for you or me or for the friends of the Lady Panc Ashash. The way you came. The other way is death."

"What do you mean?"

"I mean," he said, "that it leads straight into the slaughterhouses of the men you do not know. The Lords of the Instrumentality who are here on Fomalhaut III. There is the Lord Femtiosex, who is just and without pity. There is the Lord Limaono, who thinks that underpeople are a potential danger and should not have been started in the first place. There is the Lady Goroke, who does not know how to pray, but who tries to ponder the mystery of life and who has shown kindnesses to underpeople, as long as the kindnesses were lawful ones. And there is the Lady Arabella Underwood, whose justice no man can understand. Nor underpeople either," he added with a chuckle.

"Who is she? I mean, where did she get the funny name? It doesn't have a number in it. It's as bad as your names. Or my own," said Elaine.

"She's from Old North Australia, the stroon world, on loan to the Instrumentality, and she follows the laws she was born to. The Hunter can go through the rooms and the slaughterhouses of the Instrumentality, but could you? Could I?"

"No," said Elaine.

"Then forward," said Charley-is-my-darling, "to your death or to great wonders. May I lead the way, Elaine?"

Elaine nodded wordlessly.

The mouse-hag Baby-baby patted Elaine's sleeve, her eyes alive with strange hope. As Elaine passed Crawlie's chair, the proud, beautiful girl looked straight at her, expressionless, deadly and severe. The dog-girl D'joan followed the little procession as if she had been invited.

They walked down and down and down. Actually, it could not have been a full half-kilometer. But with the endless browns and yellows, the strange shapes of the lawless and untended underpeople, the stenches and the thick heavy air, Elaine felt as if she were leaving all known worlds behind.

In fact, she was doing precisely that, but it did not occur to her that her own suspicion might be true.

V

At the end of the corridor there was a round gate with a door of gold or brass.

Charley-is-my-darling stopped. "I can't go further," he said. "You and D'joan will have to go on. This is the forgotten antechamber between the tunnel and the upper palace. The Hunter is there. Go on. You're a person. It is safe. Underpeople usually die in there. Go on." He nudged her elbow and pulled the sliding door apart.

"But the little girl," said Elaine.

"She's not a girl," Charley-is-my darling. "She's just a dog —as I'm not a man, just a goat brightened and cut and trimmed to look like a man. If you come back, Elaine, I will love you like God or I will kill you. It depends."

"Depends on what?" asked Elaine. "And what is 'God'?"

Charley-is-my-darling smiled the quick tricky smile which was wholly insincere and completely friendly, both at the same time. It was probably the trademark of his personality in ordinary times. "You'll find out about God somewhere else, if you do. Not from us. And the depending is something you'll know for yourself. You won't have to wait for me to tell you. Go along now. The whole thing will be over in the next few minutes."

"But D'joan?" persisted Elaine.

"If it doesn't work," said Charley-is-my-darling, "we can always raise another D'joan and wait for another you. The Lady Panc Ashash has promised us that. Go on in!"

He pushed her roughly, so that she stumbled through. Bright light dazzled her and the clean air tasted as good as fresh water on her first day out of the spaceship pod.

The little dog-girl had trotted in beside her.

The door, gold or brass, clanged to behind them.

Elaine and D'joan stood still, side by side, looking forward and upward.

There are many famous paintings of that scene. Most of the paintings show Elaine in rags with the distorted, suffering face of a witch. This is strictly unhistorical. She was wearing her everyday culottes, blouse and twin over-the-shoulder purses when she went in the other end of Clown Town. That was the usual dress on Fomalhaut III at that time. She had done nothing at all to spoil her clothes, so she must have looked the same when she came out. And D'joan—well, everyone knows what D'joan looked like.

The Hunter met them.

The Hunter met them, and new worlds began.

He was a shortish man, with black curly hair, black eyes that danced with laughter, broad shoulders and long legs. He walked with a quick sure step. He kept his hands quiet at his side, but the hands did not look tough and callused, as though they had been terminating lives, even the lives of animals.

"Come up and sit down," he greeted them. "I've been waiting for you both."

Elaine stumbled upward and forward. "Waiting?" she gasped.

"Nothing mysterious," he said. "I had the viewscreen on. The one into the tunnel. Its connections are shielded, so the police could not have peeped it."

Elaine stopped dead still. The little dog-girl, one step behind her, stopped too. She tried to draw herself up to her full height. She was about the same tallness that he was. It was difficult, since he stood four or five steps above them. She managed to keep her voice even when she said:

"You know, then?"

"What?"

"All those things they said."

"Sure I know them." He smiled. "Why not?"

"But," stammered Elaine, "about you and me being lovers? That too?"

"That too," he smiled again. "I've been hearing it half my life. Come on up, sit down and have something to eat. We have a lot of things to do tonight, if history is to be fulfilled through us. What do you eat, little girl?" said he kindly to D'joan. "Raw meat or people food?"

"I'm a finished girl," said D'joan, "so I prefer chocolate cake with vanilla ice cream."

"That you shall have," said the Hunter. "Come, both of you, and sit down."

They had topped the steps. A luxurious table, already set, was waiting for them. There were three couches around it. Elaine looked for the third person who would join them. Only as she sat down did she realize that he meant to invite the dog-child.

He saw her surprise, but did not comment on it directly. Instead, he spoke to D'joan. "You know me, girl, don't you?"

The child smiled and relaxed for the first time since Elaine had seen her. The dog-girl was really strikingly beautiful when the tension went out of her. The wariness, the quietness, the potential disquiet—these were dog qualities. Now the child seemed wholly human and mature far beyond her years. Her white face had dark, dark brown eyes.

"I've seen you lots of times, Hunter. And you've told me what would happen if I turned out to be *the* D'joan. How I would spread the word and meet great trials. How I might die and might not, but people and underpeople would remember my name for thousands of years. You've told me almost everything I know— Except the things that I can't talk to you about. You know them too, but you won't talk, will you?" said the little girl imploringly.

"I know you've been to Earth," said the Hunter.

"Don't say it! Please don't say it!" pleaded the girl.

"Earth! Manhome itself?" cried Elaine. "How, by the stars, did you get there?"

The Hunter intervened. "Don't press her, Elaine. It's a big secret, and she wants to keep it. You'll find out more tonight than mortal woman was ever told before."

"What does 'mortal' mean?" asked Elaine, who disliked antique words.

"It just means having a termination of life."

"That's foolish," said Elaine. "Everything terminates. Look at those poor messy people who went on beyond the legal four hundred years." She looked around. Rich black-and-red curtains hung from ceiling to floor. On one side of the room there was a piece of furniture she had never seen before. It was like a table, but it had little broad flat doors on the front, reaching from side to side; it was richly ornamented with unfamiliar woods and metals. Nevertheless, she had more important things to talk about than furniture.

She looked directly at the Hunter (no organic disease; wounded in left arm at an earlier period; somewhat excessive exposure to sunlight; might need correction for near vision) and demanded of him: "Am I captured by you, too?"

"Captured?"

"You're a Hunter. You hunt things. To kill them, I suppose. That underman back there, the goat who calls himself Charley-is-my-darling—"

"He never does!" cried the dog-girl, D'joan, interrupting.

"Never does what?" said Elaine, cross at being interrupted.

"He never calls himself that. Other people, underpeople I mean, call him that. His name is Balthasar, but nobody uses it."

"What does it matter, little girl?" said Elaine. "I'm talking about my life. Your friend said he would take my life from me if something did not happen."

Neither D'joan nor the Hunter said anything.

Elaine heard a frantic edge go into her voice, "You heard it!" She turned to the Hunter, "You saw it on the viewscreen."

The Hunter's voice was serenity and assurance: "We three have things to do before this night is out. We won't get them done if you are frightened or worried. I know the underpeople, but I know the Lords of the Instrumentality as well—all four of them, right here. The Lords Limaono and Femtiosex and the Lady Goroke. And the Norstilian, too. They will protect you. Charley-is-my-darling might want to take your life from you because he is worried, afraid that the tunnel of Englok, where you just were, will be discovered. I have ways of protecting him and yourself as well. Have confidence in me for a while. That's not so hard, is it?"

"But," protested Elaine, "the man—or the goat—or whatever he was, Charley-is-my-darling, he said it would all happen right away, as soon as I came up here with you."

"How can anything happen," said little D'joan, "if you keep talking all the time?"

The Hunter smiled.

"That's right," he said. "We've talked enough. Now we must become lovers."

Elaine jumped to her feet, "Not with me, you don't. Not with her here. Not when I haven't found my work to do. I'm a witch. I'm supposed to do something, but I've never really found out what it was."

"Look at this," said the Hunter calmly, walking over to the

wall, and pointing with his finger at an intricate circular design.

Elaine and D'joan both looked at it.

The Hunter spoke again, his voice urgent. "Do you see it, D'joan? Do you really see it? The ages turn, waiting for this moment, little child. Do you see it? Do you see yourself in it?"

Elaine looked at the little dog-girl. D'joan had almost stopped breathing. She stared at the curious symmetrical pattern as though it were a window into enchanting worlds.

The Hunter roared, at the top of his voice, "D'joan! Joan! Joanie!"

The child made no response.

The Hunter stepped over to the child, slapped her gently on the cheek, shouted again. D'joan continued to stare at the intricate design.

"Now," said the Hunter, "you and I make love. The child is absent in a world of happy dreams. That design is a mandala, something left over from the unimaginable past. It locks the human consciousness in place. D'joan will not see us or hear us. We cannot help her go toward her destiny unless you and I make love first."

Elaine, her hand to her mouth, tried to inventory symptoms as a means of keeping her familiar thoughts in balance. It did not work. A relaxation spread over her, a happiness and quiet that she had not once felt since her childhood.

"Did you think," said the Hunter, "that I hunted with my body and killed with my hands? Didn't anyone ever tell you that the game comes to me rejoicing, that the animals die while they scream with pleasure? I'm a telepath, and I work under license. And I have my license now from the dead Lady Panc Ashash."

Elaine knew that they had come to the end of the talking. Trembling, happy, frightened, she fell into his arms and let him lead her over to the couch at the side of the black-and-gold room.

A thousand years later, she was kissing his ear and murmuring loving words at him, words that she did not even realize she knew. She must, she thought, have picked up more from the story-boxes than she ever realized.

"You're my love," she said, "my only one, my darling. Never, never leave me; never throw me away. Oh, Hunter, I love you so!"

"We part," he said, "before tomorrow is gone, but shall meet again. Do you realize that all this has only been a little more than an hour?"

Elaine blushed. "And I," she stammered, "I—I'm hungry."

"Natural enough," said the Hunter. "Pretty soon we can waken the little girl and eat together. And then history will happen, unless somebody walks in and stops us."

"But, darling," said Elaine, "can't we go on—at least for a while? A year? A month? A day? Put the little girl back in the tunnel for a while."

"Not really," said the Hunter, "but I'll sing you the song that came into my mind about you and me. I've been thinking bits of it for a long time, but now it has really happened. Listen."

He held her two hands in his two hands, looked easily and frankly into her eyes. There was no hint in him of telepathic power.

He sang to her the song which we know as "I Love You and Lost You."

> I knew you, and loved you,
>   and won you, in Kalma.
> I loved you, and won you.
>   and lost you, my darling!
> The dark skies of Waterrock
>   swept down against us.
> Lightning-lit only
>   by our own love, my lovely!
>
> Our time was a short time,
>   a sharp hour of glory—

We tasted delight
and we suffer denial.
The tale of us two
is a bittersweet story,
Short as a shot
but as long as death.

We met and we loved,
and vainly we plotted
To rescue beauty
from a smothering war.
Time had no time for us,
the minutes, no mercy.
We have loved and lost,
and the world goes on.

We have lost and have kissed,
and have parted, my darling!
All that we have,
we must save in our hearts, love.
The memory of beauty
and the beauty of memory . . .
I've loved you and won you
and lost you, in Kalma.

His fingers, moving in the air, produced a soft organ-like music in the room. She had noticed music-beams before, but she had never had one played for herself.

By the time he was through singing, she was sobbing. It was all so true, so wonderful, so heartbreaking.

He had kept her right hand in his left hand. Now he released her suddenly. He stood up.

"Let's work first. Eat later. Someone is near us."

He walked briskly over to the little dog-girl, who was still seated on the chair looking at the mandala with open, sleeping eyes. He took her head firmly and gently between his two hands and turned her eyes away from the design. She struggled momentarily against his hands and then seemed to wake up fully.

She smiled. "That was nice. I rested. How long was it—five minutes?"

"More than that," said the Hunter gently. "I want you to take Elaine's hand."

A few hours ago, and Elaine would have protested at the grotesquerie of holding hands with an underperson. This time, she said nothing, but obeyed: she looked with much love toward the Hunter.

"You two don't have to know much," said the Hunter. "You, D'joan, are going to get everything that is in our minds and in our memories. You will become us, both of us. Forevermore. You will meet your glorious fate."

The little girl shivered. "Is this really the day?"

"It is," said the Hunter. "Future ages will remember this night."

"And you, Elaine," said he to her, "have nothing to do but to love me and to stand very still. Do you understand? You will see tremendous things, some of them frightening. But they won't be real. Just stand still."

Elaine nodded wordlessly.

"In the name," said the Hunter, "of the First Forgotten One, in the name of the Second Forgotten One, in the name of the Third Forgotten One. For the love of people, that will give them life. For the love that will give them a clean death and true . . ." His words were clear but Elaine could not understand them.

The day of days was here.

She knew it.

She did not know how she knew it, but she did.

The Lady Panc Ashash crawled up through the solid floor, wearing her friendly robot body. She came near to Elaine and murmured: "Have no fear, no fear."

Fear? thought Elaine. This is no time for fear. It is much too interesting.

As if to answer Elaine, a clear, strong, masculine voice spoke out of nowhere:

This is the time for the daring sharing.

When these words were spoken, it was as if a bubble had been pricked. Elaine felt her personality and D'joan min-

gling. With ordinary telepathy, it would have been frightening. But this was not communication. It was being.

She had become Joan. She felt the clean little body in its
tidy clothes. She became aware of the girl-shape again. It was
oddly pleasant and familiar, in terribly faraway kinds of feeling, to remember that she had had that shape once—the
smooth, innocent flat chest; the uncomplicated groin; the
fingers which still felt as though they were separate and alive
in extending from the palm of the hand. But the mind—*that*
child's mind! It was like an enormous museum illuminated by
rich stained-glass windows, cluttered with variegated heaps
of beauty and treasure, scented by strange incense which
moved slowly in unpropelled air. D'joan had a mind which
reached all the way back to the color and glory of man's
antiquity. D'joan had been a Lord of the Instrumentality, a
monkey-man riding the ships of space, a friend of the dear
dead Lady Panc Ashash, and Panc Ashash herself.

No wonder the child was rich and strange: she had been
made the heir of all the ages.

*This is the time for the glaring top of the truth at the
wearing sharing,* said the nameless, clear, loud voice in her
mind. *This is the time for you and him.*

Elaine realized that she was responding to hypnotic suggestions which the Lady Panc Ashash had put into the mind
of the little dog-girl—suggestions which were triggered into
full potency the moment that the three of them came into
telepathic contact.

For a fraction of a second, she perceived nothing but aston-
ishment within herself. She saw nothing but herself—every
detail, every secrecy, every thought and feeling and contour
of flesh. She was curiously aware of how her breasts hung
from her chest, the tension of her belly-muscles holding her
female backbone straight and erect—

Female backbone?

Why had she thought that she had a female backbone?

And then she knew.

She was following the Hunter's mind as his awareness

rushed through her body, drank it up, enjoyed it, loved it all over again, this time from the inside out.

She knew somehow that the little dog-girl watched everything quietly, wordlessly, drinking in from them both the full nuance of being truly human.

Even with the delirium, she sensed embarrassment. It might be a dream, but it was still too much. She began to close her mind and the thought had come to her that she should take her hands away from the hands of Hunter and the dog-child.

But then fire came . . .

VI

Fire came up from the floor, burning about them intangibly. Elaine felt nothing . . . but she could sense the touch of the little girl's hand.

Flames around the dames, games, said an idiot voice from nowhere.

Fire around the pyre, sire, said another.

Hot is what we got, tot, said a third.

Suddenly Elaine remembered Earth, but it was not the Earth she knew. She was herself D'joan, and not D'joan. She was a tall, strong monkey-man, indistinguishable from a true human being. She/he had tremendous alertness in her/his heart as he/she walked across the Peace Square at An-fang, the Old Square at An-fang, where all things begin. She/he noticed a discrepancy. Some of the buildings were not there.

The real Elaine thought to herself, "So that's what they did with the child—printed her with the memories of other underpeople. Other ones, who dared things and went places."

The fire stopped.

Elaine saw the black-and-gold room clean and untroubled for a moment before the green white-topped ocean rushed in. The water poured over the three of them without getting them wet in the least. The greenness washed around them without pressure, without suffocation.

Elaine was the Hunter. Enormous dragons floated in the sky above Fomalhaut III. She felt herself wandering across a hill, singing with love and yearning. She had the Hunter's own mind, his own memory. The dragon sensed him, and flew down. The enormous reptilian wings were more beautiful than a sunset, more delicate than orchids. Their beat in the air was as gentle as the breath of a baby. She was not only Hunter but dragon too; she felt the minds meeting and the dragon dying in bliss, in joy.

Somehow the water was gone. So too were D'joan and the Hunter. She was not in the room. She was taut, tired, worried Elaine, looking down a nameless street for hopeless destinations. She had to do things which could never be done. The wrong me, the wrong time, the wrong place—and I'm alone, I'm alone, I'm alone, her mind screamed. The room was back again; so too were the hands of the Hunter and the little girl.

Mist began rising—

Another dream? thought Elaine. Aren't we done?

But there was another voice somewhere, a voice which grated like the rasp of a saw cutting through bone, like the grind of a broken machine still working at ruinous top speed. It was an evil voice, a terror-filling voice.

Perhaps this really was the "death" which the tunnel underpeople had mistaken her for.

The Hunter's hand released hers. She let go of D'joan.

There was a strange woman in the room. She wore the baldric of authority and the leotards of a traveler.

Elaine stared at her.

"You'll be punished," said the terrible voice, which now was coming out of the woman.

"Wh—wh—what?" stammered Elaine.

"You're conditioning an underperson without authority. I don't know who you are, but the Hunter should know better. The animal will have to die, of course," said the woman, looking at little D'joan.

Hunter muttered, half in greeting to the stranger, half in explanation to Elaine, as though he did not know what else to say: "Lady Arabella Underwood."

Elaine could not bow to her, though she wanted to.

The surprise came from the little dog girl.

I am your sister Joan, she said, *and no animal to you.*

The Lady Arabella seemed to have trouble hearing. (Elaine herself could not tell whether she was hearing spoken words or taking the message with her mind.)

I am Joan and I love you.

The Lady Arabella shook herself as though water had splashed on her. "Of course you're Joan. You love me. And I love you."

People and underpeople meet on the terms of love.

"Love. Love, of course. You're a good little girl. And so right." *You will forget me,* said Joan, *until we meet and love again.*

"Yes, darling. Good-by for now."

At last D'joan did use words. She spoke to the Hunter and Elaine, saying, "It is finished. I know who I am and what I must do. Elaine had better come with me. We will see you soon, Hunter—if we live."

Elaine looked at the Lady Arabella, who stood stock-still, staring like a blind woman. The Hunter nodded at Elaine with his wise, kind, rueful smile.

The little girl led Elaine down, down, down to the door which led back to the tunnel of Englok. Just as they went through the brass door, Elaine heard the voice of the Lady Arabella say to the Hunter: "What are you doing here all by yourself? The room smells funny. Have you had animals here? Have you killed something?"

"Yes, ma'am," said the Hunter as D'joan and Elaine stepped through the door.

"What?" cried the Lady Arabella.

Hunter must have raised his voice to a point of penetrating emphasis because he wanted the other two to hear him, too:

"I have killed, ma'am," he said, "as always—with love. This time it was a system."

They slipped through the door while the Lady Arabella's protesting voice, heavy with authority and inquiry, was still sweeping against the Hunter.

Joan led. Her body was the body of a pretty child, but her personality was the full awakening of all the underpeople who had been imprinted on her. Elaine could not understand it, because Joan was still the little dog-girl, but Joan was now also Elaine, also Hunter. There was no doubt about their movement; the child, no longer an undergirl, led the way and Elaine, human or not, followed.

The door closed behind them. They were back in the brown-and-yellow corridor. Most of the underpeople were awaiting them. Dozens stared at them. The heavy animal-human smells of the old tunnel rolled against them like thick, slow waves. Elaine felt the beginning of a headache at her temples, but she was much too alert to care.

For a moment, D'joan and Elaine confronted the under-people.

Most of you have seen paintings or theatricals based upon this scene. The most famous of all is, beyond doubt, the fantastic "one-line drawing" of San Shigonanda—the board of the background almost uniformly gray, with a hint of brown and yellow on the left, a hint of black and red on the right, and in the center the strange white line, almost a smear of paint, which somehow suggests the bewildered girl Elaine and the doom-blessed child Joan.

Charley-is-my-darling was, of course, the first to find his voice. (Elaine did not notice him as a goat-man any more. He seemed an earnest, friendly man of middle age, fighting poor health and an uncertain life with great courage. She now found his smile persuasive and charming. Why, thought Elaine, didn't I see him that way before? Have I changed?)

Charley-is-my-darling had spoken before Elaine found her wits. "He did it. Are you D'joan?"

"Am I D'joan?" said the child, asking the crowd of deformed, weird people in the tunnel. "Do you think I am D'joan?"

"No! No! You are the lady who was promised—you are the bridge-to-man," cried a tall yellow-haired old woman, whom Elaine could not remember seeing before. The woman flung herself to her knees in front of the child, and tried to get D'joan's hand. The child held her hands away, quietly, but firmly, so the woman buried her face in the child's skirt and wept.

"I am Joan," said the child, "and I am dog no more. You are people now, people, and if you die with me, you will die men. Isn't that better than it has ever been before? And you, Ruthie," said she to the woman at her feet, "stand up and stop crying. Be glad. These are the days that I shall be with you. I know your children were all taken away and killed, Ruthie, and I am sorry. I cannot bring them back. But I give you womanhood. I have even made a person out of Elaine."

"Who are you?" said Charley-is-my-darling. "Who are you?"

"I'm the little girl you put out to live or die an hour ago. But now I am Joan, not D'joan, and I bring you a weapon. You are women. You are men. You are people. You can use the weapon."

"What weapon?" The voice was Crawlie's, from about the third row of spectators.

"Life and life-with," said the child Joan.

"Don't be a fool," said Crawlie. "What's the weapon? Don't give us words. We've had words and death ever since the world of underpeople began. That's what *people* give us—good words, fine principles and cold murder, year after year, generation after generation. Don't tell me I'm a person—I'm not. I'm a bison and I know it. An animal fixed up to look like a person. Give me a something to kill with. Let me die fighting."

Little Joan looked incongruous in her young body and short stature, still wearing the little blue smock in which Elaine had first seen her. She commanded the room. She lifted her hand and the buzz of low voices, which had started while Crawlie was yelling, dropped off to silence again.

"Crawlie," she said, in a voice that carried all the way down the hall, "peace be with you in the everlasting now."

Crawlie scowled. She did have the grace to look puzzled at Joan's message to her, but she did not speak.

"Don't talk to me, dear people," said little Joan. "Get used to me first. I bring you life-with. It's more than love. Love's a hard, sad, dirty word, a cold word, an old word. It says too much and it promises too little. I bring you something much bigger than love. If you're alive, you're alive. If you're alive-with, then you know the other life is there too— both of you, any of you, all of you. Don't do anything. Don't grab, don't clench, don't possess. Just *be*. That's the weapon. There's not a flame or a gun or a poison that can stop it."

"I want to believe you," said Mabel, "but I don't know how to."

"Don't believe me," said little Joan. "Just wait and let things happen. Let me through, good people. I have to sleep for a while. Elaine will watch me while I sleep and when I get up, I will tell you why you are underpeople no longer."

Joan started to move forward—

A wild ululating screech split the corridor.

Everyone looked around to see where it came from.

It was almost like the shriek of a fighting bird, but the sound came from among them.

Elaine saw it first.

Crawlie had a knife and just as the cry ended, she flung herself on Joan.

Child and woman fell on the floor, their dresses a tangle. The large hand rose up twice with the knife, and the second time it came up red.

From the hot shocking burn in her side, Elaine knew that she must herself have taken one of the stabs. She could not tell whether Joan was still living.

The undermen pulled Crawlie off the child.

Crawlie was white with rage. "Words, words, words. She'll kill us all with her words."

A large, fat man with the muzzle of a bear on the front of an otherwise human-looking head and body, stepped around the man who held Crawlie. He gave her one tremendous slap. She dropped to the floor unconscious. The knife, stained with blood, fell on the old worn carpet. (Elaine thought automatically: restorative for her later; check neck vertebrae; no problem of bleeding.)

For the first time in her life, Elaine functioned as a wholly efficient witch. She helped the people pull the clothing from little Joan. The tiny body, with the heavy purple-dark blood pumping out from just below the rib-cage, looked hurt and fragile. Elaine reached in her left handbag. She had a surgical radar pen. She held it to her eye and looked through the flesh, up and down the wound. The peritoneum was punctured, the liver cut, the upper folds of the large intestine were perforated in two places. When she saw this, she knew what to do. She brushed the bystanders aside and got to work.

First she glued up the cuts from the inside out, starting with the damage to the liver. Each touch of the organic adhesive was preceded by a tiny spray of re-coding powder, designed to reinforce the capacity of the injured organ to restore itself. The probing, pressing, squeezing, took eleven minutes. Before it was finished, Joan had awakened, and was murmuring: "Am I dying?"

"Not at all," said Elaine, "unless these human medicines poison your dog blood."

"Who did it?"

"Crawlie."

"Why?" said the child. "Why? Is she hurt too? Where is she?"

"Not as hurt as she is going to be," said the goat-man, Charley-is-my-darling. "If she lives, we'll fix her up and try her and put her to death."

"No, you won't," said Joan. "You're going to love her. You must."

The goat-man looked bewildered.

He turned in his perplexity to Elaine. "Better have a look at Crawlie," said he. "Maybe Orson killed her with that slap. He's a bear, you know."

"So I saw," said Elaine, drily. What did the man think that thing looked like, a hummingbird?

She walked over to the body of Crawlie. As soon as she touched the shoulders, she knew that she was in for trouble. The outer appearances were human, but the musculature beneath was not. She suspected that the laboratories had left Crawlie terribly strong, keeping the buffalo strength and obstinacy for some remote industrial reason of their own. She took out a brainlink, a close-range telepathic hookup which worked only briefly and slightly, to see if the mind still functioned. As she reached for Crawlie's head to attach it, the unconscious girl sprang suddenly to life, jumped to her feet and said: "No, you don't! you don't peep me, you dirty human!"

"Crawlie, stand still."

"Don't boss me, you monster!"

"Crawlie, that's a bad thing to say." It was eerie to hear such a commanding voice coming from the throat and mouth of a small child. Small she might have been, but Joan commanded the scene.

"I don't care what I say. You all hate me."

"That's not true, Crawlie."

"You're a dog and now you're a person. You're born a traitor. Dogs have always sided with people. You hated me even before you went into that room and changed into something else. Now you are going to kill us all."

"We may die, Crawlie, but I won't do it."

"Well, you hate me, anyhow. You've always hated me."

"You may not believe it," said Joan, "but I've always loved you. You were the prettiest woman in our whole corridor."

Crawlie laughed. The sound gave Elaine gooseflesh. "Suppose I believed it. How could I live if I thought that people loved me? If I believed you, I would have to tear myself to pieces, to break my brains on the wall, to do—" The laughter changed to sobs, but Crawlie managed to resume talking: "You things are so stupid that you don't even know that you're monsters. You're not people. You never will be people. I'm one of you myself. I'm honest enough to admit what I am. We're dirt, we're nothing, we're things that are less than machines. We hide in the earth like dirt and when people kill us they do not weep. At least we were hiding. Now you come along, you and your tame human woman—" Crawlie glared briefly at Elaine— "and you try to change even that. I'll kill you again if I can, you dirt, you slut, you dog! What are you doing with that child's body? We don't even know who you are now. Can you tell us?"

The bear-man had moved up close to Crawlie, unnoticed by her, and was ready to slap her down again if she moved against little Joan.

Joan looked straight at him and with a mere movement of her eyes she commanded him not to strike.

"I'm tired," she said, "I'm tired, Crawlie. I'm a thousand years old when I am not even five. And I am Elaine now, and I am Hunter too, and I am the Lady Panc Ashash, and I know a great many more things than I thought I would ever know. I have work to do, Crawlie, because I love you, and I think I will die soon. But please, good people, first let me rest."

The bear-man was on Crawlie's right. On her left, there had moved up a snake-woman. The face was pretty and human, except for the thin forked tongue which ran in and out of the mouth like a dying flame. She had good shoulders and hips but no breasts at all. She wore empty golden brassiere cups which swung against her chest. Her hands looked as though they might be stronger than steel. Crawlie started to move toward Joan, and the snake-woman hissed.

It was the snake hiss of Old Earth.

For a second, every animal-person in the corridor stopped breathing. They all stared at the snake-woman. She hissed

again, looking straight at Crawlie. The sound was an abomi-
nation in that narrow space. Elaine saw that Joan tightened
up like a little dog, Charley-is-my-darling looked as though
he was ready to leap twenty meters in one jump, and Elaine
herself felt an impulse to strike, to kill, to destroy. The hiss
was a challenge to them all.

The snake-woman looked around calmly, fully aware of the
attention she had obtained.

"Don't worry, dear people. See, I'm using Joan's name for
all of us. I'm not going to hurt Crawlie, not unless she hurts
Joan. But if she hurts Joan, if anybody hurts Joan, they will
have me to deal with. You have a good idea who I am. We
S-people have great strength, high intelligence and no fear
at all. You know we cannot breed. People have to make us
one by one, out of ordinary snakes. Do not cross me, dear
people. I want to learn about this new love which Joan is
bringing, and nobody is going to hurt Joan while I am here.
Do you hear me, people? Nobody. Try it, and you die. I think
I could kill almost all of you before I died, even if you all
attacked me at once. Do you hear me, people? *Leave Joan
alone.* That goes for you, too, you soft human woman. I am
not afraid of you either. You there," said she to the bear-man,
"pick little Joan up and carry her to a quiet bed. She must
rest. She must be quiet for a while. You be quiet too, all you
people, or you will meet me. Me." Her black eyes roved
across their faces. The snake-woman moved forward and
they parted in front of her, as though she were the only solid
being in a throng of ghosts.

Her eyes rested a moment on Elaine. Elaine met the gaze,
but it was an uncomfortable thing to do. The black eyes with
neither eyebrow nor lashes seemed full of intelligence and
devoid of emotion. Orson, the bear-man, followed obediently
behind. He carried little Joan.

As the child passed Elaine she tried to stay awake. She
murmured, "Make me bigger. Please make me bigger. Right
away."

"I don't know how . . ." said Elaine.

The child struggled to full awakening. "I'll have work to do. Work . . . and maybe my death to die. It will all be wasted if I am this little. Make me bigger."

"But—" protested Elaine again.

"If you don't know, ask the lady."

"What lady?"

The S-woman had paused, listening to the conversation. She cut in.

"The Lady Panc Ashash, of course. The dead one. Do you think that a living Lady of the Instrumentality would do anything but kill us all?"

As the snake-woman and Orson carried Joan away, Charley-is-my-darling came up to Elaine and said, "Do you want to go?"

"Where?"

"To the Lady Panc Ashash, of course."

"Me?" said Elaine. "Now?" said Elaine, even more emphatically. "Of course not," said Elaine, pronouncing each word as though it were a law. "What do you think I am? A few hours ago I did not even know that you existed. I wasn't sure about the word 'death.' I just assumed that everything terminated at four hundred years, the way it should. It's been hours of danger, and everybody has been threatening everybody else for all that time. I'm tired and I'm sleepy and I'm dirty, and I've got to take care of myself, and besides—"

She stopped suddenly and bit her lip. She had started to say, and besides, my body is all worn out with that dream-like love-making which the Hunter and I had together. That was not the business of Charley-is-my-darling: he was goat enough as he was. His mind was goatish and would not see the dignity of it all.

The goat-man said, very gently, "You are making history, Elaine, and when you make history you cannot always take care of all the little things too. Are you happier and more important than you ever were before? Yes? Aren't you a different you from the person who met Balthasar just a few hours ago?"

Elaine was taken aback by the seriousness. She nodded.

"Stay hungry and tired. Stay dirty. Just a little longer. Time must not be wasted. You can talk to the Lady Panc Ashash. Find out what we must do about little Joan. When you come back with further instructions, I will take care of you myself. This tunnel is not as bad a town as it looks. We will have everything you could need, in the Room of Englok. Englok himself built it, long ago. Work just a little longer, and then you can eat and rest. We have everything here. 'I am the citizen of no mean city.' But first you must help Joan. You love Joan, don't you?"

"Oh, yes, I do," she said.

"Then help us just a little bit more."

With death? she thought. With murder? With violation of law? But—but it was all for Joan.

It was thus that Elaine went to the camouflaged door, went out under the open sky again, saw the great Saucer of Upper Kalma reaching out over the Old Lower City. She talked to the voice of the Lady Panc Ashash, and obtained certain instructions, together with other messages. Later, she was able to repeat them, but she was too tired to make out their real sense.

She staggered back to the place in the wall where she thought the door to be, leaned against it, and nothing happened.

"Further down, Elaine, further down. Hurry! When I used to be me, I too got tired," came the strong whisper of the Lady Panc Ashash, "but do hurry!"

Elaine stepped away from the wall, looking at it.

A beam of light struck her.

The Instrumentality had found her.

She rushed wildly at the wall.

The door gaped briefly. The strong welcome hand of Charley-is-my-darling helped her in.

"The light! The light!" cried Elaine. "I've killed us all. They saw me."

"Not yet," smiled the goat-man, with his quick crooked

intelligent smile. "I may not be educated, but I am pretty smart."

He reached toward the inner gate, glanced back at Elaine appraisingly, and then shoved a man-sized robot through the door.

"There it goes, a sweeper about your size. No memory bank. A worn-out brain. Just simple motivations. If they come down to see what they thought they saw, they will see this instead. We keep a bunch of these at the door. We don't go out much, but when we do, it's handy to have these to cover up with."

He took her by the arm. "While you eat, you can tell me. Can we make her bigger . . .?"

"Who?"

"Joan, of course. Our Joan. That's what you went to find out for us."

Elaine had to inventory her own mind to see what the Lady Panc Ashash had said on that subject. In a moment she remembered. "You need a pod. And a jelly bath. And narcotics, because it will hurt. Four hours."

"Wonderful," said Charley-is-my-darling, leading her deeper and deeper into the tunnel.

"But what's the use of it," said Elaine, "if I've ruined us all? The Instrumentality saw me coming in. They will follow. They will kill all of you, even Joan. Where is the Hunter? Shouldn't I sleep first?" She felt her lips go thick with fatigue; she had not rested or eaten since she took that chance on the strange little door between Waterrocky Road and the Shopping Bar.

"You're safe, Elaine, you're safe," said Charley-is-my-darling, his sly smile very warm and his smooth voice carrying the ring of sincere conviction. For himself, he did not believe a word of it. He thought they were all in danger, but there was no point in terrifying Elaine. Elaine was the only real person on their side, except for the Hunter, who was a strange one, almost like an animal himself, and for the Lady Panc Ashash, who was very benign, but who was, after all, a dead person. He was frightened himself, but he was afraid of fear. Perhaps they were all doomed.

In a way, he was right.

VII

The Lady Arabella Underwood had called the Lady Goroke. "Something has tampered with my mind."

The Lady Goroke felt very shocked. She threw back the inquiry. Put a probe on it.

"I did. Nothing."

Nothing?

More shock for the Lady Goroke. Sound the alert, then.

"Oh, no. Oh, no, no. It was a friendly, nice tampering." The Lady Arabella Underwood, being an Old North Australian, was rather formal: she always thought full words at her friends, even in telepathic contact. She never sent mere raw ideas.

But that's utterly unlawful. You're part of the Instrumentality. It's a crime! thought the Lady Goroke.

She got a giggle for reply.

You laugh...? she inquired.

"I just thought a new Lord might be here. From the Instrumentality. Having a look at me."

The Lady Goroke was very proper and easily shocked. We wouldn't do that!

The Lady Arabella thought to herself but did not transmit, "Not to you, my dear. You're a blooming prude." To the other she transmitted, "Forget it then."

Puzzled and worried, the Lady Goroke thought: Well, all right. Break?

"Right-ho. Break."

The Lady Goroke frowned to herself. She slapped her wall. Planet Central, she thought at it.

A mere man sat at a desk.

"I am the Lady Goroke," she said.

"Of course, my lady," he replied.

"Police fever, one degree. One degree only. Till rescinded. Clear?"

"Clear, my lady. The entire planet?"

"Yes," she said.

"Do you wish to give a reason?" His voice was respectful and routine.

"Must I?"

"Of course not, my lady."

"None given, then. Close."

He saluted and his image faded from the wall.

She raised her mind to the level of a light clear call. Instrumentality Only—Instrumentality Only. I have raised the Police fever level 1° by command. Reason, personal disquiet. You know my voice. You know me. Goroke.

Far across the city—a police ornithopter flapped slowly down the street.

The police robot was photographing a sweeper, the most elaborately malfunctioning sweeper he had ever seen.

The sweeper raced down the road at unlawful speeds, approaching three hundred kilometers an hour, stopped with a sizzle of plastic on stone, and began picking dust-motes off the pavement.

When the ornithopter reached it, the sweeper took off again, rounded two or three corners at tremendous speed and then settled down to its idiot job.

The third time this happened, the robot in the ornithopter put a disabling slug through it, flew down and picked it up with the claws of his machine.

He saw it in close view.

"Birdbrain. Old model. Birdbrain. Good they don't use those any more. The thing could have hurt A Man. Now, I'm printed from a mouse, a real mouse with lots and lots of brains."

He flew toward the central junkyard with the worn-out sweeper. The sweeper, crippled but still conscious, was trying to pick dust off the iron claws which held it.

Below them, the Old City twisted out of sight with its odd geometrical lights. The new city, bathed in its soft perpetual glow, shone out against the night of Fomalhaut III. Beyond them, the everlasting ocean boiled in its private storms.

On the actual stage the actors cannot do much with the scene of the interlude, where Joan was cooked in a single night from the size of a child five years old to the tallness of a miss fifteen or sixteen. The biological machine did work well, though at the risk of her life. It made her into a vital, robust young person, without changing her mind at all. This is hard for any actress to portray. The storyboxes have the advantage. They can show the machine with all sorts of improvements—flashing lights, bits of lightnight, mysterious rays. Actually, it looked like a bathtub full of boiling brown jelly, completely covering Joan.

Elaine, meanwhile, ate hungrily in the palatial room of Englok himself. The food was very, very old, and she had doubts, as a witch, about its nutritional value, but it stilled her hunger. The denizens of Clown Town had declared this room "off limits" to themselves, for reasons which Charley-is-my-darling could not make plain. He stood in the doorway and told her what to do to find food, to activate the bed out of the floor, to open the bathroom. Everything was very oldfashioned and nothing responded to a simple thought or to a mere slap.

A curious thing happened.

Elaine had washed her hands, had eaten and was preparing for her bath. She had taken most of her clothes off, thinking only that Charley-is-my-darling was an animal, not a man, so that it did not matter.

Suddenly she knew it did matter.

He might be an underperson but he was a man to her. Blushing deeply all the way down to her neck, she ran into the bathroom and called back to him:

"Go away. I will bathe and then sleep. Wake me when you have to, not before."

"Yes, Elaine."

"And—and—"

"Yes?"

"Thank you," she said. "Thank you very much. Do you know, I never said 'thank you' to an underperson before."

"That's all right," said Charley-is-my-darling with a smile. "Most real people don't. Sleep well, my dear Elaine. When you awaken, be ready for great things. We shall take a star out of the skies and shall set thousands of worlds on fire . . ."

"What's that?" she said, putting her head around the corner of the bathroom.

"Just a figure of speech." He smiled. "Just meaning that you won't have much time. Rest well. Don't forget to put your clothes in the ladysmaid machine. The ones in Clown Town are all worn out. But since we haven't used this room, yours ought to work."

"Which is it?" she said.

"The red lid with the gold handle. Just lift it." On that domestic note he left her to rest, while he went off and plotted the destiny of a hundred billion lives.

They told her it was midmorning when she came out of the room of Englok. How could she have known it? The brown-and-yellow corridor, with its gloomy old yellow lights, was just as dim and stench-ridden as ever.

The people all seemed to have changed.

Baby-baby was no longer a mouse-hag, but a woman of considerable force and much tenderness. Crawlie was as dangerous as a human enemy, staring at Elaine, her beautiful face gone bland with hidden hate. Charley-is-my-darling was gay, friendly and persuasive. She thought she could read expressions on the faces of Orson and the S'woman, odd though their features were.

After she had gotten through some singularly polite greetings, she demanded, "What's happening now?"

A new voice spoke up—a voice she knew and did not know.

Elaine glanced over at a niche in the wall.

The Lady Panc Ashash! And who was that with her?

Even as she asked herself the question, Elaine knew the answer. It was Joan, grown, only half a head less tall than the Lady Panc Ashash or herself. It was a new Joan, powerful, happy, and quiet; but it was all the dear little old D'joan too.

"Welcome," said the Lady Panc Ashash, "to our revolution."

"What's a revolution?" asked Elaine. "And I thought you couldn't come in here with all the thought shielding?"

The Lady Panc Ashash lifted a wire which trailed back from her robot body, "I rigged this up so that I could use the body. Precautions are no use any more. It's the other side which will need the precautions now. A revolution is a way of changing systems and people. This is one. You go first, Elaine. This way."

"To die? Is that what you mean?"

The Lady Panc Ashash laughed warmly. "You know me by now. You know my friends here. You know what your own life has been down to now, a useless witch in a world which did not want you. We may die, but it's what we do before we die that counts. This is Joan going to meet her destiny. You lead as far as the Upper City. Then Joan will lead. And then we shall see."

"You mean, all these people are going too?" Joan looked at the ranks of the underpeople, who were beginning to form into two queues down the corridor. The queues bulged wherever mothers led their children by the hand or carried small ones in their arms. Here and there the line was punctuated by a giant underperson.

They have been nothing, thought Elaine, and I was nothing too. Now we are all going to do something, even though we may be terminated for it. "May be" thought she: "shall be" is the word. But it is worth it if Joan can change the worlds, even a little bit, even for other people.

Joan spoke up. Her voice had grown with her body, but it was the same dear voice which the little dog-girl had had sixteen hours (they seem sixteen years, thought Elaine) ago, when Elaine first met her at the door to the tunnel of Englok.

Joan said, "Love is not something special, reserved for men alone.

"Love is not proud. Love has no real name. Love is for life itself, and we have life.

"We cannot win by fighting. People outnumber us, outgun us, outrun us, outfight us. But people did not create us. Whatever made people, made us too. You all know that, but will we say the name?"

There was a murmur of *no* and *never* from the crowd.

"You have waited for me. I have waited too. It is time to die, perhaps, but we will die the way people did in the beginning, before things became easy and cruel for them. They live in a stupor and they die in a dream. It is not a good dream and if they awaken, they will know that we are people too. Are you with me?" They murmured yes. "Do you love me?" Again they murmured agreement. "Shall we go out and meet the day?" They shouted their acclaim.

Joan turned to the Lady Panc Ashash. "Is everything as you wished and ordered?"

"Yes," said the dear dead woman in the robot body. "Joan first, to lead you. Elaine preceding her, to drive away robots or ordinary underpeople. When you meet real people, you will love them. If they kill you, you will love them. Joan will show you how. Pay no further attention to me. Ready?"

Joan lifted her right hand and said words to herself. The people bowed their heads before her, faces and muzzles and snouts of all sizes and colors. A baby of some kind mewed in a tiny falsetto to the rear.

Just before she turned to lead the procession, Joan turned back to the people and said, "Crawlie, where are you?"

"Here, in the middle," said a clear, calm voice far back.

"Do you love me now, Crawlie?"

"No, D'joan. I like you less than when you were a little dog. But these are my people too, as well as yours. I am brave. I can walk. I won't make trouble."

"Crawlie," said Joan, "will you love people if we meet them?"

All faces turned toward the beautiful bison-girl. Elaine could just see her, way down the murky corridor. Elaine could see that the girl's face had turned utter, dead white with emotion. Whether rage or fear, she could not tell.

At last Crawlie spoke, "No, I won't love people. And I won't love you. I have my pride."

Softly, softly, like death itself at a quiet bedside, Joan spoke. "You *can* stay behind, Crawlie. You can stay here. It isn't much of a chance, but it's a chance."

Crawlie looked at her, "Bad luck to you, dog-woman, and bad luck to the rotten human being up there beside you."

Elaine stood on tiptoe to see what would happen. Crawlie's face suddenly disappeared, dropping downward.

The snake woman elbowed her way to the front, stood close to Joan where the others could see her, and sang out in a voice as clear as metal itself:

"Sing 'poor, poor, Crawlie,' dear people. Sing 'I love Crawlie,' dear people. She is dead. I just killed her so that we would all be full of love. I love you too," said the S'woman, on whose reptilian features no sign of love or hate could be seen.

Joan spoke up, apparently prompted by the Lady Panc Ashash. "We do love Crawlie, dear people. Think of her and then let us move forward."

Charley-is-my-darling gave Elaine a little shove. "Here, you lead."

In a dream, in a bewilderment, Elaine led.

She felt warm, happy, brave when she passed close to the strange Joan, so tall and yet so familiar. Joan gave her a full smile and whispered, "Tell me I'm doing well, human woman. I'm a dog and dogs have lived a million years for the praise of man."

"You're right, Joan, you're completely right! I'm with you. Shall I go now?" responded Elaine.

Joan nodded, her eyes brimming with tears.

Elaine led.

Joan and the Lady Panc Ashash followed, dog and dead woman championing the procession.

The rest of the underpeople followed them in turn, in a double line.

When they made the secret door open, daylight flooded the corridor. Elaine could almost feel the stale odor-ridden air pouring out with them. When she glanced back into the tunnel for the last time, she saw the body of Crawlie lying all alone on the floor.

Elaine herself turned to the steps and began going up them.

No one had yet noticed the procession.

Elaine could hear the wire of the Lady Panc Ashash dragging on the stone and metal of the steps as they climbed.

When she reached the top door, Elaine had a moment of indecision and panic. "This is my life, my life," she thought. "I have no other. What have I done? Oh, Hunter, Hunter, where are you? Have you betrayed me?"

Said Joan softly behind her, "Go on! Go on. This is a war of love. Keep going."

Elaine opened the door to the upper street. The roadway was full of people. Three police ornithopters flapped slowly overhead. This was an unusual number. Elaine stopped again.

"Keep walking," said Joan, "and warn the robots off."

Elaine advanced and the revolution began.

VIII

The revolution lasted six minutes and covered one hundred and twelve meters.

The police flew over as soon as the underpeople began pouring out of the doorway.

The first one glided in like a big bird, his voice asking, "Identify! Who are you?"

Elaine said, "Go away. That is a command."

"Identify yourself," said the bird-like machine, banking steeply with the lens-eyed robot peering at Elaine out of its middle.

"Go away," said Elaine, "I am a true human and I command."

The first police ornithopter apparently called to the others by radio. Together they flapped their way down the corridor between the big buildings.

A lot of people had stopped. Most of their faces were blank, a few showing animation or amusement or horror at the sight of so many underpeople all crowded in one place.

Joan's voice sang out, in the clearest possible enunciation of the Old Common Tongue: "Dear people, we are people. We love you. We love you."

The underpeople began to chant *love, love, love* in a weird plainsong full of sharps and half-tones. The true humans shrank back. Joan herself set the example by embracing a young woman of about her own height. Charley-is-my-darling took a human man by the shoulders and shouted at him:

"I love you, my dear fellow! Believe me, I do love you. It's wonderful meeting you." The human man was startled by the contact and even more startled by the glowing warmth of the goat-man's voice. He stood mouth slack and body relaxed with sheer, utter and accepted surprise.

Somewhere to the rear a person screamed.

A police ornithopter came flapping back. Elaine could not tell if it was one of the three she had sent away, or a new one altogether. She waited for it to get close enough to hail, so that she could tell it to go away. For the first time, she wondered about the actual physical character of danger. Could the police machine put a slug through her? Or shoot flame at her? Or lift her screaming, carrying her away with its iron claws to some place where she would be pretty and clean and never herself again? "Oh, Hunter, Hunter, where are you now? Have you forgotten me? Have you betrayed me?"

The underpeople were still surging forward and mingling

with the real people, clutching them by their hands or their garments and repeating in the queer medley of voices:

"I love you. Oh, please, I love you! We are people. We are your sisters and brothers . . ."

The snake-woman wasn't making much progress. She had seized a human man with her more-than-iron hand. Elaine hadn't seen her saying anything, but the man had fainted dead away. The snake woman had him draped over her arm like an empty overcoat and was looking for somebody else to love.

Behind Elaine a low voice said, "He's coming soon."

"Who?" said Elaine to the Lady Panc Ashash, knowing perfectly well whom she meant, but not wanting to admit it, and busy with watching the circling ornithopter at the same time.

"The Hunter, of course," said the robot with the dear dead lady's voice. "He'll come for you. You'll be all right. I'm at the end of my wire. Look away, my dear. They are about to kill me again and I am afraid that the sight would distress you."

Fourteen robots, foot models, marched with military decision into the crowd. The true humans took heart from this and some of them began to slip away into doorways. Most of the real people were still so surprised that they stood around with the underpeople pawing at them, babbling the accents of love over and over again, the animal origin of their voices showing plainly.

The robot sergeant took no note of this. He approached the Lady Panc Ashash only to find Elaine standing in his way.

"I command you," she said, with all the passion of a working witch, "I *command* you to leave this place."

His eye-lenses were like dark-blue marbles floating in milk. They seemed swimmy and poorly focused as he looked her over. He did not reply but stepped around her, faster than her own body could intercept him. He made for the dear, dead Lady Panc Ashash.

Elaine, bewildered, realized that the Lady's robot body

seemed more human than ever. The robot-sergeant confronted her.

This is the scene which we all remember, the first authentic picture tape of the entire incident:

The gold and black sergeant, his milky eyes staring at the Lady Panc Ashash.

The Lady herself, in the pleasant old robot body, lifting a commanding hand.

Elaine, distraught, half-turning as though she would grab the robot by his right arm. Her head is moving so rapidly that her black hair swings as she turns.

Charley-is-my-darling shouting, "I love, love, love!" at a small handsome man with mouse-colored hair. The man is gulping and saying nothing.

All this we know.

Then comes the unbelievable, which we now believe, the event for which the stars and skylanes were unprepared.

Mutiny.

Robot mutiny.

Disobedience in open daylight.

The words are hard to hear on the tape, but we can still make them out. The recording device on the police ornithopter had gotten a square fix on the face of the Lady Panc Ashash. Lip-readers can see the words plainly; non-lip readers can hear the words the third or fourth time the tape is run through the eyebox.

Said the Lady, "Overridden."

Said the sergeant, "No, you're a robot."

"See for yourself. Read my brain. I am a robot. I am also a woman. You cannot disobey people. I am people. I love you. Furthermore, you are people. You think. We love each other. Try. Try to attack."

"I—I cannot," said the robot sergeant, his milky eyes seeming to spin with excitement. "You love me? You mean I'm *alive? I exist?*"

"With love, you do," said the Lady Panc Ashash. "Look at

her," said the Lady, pointing to Joan, "because she has brought you love."

The robot looked and disobeyed the law. His squad looked with him.

He turned back to the Lady and bowed to her: "Then you know what we must do, if we cannot obey you and cannot disobey the others."

"Do it," she said sadly, "but know what you are doing. You are not really escaping two human commands. You are making a choice. You. That makes you men."

The sergeant turned to his squad of man-sized robots: "You hear that? She says we are men. I believe her. Do you believe her?"

"We do," they cried almost unanimously.

This is where the picture-tape ends, but we can imagine how the scene was concluded. Elaine had stopped short, just behind the sergeant-robot. The other robots had come up behind her. Charley-is-my-darling had stopped talking. Joan was in the act of lifting her hands in blessing, her warm brown dog eyes gone wide with pity and understanding.

People wrote down the things that we cannot see.

Apparently the robot-sergeant said, "Our love, dear people, and good-by. We disobey and die." He waved his hand to Joan. It is not certain whether he did or did not say, "Goodby, our lady and our liberator." Maybe some poet made up the second saying; the first one, we are sure about. And we are sure about the next word, the one which historians and poets all agree on. He turned to his men and said, "Destruct."

Fourteen robots, the black-and-gold sergeant and his thirteen silver-blue foot soldiers, suddenly spurted white fire in the street of Kalma. They detonated their suicide buttons, thermite caps in their own heads. They had done something with no human command at all, on an order from another robot, the body of the Lady Panc Ashash, and she in turn had no human authority but merely the word of the little dog-girl Joan, who had been made an adult in a single night.

Fourteen white flames made people and underpeople turn their eyes aside. Into the light there dropped a special police ornithopter. Out of it came the two Ladies, Arabella Underwood and Goroke. They lifted their forearms to shield their eyes from the blazing dying robots. They did not see the Hunter, who had moved mysteriously into an open window above the street and who watched the scene by putting his hands over his eyes and peeking through the slits between his fingers. While the people still stood blinded, they felt the fierce telepathic shock of the mind of the Lady Goroke taking command of the situation. That was her right, as a Chief of the Instrumentality. Some of the people, but not all of them, felt the outre countershock of Joan's mind reaching out to meet the Lady Goroke.

"I command," thought the Lady Goroke, her mind kept open to all beings.

"Indeed you do, but I love, I love you," thought Joan.

The first-order forces met.

They engaged.

The revolution was over. Nothing had really happened, but Joan had forced people to meet her. This was nothing like the poem about people and underpeople getting all mixed up. The mixup came much later, even after the time of C'mell. The poem is pretty, but it is dead wrong, as you can see for yourself:

> You should ask me,
>   Me, me, me,
> Because I know—
> I used to live
>   On the Eastern Shore.
> Men aren't men,
> And women aren't women,
> And people aren't people any more.

There is no Eastern Shore on Fomalhaut III anyhow; the people/underpeople crisis came much later than this. The revolution had failed, but history had reached its new turning-point, the quarrel of the two Ladies. They left their minds open out of sheer surprise. Suicidal robots and world-loving dogs were unheard of. It was bad enough to have illegal underpeople on the prowl, but these new things—ah!

Destroy them all, said the Lady Goroke.

"Why?" thought the Lady Arabella Underwood.

Malfunction, replied Goroke.

"But they're not machines!"

Then they're animals—underpeople. Destroy! Destroy!

Then came the answer which has created our own time. It came from the Lady Arabella Underwood, and all Kalma heard it:

Perhaps they are people. They must have a trial.

The dog-girl Joan dropped to her knees. "I have succeeded, I have succeeded, I have succeeded! You can kill me, dear people, but I love, love, love you!"

The Lady Panc Ashash said quietly to Elaine, "I thought I would be dead by now. Really dead, at last. But I am not. I have seen the worlds turn, Elaine, and you have seen them turn with me."

The underpeople had fallen quiet as they heard the high-volume telepathic exchange between the two great Ladies.

The real soldiers dropped out of the sky, their ornithopters whistling as they hawked down to the ground. They ran up to the underpeople and began binding them with cord.

One soldier took a single look at the robot body of the Lady Panc Ashash. He touched it with his staff, and the staff turned cherry-red with heat. The robot-body, its head suddenly drained, fell to the ground in a heap of icy crystals.

Elaine walked between the frigid rubbish and the red-hot staff. She had seen Hunter.

She missed seeing the soldier who came up to Joan, started to bind her and then fell back weeping, babbling, "She loves me! She loves me!"

The Lord Femtiosex, who commanded the inflying soldiers, bound Joan with cord despite her talking.

Grimly he answered her; "Of course you love me. You're a good dog. You'll die soon, doggy, but till then, you'll obey."

"I'm obeying," said Joan, "but I'm a dog *and* a person. Open your mind, man, and you'll feel it."

Apparently he did open his mind and felt the ocean of love riptiding into him. It shocked him. His arm swung up and back, the edge of the hand striking at Joan's neck for the ancient kill.

"No, you don't," thought the Lady Arabella Underwood. "That child is going to get a proper trial."

He looked at her and glared. Chief doesn't strike Chief, my Lady. Let go my arm.

Thought the Lady Arabella at him, openly and in public: "A trial, then."

In his anger he nodded at her. He would not think or speak to her in the presence of all the other people.

A soldier brought Elaine and Hunter before him. "Sir and master, these are people, not underpeople. But they have dog-thoughts, cat-thoughts, goat-thoughts and robot-ideas in their heads. Do you wish to look?"

"Why look?" said the Lord Femtiosex, who was as blond as the ancient pictures of Baldur, and oftentimes that arrogant as well. "The Lord Limaono is arriving. That's all of us. We can have the trial here and now."

Elaine felt cords bite into her wrists; she heard the Hunter murmur comforting words to her, words which she did not quite understand.

"They will not kill us," he murmured, "though we will wish they had, before this day is out. Everything is happening as she said it would, and—"

"Who is that she?" interrupted Elaine.

"She? The lady, of course. The dear dead Lady Panc Ashash, who has worked wonders after her own death, merely with the print of her personality on the machine. Who do you think told me what to do? Why did we wait for you to condition Joan to greatness? Why did the people way down in Clown Town keep on raising one D'joan after another, hoping that hope and a great wonder would occur?"

"You knew?" said Elaine. "You knew ... before it happened?"

"Of course," said the Hunter, "not exactly, but more or less. She had had hundreds of years after death inside that computer. She had time for billions of thoughts. She saw how it would be if it had to be, and I—"

"Shut up, you people!" roared the Lord Femtiosex. "You are making the animals restless with your babble. Shut up, or I will stun you!"

Elaine fell silent.

The Lord Femtiosex glanced around at her, ashamed at having made his anger naked before another person. He added quietly: "The trial is about to begin. The one that the tall lady ordered."

IX

You all know about the trial, so there is no need to linger over it. There is another picture of San Shigonanda, the one from his conventional period, which shows it very plainly.

The street had filled full of real people, crowding together to see something which would ease the boredom of perfection and time. They all had numbers or number-codes instead of names. They were handsome, well, dully happy. They even looked a great deal alike, similar in their handsomeness, their health and their underlying boredom. All of them had a total of four hundred years to live. None of them knew real war, even though the extreme readiness of the soldiers showed vain practice of hundreds of years. The people were beautiful, but they felt themselves useless, and they were quietly desperate without knowing it themselves. This is all clear from the painting, and from the wonderful way that San Shigonanda has of forming them in informal ranks and letting the calm blue light of day shine down on their handsome, hopeless features.

With the underpeople, the artist performs real wonders.

Joan herself is bathed in light. Her light brown hair and her doggy brown eyes express softness and tenderness. He even conveys the idea that her new body is terribly new and strong, that she is virginal and ready to die, that she is a mere girl and yet completely fearless. The posture of love shows in her legs: she stands lightly. Love shows in her hands: they are turned outward toward the judges. Love shows in her smile: it is confident.

And the judges!

The artist has them, too. The Lord Femtiosex, calm again, his narrow sharp lips expressing perpetual rage against a universe which has grown too small for him. The Lord Limaono, wise, twice-reborn, sluggardly, but alert as a snake behind the sleepy eyes and the slow smile. The Lady Arabella Underwood, the tallest true-human present, with her Norstrilian pride and the arrogance of great wealth, along with the capricious tenderness of great wealth, showing in the way that she sat, judging her fellow judges instead of the prisoners. The Lady Goroke, bewildered at last, frowning at a play of fortune which she does not understand. The artist has it all.

And you have the real viewtapes, too, if you want to go to a museum. The reality is not as dramatic as the famous painting, but it has value of its own. The voice of Joan, dead these many centuries, is still strangely moving. It is the voice of a dog-carved-into-man, but it is also the voice of a great lady. The image of the Lady Panc Ashash must have taught her that, along with what she had learned from Elaine and Hunter in the antechamber above the Brown and Yellow Corridor of Englok.

The words of the trial, they too have survived. Many of them have become famous, all across the worlds.

Joan said, during inquiry, "But it is the duty of life to find more than life, and to exchange itself for that higher goodness."

Joan commented, upon sentence. "My body is your property, but my love is not. My love is my own, and I shall love you fiercely while you kill me."

When the soldiers had killed Charley-is-my-darling and were trying to hack off the head of the S'woman until one of them thought to freeze her into crystals, Joan said:

"Should we be strange to you, we animals of earth that you have brought to the stars? We shared the same sun, the same oceans, the same sky. We are all from Manhome. How do you know that we would not have caught up with you if we had all stayed at home together? My people were dogs. They loved you before you made a woman-shaped thing out of my mother. Should I not love you still? The miracle is not that you have made people out of us. The miracle is that it took us so long to understand it. We are people now, and so are you. You will be sorry for what you are going to do to me, but remember that I shall love your sorrow, too, because great and good things will come out of it."

The Lord Limaono slyly asked, "What is a 'miracle'?"

And her words were, "There is knowledge from Earth which you have not yet found again. There is the name of the Nameless one. There are secrets hidden in time from you. Only the dead and the unborn can know them right now: I am both."

The scene is familiar, and yet we will never understand it.

We know what the lords Femtiosex and Limaono thought they were doing. They were maintaining established order and they were putting it on tape. The minds of men can live together only if the basic ideas are communicated. Nobody has, even now, found out a way of recording telepathy directly into an instrument. We get pieces and snatches and wild jumbles, but we never get a satisfactory record of what one of the great ones was transmitting to another. The two male chiefs were trying to put on record all those things about the episode which would teach careless people not to play with the lives of the underpeople. They were even trying to make underpeople understand the rules and designs by virtue of which they had been transformed from animals into the highest servants of man. This would have been hard to do, given the bewildering events of the last few hours, even from one Chief of the Instrumentality to another; for the general public, it was almost impossible. The outpouring from the Brown and Yellow Corridor was wholly unexpected, even though the Lady Goroke had surprised D'joan; the mutiny of the robot police posed problems which would have to be discussed halfway across the galaxy. Furthermore, the dog-girl was making points which had some verbal validity. If they were left in the form of mere words without proper context, they might affect heedless or impressionable minds. A bad idea can spread like a mutated germ. If it is at all interesting, it can leap from one mind to another halfway across the universe before it has a stop put to it. Look at the ruinous fads and foolish fashions which have nuisanced mankind even in the ages of the highest orderliness. We today know that variety, flexibility, danger and the seasoning of a little hate can make love and life bloom as they never bloomed before; we know it is better to live with the complications of thirteen thousand old languages resurrected from the dead ancient past than it is to live with the cold blind-alley perfection of the Old Common Tongue. We know a lot of things which the Lords Femtiosex and Limaono did not, and before we consider them stupid or cruel, we must remember that centuries passed before mankind finally came to grips with the problem of the underpeople and decided what "life" was within the limits of the human community.

Finally, we have the testimony of the two Lords themselves. They both lived to very advanced ages, and toward the end of their lives they were worried and annoyed to find that the episode of D'joan overshadowed all the bad things which had not happened during their long careers—bad things which had labored to forestall for the protection of the planet Fomalhaut III—and they were distressed to see themselves portrayed as casual, cruel men when in fact they were nothing of the sort. If they had seen that the story of Joan on Fomalhaut III would get to be what it is today—one of the great romances of mankind, along with the story of C'mell or the romance of the lady who sailed *The Soul*—they would not only have been disappointed, but they would have been justifiably angry at the fickleness of mankind as well. Their roles are clear, because they made them clear. The Lord Femtiosex accepts the responsibility for the notion of fire; the Lord Limaono agrees that he concurred in the decision. Both of them, many years later, reviewed the tapes of the scene and agreed that something which the Lady Arabella Underwood had said or thought—

Something had made them do it.

But even with the tapes to refresh and clarify their memories, they could not say what.

We have even put computers on the job of cataloguing every word and every inflection of the whole trial, but they have not pinpointed the critical point either.

And the Lady Arabella—nobody ever questioned her. They didn't dare. She went back to her own planet of Old North Australia, surrounded by the immense treasure of the santaclara drug, and no planet is going to pay at the rate of two thousand million credits a day for the privilege of sending an investigator to talk to a lot of obstinate, simple, wealthy Norstrilian peasants who will not talk to offworlders anyhow. The Norstrilians charge that sum for the admission of any guest not selected by their own invitation; so we will never know what the lady Arabella Underwood said or did after she went home. The Norstrilians said they did not wish to discuss the matter, and if we do not wish to go back to living a mere seventy years we had better not anger the only planet which produces stroon.

And the Lady Goroke—she, poor thing, went mad.

People did not know it till later, but there was no word to be gotten out of her. She performed the odd actions which we now know to be a part of the dynasty of Lords Jestocost, who forced themselves by diligence and merit upon the Instrumentality for two hundred and more years. But on the case of Joan she had nothing to say.

The trial is therefore a scene about which we know everything—and nothing.

We think that we know the physical facts of the life of D'joan who became Joan. We know about the Lady Panc Ashash who whispered endlessly to the underpeople about a justice yet to come. We know the whole life of the unfortunate Elaine and of her involvement with the case. We know that there were in those centuries, when underpeople first developed, many warrens in which illegal underpeople used their near-human wits, their animal cunning and their gift of speech to survive even when mankind had declared them surplus. The Brown and Yellow Corridor was not by any means the only one of its kind. We even know what happened to the Hunter.

For the other underpeople—Charley-is-my-darling, Baby-baby, Mabel, the S'woman, Orson and all the others—we have the tapes of the trial itself. They were not tried by anybody. They were put to death by the soldiers on the spot, as soon as it was plain that their testimony would not be needed. As witnesses, they could live a few minutes or an hour; as animals, they were already outside the regulations.

Ah, we know all about that now, and yet know nothing. Dying is simple, though we tend to hide it away. The *how* of dying is a minor scientific matter; the when of dying is a problem to each of us, whether he lives on the old-fashioned 400-year-life planets or on the radical new ones where the freedoms of disease and accident have been reintroduced; the *why* of it is still as shocking to us as it was to pre-atomic man, who used to cover farmland with the boxed bodies of his dead. These underpeople died as no animals had ever died before. Joyfully.

One mother held her children up for the soldier to kill them all.

She must have been of rat origin, because she had sep-tuplets in closely matching form.

The tape shows us the picture of the soldier getting ready.

The rat-woman greets him with a smile and holds up her seven babies. Little blondes they are, wearing pink or blue bonnets, all of them with glowing cheeks and bright little blue eyes.

"Put them on the ground," said the soldier. "I'm going to kill you and them too." On the tape, we can hear the nervous peremptory edge of his voice. He added one word, as though he had already begun to think that he had to justify himself to these underpeople. "Orders," he added.

"It doesn't matter if I hold them, soldier. I'm their mother. They'll feel better if they die easily with their mother near. I love you, soldier. I love all people. You are my brother, even though my blood is rat blood and yours is human. Go ahead and kill them soldier. I can't even hurt you. Can't you understand it? *I love you, soldier.* We share a common speech, common hopes, common fears, and a common death. That is what Joan has taught us all. Death is not bad, soldier. It just comes badly, sometimes, but you will remember me after you have killed me and my babies. You will remember that I love you now—"

The soldier, we see on the tape, can stand it no longer. He clubs his weapon, knocks the woman down; the babies scatter on the ground. We see his booted heel rise up and crush down against their heads. We hear the wet popping sound of the little heads breaking, the sharp cut-off of the baby wails as they die. We get one last view of the rat-woman herself. She has stood up again by the time the seventh baby is killed. She offers her hand to the soldier to shake. Her face is dirty and bruised, a trickle of blood running down her left cheek. Even now, we know she is a rat, an underperson, a modified animal, a nothing. And yet we, even we across the centuries, feel that she had somehow become more of a person than we are—that she dies human and fulfilled. We know that she has triumphed over death: we have not.

We see the soldier looking straight at her with eerie horror, as though her simple love were some unfathomable device from an alien source.

We hear her next words on the tape:

"Soldier, I love all of you—"

His weapon could have killed her in a fraction of a second, if he had used it properly. But he didn't. He clubbed it and hit her, as though his heat-remover had been a wooden club and himself a wild man instead of part of the elite guard of Kalma.

We know what happens then.

She falls under his blows. She points. Points straight at Joan, wrapped in fire and smoke.

The rat-woman screams one last time, screams into the lens of the robot camera as though she were talking not to the soldier but to all mankind:

"You can't kill *her.* You can't kill love. I love you, soldier, love you. You can't kill *that.* Remember—"

His last blow catches her in the face.

She falls back on the pavement. He thrusts his foot, as we can see by the tape, directly on her throat. He leaps forward in an odd little jig, bringing his full weight down on her fragile neck. He swings while stamping downward, and we then see his face, full on in the camera.

It is the face of a weeping child, bewildered by hurt and shocked by the prospect of more hurt to come.

He had started to do his duty, and duty had gone wrong, all wrong.

Poor man. He must have been one of the first men in the new worlds who tried to use weapons against love. Love is a sour and powerful ingredient to meet in the excitement of battle.

All the underpeople died that way. Most of them died smiling, saying the word "love" or the name "Joan."

The bear-man Orson had been kept to the very end.

He died very oddly. He died laughing.

The soldier lifted his pellet-thrower and aimed it straight

at Orson's forehead. The pellets were 22 millimeters in diameter and had a muzzle velocity of only 125 meters per second. In that manner, they could stop recalcitrant robots or evil underpeople, without any risk of penetrating buildings and hurting the true people who might be inside, out of sight.

Orson looks, on the tape the robots made, as though he knows perfectly well what the weapon is. (He probably did. Underpeople used to live with the danger of a violent death hanging over them from birth until removal.) He shows no fear of it, in the pictures we have; he begins to laugh. His laughter is warm, generous, relaxed—like the friendly laughter of a happy foster-father who has found a guilty and embarrassed child, knowing full well that the child expects punishment but will not get it.

"Shoot, man. You can't kill me, man. I'm in your mind. I love you. Joan taught us. Listen man. There is no death. Not for love. Ho, ho, ho, poor fellow, don't be afraid of me. Shoot! You're the unlucky one. You're going to live. And remember. And remember. And remember. I've made you human, fellow."

The soldier croaks, "What did you say?"

"I'm saving you, man. I'm turning you into a real human being. With the power of Joan. The power of love. Poor guy! go ahead and shoot me if it makes you uncomfortable to wait. You'll do it anyhow."

This time we do not see the soldier's face, but the tightness of his back and neck betray his own internal stress.

We see the big broad bear face blossom forth in an immense splash of red as the soft heavy pellets plow into it.

Then the camera turns to something else.

A little boy, probably a fox, but very finished in his human shape.

He was bigger than a baby, but not big enough, like the larger underchildren, to have understood the deathless importance of Joan's teaching.

He was the only one of the group who behaved like an ordinary underperson. He broke and ran.

He was clever: He ran among the spectators, so that the soldier could not use pellets or heat-reducers on him without hurting an actual human being. He ran and jumped and dodged, fighting passively but desperately for his life.

At last one of the spectators—a tall man with a silver hat —tripped him up. The fox-boy fell to the pavement, skinning his palms and knees. Just as he looked up to see who might be coming at him, a bullet caught him neatly in the head. He fell a little way forward, dead.

People die. We know how they die. We have seen them die shy and quiet in the Dying Houses. We have seen others go into the 400-year-rooms, which have no door-knobs and no cameras on the inside. We have seen pictures of many dying in natural disasters, where the robot crews took picture-tapes for the record and the investigation later on. Death is not uncommon, and it is very unpleasant.

But this time, death itself was different. All the fear of death—except for the one little fox-boy, too young to understand and too old to wait for death in his mother's arms—had gone out of the underpeople. They met death willingly, with love and calmness in their bodies, their voices, their demeanor. It did not matter whether they lived long enough to know what happened to Joan herself: they had perfect confidence in her, anyway.

This indeed was the new weapon, love and the good death.

Crawlie, with her pride, had missed it all.

The investigators later found the body of Crawlie in the corridor. It was possible to reconstruct who she had been and what had happened to her. The computer in which the bodiless image of Lady Panc Ashash survived for a few days after the trial was, of course, found and disassembled. Nobody thought at the time to get her opinions and last words. A lot of historians have gnashed their teeth over that.

The details are therefore clear. The archives even preserve the long interrogation and responses concerning Elaine, when she was processed and made clear after the trial. But we do not know how the idea of "fire" came in.

Somewhere, beyond sight of the tape-scanner, the word must have been passed between the four Chiefs of the Instrumentality who were conducting the trial. There is the protest of the Head of Birds (Robot), or police chief of Kalma, a Subchief named Fisi.

The records show his appearance. He comes in at the right side of the scene, bows respectfully to the four Chiefs and lifts his right hand in the traditional sign for "beg to interrupt," an odd twist of the elevated hand which the actors have found it very difficult to copy when they tried to put the whole story of Joan and Elaine into a single drama. (In fact, he had no more idea that future ages would be studying his casual appearance than did the others. The whole episode was characterized by haste and precipitateness, in the light of what we now know.) The Lord Limaono says:

"Interruption refused. We are making a decision."

The Chief of Birds spoke up anyhow.

"My words are for your decision, my Lords and my Ladies."

"Say it, then," commanded the Lady Goroke, "but be brief."

"Shut down the viewers. Destroy that animal. Brainwash the spectators. Get amnesia yourselves, for this one hour. This whole scene is dangerous. I am nothing but a supervisor of ornithopters, keeping perfect order, but I—"

"We have heard enough," said the Lord Femtiosex. "You manage your birds and we'll run the worlds. How do you dare to think 'like a Chief'? We have responsibilities which you can't even guess at. Stand back."

Fisi, in the pictures, stands back, his face sullen. In that particular frame of scenes, one can see some of the spectators going away. It was time for lunch and they had become hungry; they had no idea that they were going to miss the greatest atrocity in history, about which a thousand and more grand operas would be written.

Femtiosex then moved to the climax. "More knowledge, not less, is the answer to this problem. I have heard about something which is not as bad as the Planet Shayol, but which can do just as well for an exhibit on a civilized world. You there," said he to Fisi, the Chief of Birds, "bring oil and a spray. Immediately."

Joan looked at him with compassion and longing, but she said nothing. She suspected what he was going to do. As a girl, as a dog, she hated it; as a revolutionary, she welcomed it as the consummation of her mission.

The Lord Femtiosex lifted his right hand. He curled the ring finger and the little finger, putting his thumb over them. That left the first two fingers extended straight out. At that time, the sign from one Chief to another, meaning, "private channels, telepathic, immediate." It has since been adopted by underpeople as their emblem for political unity.

The four Chiefs went into a tracelike state and shared the judgment.

Joan began to sing in a soft, protesting, dog-like wail, using the off-key plainsong which the underpeople had sung just before their hour of decision when they left the Brown and Yellow Corridor. Her words were nothing special, repetitions of the "people, dear people, I love you" which she had been communicating ever since she came to the surface of Kalma. But the way she did it was defied imitation across the centuries. There are thousands of lyrics and melodies which call themselves, one way and another, "The Song of Joan," but none of them come near to the heart-wrenching pathos of the original tapes. The singing, like her own personality, was unique.

The appeal was deep. Even the real people tried to listen, shifting their eyes from the four immobile Chiefs of the Instrumentality to the brown-eyed singing girl. Some of them just could not stand it. In true human fashion, they forgot why they were there and went absent-mindedly home to lunch.

Suddenly Joan stopped.

Her voice ringing clearly across the crowd, she cried out: "The end is near, dear people. The end is near."

Eyes all shifted to the two Lords and the two Ladies of the

Instrumentality. The Lady Arabella Underwood looked grim after the telepathic conference. The Lady Goroke was haggard with wordless grief. The two Lords looked severe and resolved.

It was the Lord Femtiosex who spoke.

"We have tried you, animal. Your offense is great. You have lived illegally. For that the penalty is death. You have interfered with robots in some manner which we do not understand. For that brand-new crime, the penalty should be more than death; and I have recommended a punishment which was applied on a planet of the Violet Star. You have also said many unlawful and improper things, detracting from the happiness and security of mankind. For that the penalty is reeducation, but since you have two death sentences already, this does not matter. Do you have anything to say before I pronounce sentence?"

"If you light a fire today, my lord, it will never be put out in the hearts of men. You can destroy me. You can reject my love. You cannot destroy the goodness in yourselves, no matter how much goodness may anger you—"

"Shut up!" he roared. "I asked for a plea, not a speech. You will die by fire, here and now. What do you say to that?"

"I love you, dear people."

Femtiosex nodded to the men of the Chief of Birds, who had dragged a barrel and a spray into the street in front of Joan.

"Tie her to that post," he commanded. "Spray her. Light her. Are the tape-makers in focus? We want this to be recorded and known. If tho underpeople try this again, they will see that mankind controls the worlds." He looked at Joan and his eyes seemed to go out of focus. In an unaccustomed voice he said, "I am not a bad man, little dog-girl, but you are a bad animal and we must make an example of you. Do you understand that?"

"Femtiosex," she cried, leaving out his title, "I am very sorry for you. I love you too."

With these words of hers, his face became clouded and

angry again. He brought his right hand down in a chopping gesture.

Fisi copied the gesture and the men operating the barrel and spray began to squirt a hissing stream of oil on Joan. Two guards had already chained her to the lamp post, using an improvised chain of handcuffs to make sure that she stood upright and remained in plain sight of the crowd.

"Fire," said Femtiosex.

Elaine felt the Hunter's body, beside her, cramp sharply. He seemed to strain intensely. For herself, she felt the way she had felt when she was defrozen and taken out of the adiabatic pod in which she had made the trip from earth—sick to her stomach, confused in her mind, emotions rocking back and forth inside her.

Hunter whispered to her, "I tried to reach her mind so that she would die easy. Somebody else got there first. I . . . don't know who it is."

Elaine stared.

The fire was being brought. Suddenly it touched the oil and Joan flamed up like a human torch.

X

The burning of D'joan at Fomalhaut took very little time, but the ages will not forget it.

Femtiosex had taken the cruelest step of all.

By telepathic invasion he had suppressed her human mind, so that only the primitive canine remained.

Joan did not stand still like a martyred queen.

She struggled against the flames which licked her and climbed her. She howled and shrieked like a dog in pain, like an animal whose brain—good though it is—cannot comprehend the senselessness of human cruelty.

The result was directly contrary to what the Lord Femtiosex had planned.

The crowd of people stirred forward, not with curiosity but

because of compassion. They had avoided the broad areas of the street on which the dead underpeople lay as they had been killed, some pooled in their own blood, some broken by the hands of robots, some reduced to piles of frozen crystal. They walked over the dead to watch the dying, but their watching was not the witless boredom of people who never see a spectacle; it was the movement of living things, instinctive and deep, toward the sight of another living thing in a position of danger and ruin.

Even the guard who had held Elaine and Hunter by gripping Hunter's arm—even he moved forward a few unthinking steps. Elaine found herself in the first row of the spectators, the acrid, unfamiliar smell of burning oil making her nose twitch, the howls of the dying dog-girl tearing through her eardrums into her brain. Joan was turning and twisting in the fire now, trying to avoid the flames which wrapped her tighter than clothing. The odor of something sickening and strange reached the crowd. Few of them had ever smelled the stink of burning meat before.

Joan gasped.

In the ensuing seconds of silence, Elaine heard something she had never expected to hear before— the weeping of grown human beings. Men and women stood there sobbing and not knowing why they sobbed.

Femtiosex loomed over the crowd, obsessed by the failure of his demonstration. He did not know that the Hunter, with a thousand kills behind him, was committing the legal outrage of peeping the mind of a Chief of the Instrumentality.

The Hunter whispered to Elaine, "In a minute I'll try it. She deserves something better than that ..."

Elaine did not ask what. She too was weeping.

The whole crowd became aware that a soldier was calling. It took them several seconds to look away from the burning, dying Joan.

The soldier was an ordinary one. Perhaps he was the one who had been unable to tie Joan with bonds a few minutes ago, when the Lords decreed that she be taken into custody.

He was shouting now, shouting frantically and wildly, shaking his fist at the Lord Femtiosex. "You're a liar, you're a coward, you're a fool, and I challenge you—"

The Lord Femtiosex became aware of the man and of what he was yelling. He came out of his deep concentration and said, mildly for so wild a time: "What do you mean?"

"This is a crazy show. There is no girl here. No fire. Nothing. You are hallucinating the whole lot of us for some horrible reason of your own, and I'm challenging you for it, you animal, you fool, you coward."

In normal times even a Lord had to accept a challenge or adjust the matter with clear talk.

This was no normal time.

The Lord Femtiosex said, "All this is real. I deceive no one."

"If it's real, Joan, I'm with you!" shrieked the young soldier. He jumped in front of the jet of oil before the other soldiers could turn it off and then he leapt into the fire beside Joan.

Her hair had burned away but her features were still clear. She had stopped the doglike whining shriek. Femtiosex had been interrupted. She gave the soldier, who had begun to burn as he stood voluntarily beside her, the smiles. Then she frowned, the gentlest and most feminine of smiles. Then she frowned, as though there were something which she should remember to do, despite the pain and terror which surrounded her.

"Now!" whispered the Hunter. He began to hunt the Lord Femtiosex as sharply as he had ever sought the alien, native minds of Fomalhaut III.

The crowd could not tell what had happened to the Lord Femtiosex. Had he turned coward? Had he gone mad? (Actually, the Hunter, by using every gram of the power of his mind, had momentarily taken Femtiosex courting in the skies; he and Femtiosex were both male bird-like beasts, singing wildly for the beautiful female who lay hidden in the landscape far, far below.)

Joan was free, and she knew she was free.

She sent out her message. It knocked both Hunter and Femtiosex out of thinking; it flooded Elaine; it made even Fisi, the Chief of Birds, breathe quietly. She called so loudly that within the hour messages were pouring in from the other cities to Kalma, asking what had happened. She thought a single message, not words. But in words it came to this:

"Loved ones, you kill me. This is my fate. I bring love, and love must die to live on. Love asks nothing, does nothing. Love thinks nothing. Love is knowing yourself and knowing all other people and things. Know—and rejoice. I die for all of you now, dear ones—"

She opened her eyes for a last time, opened her mouth, sucked in the raw flame and slumped forward. The soldier, who had kept his nerve while his clothing and body burned, ran out of the fire, afire himself, toward his squad. A shot stopped him and he pitched flat forward.

The weeping of the people was audible throughout the streets. Underpeople, tame and licensed ones, stood shamelessly among them and wept too.

The Lord Femtiosex turned wearily back to his colleagues.

The face of Lady Goroke was a sculptured, frozen caricature of sorrow.

He turned to the Lady Arabella Underwood. "I seem to have done something wrong, my lady. Take over, please."

The Lady Arabella stood up. She called to Fisi, "Put out that fire."

She looked out over the crowd. Her hard, honest Norstrilian features were unreadable. Elaine, watching her, shivered at the thought of a whole planet full of people as tough, obstinate and clever as these.

"It's over," said the Lady Arabella. "People, go away. Robots, clean up. Underpeople, to your jobs."

She looked at Elaine and the Hunter. "I know who you are and I suspect what you have been doing. Soldiers, take them away."

The body of Joan was fire-blackened. The face did not look

particularly human any more; the last burst of fire had caught her in the nose and eyes. Her young, girlish breasts showed with heart-wrenching immodesty that she had been young and female once. Now she was dead, just dead.

The soldiers would have shoveled her into a box if she had been an underperson. Instead, they paid her the honors of war that they would have given to one of their own comrades or to an important civilian in time of disaster. They unslung a litter, put the little blackened body on it and covered the body with their own flag. No one had told them to do so.

As their own soldier led them up the road toward the Waterrock, where the houses and offices of the military were located, Elaine saw that he too had been crying.

She started to ask him what he thought of it, but Hunter stopped her with a shake of the head. He later told her that the soldier might be punished for talking with them.

When they got to the office, they found the Lady Goroke already there.

The Lady Goroke already there . . . It became a nightmare in the weeks that followed. She had gotten over her grief and was conducting an inquiry into the case of Elaine and D'joan.

The Lady Goroke already there . . . She was waiting when they slept. Her image, or perhaps herself, sat in on all the endless interrogations. She was particularly interested in the chance meeting of the dead Lady Panc Ashash, the misplaced witch Elaine, and the non-adjusted man, the Hunter.

The Lady Goroke already there . . . She asked them everything, but she told them nothing.

Except for once.

Once she burst out, violently personal after endless hours of formal, official work, "Your minds will be cleansed when we get through, so it wouldn't matter how much else you know. Do you know that this has hurt me—me!—all the way to the depths of everything I believe in?"

They shook their heads.

"I'm going to have a child, and I'm going back to Manhome to have it. And I'm going to do the genetic coding myself. I'm going to call him Jestocost. That's one of the Ancient Tongues, the Paroskii one, for 'cruelty,' to remind him where he comes from, and why. And he, or his son, or *his* son will bring justice back into the world and solve the puzzle of the underpeople. What do you think of that? On second thought, don't think. It's none of your business, and I am going to do it anyway."

They stared at her sympathetically, but they were too wound up in the problems of their own survival to extend her much sympathy or advice. The body of Joan had been pulverized and blown into the air, because the Lady Goroke was afraid that the underpeople would make a *goodplace* out of it; she felt that way herself, and she knew that if she herself were tempted, the underpeople would be even more tempted.

Elaine never knew what happened to the bodies of all the other people who had turned themselves, under Joan's leadership, from animals into mankind, and who had followed the wild, foolish march out of the Tunnel of Englok into the Upper City of Kalma. Was it really wild? Was it really foolish? If they had stayed where they were, they might have had a few days or months or years of life, but sooner or later the robots would have found them and they would have been exterminated like the vermin which they were. Perhaps the death they had chosen was better. Joan *did* say, "It's the mission of life always to look for something better than itself, and then to try to trade life itself for meaning."

At last, the Lady Goroke called them in and said, "Good-by, you two. It's foolish, saying good-by, when an hour from now you will remember neither me nor Joan. You've finished your work here. I've set up a lovely job for you. You won't have to live in a city. You will be weather-watchers, roaming the hills and watching for all the little changes which the machines can't interpret fast enough. You will have whole lifetimes of marching and picnicking and camping together.

I've told the technicians to be very careful, because you two are very much in love with each other. When they reroute your synapses, I want that love to be there with you."

They each knelt and kissed her hand. They never wittingly saw her again. In later years they sometimes saw a fashionable ornithopter soaring gently over their camp, with an elegant woman peering out of the side of it; they had no memories to know that it was the Lady Goroke, recovered from madness, watching over them.

Their new life was their final life.

Of Joan and the Brown and Yellow Corridor, nothing remained.

They were both very sympathetic toward animals, but they might have been this way even if they had never shared in the wild political gamble of the dear dead Lady Panc Ashash.

One time a strange thing happened. An underman from an elephant was working in a small valley, creating an exquisite rock garden for some important official of the Instrumentality who might later glimpse the garden once or twice a year. Elaine was busy watching the weather, and the Hunter had forgotten that he had ever hunted, so that neither of them tried to peep the underman's mind. He was a huge fellow, right at the maximum permissible size—five times the gross stature of a man. He had smiled at them friendlily in the past.

One evening he brought them fruit. Such fruit! Rare off-world items which a year of requests would not have obtained for ordinary people like them. He smiled his big, shy, elephant smile, put the fruit down and prepared to lumber off.

"Wait a minute," cried Elaine, "why are you giving us this? Why us?"

"For the sake of Joan," said the elephant man.

"Who's Joan?" said the Hunter.

The elephant man looked sympathetically at them. "That's all right. You don't remember her, but I do."

"But what did Joan do?" said Elaine.

"She loved you. She loved us all," said the elephant man. He turned quickly, so as to say no more. With incredible deftness for so heavy a person, he climbed speedily into the fierce lovely rocks above them and was gone.

"I wish we had known her," said Elaine. "She sounds very nice."

In that year there was born the man who was to be the first Lord Jestocost.

BRECKENRIDGE AND THE CONTINUUM

Robert Silverberg

An anthology of this sort is by definition a record of its compiler's personal preferences. As a reader, I am most excited by the kind of science fiction that offers conscious-ness-expanding views of wondrous reaches of space and time —fiction that creates myths about the future. Not surpris-ingly, in my own fiction I often attempt to create the sort of effects I most cherish when reading, and in such long works as Son of Man, Tower of Glass, Downward to the Earth, *and others I have offered my repayment for the pleasures science fiction has given me. To illustrate my personal preoccupation with the myth-making qualities of science fiction, however, I have selected a shorter and more recent work, a story that is in some ways homage to the structuralist theories of Claude Lévi-Strauss, but is primarily intended to convey*

*that quality of dreamlike clarity, of sharp-edged mythopoei-
sis, that for me is science fiction's most potent trait.*

THEN Breckenridge said, "I suppose I could tell you
the story of Oedipus King of Thieves tonight."

The late-afternoon sky was awful: gray, mottled, fierce. It
resonated with a strange electricity. Breckenridge had never
grown used to that sky. Day after day, as they crossed the
desert, it transfixed him with the pain of incomprehensible
loss.

"Oedipus King of Thieves," Scarp murmured. Arios nodded. Horn looked toward the sky. Militor frowned.
"Oedipus," said Horn. "King of Thieves," Arios said.

Breckenridge and his four companions were camped in a
ruined pavilion in the desert—a handsome place of granite
pillars and black marble floors, constructed perhaps for some
delicious paramour of some forgotten prince of the city-
building folk. The pavilion lay only a short distance outside
the walls of the great dead city that they would enter, at last,
in the morning. Once, maybe, this place had been a summer
resort, a place for sherbet and swimming, in that vanished
time when this desert had bloomed and peacocks had
strolled through fragrant gardens. A fantasy out of the *Thousand and One Nights:* long ago, long ago, thousands of years
ago. How confusing it was for Breckenridge to remember
that that mighty city, now withered by time, had been
founded and had thrived and had perished all in an era far
less ancient than his own. The bonds that bound the continuum had loosened. He flapped in the time-gales.

"Tell your story," Militor said.

They were restless; they nodded their heads, they shifted
positions. Scarp added fuel to the campfire. The sun was
dropping behind the bare low hills that marked the desert's
western edge; the day's smothering heat was suddenly rush-
ing skyward, and a thin wind whistled through the colonnade

of grooved gray pillars that surrounded the pavilion. Grains of pinkish sand danced in a steady stream across the floor of polished stone on which Breckenridge and those who traveled with him squatted. The lofty western wall of the nearby city was already sleeved in shadow.

Breckenridge drew his flimsy cloak closer around himself. He stared in turn at each of the four hooded figures facing him. He pressed his fingers against the cold smooth stone to anchor himself. In a low droning voice he said, "This Oedipus was monarch of the land of Thieves, and a bold and turbulent man. He conceived an illicit desire for Euridice his mother. Forcing his passions upon her, he grew so violent that in their coupling she lost her life. Stricken with guilt and fearing that her kinsmen would exact reprisals, Oedipus escaped his kingdom through the air, having fashioned wings for himself under the guidance of the magician Prospero; but he flew too high and came within the ambit of the chariot of his father Apollo, god of the sun. Wrathful over this intrusion, Apollo engulfed Oedipus in heat, and the wax binding the feathers of his wings was melted. For a full day and a night Oedipus tumbled downward across the heavens, plummeting finally into the ocean, sinking through the sea's floor into the dark world below. There he dwells for all eternity, blind and lame; but each spring he reappears among men, and as he limps across the fields green grasses spring up in his tracks."

There was silence. Darkness was overtaking the sky. The four rounded fragments of the shattered old moon emerged and commenced their elegant, baffling saraband, spinning slowly, soaking one another in shifting patterns of cool white light. In the north the glittering violet and green bands of the aurora flickered with terrible abruptness, like the streaky glow of some monstrous searchlight. Breckenridge felt himself penetrated by gaudy ions, roasting him to the core. He waited, trembling.

"Is that all?" Militor said eventually. "Is that how it ends?"

"There's no more to the story," Breckenridge replied. "Are you disappointed?"

"The meaning is obscure. Why the incest? Why did he fly too high? Why was his father angry? Why does Oedipus reappear every spring? None of it makes sense. Am I too shallow to comprehend the relationships? I don't believe that I am."

"Oh, it's old stuff," said Scarp. "The tale of the eternal return. The dead king bringing the new year's fertility. Surely you recognize it, Militor." The aurora flashed with redoubled frenzy, a coded beacon, crying out, SPACE AND TIME, SPACE AND TIME, SPACE AND TIME. "You should have been able to follow the outline of the story," Scarp said. "We've heard it a thousand times in a thousand forms."

—SPACE AND TIME—

"Indeed we have," Militor said. "But the components of any satisfying tale have to have some logical necessity of sequence, some essential connection." —SPACE— "What we've just heard is a mass of random floating fragments. I see the semblance of myth but not the inner truth."

—TIME—

"A myth holds truth," Scarp insisted, "no matter how garbled its form, no matter how many irrelevant interpolations have entered it. The interpolations may even be one species of truth, and not the lowest species at that."

The Dow-Jones Industrial Average, Breckenridge thought, closed today at 1100432.86—

"At any rate, he told it poorly," Arios observed. "No drama, no intensity, merely a bald outline of events. I've heard better from you on other nights, Breckenridge. Sheherazade and the Forty Giants—now, that was a story! Don Quixote and the Fountain of Youth, yes! But this—this—"

Scarp shook his head. "The strength of a myth lies in its content, not in the melody of its telling. I sense the inherent power of tonight's tale. I find it acceptable."

"Thank you," Breckenridge said quietly. He threw sour glares at Militor and Arios. It was hateful when they quibbled over the stories he told them. What gift did he have for these four strange beings, anyhow, except his stories? When they received that gift with poor grace they were denying him his sole claim to their fellowship.

A million years from nowhere . . .

SPACE—TIME

Apollo—Jesus—Apollo—

The wind grew chillier. No one spoke. Beasts howled on the desert. Breckenridge lay back, feeling an ache in his shoulders, and wriggled against the cold stone floor.

Merry my wife, Cassandra my daughter, Noel my son—

SPACE—TIME—

SPACE—

His eyes hurt from the aurora's frosty glow. He felt himself stretched across the cosmos, torn between then and now—breaking, breaking, ripping into fragments like the moon—

The stars had come out. He contemplated the early constellations. They were unfamiliar; no matter how often Scarp or Horn pointed out the patterns to him, he saw only random sprinklings of light. In his other life he had been able to identify at least the more conspicuous constellations, but they did not seem to be here. How long does it take to effect a complete redistribution of the heavens? A million years? Ten million? Thank God Mars and Jupiter still were visible, the orange dot and the brilliant white one, to tell him that this place was his own world, his own solar system. Images danced in his aching skull. He saw everything double, suddenly. There was Pegasus, there was Orion, there was Sagittarius. An overlay, a mask of realities superimposed on realities.

"Listen to this music," Horn said after a long while, producing a fragile device of wheels and spindles from beneath his cloak. He caressed it and delicate sounds came forth: crystalline, comforting, the music of dreams, sliding into the range of audibility with no perceptible instant of attack. Shortly Scarp began a wordless song, and, one by one, the others joined him, first Horn, then Militor, and lastly, in a dry, buzzing monotone, Arios.

"What are you singing?" Breckenridge asked.

"The hymn of Oedipus King of Thieves," Scarp told him.

Had it been such a bad life? He had been healthy, properous, and beloved. His father was managing partner of Falkner, Breckenridge & Co., one of the most stable of the Wall Street houses, and Breckenridge, after coming up through the ranks in the family tradition, putting in his time as a customer's man and his time in the bond department and as a floor trader, was a partner too, only ten years out of Dartmouth. What was wrong with that? His draw in 1972 was $83,500—not as much as he had hoped for out of a partnership, but not bad, not bad at all, and next year might be much better. He had a wife and two children, an apartment on East 73rd Street, a country cabin on Candlewood Lake, a fair-sized schooner that he kept in a Gulf Coast marina, and a handsome young mistress in an apartment of her own on the Upper West Side. What was wrong with that? When he burst through the fabric of the continuum and found himself in an unimaginably altered world at the end of time, he was astonished not that such a thing might happen but that it had happened to someone as settled and well-established as himself.

While they slept, a corona of golden light sprang into being along the top of the city wall. The glow awakened Breckenridge, and he sat up quickly, thinking that the city was on fire. But the light seemed cool and supple, and appeared to be propagated in easy rippling waves, more like the aurora than like the raw blaze of flames. It sprang from the very rim of the wall and leaped high, casting blurred, rounded shadows at cross-angles to the sharp crisp shadows that the fragmented moon created. There also seemed to be a deep segment of blackness in the side of the wall. Looking closely, Breckenridge saw that the huge gate on the wall's western face was standing open. Without telling the others, he left the camp and crossed the flat sandy wasteland, coming to the gate after a brisk march of about an hour. Nothing prevented him from entering.

Just within the wall was a wide cobbled plaza, and beyond that stretched broad avenues lined with buildings of a strange sort: rounded and rubbery, porous of texture, all humps and parapets. Black unfenced wells at the center of each major intersection plunged to infinite depths. Breckenridge had been told that the city was empty—that it had been uninhabited for centuries, since the spoiling of the climate in this part of the world—and so he was surprised to find it occupied. Pale figures flitted silently about, moving like wraiths, as though there were empty space between their feet and the pavement. He approached one and another and a third, but when he tried to speak no words would leave his lips. He seized one of the city dwellers by the wrist, a slender black-haired girl in a soft gray robe, and held her tightly, hoping that contact would lead to contact. Her dark somber eyes studied him without show of fear and she made no effort to break away. I am Noel Breckenridge, he said—Noel III— and I was born in the town of Greenwich, Connecticut, in the year of our lord 1940, my wife's name is Merry and my daughter is Cassandra and my son is Noel Breckenridge IV, and I am not as coarse or stupid as you may think me to be. She made no reply and showed no change of expression. He asked, Can you understand anything I'm saying to you? Her face remained wholly blank. He asked, Can you even hear the sound of my voice? There was no response. He went on: What is your name? What is this city called? When was it abandoned? What year is this on any calendar that I can comprehend? What do you know about me that I need to know? She continued to regard him in an altogether neutral way. He pulled her against his body and gripped her thin shoulders with his fingertips and kissed her urgently, forcing his tongue between her teeth. An instant later he found himself sprawled not far from the campsite with his face in the sand and sand in his mouth. Only a dream, he thought wearily, only a dream.

He was having lunch with Harry Munsey at the Merchants and Shippers Club: sleek chrome-and-redwood premises sixty stories above William Street in the heart of the financial district. Subdued light fixtures glowed like pulsing red suns; waiters moved past the tables like silent moons. The club was over a century old, although the skyscraper in which it occupied a penthouse suite had only been erected in 1968—its fourth home, or maybe its fifth. Membership was limited to white male Christians, sober and responsible, who held important positions in the New York securities industry. There was nothing in the club's written constitution which explicitly limited its membership to white male Christians, but, all the same, there had never been any members who had not been white, male, and Christian. No one with a firm grasp of reality thought there ever would be.

Harry Munsey, like Noel Breckenridge, was white, male, and Christian. They had gone to Dartmouth together and they had entered Wall Street together, Breckenridge going into his family's firm and Munsey into his, and they had lunch together almost every day and saw each other almost every Saturday night, and each had slept with the other's wife, though each believed that the other knew nothing about that.

On the third martini Munsey said, "What's bugging you today, Noel?"

A dozen years ago Munsey had been an all-Ivy halfback; he was a big, powerful man, bigger even than Breckenridge, who was not a small man. Munsey's face was pink and unlined and his eyes were alive and youthful, but he had lost all his hair before he turned thirty.

"Is something bugging me?"

"Something's bugging you, yes. Why else would you look so uptight after you've had two and a half martinis?"

Breckenridge had found it difficult to grow used to the sight of the massive bright dome that was Munsey's skull.

He said, "All right. So I'm bugged."

"Want to talk about it?"

"No."

"Okay," Munsey said.

Breckenridge finished his drink. "As a matter of fact, I'm oppressed by a sophomoric sense of the meaninglessness of life, if you have to know."

"Really?"

"Really."

"The meaninglessness of life?"

"Life is empty, dumb, and mechanical," Breckenridge said.

"*Your* life?"

"Life."

"I know a lot of people who'd like to live your life. They'd trade with you, even up, asset for asset, liability for liability, life for life."

Breckenridge shook his head. "They're fools, then."

"It's that bad?"

"It all seems so pointless, Harry. Everything. We have a good time and con ourselves into thinking it means something. But what is there, actually? The pursuit of money? I have enough money. After a certain point it's just a game. French restaurants? Trips to Europe? Drinking? Sex? Swimming pools? Jesus! We're born, we grow up, we do a lot of stuff, we grow old, we die. Is that all? Jesus, Harry, is that *all*?"

Munsey looked embarrassed. "Well, there's family," he suggested. "Marriage, fatherhood, knowing that you're linking yourself into the great chain of life. Bringing forth a new generation. Transmitting your ideals, your standards, your traditions, everything that distinguishes us from the apes we used to be. Doesn't that count?"

Shrugging, Breckenridge said, "All right. Having kids, you say. We bring them into the world, we wipe their noses, we teach them to be little men and women, we send them to the right schools and get them into the right clubs, and they grow up to be carbon copies of their parents: lawyers or brokers or clubwomen or whatever—"

The lights fluttering. The aurora: red, green, violet, red, green. The straining fabric; the moon, the broken moon; the aurora; the lights; the fire atop the walls—

"—or else they grow up and deliberately fashion themselves into the opposites of their parents, and somewhere along the way the parents die off, and the kids have kids, and the cycle starts around again. Around and around, generation after generation, Noel Breckenridge III, Noel Breckenridge IV, Noel Breckenridge XVI—"

Arios—Scarp—Militor—Horn—

The city—the gate—

"—making money, spending money, living high, building nothing real, just occupying space on the planet for a little while, and what for? What for? What does it all mean?"

The granite pillars—the aurora—SPACE AND TIME—

"You're on a bummer today, Noel," Munsey said.

"I know. Aren't you sorry you asked what was bugging me?"

"Not particularly. Everybody goes through a phase like this."

"When he's seventeen, yes."

"And later, too."

"It's more than a phase," Breckenridge said. "It's a sickness. If I had any guts, Harry, I'd drop out. Drop right out and try to work out some meanings in the privacy of my own head."

"Why don't you? You can afford it. Go on. Why not?"

"I don't know," said Breckenridge.

Such strange constellations. Such a terrible sky.

Such a cold wind blowing out of tomorrow.

"I think it may be time for another martini," Munsey said.

They had been crossing the desert for a long time now
—forty days and forty nights, Breckenridge liked to tell himself, but probably it had been longer than that—and they
moved at an unsparing pace, marching from dawn to sunset
with as few rest periods as possible. The air was thin. His
lungs felt leathery. Because he was the biggest man in the
group, he carried the heaviest pack. That didn't bother him.

What did bother him was how little he knew about this
expedition, its purposes, its origin, even how he had come to
be part of it. But asking such questions seemed somehow
naive and awkward, and he never did. He went along, doing
his share—making camp, cleaning up in the morning—and
tried to keep his companions amused with his stories. They
demanded stories from him every night. "Tell us your
myths," they urged. "Tell us the legends and fables you
learned in your childhood."

After weeks of sharing this trek with them he knew little
more about the other four than he had at the outset. His
favorite among them was Scarp, who was sympathetic and
flexible. He like the hostile, contemptuous Militor the least.
Horn—dreamy, poetic, unworldly, aloof—was beyond his
reach; Arios, the most dry and objective and scientific of the
group, did not seem worth trying to reach. So far as Breckenridge could determine they were human, although their
skins were oddly glossy and of a peculiar olive hue, something on the far side of swarthy. They had strange noses,
narrow, high-bridged noses of a kind he had never seen before, extremely fragile, like the noses of pure-bred society
women carried to the ultimate possibilities of their design.

The desert was beautiful. A gaudy desolation, all dunes and
sandy ripples, streaked blue and red and gold and green with
brilliant oxides.

Sometimes when the aurora was going full blast—SPACE!
TIME! *Space! Time!*—the desert seemed to be merely a mirror for the sky. But in the morning, when the electronic
furies of the aurora had died away, the sand still reverberated
with its own pulses of bright color.

And the sun—pale, remorseless—Apollo's deathless fires—
*I am Noel Breckenridge and I am nine years old and this
is how I spent my summer vacation—*
Oh Lord Jesus forgive me.

Scattered everywhere on the desert were outcroppings of
ancient ruins—colonnades, halls of statuary, guardposts, summer pavilions, hunting lodges, the stumps of antique walls,
and invariably the marchers made their camp beside one of
these. They studied each ruin, measured its dimensions,
recorded its salient details, poked at its sand-shrouded foun-
dations. Around Scarp's neck hung a kind of mechanized
map, a teardrop-shaped black instrument that could be made
to emit—

PING!

—sounds which daily guided them toward the next ruin in
the chain leading to the city. Scarp also carried a compact
humming machine that generated sweet water from hand-
fuls of sand. For solid food they subsisted on small yellow
pellets, quite tasty.

PING!

At the beginning Breckenridge had felt constant fatigue,
but under the grinding exertions of the march he had grown
steadily in strength and endurance, and now he felt he could
continue forever, never tiring, parading—

PING!

—endlessly back and forth across this desert which perhaps spanned the entire world. The dead city, though, was
their destination, and finally it was in view. They were to
remain there for an indefinite stay. He was not yet sure
whether these four were archaeologists or pilgrims. Perhaps
both, he thought. Or maybe neither. Or maybe neither.

"How do you think you can make your life more
meaningful, then?" Munsey asked.

"I don't know. I don't have any idea what would work for

me. But I do know who the people are whose lives *do* have meaning."

"Who?"

"The creators, Harry. The shapers, the makers, the begetters. Beethoven, Rembrandt, Dr. Salk, Einstein, Shakespeare, that bunch. It isn't enough just to live. It isn't even enough just to have a good mind, to think clear thoughts. You have to add something to the sum of humanity's accomplishments, something real, something valuable. You have to *give*. Mozart. Newton. Columbus. Those who are able to reach into the well of creation, into that hot boiling chaos of raw energy down there, and pull something out, shape it, make something unique and new out of it. Making money isn't enough. Making more Breckenridges or Munseys isn't enough, either. You know what I'm saying, Harry? The well of creation. The reservoir of life, which is God. Do you ever think you believe in God? Do you wake up in the middle of the night sometimes saying, Yes, yes, there *is* Something after all, I believe, I believe! I'm not talking about churchgoing now, you understand. Churchgoing's nothing but a conditioned reflex these days, a twitch, a tic. I'm talking about faith. Belief. The state of enlightenment. I'm not talking about God as an old man with long white whiskers, either, Harry. I mean something abstract, a force, a power, a current, a reservoir of energy underlying everything and connecting everything. God is that reservoir. That reservoir is God. I think of that reservoir as being something like the sea of molten lava down beneath the earth's crust: it's there, it's full of heat and power, it's accessible for those who know the way. Plato was able to tap into the reservoir. Van Gogh. Joyce. Schubert. El Greco. A few lucky ones know how to reach it. Most of us can't. Most of us can't. For those who can't, God is dead. Worse—for them, He never lived at all. Oh, Christ, how awful it is to be trapped in an era where everybody goes around like some sort of zombie, cut off from the energies of the spirit, ashamed even to admit there are such energies. I hate it. I hate the whole stinking twentieth century, do you know

that? Am I making any sense? Do I seem terribly drunk? Am
I embarrassing you, Harry? Harry? Harry?"

In the morning they struck camp and set out on the
final leg of their journey toward the city. The sand here had
a disturbing crusty quality: white saline outcroppings gave
Breckenridge the feeling that they were crossing a tundra
rather than a desert. The sky was clear and pale, and in its
bleached cloudlessness it took on something of the quality of
a shield, of a mirror, seizing the morning heat that rose from
the ground and hurling it inexorably back, so that the five
marchers felt themselves trapped in an infinite baffle of
unendurable dry smothering warmth.

As they moved cityward Militor and Arios chattered com-
pulsively, falling after a while into a quarrel over certain
obscure and controversial points of historical theory. Breckenridge had heard them have this argument at least a dozen
times in the last two weeks, and no doubt they had been
battling it out for years. The main area of contention was the
origin of the city. Who were its builders? Militor believed
they were colonists from some other planet—strangers to
Earth, representatives of some alien species of immeasurable
grandeur and nobility—who had crossed space thousands of
years ago to build this gigantic monument on Asia's flank.
Nonsense, retorted Arios: the city was plainly the work of
human beings, unusually gifted and energetic but human
nonetheless. Why multiply hypotheses needlessly? Here is
the city; humans have built many cities nearly as great as this
one in their long history; this city is only quantitatively superior to the others, merely a little bigger, merely a bit more
daringly conceived. To invoke extraterrestrial architects is to
dabble gratuitously in fantasy. But Militor maintained his
position. Humans, he said, were plainly incapable of such
immense constructions. Neither in this present decadent
epoch, when any sort of effort is too great, nor at any time
in the past, could human resources have been equal to such

a task as the building of this city must have been. Breckenridge had his doubts about that, having seen what the twentieth century had accomplished. He tended to side with
Arios. But indeed the city was extraordinary, Breckenridge
admitted: an ultimate urban glory, a supernal Babylon, a
consummate Persepolis, the soul's own hymn in brick and
stone. The wall that girdled it was at least two hundred feet
high—why pour so much energy into a wall? were no better
means of defense at hand, or was the wall mere exuberant
decoration?—and, judging by the easy angle of its curve, it
must be hundreds of miles in circumference. A city larger
than New York, more sprawling than even Los Angeles, a
giant antenna of turbulent consciousness set like a colossal
gem into this vast plain, a throbbing antenna for all the radi-
ance of the stars: yes, it was overwhelming, it was devastating
to contemplate the planning and the building of it; it seemed
almost to require the hypothesis of a superior alien race. And
yet he refused to accept that hypothesis. Arios, he thought,
I am with you.

The city was uninhabited, a hulk, a ruin. Why? What had
happened here to turn this garden plain into a salt-crusted
waste? The builders grew too proud, said Militor. They
defied the gods, they overreached even their own powers,
and stumbling, fell headlong into decay. The life went out of
the soil, the sky gave no rain, the spirit lost its energies; the
city perished and was forgotten, and was whispered about by
mythmakers, a city out of time, a city at the end of the world,
a mighty mass of dead wonders, a habitation for jackals, a
place where no one went. We are the first in centuries, said
Scarp, to seek this city.

Halfway between dawn and noon they reached the wall
and stood before the great gate. The gate alone was fifty feet
high, a curving slab of burnished blue metal set smoothly into
a recess in the tawny stucco of the wall. Breckenridge saw no
way of opening it, no winch, no portcullis, no handles, no
knobs. He feared that the impatient Militor would merely
blow a hole in it. But, groping along the base of the gate, they

found a small doorway, man-high and barely man-wide, near the left-hand edge. Ancient hinges yielded at a push. Scarp led the way inside.

The city was as Breckenridge remembered it from his dream: the cobbled plaza, the broad avenues, the humped and rubbery buildings. The fierce sunlight, deflected and refracted by the undulant roof lines, reverberated from every flat surface and rebounded in showers of brilliant energy. Breckenridge shaded his eyes. It was as though the sky were full of pulsars. His soul was frying on a cosmic griddle, cooking in a torrent of hard radiation.

The city was inhabited.

Faces were visible at windows. Elusive figures emerged at street corners, peered, withdrew. Scarp called to them; they shrank back into the hard-edged shadows.

"Well?" Arios demanded. "They're human, aren't they?"

"What of it?" said Militor. "Squatters, that's all. You saw how easy it was to push open that door. They've come in out of the desert to live in the ruins."

"Maybe not. Descendants of the builders, I'd say. Perhaps the city never really was abandoned." Arios looked at Scarp. "Don't you agree?"

"They might be anything," Scarp said. "Squatters, descendants, synthetics, even servants without masters, living on, waiting, living on, waiting—"

"Or projections cast by ancient machines," Militor said. "No human hand built this city."

Arios snorted. They advanced quickly across the plaza and entered onto the first of the grand avenues. The buildings flanking it were sealed. They proceeded to a major intersection, where they halted to inspect an open circular pit, fifteen feet in diameter, smooth-rimmed, descending into infinite darkness. Breckenridge had seen many such dark wells in his vision of the night before. He did not doubt now that he had left his sleeping body and had made an actual foray into the city last night.

Scarp flashed a light into the well. A copper-colored metal ladder was visible along one face.

"Shall we go down?" Breckenridge asked.

"Later," said Scarp.

The famous anthropologist had been drinking steadily all through the dinner party—wine, only wine, but plenty of it—and his eyes seemed glazed, his face flushed. Nevertheless, he continued to talk with superb clarity of perception and elegant precision of phrase, hardly pausing at all to construct his concepts. Perhaps he's merely quoting his own latest book from memory, Breckenridge thought as he strained to follow the flow of ideas. "—a comparison between myth and what appears to have largely replaced it in modern societies, namely, politics. When the historian refers to the French Revolution, it is always as a sequence of past happenings—a non-reversible series of events, the remote consequences of which may still be felt at present. But to the French politician, as well as to his followers, the French Revolution is both a sequence belonging to the past—as to the historian—and an everlasting pattern which can be detected in the present French social structure and which provides a clue for its interpretation, a lead from which to infer the future developments. See, for instance, Michelet, who was a politically-minded historian. He describes the French Revolution thus: 'This day . . . everything was possible . . . Future became present . . . that is, no more time, a glimpse of eternity.'" The great man reached decisively for another glass of claret. His hand wavered; the glass toppled; a dark red torrent stained the tablecloth. Breckenridge experienced a sudden terrifying moment of complete disorientation, as though the walls and floor were shifting places. He saw a parched desert plateau, four hooded figures, a blazing sky of strange constellations, a pulsating aurora sweeping the heavens with cold fire. A mighty walled city dominated the plain, and its frosty shadow, knifeblade-sharp, cut across Breckenridge's path. He shivered. The woman on Breckenridge's right laughed lightly and began to recite:

I saw Eternity the other night
Like a great ring of pure and endless light.
All calm, as it was bright;
And round beneath it, Time in hours, days, years,
Driv'n by the spheres
Like a vast shadow mov'd; in which the world
And all her train were hurl'd.

"Excuse me," Breckenridge said. "I think I'm unwell." He rushed from the dining room. In the hallway he turned toward the washroom and found himself staring into a steaming tropical marsh, all ferns and horsetails and giant insects. Dragonflies the size of pigeons whirred past him. The sleek rump of a brontosaurus rose like a bubbling aneurysm from the black surface of the swamp. Breckenridge recoiled and staggered away. On the other side of the hall lay the desert under the lash of a frightful noonday sun. He gripped the frame of a door and held himself upright, trembling, as his soul oscillated wildly across the hallucinatory eons. "I am Scarp," said a quiet voice within him. "You have come to the place where all times are one, where all errors can be unmade, where past and future are fluid and subject to redefinition." Breckenridge felt powerful arms encircling and supporting him. "Noel? Noel? Here, sit down." Harry Munsey. Shiny pink skull, searching blue eyes. "Jesus, Noel, you look like you're having some kind of bad trip. Merry sent me after you to find out—"

"It's okay," Breckenridge said hoarsely. "I'll be all right."

"You want me to get her?"

"I'll be *all right*. Just let me steady myself a second." He rose uncertainly. "Okay. Let's go back inside."

The anthropologist was still talking. A napkin covered the wine stain and he held a fresh glass aloft like a sacramental chalice. "The key to everything, I think, lies in an idea that Franz Boas offered in 1898: 'It would seem that mythological worlds have been built up only to be shattered again, and that new worlds were built from the fragments.' "

Breckenridge said, "The first men lived underground and there was no such thing as private property. One day there was an earthquake and the earth was rent apart. The light of day flooded the subterranean cavern where mankind dwelled. Clumsily, for the light dazzled their eyes, they came upward into the world of brightness and learned how to see. Seven days later they divided the fields among themselves and began to build the first walls as boundaries marking the limits of their land."

By midday the city dwellers were losing their fear of the five intruders. Gradually, in twos and threes, they left their hiding places and gathered around the visitors, until a substantial group collected. They were dressed simply, in light robes, and they said nothing to the strangers, though they whispered frequently to one another. Among the group was the slender, dark-haired girl of Breckenridge's dream. "Do you remember me?" he asked. She smiled and shrugged and answered softly in a liquid, incomprehensible language. Arios questioned her in six or seven tongues, but she shook her head to everything. Then she took Breckenridge by the hand and led him a few paces away, toward one of the street wells. Pointing into it, she smiled. She pointed to Breckenridge, pointed to herself, to the surrounding buildings. She made a sweeping gesture taking in all the sky. She pointed again into the well. "What are you trying to tell me?" he asked her. She answered in her own language. Breckenridge shook his head apologetically. She did a simple pantomime:

eyes closed, head lolling against pressed-together hands. An image of sleep, certainly. She pointed to him. To herself. To the well. "You want me to sleep with you?" he blurted. "Down there?" He had to laugh at his own foolishness. It was ridiculous to assume the persistence of a cowardly, euphemistic metaphor like that across so many millennia. He gaped stupidly at her. She laughed—a silvery, tinkling laugh—and danced away from him, back toward her own people.

Their first night in the city they made camp in one of the great plazas. It was an octagonal space surrounded by low green buildings, sharp-angled, each faced on its plaza side with mirror-bright stone. About a hundred of the city dwellers crouched in the shadows on the plaza's periphery, watching them. Scarp sprinkled fuel pellets and kindled a fire; Militor distributed dinner; Horn played music as they ate; Arios, sitting apart, dictated a commentary into a recording device he carried, the size and texture of a large pearl. Afterward, they asked Breckenridge to tell a story, as usual, and he told them the tale of how death came to the world.

"Once upon a time," he began, "there were only a few people in the world and they lived in a green and fertile valley, where winter never came and gardens bloomed all the year round. They spent their days laughing and swimming and lying in the sun, and in the evenings they feasted and sang and made love, and this went on without change, year in, year out, and no one ever fell ill or suffered from hunger, and no one ever died. Despite the serenity of this existence, one man in the village was unhappy. His name was Faust, and he was a restless, intelligent man with intense, burning eyes and a lean, unsmiling face. Faust felt that life must consist of something more than swimming and making love and plucking ripe fruit off vines. There is something else to life, Faust insisted, something unknown to us, something that eludes our grasp, something the lack of which keeps us from being truly happy. We are incomplete, he said.

"The others listened to him and at first they were puzzled, for they had not known they were unhappy or incomplete; they had mistaken the ease and placidity of their existence for happiness. But after a while they started to believe that Faust might be right. They had not known how vacant their lives were until Faust had pointed it out. What can we do, they asked? How can we learn what the thing is that we lack? A wise old man suggested that they might ask the gods. So they elected Faust to visit the god Prometheus, who was said to be a friend to mankind, and ask him. Faust crossed hill and dale, mountain and river, and came at last to Prometheus on the storm-swept summit where he dwelled. He explained the situation and said, Tell me, O Prometheus, why we feel so incomplete. The god replied. It is because you do not have the use of fire. Without fire there can be no civilization; you are uncivilized, and your barbarism makes you unhappy. With fire you can cook your food and enjoy many interesting new flavors. With fire you can work metals, and create effective weapons and other tools. Faust considered this and said, But where can we obtain fire? What is it? How is it used?

"I will bring fire to you, Prometheus answered.

"Prometheus then went to Zeus, the greatest of the gods, and said, Zeus, the humans desire fire, and I seek your permission to bestow it upon them. But Zeus was hard of hearing and Prometheus lisped badly and in the language of the gods the words for 'fire' and for 'death' were very similar, and Zeus misunderstood and said, How odd of them to desire such a thing, but I am a benevolent god, and deny my creatures nothing that they crave. So Zeus created a woman named Pandora and put death inside her and gave her to Prometheus, who took her back to the valley where mankind lived. Here is Pandora, said Prometheus. She will give us fire.

"As soon as Prometheus took his leave Faust came forward and embraced Pandora and lay with her. Her body was hot as flame, and as he held her in his arms death came forth from her and entered him, and he shivered and grew feverish, and cried out in ecstasy, This is fire! I have mastered fire! Within the hour death began to consume him, so that he grew weak and thin, and his skin became parched and yellowish, and he trembled like a leaf in a breeze. Go! he cried to the others. Embrace her! She is the bringer of fire! And he staggered off into the wilderness beyond the valley's edge, murmuring, Thanks be to Prometheus for this gift. He lay down beneath a huge tree, and there he died, and it was the first time that death had visited a human being. And the tree died also.

"Then the other men of the village embraced Pandora, one after another, and death entered into them too, and they went from her to their own women and embraced them, so that soon all the men and women of the village were ablaze with death, and one by one their lives reached an end. Death remained in the village, passing into all who lived and into all who were born from their loins, and this is how death came to the world. Afterward during a storm, lightning struck the tree that had died when Faust had died, and set it ablaze, and a man whose name is forgotten thrust a dry branch into the blaze and lit it, and learned how to build a fire and how to keep the fire alive, and after that time men cooked their food and used fire to work metal into weapons, and so it was that civilization began."

It was time to investigate one of the wells. Scarp, Arios, and Breckenridge would make the descent, with Militor and Horn remaining on the surface to cope with contingencies. They chose a well half a day's march from their campsite, deep into the city, a big one, broader and deeper than most they had seen. At its rim Scarp mounted a spherical fist-sized light that cast a dazzling blue-white beam into the opening. Then, lightly swinging himself out onto the metal ladder, he began to climb down, shrouded in a nimbus of molten brightness. Breckenridge peered after him. Scarp's head and shoulders remained visible for a long while, dwindling until he was only a point of darkness in motion deep within the cone of light, and then he could no longer be seen. "Scarp?" Breckenridge called. After a moment came a muffled reply out of the depths. Scarp had reached the bottom, somewhere beyond the range of the beam, and wanted them to join him.

Breckenridge followed. The descent seemed infinite. There was a stiffness in his left knee. He became a mere automaton mechanically seizing the rungs; they were warm in his hands. His eyes, fixed on the pocked gray skin of the well's wall inches from his nose, grew glassy and unfocused. He passed through the zone of light as though sliding through the face of a mirror and moved downward in darkness without a change of pace until his boot slammed unexpectedly into a solid floor where he had thought to encounter the next rung. The left boot; his knee, jamming, protested. Scarp lightly touched his shoulder. "Step back here next to me," he said. "Take sliding steps and make sure you have a footing. For all we know, we're on some sort of ledge with a steep drop on all sides."

They waited while Arios came down. His footfalls were like thunder in the well—*boom, boom, boom,*—transmitted and amplified by the rungs. Then the men at the surface lowered the light, fixed to the end of a long cord, and at last they could look around.

They were in a kind of catacomb. The floor of the well was a platform of neatly dressed stone slabs which gave access to horizontal tunnels several times a man's height, stretching away to right and left, to fore and aft. The mouth of the well was a dim dot of light far above. Scarp, after inspecting the perimeter of the platform, flashed the beam into one of the tunnels, stared a moment, and cautiously entered. Breckenridge heard him cough, "You told us a story once about the King of the Dead Lands, Breckenridge. What was his name?"

"Thanatos."

"Thanatos, yes. This must be his kingdom. Come and look."

Arios and Breckenridge exchanged shrugs. Breckenridge stepped into the tunnel. The walls on both sides were lined from floor to ceiling with tiers of coffins, stacked eight or ten high and extending as far as the light beam reached. The coffins were glass-faced and covered over with dense films of dust. Scarp drew his fingers through the dust over one coffin and left deep tracks; clouds rose up, sending Breckenridge back, coughing and choking, to stumble into Arios. When the dust cleared they could see a figure within, seemingly asleep, the nude figure of a young man lying on his back. His expression was one of great serenity. Breckenridge shivered. Death's kingdom, yes, the place of Thanatos, the house of Pluto. He walked down the row, wiping coffin after coffin. An old man. A child. A young woman. An older woman. A whole population lay embalmed here. I died long ago, he thought, and I don't even sleep. I walk about beneath the earth. The silence was frightening here. "The people of the city?" Scarp asked. "The ancient inhabitants?"

"Very likely," said Arios. His voice was as crisp as ever. He alone was not trembling. "Slain in some inconceivable massacre? But what? But how?"

"They appear to have died natural deaths," Breckenridge pointed out. "Their bodies look whole and healthy. As though they were lying here asleep. Not dead, only sleeping."

"A plague?" Scarp wondered. "A sudden cloud of deadly gas? A taint of poison in their water supply?"

"If it had been sudden," said Breckenridge, "how would they have had time to build all these coffins? This whole tunnel—catacomb upon catacomb—" A network of passageways spanning the city's entire subterrane. Thousands of coffins. Millions. Breckenridge felt dazed by the presence of death on such a scale. The skeleton with the scythe, moving briskly about its work. Severed heads and hands and feet scattered like dandelions in the springtime meadow. The reign of Thanatos, King of Swords, Knight of Wands.

Thunder sounded behind them. Footfalls in the well.

Scarp scowled. "I told them to wait up there. That fool Militor—"

Arios said, "Militor should see this. Undoubtedly it's the

resting place of the city dwellers. Undoubtedly these are human beings. Do you know what I imagine? A mass suicide. A unanimous decision to abandon the world of life. Years of preparation. The construction of tunnels, of machines for killing, a whole vast apparatus of immolation. And then the day appointed—long lines waiting to be processed—millions of men and women and children passing through the machines, gladly giving up their lives, going willingly to the coffins that await them—"

"And then," Scarp said, "there must have been only a few left and no one to process them. Living on, caretakers for the dead, perhaps, maintaining the machinery that preserves these millions of bodies."

"Preserves them for what?" Arios asked.

"The day of resurrection," said Breckenridge.

The footfalls in the well grew louder. Scarp glanced toward the tunnel's mouth. "Militor?" he called. "Horn?" He sounded angry. He walked toward the well. "You were supposed to wait for us up—"

Breckenridge heard a grinding sound and whirled to see Arios tugging at the lid of a coffin—the one that held the serene young man. Instinctively he moved to halt the desecration, but he was too slow; the glass plate rose and Arios broke the seals, and, with a quick whooshing sound, a burst of greenish vapor rushed from the coffin. It hovered a moment in midair, speared by Arios' beam of light; then it congealed into a yellow precipitant and broke in a miniature rainstorm that stained the tunnel's stone floor. To Breckenridge's horror the young man's body jerked convulsively. Muscles tightened into knots and almost instantly relaxed. "He's alive!" Breckenridge cried.

"Was," said Scarp.

Yes. The figure in the glass case was motionless. It changed color and texture, turning black and withered. Scarp shoved Arios aside and slammed the lid closed, but that could do no good now. A dreadful new motion commenced within the coffin. In moments something shriveled and twisted lay before them.

"Suspended animation," said Arios. "The city builders—they lie here, as human as we are, sleeping, not dead, sleeping. Sleeping! Militor! Militor, come quickly!"

Feingold said, "Let me see if I have it straight. After the public offering our group will continue to hold 83 percent of the Class B stock and 34 percent of the voting common, which constitutes a controlling block. We'll let you have 100,000 five-year warrants and we'll agree to a conversion privilege on the 1992 6 1/2 percent debentures, plus we allow you the stipulated underwriting fee, providing your Argentinian friend takes up the agreed-upon allotment of debentures and follows through on his deal with us in Colorado. Okay? Now, then, assuming the SEC has no objections, I'd like to outline the proposed interlocking directorates with Heitmark A.G. in Liechtenstein and Hellaphon S.A. in Athens, after which—"

The high, clear, rapid voice went on and on. Breckenridge toyed with his lunch, smiled frequently, nodded whenever he felt it was appropriate, and otherwise remained disconnected, listening only with the automatic-recorder part of his mind. They were sitting on the terrace of the open-air restaurant in Tiberias, at the edge of the Sea of Galilee, looking across the bleak, brown Syrian hills on the far side. The December air was mild, the sun bright. Last week Breckenridge had visited Monaco, Zurich, and Milan. Yesterday Tel Aviv, tomorrow Haifa, next Tuesday Istanbul. Then on to Nairobi, Johannesburg, Peking, Singapore. Finally San Francisco and then home. Zap! Zap! A crazy round-the-world scramble in twenty days, cleaning up a lot of international business for the firm. It could all have been handled by telephone, or else some of these foreign tycoons could have come to New York, but Breckenridge had volunteered to do the junket. Why? Why? Sitting here ten thousand miles from home having lunch with a man whose office was down the street from his own. Crazy. Why all this running, Noel? Where do you think you'll get?

"Some more wine?" Feingold asked. "What do you think of this Israeli stuff, anyway?"

"It goes well with the fish." Breckenridge reached for Feingold's copy of the agreement. "Here, let me initial all that."

"Don't you want to check it over first?"

"Not necessary. I have faith in you, Sid."

"Well, I wouldn't cheat you, that's true. But I could have made a mistake. I'm capable of making mistakes."

"I don't think so," Breckenridge said. He grinned. Feingold grinned. Behind the grin there was something chilly. Breckenridge looked away. You think I'm bending over backwards to treat you like a gentleman, he thought, because you know what people like me are really supposed to think about Jews, and I know you know, and you know I know you know, and—and—well, screw it, Sid. Do I trust you? Maybe I do. Maybe I don't. But the basic fact is that I just don't care. Stack the deck any way you like, Feingold. I just don't care. I wish I was on Mars. Or Pluto. Or in the year Two Billion. Zap! Right across the whole continuum! Noel Breckenridge, freaking out! He heard himself say, "Do you want to know my secret fantasy, Sid? I dream of waking up Jewish one day. It's so damned boring being a gentile, do you know that? I feel so bland, so straight, so sunny. I envy you all that feverish kinky complexity of soul. All that history. Ghettos, persecutions, escapes, schemes for survival and revenge, a sense of tribal unity born out of shared pain. It's so hard for a goy to develop some honest paranoia, you know? Let alone a little schiziness." Feingold was still grinning. He filled Breckenridge's wine glass again. He showed no sign of having heard anything that might offend him. Maybe I didn't say anything, Breckenridge thought.

Feingold said, "When you get back to New York, Noel, I'd like you out to our place for dinner. You and your wife. A weekend, maybe. Logs on the fire, thick steaks, plenty of good wine. You'll love our place." Three Israeli jets roared low over Tiberias and vanished in the direction of Lebanon. "Will you come? Can you fit it into your schedule?"

Some possible structural hypotheses:

LIFE AS MEANINGLESS CONDITION

Breckenridge on Wall Street	The four seekers moving randomly	The dead city

* * *

LIFE RENDERED MEANINGFUL THROUGH ART

Breckenridge recollects ancient myths	The four seekers elicit his presence and request the myths	The dead city inhabited after all. The inhabitants listen to Breckenridge

* * *

THE IMPACT OF ENTROPY

His tales are garbled dreams	The seekers quarrel over theory	The city dwellers speak an unknown language

* * *

ASPECTS OF CONSCIOUSNESS

He is a double self	The four seekers are unsure of the historical background	Most of the city dwellers are asleep

His audience was getting larger every night. They came from all parts of the city, silently arriving, drawn at sundown to the place where the visitors camped. Hundreds, now, squatting beyond the glow of the campfire. They listened intently, nodded, seemed to comprehend, murmured occasional comments to one another. How strange: they seemed to comprehend.

"The story of Samson and Odysseus," Breckenridge announced. "Samson is blind but mighty. His woman is known as Delilah. To them comes the wily chieftain Odysseus, making his way homeward from the land of Ithaca. He penetrates the maze in which Samson and Delilah live and hires himself to them as bond servant, giving his name as No Man. Delilah entices him to carry her off, and he abducts her. Samson is aware of the abduction but is unable to find them in the maze. He cries out in pain and rage, No Man steals my wife! No Man steals my wife! His servants are baffled by this and take no action. In fury Samson brings the maze crashing down on himself and dies, while Odysseus carries Delilah off to Sparta, where she is seduced by Paris, Prince of Troy. Odysseus thus loses her and by way of gaining revenge he seduces Helen, the Queen of Troy, and the Trojan War begins."

And then he told the story of how mankind was created:

"In the beginning there was only a field of white sand. Lightning struck it, and where the lightning hit the sand it coagulated into a vessel of glass, and rainwater ran into the vessel and brought it to life, and from the vessel a she-wolf was born. Thunder entered her womb and fertilized her and she gave birth to twins, and they were not wolves but a human boy and a human girl. The wolf suckled the twins until they reached adulthood. Then they copulated and engendered children of their own. Because they were ashamed of their nakedness they killed the old wolf and made garments from her hide."

And he told them the myth of the wandering Jew, who scoffed at God and was condemned to drift through time until he himself was able to become God.

And he told them of the Golden Age and the Iron Age and the Age of Uranium.

And he told them how the waters and winds came into being, and the seasons, the months, day and night.

And he told them how art was born:
"Out of a hole in space pours a stream of pure life-force. Many men and women attempted to seize the flow, but they were burned to ashes by its intensity. At last, however, a man devised a way. He hollowed himself out until there was nothing at all inside his body, and had himself dragged by a faithful dog to the place where the stream of energy descended from the heavens. Then the life force entered him and filled him, and instead of destroying him it took possession of him and restored him to life. But the force overflowed within him, brimming over, and the only way he could deal with that was to fashion stories and sculptures and songs, for otherwise the force would engulf him and drown him. His name was Gilgamesh and he was the first of the artists of mankind."

The city dwellers came by the thousands now. They listened and wept at Breckenridge's words.

Hypothesis of structural resolution:

He finds creative fulfillment	The four seekers have bridged space and time to bring life out of death	The sleeping city dwellers will be awakened

Gradually the outlines of a master myth took place: the creation, the creation of man, the origin of private property, the origin of death, the loss of innocence, the loss of faith, the end of the world, the coming of the redeemer to start the cycle anew. Soon the structure would be complete. When it was, Breckenridge thought, perhaps rains would fall on the desert, perhaps the world would be reborn.

Breckenridge slept. Sleeping, he experienced an inward glow of golden light. The girl he had encountered before came to him and took his hand and led him through the city. They walked for hours, it seemed, until they came to a well different from all the others, rectangular rather than circular and surrounded at street level by a low railing of bright metal mesh. "Go down into this one," she told him. "When you reach the bottom, keep walking until you reach the room where the mechanisms of awakening are located." He looked at her in amazement, realizing that her words had been comprehensible. "Are you speaking my language," he asked, "or am I speaking yours?" She answered by smiling and pointing toward the well.

He stepped over the railing and began his descent. The well was deeper than the other one; the air in its depths was stale and dry. The golden glow lit his way for him to the bottom and thence along a low passageway with a rounded vault of a ceiling. After a long time he came to a large, brightly lit room filled with sleek gray machinery. It was much like the computer room at any large bank. Mounted on the walls were control panels, labeled in an unknown language but also marked with sequential symbols:

I II III IIII IIIII

While he studied these he became aware of a sliding, hissing sound from the corridor beyond. He thought of sturdy metal cables passing one against the other, but then into the control room slowly came a creature something like a scorpion in form, considerably greater than a man in size. Its curved tubular thorax was dark and of a waxen texture; a dense mat of brown bristles, thick as straws, sprouted on its abdomen; its many eyes were bright, alert, and malevolent. Breckenridge snatched up a steel bar that lay near his feet and tried to wield it like a lance as the monster approached. From its jaws, though, there looped a sudden lasso of newly spun silken thread that caught the end of the bar and jerked it from Breckenridge's grasp. Then a second loop, entangling his arms and shoulders. Struggle was useless. He was caught. The creature pulled him closer. Breckenridge saw fangs, powerful palpi, a scythe of a tail in which a dripping stinger had become erect. Breckenridge writhed in the monster's grip. He felt neither surprise nor fear; this seemed a necessary working out of some ancient foreordained pattern.

A cool silent voice within his skull said, "Who are you?"

"Noel Breckenridge of New York City, born A.D. 1940."

"Why do you intrude here?"

"I was summoned. If you want to know why, ask someone else."

"Is it your purpose to awaken the sleepers?"

"Very possibly," Breckenridge said.

"So the time has come?"

"Maybe it has," said Breckenridge. All was still for a long moment. The monster made no hostile move. Breckenridge grew impatient. "Well, what's the arrangement?" he said finally.

"The arrangement?"

"The terms under which I get my freedom. Am I supposed to tell you a lot of diverting stories? Will I have to serve you six months out of the year, forever more? Is there some precious object I'm obliged to bring you from the bottom of the sea? Maybe you have a riddle that I'm supposed to answer."

The monster made no reply.

"Is that it?" Breckenridge demanded. "A riddle?"

"Do you want it to be a riddle?"

"A riddle, yes."

There was another endless pause. Breckenridge met the beady gaze steadily. At last the voice said, "A riddle. A riddle. Very well. Tell me the answer to this. What goes on four legs in the morning, on two legs in the afternoon, on three legs in the evening?"

Breckenridge repeated it. He pondered. He frowned. He coughed. Then he laughed. "A baby," he said, "crawls on all fours. A grown man walks upright. An old man requires the assistance of a cane. Therefore the answer to your riddle is—"

He left the sentence unfinished. The gleam went out of the monster's eye; the silken loop binding Breckenridge dissolved; the creature began slowly and sadly to back away, withdrawing into the corridor from which it came. Its hissing, rustling sound persisted for a time, growing ever more faint.

Breckenridge turned and without hesitation pulled the switch marked I.

The aurora no longer appears in the night sky. A light rain has been falling frequently for some days, and the desert is turning green. The sleepers are awakening, millions of them, called forth from their coffins by the workings of automatic mechanisms. Breckenridge stands in the central plaza of the city, arms outspread, and the city dwellers, as they emerge from the subterranean sleeping places, make their way toward him. I am the resurrection and the life, he thinks. I am Orpheus the sweet singer. I am Homer the blind. I am Noel Breckenridge. He looks across the eons to Harry Munsey. "I was wrong," he says. "There's meaning everywhere, Harry. For Sam Smith as well as for Beethoven. For Noel Breckenridge as well as for Michelangelo. Dawn after dawn, simply being alive, being part of it all, part of the cosmic dance of life—that's the meaning, Harry. Look! Look!" The sun is high now, not a cruel sun but a mild, gentle one, its heat softened by a humid haze. This is the dreamtime, when all mistakes are unmade, when all things become one. The city folk surround him. They come closer. Closer yet. They reach toward him. He experiences a delicious flash of white light. The world disappears.

"JFK Airport," he told the taxi driver. The cab zoomed away. From the front seat came the voice of the radio with today's closing Dow-Jones Industrials: 948.72, down 6.11. He reached the airport by half past five, and at seven he boarded a Pan Am flight for London. The next morning at nine, London time, he cabled his wife to say that he was well and planned to head south for the winter. Then he reported to the Air France counter for the nonstop flight to Morocco. Over the next week he cabled home from Rabat, Marrakech and Timbuktu in Mali. The third cable said:

GUESS WHAT STOP I'M REALLY IN TIMBUKTU STOP HAVE RENTED JEEP STOP I SET OUT INTO SAHARA TOMORROW STOP AM VERY HAPPY STOP YES STOP VERY HAPPY STOP VERY VERY HAPPY STOP STOP STOP

It was the last message he sent. The night it arrived in New York there was a spectacular celestial display, an aurora that brought thousands of people out into Central Park. There was rain in the southeastern Sahara four days later, the first recorded precipitation there in eight years and seven months. An earthquake was reported in southern Sicily, but it did little damage. Things were much quieter after that for everybody.

About the Editor

ROBERT SILVERBERG was born in New York and graduated from Columbia University. He now lives near San Francisco. He is the author of countless short stories and many novels. He has also had a substantial career as a nonfiction writer specializing in archaeological and historical themes. He is a past president of the Science Fiction Writers of America and was American guest of honor at the World Science Fiction Convention in Heidelberg, 1970. He has won the Hugo twice and the Nebula Award four times. His hobbies are gardening and travel. When he has time, his special interests include contemporary literature and music, medieval geography, and the raising of fuchsias and cacti.